The Worst Duke in the World

The Duke was stammering adorably again, and Jane felt her temperature go up several additional degrees. Another idea came to her and she didn't waste any time wondering if it meant she was good or bad. She said:

"I think we ought to kiss each other."

He looked surprised. And then so happy that her own heart gave a leap of joy within her.

"Do you really, Miss Kent?"

"Yes. Your Grace."

"Then let's do that. If you're sure?"

"I'm very sure."

"I say, how *ripping*."

With one gloved hand still holding the reins, the Duke raised his other gloved hand to his mouth, took the tip of one finger between his teeth, tugged his hand free, and in a very dashing way spat out his glove and let it drop down into the curricle's well at their feet. Then that newly bare hand was warmly cupping her cheek, and the Duke brought his face closer to her own, and then his incredibly attractive mouth was on hers, and Jane, her lips eagerly parting, felt her bones melt away into wonderful nothingness as white-hot sensation took hold of her . . .

By Lisa Berne

THE WORST DUKE IN THE WORLD
ENGAGED TO THE EARL
THE BRIDE TAKES A GROOM
THE LAIRD TAKES A BRIDE
YOU MAY KISS THE BRIDE

Lisa Berne

The Worst Duke in the World

The Penhallow Dynasty

AVONBOOKS

An Imprint of HarperCollins*Publishers*

This is a work of fiction. Names, characters, places, and incidents are products of the author's imagination or are used fictitiously and are not to be construed as real. Any resemblance to actual events, locales, organizations, or persons, living or dead, is entirely coincidental.

First Avon Books mass market printing: January 2021

Print Edition ISBN: 978-0-06-285237-3
Digital Edition ISBN: 978-0-06-285238-0

Cover design by Amy Halperin
Cover illustration © Anna Kmet
Author photo by Shoop Studios

FIRST EDITION

21 22 23 24 25 QGM 10 9 8 7 6 5 4 3 2 1

For Cheryl Pienkta. Of course.

Acknowledgments

With oodles of gratitude to these amazing people:
Lucia Macro
Sophie Jordan
Julia Quinn
Leslie Ruder
Frauke Spanuth
And to you, dear reader.
Thank you! ♥

THE WORST
DUKE IN THE
WORLD

Chapter 1

Somerset County, England
February 1817

His Grace the Duke of Radcliffe had reached the last of the wide marble steps that led from his house onto the graveled sweep and was just about to execute a gentle left turn when from above and behind him came a piercing voice which throbbed with annoyance and disapproval.

"Anthony."

He turned and looked up.

On the broad covered portico stood his sister Margaret, clad in habitual black from the lacy cap on her head to the trailing draperies of her gown and incredibly flat slippers. Her back was ramrod straight, her brows were drawn together, and her lips compressed into a thin, tight line. She had, in fact, the darkly ominous air of an avenging angel. All she lacked was a fiery sword. He said:

"Hullo, Meg."

Rather than responding to his civil greeting in kind, her frown only deepened. "Where do you think you're going?"

"To the stables."

"Why?"

"To get my horse."

"For what purpose are you getting your horse?"

He squinted up at her. Really, sometimes Margaret asked the most obvious of questions. "To go riding."

"Where?"

"To see Penhallow over at Surmont Hall. Apparently the enmity between our respective pigmen has been escalating."

"Indeed," said Margaret, although in a noticeably flat way.

"Yes, Johns says Cremwell has been threatening to sneak over from the Hall and put calomel in the Duchess' slops. Can't have that, you know. Very unsporting." Anthony watched with mild interest as Margaret's eyes began snapping with anger.

"Why you had to name that revolting pig 'Duchess' is beyond me."

"I didn't *have* to, Meg. And it was you who inspired me—don't you remember? Saying that I cared more for the new piglet than I did Selina. Which, of course, was not entirely untrue."

At this frank reference to his wife, dead these five years, and the unvarnished truth of his marriage—a dry, sepulchral, mutually loveless match of convenience—Margaret said, with more tartness than seemed strictly necessary:

"Your remarks, Anthony, are insupportable. Selina, may I remind you, was the daughter of an earl, and comported herself at all times with the dignity appropriate to her station in life. Moreover, if she had known you named a pig after her—"

"You're off the mark there, old girl. I didn't name the pig 'Selina,' after all."

"Off the *mark*? Why, you—you're—flippant—and feckless—and—and—" Margaret actually sputtered, briefly fell silent, then gathered herself again for her *riposte*, as might a duelist prepare for the killing blow. "Your juvenile absence of seriousness on the subject is an affront to anyone with a particle of sensibility."

"I assure you, Meg, I'm very serious about my pigs."

"*And*," she went on, unheeding, "the manner in which you fraternize with your pigman is a complete betrayal of your rank."

"Is that what you came out onto the portico to tell me? Far be it from me to throw your own words back into your face, but you've said that many times before. Also, you'll get chilled standing there without a shawl."

"I came out to inform you," Margaret said, in the tone of one forced to call upon the last vestiges of extraordinary self-control in the face of unbearable provocation, "that instead of gallivanting off to Surmont Hall to chat about pigs with Gabriel Penhallow, you're shortly expected at tea, in your own drawing-room, where you are to carry on—if at all humanly possible—a polite conversation with the Preston-Carnabys."

"Who?"

"The Preston-Carnabys, whose daughter, as I have already explained to you twice today, you are to inspect with an eye toward matrimony."

Anthony groaned. "Oh, for God's sake, Meg, another one?"

"Yes, *another one*. It has evidently escaped your notice that you have but the one son, which leaves you in a very precarious position. You must marry again."

"Five years with Selina was enough."

"Your feelings in the matter, Anthony, are irrelevant. You have a duty to the family and to your ancient lineage. The Preston-Carnabys are our guests, and—"

"Your guests. I didn't invite them."

"They are our guests," Margaret said with steel in her voice, "who have come all the way from Yorkshire. Incidentally, Nurse tells me that Wakefield has not been seen since breakfast, *and* I got a note from the vicar saying that Wakefield didn't come for his lessons, *and* your tenant farmer Moore stopped by to complain that Wakefield was seen attempting to ride one of his bulls—all of which means, I daresay, that he could be anywhere by now."

"Oh, Wake's somewhere about, you know."

"Your only child and heir is missing."

"Not missing, Meg. Just not here. When I was his age I could spend half the day up a tree, or fishing by the river."

"And look how *you* turned out. When Wakefield returns, I expect you to discipline him with the utmost stringency. He's a marquis, after all, and ought to act like one."

"He's eight."

"And in line to inherit one of the most illustrious dukedoms in the country."

"Very well, stale bread and water for a week. Maybe a few turns on the rack, too."

In the silence that fell between them after this last utterance, Anthony watched with the same mild interest as Margaret's face turned so vehemently and comprehensively brilliant a red that she gave the appearance of one wearing an odd (and off-putting) theatrical mask. Finally she hissed:

"You—you're—you're . . ."

"Yes?" he said, politely.

"You're a very bad duke!"

"Am I?" he said, still politely.

"Yes! In fact, you're the worst duke in the world!"

"Well then." Warm and cozy in his wool greatcoat and tall hat, his hands stuck comfortably into his pockets, Anthony stood looking up at Margaret on the portico. The black hem of her gown fluttered in a sharp wintry wind, her eyes were watering in the cold, and her teeth chattered ever so slightly. He knew from extensive experience that she would go on standing there until she gained her point, no matter how long it took. Little did he want on his conscience the nasty bout of pleurisy that might develop if she stayed like this much longer, so he said:

"I'll talk to Wakefield, Meg. Now, if you'll excuse me, I'll stop by the stables to tell them I don't want my horse after all. Then I'll come back for tea."

She eyed him narrowly, then nodded and turned around. A footman had obviously been awaiting her return to the house, for the door swung open wide to admit her, and then was closed very, very gently by the same invisible hand within. Had it not been beneath her, Anthony knew that Margaret would have loved nothing better than personally slamming the great oak door shut in a way that would have made her sentiments known to everyone within a fifty-foot radius.

He gave a little sigh.

Poor old Margaret.

He wished *she* would marry again.

At eighteen she had been wed to Selina's older brother, who had died after only two years of marriage. His heir, Selina's younger brother, had promptly booted the widowed Margaret out of the house, and so she had come back home to Hastings where she and Selina had—beneath a brittle veneer of civility—lived under the same roof as might two queens jockey for the same throne, an uneasy state of affairs which lasted until Selina's death, five long years later.

Now here they were.

He a widower at thirty-one, she a widow at thirty-three. She still wore black for the late Viscount Peete, which was a mystery to Anthony, as Skiffy Featherington had not only been exceedingly stupid, he had also been vain, arrogant, and among the most extreme of the so-called Dandy set—notorious throughout half of England for the immense shoulder-padding in his coats, the soaring height of his shirt-points, the half-dozen fobs jangling from his waist, and the jeweled quizzing-glass he carried with him everywhere including (it was rumored) bed, bathtub, and privy.

Well, life was full of mysteries, wasn't it?

By way of further example, why had blight returned this past autumn to the northeastern apple orchards after a full decade of untroubled health and productivity?

And was it true that the long white blurry swath in the night sky wasn't a celestial sort of exhalation, as he'd been taught in his youth, but was instead, thanks to the revelations of modern telescopes, an immense grouping of distant stars?

Too, recently he had found himself wondering why the self-styled village oracle, Mrs. Roger, had come up to him the last time he was in Riverton and said, nodding her head in a highly significant manner, *You're next, Yer Grace.*

Also, would Margaret ever stop presenting him with marital candidates, or would this dispiriting parade of hopeful females go on forever?

Anthony turned away from the marble steps and began walking toward the stables, and as he passed a large and perfectly rounded shrub, a small form leaped out from behind it and onto the graveled path, shouting in a high-pitched childish treble:

"Boo!"

Anthony paused and calmly regarded his son, who in turn looked very disappointed.

"Oh, Father, you *never* jump."

"Nerves of iron," explained Anthony. "Only way a chap could survive in this family. How long have you been hiding behind that shrub?"

"Ages. I heard everything you and Aunt Margaret said. I say, Father, are you going to marry Miss Thingummy?"

"Who?"

"You know, the lady from Yorkshire."

"Doubtful."

"Well, that's good. I saw her in the drawing-room, Father, and she asked who I was, and when I told her, she said I ought to be away at school, and then I told her I didn't want to go, and she said I was a foolish little boy and that *you're* a nonglickful father."

"Do you mean neglectful?"

"Yes, that's what I said. And then *she* said that the first thing she'll do after she marries you will be to pack me off to Eton."

"Fat chance of that. You'd run away and join the Navy."

"Yes, that's what I told her! And guess what she said then, Father?"

"She complimented you on your patriotic spirit."

"No, she said I was not only a foolish little boy, but a horrid one too."

"Hardly an endearing strategy to get me to marry her," remarked Anthony. "I wonder why she didn't think you'd repeat what she said to you."

Wakefield smiled a distinctly gleeful smile. "I *told* her I would, Father, and then she gave me a half-crown to keep my mouth shut."

"And yet here you are, telling me."

"Aren't you glad I did?"

"Well, yes," Anthony admitted. "You've given me all the insight I need into Miss Thingummy's character."

"I think *you* ought to give me a half-crown for that."

"Don't push your luck. You're already deep into morally ambiguous territory. By the way, what were you doing in the drawing-room?"

"Hiding from Nurse."

"Why?"

"She keeps trying to give me castor oil, and it's *foul*."

Anthony nodded, and resumed walking again. "She dosed me with that when I was a lad. Said it would fatten me up."

Briskly taking two or three strides to one of his own, Wakefield kept pace alongside him. "It didn't work, Father."

"No, it only made me bilious. Does she think you're too thin also?"

"Yes. She says I'll grow up to be a scarecrow like you if I don't watch out."

"A scarecrow? How unkind of Nurse to say that."

"I stuck up for you, Father."

"Did you, Wake? That was ripping of you."

"Yes, I told her you don't look like a scarecrow—you're more like a crane. Because your legs are awfully long, you know."

"They may be long, my boy, but at least they reach the ground."

Wakefield thought this over, and grinned. "I say, Father, you're the most complete hand."

"One does try."

"So will you talk to Nurse, then?"

"Yes. Henceforth no drop of castor oil is to pass betwixt your unwilling lips. This is my ducal decree. Let no man—or nurse—flout it with impunity."

Wakefield gave a joyful skip. "That's capital, Father, thanks ever so much."

"You're welcome. Speaking of hiding in the drawing-room, why didn't you go to the vicarage today for your lessons?"

"I wanted to, of course," said Wakefield, looking up at him with brown eyes that had somehow gotten all big and glistening, like those of a sweet, vulnerable fawn. "But there were so many more important things I had to do, Father."

"Like what?"

"Well, for one, yesterday I told Johns I'd stand guard over the Duchess for a while, so he could go get his breakfast. He'd told me about Cremwell's evil plan, you see, and he stayed by the Duchess' pig-cote all night. And when he got back, *I* was hungry, so I went to Mrs. Gregg's cottage. Because she makes the most dilickable muffins, Father."

"Do you mean delectable?"

"Yes, that's what I said. You ought to try them. So I had nuncheon with Mrs. Gregg, and then I *was* going to the vicarage, but I passed Mr. Moore's field and saw that bull of his, Old Snorter, and thought I'd give it a go. So after I fell off, I had to run away from Old Snorter *and* Mr. Moore, who was shouting like anything. Then I tripped over a tree-root and scraped away half the skin on my arm—"

"Did you really?"

"Well, no, but I *was* bleeding a bit, and luckily Miss Trevelyan came by on one of her walks, and she took me back to her house and put a sticking-plaster on it, and then I was hungry again, so Miss Humphrey made some sandwiches for me, and then we all went into the library so Miss Trevelyan could read aloud to us from the book she's writing, which was jolly good fun, and Miss Humphrey also brought in some biscuits. I saved one for you, Father."

Wakefield pulled from the pocket of his coat a vaguely circular object. "See? It's only a tiny bit crumbled."

He offered it to Anthony, who accepted it, blew off what looked like some dog hairs, and took a bite. "I say, it *is* good."

Wakefield looked pleased. "Isn't it? I ate five of them."

Anthony took another bite, then said, "Look here, old chap, these are all very worthy activities, but you and I made a bargain. I agreed to let you stay at home and not go off to school, and you agreed to have lessons with Mr. Pressley. So you ought to stick to the bargain, don't you think?"

Wakefield opened his mouth, closed it, kicked at the gravel, hopped on one foot, lagged behind, ran to catch up, and finally said, "Yes, Father."

"Splendid. Want the last bite?"

"Yes, please." Wakefield took what was left of the biscuit and ate it. "I say, Father, I don't think Aunt Margaret meant it when she said you're the worst duke in the world."

"Oh yes, she did," answered Anthony dispassionately.

"There's probably worse ones in China, Father, or in the Colonies, or Antarctica."

"You're a great comfort to me, my boy."

"One does try."

Anthony ruffled his son's tawny hair, repressed a sigh at the thought of the predictably ghastly tea that lay ahead of him, and then the two of them passed into the stables which smelled so pleasantly of horse, hay, liniment, cheroot, and manure.

Meanwhile, over at Surmont Hall . . .

Shivering, Jane Kent stood on the porch of the intimidatingly vast old house, gazing with considerable uneasiness at the massive door of dark knotted wood and the polished knocker which was just a little above her eye-level. She was uncomfortably aware that the hem of her shabby old gown was rather short, showing far too much of her scrawny ankles in equally shabby stockings and also entirely failing to conceal the fact that her dark half-boots, though sturdy, were (unfortunately) shabby too.

She tightened her grip on the small battered valise she held in both hands, additionally aware that she was ravenously hungry, underdressed for the winter weather, not as clean as she would like after traveling in various dingy coaches for four days, and that in the tatty reticule she carried looped around her bony wrist was all the money she had left in the world.

Three pounds, four shillings, and sixpence.

No, wait, that was wrong.

She had given the shillings to a nice old man named John Roger who had conveyed her from the village—Riverton—in his gig. He hadn't wanted to take the money, but she had insisted.

It was his wife, curiously enough, who had helped her find her way here.

Jane had just climbed out of the coach from Bristol, and was standing, stiff and cold and bewildered, on the high street, when a stout old lady had come marching up and said in a satisfied way:

You're right on time.

Of course, the old lady, who then introduced herself as Mrs. Roger, could have been referring to the coach's traveling schedule, but somehow Jane didn't think that was quite what she had meant. Still, before she could gather her scattered wits to try and frame a rational inquiry, Mrs. Roger had taken her over to where her husband happened to be standing with his gig and horse, hustled Jane up onto the high front seat, and said:

You're to ask for old Mrs. Penhallow.

More bewildered than ever, Jane had thought about the fragile, yellowed letter she had in her possession, and only said, haltingly:

At Surmont Hall?

Mrs. Roger had looked up at her and calmly answered, *Well, of course.*

And just for a second Jane felt like she had asked a stupid question.

A loud complaining rumble from her empty stomach abruptly reminded her that she'd been standing on the wide gracious porch of Surmont Hall like a wax dummy. Well, it was now or never, she supposed.

So Jane lifted her hand and rapped the knocker in a way that sounded, she hoped, neither too assertive nor too timid—the easy, casual knock of a person who was certainly going to be admitted into this very, very grand house despite looking as if she really ought to be going around the back to the servants' entrance and begging for a bowl of soup.

Which she might, in fact, shortly be doing.

A blast of cold sharp wind whipped at the hems of Jane's gown and pelisse and, as if embodied in an unseen malevolent hand, it also ripped from her head her old flat-crowned straw bonnet, which flew high into the air, did three or four jaunty somersaults, and landed gracefully onto the tranquil waters of the large ornamental pond which lay beyond the curving graveled carriage sweep.

Jane was just about to go darting after it (as it was her only hat) when the big dark door opened and instead she was startled into immobility again. A beautifully dressed, well-fed, very clean young footman stood there, looking inquiringly at her.

"May I help you, miss?"

"Yes, please." Jane realized that her voice had emerged

all weak and croaky, like that of a despairing frog, perhaps, and hastily she cleared her throat. "I've—I've come to see Mrs. Penhallow."

"Which one, miss?"

Jane gaped at the footman. Was this a trick question? How many Mrs. Penhallows could there possibly be? A dozen—a hundred—a thousand? Into her muddled mind came Mrs. Roger's instructions and she said rather wildly, "The—ah—older Mrs. Penhallow, if you please."

A little doubtfully, the footman said, "Is she expecting you, miss?"

"I—I have a letter." This was true, although Jane was miserably conscious that her answer was more than a little opaque. Her stomach rumbled again, as if to helpfully remind her of just how miserable things were.

"Very well, miss. Won't you please come inside?" The footman stepped aside, and gratefully Jane went into the light and warmth of an immense high-ceilinged hall, catching quick glimpses of an enormous fireplace flanked by gleaming suits of armor, a coat of arms carved into the massive chimney-piece, a large and unnerving display of old weapons on one wall, a wide curving staircase leading to the upstairs.

Everything was so big—and it made her feel so very small.

Jane shrank a little inside her pelisse, feeling extremely out of place among all this elegance and grandeur, and also hoping she hadn't tracked mud inside. Her idea back in Nantwich, to upend her life because of a yellowy old letter discovered by chance, had seemed so brilliant and important at the time, but now it struck her as reckless, demented, asinine, ruinous folly.

Still, maybe there would be soup.

She thought of a nice fragrant steaming hot bowl of

it, filled with, say, chunks of beef, and with carrots and parsnips and onions. Maybe some celery and diced potatoes, too.

Then she pictured a lovely thick slice of fresh bread, with a spongy tender crumb and a crisp chewy crust.

No, *two* slices. Why not?

In her mind's eye she pictured herself lavishly spreading onto the bread as much butter as she liked.

Lots and lots of it, fresh-churned and creamy, with a little sprinkle of salt, perhaps.

Covering every bit of the slice, all the way to the crust.

She would eat these two buttery slices very methodically—it would give her soup a chance to cool a little.

Next she imagined *another* slice of bread, which she wouldn't butter, but would instead dip into her soup. It would soak up the rich beefy broth, and get all soft and drippy, and she'd have to carefully bite at it so as not to spill a single drop.

After that, she'd spoon up everything else.

Then, when she had nearly finished the bowl, she would use some more bread to mop up the last of the broth, wiping her bowl clean.

Of course, there would be plenty more soup and bread, and it would be perfectly all right for her to have seconds, so—

Jane realized that she was salivating, and that drool was just about to start spooling out of the side of her mouth. Quickly she swallowed. As she did, she heard, from within a corridor off the hall, a man say, in a deep, cool, aristocratic-sounding voice tinged with faint amusement:

"Cremwell's been telling me that Johns—the Hastings pigman—has been grossly insulting him in the Riverton pubs, denigrating his professional expertise, mocking his appearance, and casting aspersions on his mother's fidelity."

"Dear me," said another voice, a woman's, also very cool and aristocratic. "The passions of these pigmen! You ought, perhaps, to speak with Radcliffe, before they come to actual blows."

Nervously Jane turned toward these new voices and, her fingers clenched tight on the handle of her valise, watched as from the corridor came two people walking side by side.

One was a tall, broad-shouldered, excessively good-looking man in his early thirties, with neatly cropped brown hair and penetrating dark eyes, and dressed very fine in a dark blue jacket, dark breeches, and tall glossy boots.

The other person was a handsome, slender old lady, very straight and graceful, with silvery curls and sharp blue eyes, and clad in a soft dove-gray gown of marvelous elegance and simplicity.

Jane stared at her, her heart thumping hard within her chest, hearing in her mind once again Mrs. Roger's firm voice:

You're to ask for old Mrs. Penhallow.

She took a few tentative steps forward. "Please, ma'am—are you—may I speak with you, please?" Her voice felt to her as if it were being swallowed up in this enormous hall, but apparently it was loud enough to attract the attention of the handsome man and the elegant old lady, for they both paused and turned to look at her.

The old lady's reaction was more intense—far, far more intense—than Jane could ever have anticipated.

At first moving over Jane with mild curiosity, those sharp blue eyes suddenly widened, her mouth went slack, and the old lady gasped out:

"Titus!"

Her face gone white as snow, she staggered back and would have fallen if not for the swift action of the man beside her, who wrapped his arm around her to keep her upright.

The old lady didn't faint, but she certainly looked as if she had seen a ghost.

Chapter 2

Tugging her skirt down to cover her exposed ankles as best she could, Jane sat gingerly on the edge of a sofa which was upholstered in soft pink and embroidered in a repeating motif of roses, from buds to blooms. It was a very charming and elegant sofa, which was why she was trying to occupy as little of it as possible, all too conscious of how grubby her gown was. Nervous tension was skittering up and down her spine in a very uncomfortable way, and she felt like a gray bedraggled sparrow which had somehow landed amidst a family of sleek, shining swans.

Grouped around her in this cozy and comfortable saloon was the old lady, Mrs. Henrietta Penhallow, who had rallied and was now sitting bolt upright with her blue eyes fixed on Jane with a painful intensity; her grandson, the handsome, aristocratic Mr. Gabriel Penhallow, whose manner was civil, but reserved and watchful; and his pretty wife, Livia, who had come from the nursery where she had been with their children and now sat next to Jane on the flowery pink sofa, her forest-green eyes wide and wondering.

Maybe, Jane thought rather miserably, she should have

simply gone around to the back of the house, begged for a bowl of soup, and crept away. What on earth was she doing here? She glanced over to the doorway, half-wondering if she should make a dash for it.

"You say you have a letter, Miss Kent?" said the old lady.

"Yes, ma'am." Abandoning the idea of a hasty retreat, however appealing, Jane reached down to the valise which she had set next to her feet, opened it, and pulled from it an old, crumbling chapbook entitled *Four Hundred Practical Aspects of Vinegar As Used to Reduce Corpulence, Purify the Humours, Improve the Complexion, and Attract a Most Desirable Spouse.*

Carefully she opened the little book; between the first pages was the old yellowed letter. She took hold of it and leaned across the low table that separated her and the old lady. "Here it is."

With equal carefulness Henrietta Penhallow took the letter, and Jane, rigid with anxiety, watched as her eyes moved rapidly across the lines and down the page, then did it twice more.

"Well, Grandmama?" said Gabriel Penhallow.

The old lady gave him the letter to read, and when he was finished, he silently passed it along to his wife Livia. Jane didn't need to look at it again to know its contents; she had read it so many times she knew it all by heart.

4 October 1780

My darling Charity,

I long to see you—to hold you in my arms again—to put an end to this curst sneaking about. First I've got this curricle race against Calthrop—I'm honor-bound to it, you know, I can't back out—which of course I shall win as he is a ham-handed ass despite his claims of being a superior whip—but it will take me to Brighton and back, which means the soonest I can come for you will be Thursday next. Hey ho! Be packed and ready, my dearest girl—meet me at the church on Decker Street, I'll be waiting for you at noon with the parson standing by and a special license in my pocket. Man and wife at last! We'll dash to France for a bit, till the flap of our elopement dies down, and then I'll take you to Surmont Hall to meet my family. I know they will come to love you as I do. And Somerset is beautiful country, you'll enjoy it very much, I'm sure.

We shall be the happiest couple in the world, you and I.

Yours forever,
Titus

Gently Livia gave the letter back to Jane, and she slid it between the pages of the old chapbook, then put it on the table.

Gabriel Penhallow said, "Is that Titus' handwriting, Grandmama?"

"Yes. I've no doubt it's genuine." Old Mrs. Penhallow looked to Jane, studying her all over again with that same eager, painful curiosity. "Charity was your grandmother, you say?"

"Yes, ma'am."

"But why this delay? It's been nearly forty years since—" The shadow of old grief, freshly renewed, passed across Mrs. Penhallow's face, but somehow she sat up even straighter. "It's been nearly forty years since my son Titus died."

Jane leaned forward again. "He died, ma'am? I'm so sorry. I didn't know."

"Yes. He perished in that race. Apparently his opponent—Edmund Calthrop—rammed his curricle against Titus', which sent Titus and his team off an embankment. Richard—my husband—well, I had to restrain him from going after Calthrop, who, in any event, fled to the Netherlands where he was shortly killed himself, in some kind of vulgar barroom quarrel. As for my poor impetuous Titus—they found a special license in a pocket of his waistcoat, though it hadn't yet been filled out with names."

"So he never came for Charity," Livia said softly. "He meant to, though, didn't he? How very sad. What happened to her, Miss Kent?"

"She died, ma'am, not long after giving birth to a son, Josiah—my father—but I never knew much about her. It was only when my great-grandmother, Charity's mother, was very old, and began to speak more freely, that I learned a little more. She kept talking about Charity's terrible fall, the shame of the family, and how Charity stubbornly refused to name the father of her baby."

Old Mrs. Penhallow was slowly shaking her silvery head. "If only she had. How differently things might have turned out."

Into Jane's mind came an image of the cold, drafty, tumbledown little house in which she had lived for all her life back in Nantwich. It could easily have fit into the massive hall through which she had just passed, and with room to spare. But before she let herself fall into a dangerously wistful dream of what might have been, she gave herself a little shake and went on:

"Yes, well—Charity never did say, ma'am. And when I found the letter a few months ago, hidden inside that chapbook, it was another piece I thought I could add to the puzzle." Jane drew a deep breath and took the plunge, hoping she wouldn't sound ridiculous, impertinent, or both, and thus promptly booted out of the house by the outraged Penhallows. "You see, I—I wondered if Titus was the father of Charity's baby."

"He most certainly was the father, and therefore your grandfather," Mrs. Penhallow said. "You need only to look at his portrait. Gabriel, if you would bring it to Miss Kent?"

"Of course." Gabriel Penhallow rose to his feet, took from the fireplace mantel a small framed painting, and extended it to Jane, who carefully received it in both hands and stared down at it, her breath catching in her throat. It was uncannily like looking at her own reflection in a mirror. The same wavy hair, the color of palest straw. Eyes of an unusual gray, with thick dark eyelashes and above, dark winged eyebrows. Even the same pointed chin. "My God."

"Yes," said Mrs. Penhallow. "The likeness is unmistakable, which explains my shock upon seeing you in the Great Hall. For further confirmation, you may wish at some point to see Titus' other portraits, most of which hang in our Picture Gallery. Well! It seems, Miss Kent, that I am, in fact, your great-grandmother."

Jane stared at that handsome lined face opposite her, her hands gripped tight on the portrait frame as if it were the only solid thing in a topsy-turvy world. Was it really possible that her wild and rather desperate guess had been correct?

Old Mrs. Penhallow continued firmly, answering Jane's unspoken question: "Yes, thanks to the letter, your astonishing resemblance to Titus, and the license that was found in his pocket, I have no doubt. I'm your great-grandmother, and Gabriel is your cousin."

Jane stared at them both, amazed, thrilled, her heart beating violently in her chest with a kind of stunned happiness.

"A day of wonders, to be sure," remarked Gabriel Penhallow, his manner a little less cool, his expression a little less reserved. "A long-lost relation turning up on one's doorstep. One feels quite like a character in a storybook."

"One certainly does," responded Mrs. Penhallow. "A feeling I've had more than once in my long, long life. Miss Kent, may I inquire as to your age?"

"I'm twenty, ma'am."

"Indeed? You look younger. Perhaps it's the slightness of your person."

Slightness of your person. Jane had to repress a sudden crazy desire to laugh. What a tactful way to say *skeletally thin.* Politely she replied, "Perhaps, ma'am."

"How very extraordinary this all is!" Livia exclaimed. "Jane—if you don't mind my calling you that?—I have so many questions! Which I hope isn't horribly rude of me? Oh—here's Mary with tea. Thank you, Mary, I'll move this little book so you can set down the tray."

As the maidservant placed on the low table a large, laden silver tray, Jane could feel saliva pooling in her mouth again and she forced herself to tear her gaze away from a plate heaped high with what looked to be ham sandwiches, cut attractively on the diagonal. Lord, oh Lord, there were devilled eggs too, and muffins, and a whole entire seedcake, dotted with caraway seeds and fragrant with cinnamon that teased at her nostrils in the most seductive way.

Sternly Jane instructed her stomach not to rumble again, and for a few moments she felt that same disconcerting urge to laugh. Here she was, having miraculously found these interesting (and also slightly terrifying) new family members, thinking—once again—about food.

Well, who could blame her?

After two long years without much to eat, a certain interest in the subject was only natural.

"Four Hundred Practical Aspects of Vinegar . . ." Livia had picked up the chapbook and was looking with fresh wonder at the title. "*. . . As Used to Reduce Corpulence, Purify the Humours, Improve the Complexion, and Attract a Most Desirable Spouse.* Jane, why did Charity keep Titus' letter in this? Did it have a special significance for her?"

Jane turned to face Livia, which was a fairly effective way of keeping the tea-tray out of her direct line of sight, although peripheral vision was still a bit of a problem. "Charity's parents had a little print-shop in London, ma'am. They put out all kinds of pamphlets and chapbooks, mostly with—ah—advice like this. Apparently all written by my great-grandfather."

"Very creative," said old Mrs. Penhallow dryly, and gave a sudden crack of laughter. "Oh, I can easily imagine Titus wandering into a shop like that, and buying several of these pamphlets as a joke to dispense among his friends! Ever one for a lark, my darling madcap Titus. That must have been how he met Charity."

"And so perhaps Charity tucked his letter into one of her family's chapbooks," said Livia. "But you only discovered it a few months ago, Jane?"

"Yes, ma'am. My great-grandmother died this past autumn, and with my parents long gone, it was just me left. I knew I couldn't afford to stay in our house much longer, so I started clearing out the old trunks and boxes stored in our attic. That's how I found the chapbook with the letter, in a little valise of Charity's. This same one." She nodded at the valise next to her feet, saw her skinny exposed ankles again, and gently set aside Titus' portrait so she could tug her skirt down an inch or two. Titus: her *grandfather*!

"And to think," said Mrs. Penhallow, with longing in her voice, "I might have seen you years ago, Miss Kent, and your father, perhaps, in London."

"No, ma'am, you wouldn't have," replied Jane. "My great-grandfather died of an apoplexy not long after the failed elopement, and without him to provide all the writing, the print-shop went under, so my great-grandmother took Charity back to the little town she herself had been raised in—Nantwich."

"That's near Liverpool, I believe?" Mrs. Penhallow asked.

"Yes, ma'am."

"It must have taken you quite a while to get here."

"Yes, ma'am."

"Had you a companion of any sort? A maid?"

"No, ma'am."

"How very enterprising of you, Miss Kent."

Enterprising. Jane choked back another laugh. A diplomatic way to describe an unpleasant, uncomfortable, nerve-wracking journey. Still, it sounded like a compliment, so she said, "Thank you, ma'am."

"But Jane," Livia said, "with the print-shop gone, how did you and your family get on? Were you happy growing up in Nantwich? What happened to your parents? Were you frightened, traveling all by yourself? Also—"

"While these are all questions whose answers I am equally interested to hear," interposed Gabriel Penhallow, in his dark eyes a subtle gleam of affectionate humor as he turned them upon his wife, "may I suggest that further inquiries be postponed until we've all had some tea?"

Jane looked with admiration and gratitude at him.

What an excellent idea.

In fact, it was the best idea anyone, in the whole history of the world, had ever had.

Her cousin Gabriel was obviously a *genius*.

Jane hitched herself around on the sofa so that she was facing the tea-tray again, as it now seemed safe to do so, and folded her hands in her lap, just as might a person do who could wait forever for tea. But she did permit herself to look, rather gloatingly, at the big silver teapot, the empty cups and little plates just waiting to be filled, at the elegant linen napkins, and, of course, at the cake, the muffins, the devilled eggs, the sandwiches.

What would she have first?

Into her mind popped an image of herself with grotesque bulging cheeks, just like a chipmunk, having inserted into her mouth four eggs, two on each side.

"Oh yes, of course, Gabriel, you're absolutely correct," said Livia, smiling at him and then at Jane. "I'll pour out right away. Jane, won't you please help yourself to anything you like?"

"Thank you, ma'am," Jane answered, and, making herself move very slowly, she took a plate, and onto the plate she put a muffin and a sandwich.

She had taken three bites of her sandwich before she realized, glancing at Livia beside her, that she should have taken a napkin.

Flushing hotly, she reached out to get one from the silver tray.

As they had their tea, nobody said a word about Jane's deliberate but methodical consumption of food and drink which was probably greater in total volume than that which Mrs. Penhallow, Gabriel, and Livia had collectively among the three of them. In between bites, she told them that Great-grandmother Kent had taken in sewing to make money, and had tried without much success to train Jane up to do the same, and also that her father Josiah had at eighteen married the daughter of a blacksmith, but they had both been taken by the cholera epidemic back in '02 when Jane was five, and finally she described how poor Great-grandmother's bitter spirit from first to last had rather alienated the Kent family from their neighbors, and so Jane had really left nothing—and no one—behind when she had embarked on her momentous trip to Surmont Hall.

As she talked and ate and drank, Jane couldn't help but notice that old Mrs. Penhallow was gazing at her the whole time, as if more hungry for the sheer sight of her than for the food—barely touched—on her plate. And when tea was over, and Livia suggested that Jane might like to go upstairs to the bedchamber which had been prepared for her and rest for a while, and Jane, realizing that she was exhausted to the bone, had willingly agreed, and gotten up, valise in hand, and thanked them all from the bottom of her heart, Henrietta had stood up too, and went to Jane, and hugged her for a long, long time. And then she softly said:

"Welcome home, my dear."

Anthony leaned his elbow on the stone balustrade of the Duchess' pen, cupping his chin in one hand, and with the other hand he used a stick to scratch the broad, hairy pink back below him. The Duchess grunted with pleasure, but there was no answering smile on Anthony's face.

For his mood was melancholy.

It had taken three full days for the Preston-Carnabys to finally realize that no offer of marriage was forthcoming, had been forthcoming, or would ever be forthcoming, no matter how tangled up he got in subjunctive verb forms.

Or did he mean the present perfect progressive?

Good Lord, who knew and who cared?

The point was, those were three days of his life he would never get back.

The teas, the strolls, the rides, the dinners that seemed to go on forever. The labored conversations. Margaret's hard relentless eyes boring into him. The Preston-Carnabys leaning on his every word as if jewels fell from his mouth every time he opened it, which only made him feel less and less like saying anything at all. And to add insult to injury, after luncheon today Margaret had ruthlessly inveigled him into showing Miss Preston-Carnaby around the conservatory, a ploy so blatant that he wanted with all his heart to immediately decamp somewhere else—*anywhere* else—in a very rude and undukish way.

Luckily, Miss Preston-Carnaby (who had been positively foaming at the mouth with spurious compliments about Wakefield) had an adverse reaction to the Siberian irises which were Margaret's pride and joy, not to say obsession, and so Anthony was able inside of ten minutes to lead her, with streaming eyes and dripping nostrils, out of the dangerous privacy of the conservatory and return her forthwith to her parents who lay in wait just outside the door, practically with tails twitching, like stalking lions eyeing their innocent prey (him), after which he bowed himself away and escaped for a much-needed interval of respite in his library, where he found balm for his wounds within the ever-fascinating pages of Dinkle's *Advanced Concepts in Piggery.*

Margaret had found him there an hour or so later, with his feet up on his desk and his chair tipped back, deep in a gripping section on exudative dermatitis. In an unpleasantly icy way she had informed him that the Preston-Carnabys had left in high dudgeon for their home in Yorkshire, and he had made the mistake of saying "About time," and she had angrily shoved his feet off the desk and nearly sent him sprawling, and then with what struck him as a triumphant sort of malice (or a malicious sort of triumph) she issued her *coup de grâce*, saying she had already written to her acquaintance the Countess of Silsbury, extending a cordial invitation to her and her charming, delightful, beautiful, accomplished, and highly eligible daughter, Lady Felicia Merifield, to come stay at Hastings for as long as they liked.

Good God, Meg, we're not a blasted inn, he had protested, but to no avail.

Margaret had sent her letter by express.

Anthony now reached out with the stick to expertly scratch just behind the Duchess' ears, a highly sensitive area of her anatomy, and she responded with further happy grunts.

Oh, to be a pig, he thought gloomily.

Eat, wallow, sleep, and be scratched where it felt good.

Why couldn't *his* life be that simple?

But no—he had apple blights to worry about, and Margaret's incessant machinations to evade as best he could, and Mrs. Roger's sinister comment to dwell upon.

You're next, Yer Grace.

Just what the devil did she mean by that?

In a perfect world, via this mysterious utterance she would have been giving him a prescient sort of wink to let him know that the premier Hastings pumpkin (at present a mere twinkle in his head gardener McTavish's eye), which would be offered up at this year's competition at the annual harvest *fête*, would finally best Miss Humphrey's pumpkin, after several painful years of second-place ribbons rather than the treasured gilt cup.

But alas, this was not a perfect world.

Far from it.

To this he could attest.

Also, Mrs. Roger had never, to his limited knowledge, manifested the slightest interest in pumpkins, so it seemed unlikely that she had been referring to his aspirations in that regard.

"Foot-and-mouth," a voice said, sounding aggrieved.

Anthony turned his head to see that his pigman Johns had come stumping up to the pig-cote, and now stood looking over the balustrade, his big round red face creased in bitter lines.

"I beg your pardon?" Anthony said, resisting the urge to look nervously down at his own feet which, so far as he knew, were in tiptop condition.

"That there Cremwell's been saying the Duchess has foot-and-mouth, guv'nor."

"A filthy lie."

"You're not wrong there. I mean, *look* at those hooves, guv'nor. Ever seen anything more beautiful in your life?"

"Well," said Anthony, hesitating, torn between honesty and loyalty, but Johns was on a roll.

"It hurts, don't it, to know that damned blabby lick-spittle's spreading such things about. And here's me, despite all *his* flams and clankers, the very soul of politeness! But it's trying, guv'nor, very trying. Why, old Moore came shamble-legging up to me yesterday, blathering on about vinegar remedies till it was all I could do to not land him a facer."

"Vinegar remedies? What rot. I'd have been incensed too."

"Right waspish I was, guv'nor, that I'll not deny." Johns shook his head morosely. "But it's just this sort of ill-meaning tittle-tattle that might sway them there judges come festival time."

"By God, so it might," said Anthony, much struck. "We can't have that."

"Weren't you gonta tell Mr. Penhallow to make Cremwell stubble it, guv'nor?"

"Well, I was, Johns, if not quite in those terms, but I've been tethered to the ancestral pile by the miserable chains of hospitality." Even as Anthony said this, he felt a sudden burst of exuberance overtake him. The Preston-Carnabys were now little more than an exhausting memory, and he was (for now) a free man again. This, he thought jubilantly, straightening up, was no doubt how mighty Samson felt upon regaining his strength in the temple, casting off his shackles and toppling all those pillars.

Although, of course, he *did* die right after that.

A sobering detail.

Anthony cast a glance past the Duchess' pig-cote and to the lake beyond, where, on the opposite shore, stood the full-scale replica of a Greek temple built by his great-grandfather Osbert who, for some obscure reason, had seemed to think it an appropriate use of ducal resources.

It was easy to imagine Samson, arms outstretched, poised between two of those massive columns.

As he gazed thoughtfully across the lake, it also occurred to Anthony that it had been quite a while since his last haircut.

Hadn't Margaret been nagging him about that, in fact? He seemed to recall some pointed remarks on the subject recently at breakfast, but as he preferred at all times to read the papers while he had his eggs, toast, and so on, his memory was rather vague.

Dismissing the question from his mind, he handed the Duchess' stick to Johns, gave a loud whistle, and said cheerfully:

"I'm off, then."

Four dogs came dashing out of the nearby woods with flattering alacrity. Bounding on long powerful legs, his wolfhound Breen came first, followed by—rather neatly in order of size—two dogs of uncertain parentage, Joe (possible retriever) and Sam (maybe a shepherd), and finally the lame little pug Snuffles, a runt and Wakefield's favorite among the four, whom Anthony had rescued from certain extinction at the hands of the small-minded village draper. Strictly speaking, Snuffles didn't dash—given the infinitesimal length of his legs, his run was more like a lolloping skitter, but it was, as he and Wakefield often agreed, the most adorable thing they had ever seen.

"Come on, you lot," he said to them, and together they made their way to the stables where he left them to hobnob with the horses and shamelessly importune the grooms for treats. And then he was on his horse and on his way to Surmont Hall.

Oh dear, Jane thought anxiously, she was going to be late.

She had overslept (again)—what she'd intended to be only a brief afternoon nap turned into a deep sleep of some three or four hours—and she'd gotten lost (again) in the dizzying maze of corridors, galleries, hallways, and staircases within this vast, ancient house.

Too, if truth be told, she had wandered (again, but by accident this time) into the Picture Gallery, and it was impossible not to stop and stare at the portraits of Grandfather Titus, marveling (again) at their uncanny resemblance to herself. Also, it was helpful to see the paintings of her cousin Gabriel when he was a little boy, and Great-grandmother Henrietta, too, as a girl, for it was a reassuring reminder that they too had once been actual children and, perhaps, not quite as self-assured as they were now as fully fledged adults. Jane also marveled once more at how nice everyone had been to her these past few days, how kind and accepting of her, as if she weren't a little lost sparrow but actually a swan like them. Nantwich seemed further and further away, and with each passing hour she was beginning, slowly but surely, to feel more and more at home here.

Breathlessly Jane turned a corner, found herself at last in the hallway which led to the Little Drawing-room, and—still amazed at finding herself in a house so large that the various rooms actually had names—hurried to the open door, then stopped abruptly on the threshold when she saw that the family, at the moment represented by Great-grandmother Henrietta and Livia, had two guests for tea.

This would be her first real encounter with people from the neighborhood.

Reflexively Jane ran her hands along the smooth pale-green muslin of her gown—one of Livia's, actually, which she had generously given to Jane. Great-grandmother had directed one of the maidservants to quickly alter it to accommodate Jane's very different dimensions, and had also consigned forevermore to the rubbish heap the old, dirty gown in which Jane had traveled from Nantwich, saying that it wasn't even fit to be cut down into floor-rags.

Jane had not been sorry to see it go.

She glanced down at the hem of her new gown, saw with satisfaction that her ankles were neatly concealed, and also noticed with satisfaction that three days of food and sleep and baths and also kindness did wonders for one's confidence, then stepped into the room feeling more like herself than she had in a long, long time.

"Here she is," said Great-grandmother Henrietta, smiling at Jane, and introduced her to Miss Humphrey, a plump bespectacled middle-aged lady with lustrous brown hair and kind soft eyes, and to Miss Trevelyan, also middle-aged, slim, elegant, vigorous-looking, dressed in a plum-colored gown of modish cut and with a dashing coiffure of graying curls swept high on her head.

"You're quite the nine days' wonder, Miss Kent," said Miss Trevelyan, who had stood up to affably shake hands with Jane. "To think that you've only recently learned your true identity! How delightful. You may inspire me to try my hand at a novel—it would make a splendid plot, you know. A lovely young woman, born to a life of humble obscurity, discovers at twenty she's actually a member of one of England's oldest and most distinguished families."

Miss Trevelyan paused, on her face a look of dreamy enthusiasm, then went on thoughtfully:

"Although it would hardly be innovative, would it? Been done to death, really. Also, it would probably be better if the young woman turned out to be a princess or a duchess or something along those lines—especially if there's some sort of dark, enigmatic hero, too, with a fine curling lip of disdain. I daresay the book would sell better that way."

"Oh—I—would it indeed, ma'am?" said Jane, rather blankly.

"Miss Trevelyan is a writer," explained Livia, and Jane, having eyed her new acquaintance with respect and not a little awe, went to sit on the sofa closest to where the tea-tray would, she hoped, shortly be placed. She said to Miss Trevelyan:

"What sort of books do you write, ma'am?"

"History mostly, Miss Kent. Just now I'm on a Tudor jag—all six wives of the monstrous Henry, each with their own book. I'm nearly finished with Anne of Cleves." Miss Trevelyan sat back down next to Miss Humphrey, who said with fond admiration:

"Sarah's Anne Boleyn *and* Katherine of Aragon books were tremendous sellers."

"Yes, they paid for the new roof," said Miss Trevelyan, with justifiable pride, "and Jane Seymour fixed the drains. If Anne of Cleves does as well as she ought, you'll have that extension to the greenhouse you've been wanting, my dear Arabella."

"Oh, that'll be lovely." Miss Humphrey smiled at Miss Trevelyan. "I'd love to have a whirl at growing some more winter salads. One does crave something fresh and green when it's so cold out."

This was going better than Jane could have hoped. Miss Trevelyan and Miss Humphrey were so nice, and didn't seem to care one jot about her decidedly odd background. Her trepidations fell away, and she felt her shoulders, held tight with tension, begin to relax. Bravely she said:

"It's embarrassing to admit, but I always thought her name was Anne of *Cloves*. And I imagined her walking around the palace smelling so nice."

"Funny you should say that, Miss Kent," replied Miss Trevelyan, "as Henry Tudor went about telling everyone that poor Anne smelled bad, which is quite the rich remark coming from a man with a suppurating ulcer on his leg that stank to high heaven."

"He should have tried a turpentine compress," Jane said without thinking, then blushed when Miss Trevelyan looked at her with bright curious eyes and said:

"Medical, are you, Miss Kent?"

"Oh no, ma'am. I was quoting from an old—ah—remedy of my great-grandfather's. He wrote pamphlets filled with such things for a living—we had a whole trunkful of them in our house, and as there wasn't much else to read, I pored over them again and again. So I'm afraid my brain is quite filled with these remedies."

"My mother was a great proponent of farina cataplasms," said Miss Humphrey nostalgically. "She always said there was nothing else so soothing for veinous palpitations."

"Yes, and she also let those quacks in Bath wrap her feet in vinegar-infused cloths for hours on end," retorted Miss Trevelyan. "And only consider what happened then."

"It *was* rather dreadful, having all her toenails fall off," Miss Humphrey agreed. "Poor Mama! Yet she never lost her faith in medicine."

"On a different subject," said Great-grandmother Henrietta, "I've been thinking that as Jane's education has, through no fault of her own, been sadly neglected, she would benefit from some lessons with Mr. Pressley."

"Lessons?" echoed Jane in surprise. Well, she would certainly enjoy acquiring some more learning, because if she had been wrong about Anne of Cloves—Cleves—it stood to reason there were probably quite a few more gaps in her understanding of the world. It would be nice, though, if this Mr. Pressley wasn't like the schoolmaster back in Nantwich, who, it was well known, drank so much that his young students often had to troop over to his favorite tavern, pour a bucket of water over his head, and together convey him back to the schoolhouse, two boys to each limb and one to keep his head from dragging on the ground.

"Yes, lessons in geography, history, science, mathematics, English grammar, and so on, my dear," answered Great-grandmother. "I've sent a note round to the vicarage, and Mr. Pressley says you're welcome to begin tomorrow."

"Tomorrow?" Jane said, feeling a little dazed. Great-grandmother clearly wasn't one to let the grass grow under *her* feet.

"That's right, my dear. You'll certainly be one of his older pupils, but I understand the range of his scholarship is impressive."

"Oh yes, he's an Oxford man," said Miss Trevelyan. "If he hadn't been a younger son and put to the yoke, you know, I do think he would have been a brilliant scholar."

"Mr. Pressley doesn't seem to mind being a vicar," Livia observed. "He's so pleasant to talk to. And I always enjoy his sermons."

"Yes, nice and short," Miss Trevelyan said approvingly.

"He has only the one pupil at the moment, I believe," said Miss Humphrey. "The Duke's son. Dear little Wakefield. He came to visit us the other day, and we had *such* a nice chat."

"Speaking of the Duke," said Livia, "he stopped by to talk to Gabriel, and I invited him to join us for tea. I expect they'll be here shortly."

A duke! A thrill ran through Jane from head to toe, and she turned her eyes expectantly to the doorway. Great-grandmother Kent had avidly, if disparagingly, followed any snippet of news that reached Nantwich about the Royal Family and the nobility in general, and so Jane was well positioned to know that dukes were just below the royals in rank and consequence.

Apparently her new relations, the Penhallows, were indeed—as Miss Trevelyan had said—one of England's oldest and most distinguished families, but how exciting to meet a real live duke! And how grand he must be!

It would be unlikely that he'd sweep into the room clad in, say, an ermine-trimmed velvet cape which would trail behind him by several feet, as that would necessitate having a couple of pages to follow him about to keep it from getting tangled around chair legs, but still, there was bound to be such an air of stately magnificence about him—and grandeur—and quite possibly hauteur. Jane wondered if she should curtsy. And what should she say?

Something noble and lofty and stunningly clever?

For example, something about art? Philosophy? Literature? History?

Unfortunately she didn't know much about any of those things.

What if the Duke asked her about them? Ideally, he might happen to mention Henry Tudor, and thanks to Miss Trevelyan, Jane now reliably knew something about his wives *and* the smelly ulcer on his leg.

Sounds of deep voices, out in the hallway, reached Jane's ears. One of them belonged to Cousin Gabriel, and the other was unknown to her.

Now she could hear footsteps approaching.

They were almost here!

Jane noticed that in her excitement she had been holding her breath, and made herself quietly exhale. She glanced around and saw that nobody else was looking particularly agitated, but maybe (hard as it was to believe) when one spent a lot of time traveling in such elevated circles one got used to being around dukes. Back in Nantwich the thought had never, ever crossed her mind—that one day she would be in the same room as an actual duke.

Cousin Gabriel came into the drawing-room, and with him was a tall, wiry-looking man of about the same age who had a great deal of tawny light-brown hair. He wore a plain dark blue jacket, a carelessly tied neckcloth, dark breeches, and tall, rather scuffed black boots.

Jane stared.

Why, he was quite ordinary-looking. In fact, he rather reminded her of a fellow one might see lounging around a Nantwich stable-yard, or herding a flock of sheep to the market square.

And so, when Cousin Gabriel introduced her to His Grace the Duke of Radcliffe, Jane smiled politely up into his long thin face, but with a mild sense of disillusionment which she tried very hard to conceal. Unfortunately, she had one of those countenances which—as Great-grandmother Kent had often remarked, in a rather sour way—could be all too expressive.

Chapter 3

Anthony sat down in a comfortable armchair, crossed one leg over the other, and looked around the room. Penhallow was talking to Miss Trevelyan, his wife Livia was chatting with Miss Humphrey, old Mrs. Penhallow had a faintly sardonic expression on her face, and the other person, a slim, flaxen-haired girl—what *was* her name? He'd already forgotten it—was gazing at him in a manner with which he was all too familiar.

She was looking disappointed.

Old Mrs. Penhallow said, "I trust, Duke, that you and Gabriel have between you resolved the pressing issue of your pigmen's dispute."

Her tone did not, in Anthony's opinion, convey serious concern over the matter, so rather than regale her with a thoughtful, nuanced reply which encompassed the subtler aspects of this complex and exceedingly delicate situation, he merely said, "Well, we hope so, ma'am."

Mrs. Penhallow nodded, in a way that could only be described as satirical. Anthony uncrossed his left leg from over his right leg, then crossed his right leg over his left, and began to gently swing his uppermost foot back and forth. It was really only the imminent arrival of the tea-tray that was keeping him here. If he wanted sardonic glances sent his way, he could just go home and talk to Margaret.

"I believe, Duke, that your son Wakefield remains at home, instead of going off to school?"

"Yes."

"A rather unusual arrangement."

"Perhaps."

"Didn't you yourself go off to school when you were that age?"

"For a while, ma'am."

"I see."

Anthony braced himself for further interrogation on that point, but Mrs. Penhallow went on:

"Wakefield is a pupil of Mr. Pressley's, is he not?"

"Yes, that's right."

"And are you satisfied with his progress?"

"Quite."

"I'm pleased to hear it, as Miss Kent's going to begin lessons with Mr. Pressley tomorrow."

"Who is?"

"My great-granddaughter."

"Ah."

Mrs. Penhallow gave him a slight, caustic smile. "I refer, of course, to the young lady sitting opposite you, Duke."

Anthony looked across the low table to the sofa on which the gray-eyed girl sat, and tried to piece together what little he knew of the situation. Mrs. Penhallow had a great-granddaughter here at Surmont Hall, who, having appeared seemingly out of nowhere, was going to have lessons with Mr. Pressley. Speaking of unusual arrangements, wasn't this one as well? He vaguely remembered Margaret having a governess, or a series of them—it was difficult to recall as they all seemed to be tyrannical, severely dressed women who sported a deeply intimidating pince-nez.

"Will he mind?" said the gray-eyed girl—Miss Kent—and Anthony found himself jolted out of misty memory into the present again where, he was pleased to recollect, he knew no one who wore a pince-nez. He answered:

"Will who mind?"

"Your son Wakefield."

"Mind what?"

"If I have lessons too."

"Why would he?"

Miss Kent's delicate dark brows drew together ever so slightly, as if she were puzzled. "I mean—will Wakefield object to sharing Mr. Pressley's time with me."

Anthony thought about it. "I can't see why he would. But of course, you can ask him yourself if you like."

"Duke," said old Mrs. Penhallow, "you're a most unusual parent."

He gave her a wry smile. "So my sister says."

"How *is* dear Lady Margaret?" In the old lady's voice was the same satirical tone, which reminded him that between these two formidable women absolutely no love was lost. Just the other day Margaret made a waspish remark about how Henrietta Penhallow must have been completely addled to allow her only grandson to marry such an inauspicious person as Livia, and also to think herself (or her head gardener) capable of growing decent roses of Provins. To which Anthony had replied that he found Livia rather an auspicious person, a phrase which made little sense in retrospect, but a fellow couldn't stand idly by and allow Margaret to go on snobbishly insulting a perfectly nice lady who, whatever her origins, was also a dab hand at raising Blue Andalusian chickens. An unpleasant scene had followed, which concluded with Margaret storming out of his library and slamming the door with such violence that two paintings had fallen off the wall.

Anthony now answered:

"Oh, she's fine. Busy."

"You've had houseguests, I understand?"

"Unfortunately, yes."

"Dear me, how inhospitable of you, Duke."

Well, this was certainly putting him in a bad light. Nor did he particularly care to explain and so paint himself for the harassed, ruthlessly pursued single man that he was. "I say, here's tea," Anthony said with relief, especially as the conversation then became more general.

Miss Humphrey asked after Titania, Lucy, and baby Daniel, the three young children of Livia and Gabriel; Mrs. Penhallow mentioned receiving an interesting letter from her former companion, Mrs. Markson, who was traveling in Europe with her husband, Mr. Pressley's predecessor, and with Miss Gwendolyn Penhallow, the younger sister of Gabriel's cousin Hugo; and also Miss Trevelyan issued a scathing critique of Lady Caroline Lamb's scandalous, gossipy novel *Glenarvon*, primarily finding fault with its sensationalist themes and its sloppy writing, which included the murder of a character who was later shown to still be alive.

Anthony listened as he made his way through several small iced butter-cakes, a plate he'd filled with delicious fish-paste sandwiches, and four sweet York biscuits. He noticed that Miss Kent wasn't saying much either, and that she seemed to have quite an appetite. As he watched her take two more biscuits, he also noticed that she had long-fingered, capable-looking hands, with very slim wrists and a prominent, knobby bone showing in the delicate juncture between arm and hand.

Then he watched as one of those interesting and beautiful hands also took another sandwich. And saw with a little ripple of alarm that there were only two sandwiches left. So he took one, and ate it.

Then he saw Miss Kent take another butter-cake, leaving only three left. She ate it, without hurry but with great precision, and had a sip of her tea.

Surreptitiously Anthony glanced around. Everyone else—with the exception of Miss Kent, who apparently had at least one hollow limb—seemed to have finished their tea. So he took one of the three remaining butter-cakes, ate that, and took another one which he also ate.

That left one butter-cake, one sandwich, and three York biscuits.

He took a fortifying swallow of tea, then looked across the low table and into Miss Kent's big, gray, dark-lashed eyes. And he saw that she was looking right back at him, on her face a determined expression. (Which, he thought, was preferable to a disappointed one.)

And before he could do anything about it, she took the last butter-cake.

She ate it in two bites.

There was a trace of icing on her upper lip when she was done, and Anthony watched, fascinated, as delicately she licked it away with the tip of her tongue.

She could have used a napkin, of course, yet he found himself rather glad she hadn't.

All the icing was gone from that nicely shaped upper lip, the very color of—well, in point of fact, the glorious pink color of a Provins rose in full bloom.

Rather dreamily Anthony wondered if she would lick her lip again, just to be sure.

And Miss Kent, striking like an adder, made her next move, which was to take two of the three remaining York biscuits.

Anthony snapped to attention. Even in his indignation, however, he had to grudgingly admire her rapacious boldness. But he wasn't going to let himself be blinded by admiration.

He reached out to take the last biscuit.

This he ate with marked efficiency, but here again, Miss Kent beat him all to flinders. Never had he seen someone eat biscuits so rapidly while at the same time managing to look so cool and prim. It was an art form, one which Miss Kent had clearly taken to its highest level.

Appreciation notwithstanding, Anthony was aware of a certain tension humming within him.

For there was one sandwich left.

He looked at it, and then at Miss Kent. She was looking at him, and then, as if casually, dropped her gaze to the table between them.

"I say," he said, cunningly, "fine weather we've been having."

"It does seem to have warmed up over the past few days," she agreed.

Ha *ha*, he thought. Got her to look at me, not the sandwich. He went on, "It snowed last week, you know."

"Oh, did it?"

"Yes, just a little."

"I wasn't here then."

"Where were you?"

"Traveling here from Nantwich."

Damn. "Nantwich" sounded too much like "sandwich." Anthony willed himself to keep his eyes on Miss Kent's face. "That's in the north, isn't it?"

"Yes, not far from Liverpool."

"Is that where you're from?"

"Yes, that's right."

"I didn't know the Penhallows had a northern branch of the family."

"There are two, Great-grandmother says—one up in Cumbria, and another further north, in the Scottish Highlands. But not in Nantwich."

Damn again. Don't look down, old chap, don't look down, Anthony sternly told himself. "So you're from a twig of the family, then?"

Miss Kent smiled a little. "That's a good way to put it. Titus Penhallow was my grandfather."

"Titus? I've never heard of him."

"He was a son of Great-grandmother's."

"Oh, I see."

"There's a portrait of him over on the mantel."

Miss Kent gestured with one of those beautiful hands of hers, and Anthony looked over to the wide beveled mantelpiece, which held several smallish paintings, a white marble bust of Shakespeare, a mahogany-inlaid clock, and a tall crystal vase filled with exquisite pink flowers. This last item Anthony surveyed with no small degree of pleasure, as it put paid to Margaret's vindictive assertion that the Penhallow hothouse was unable to properly grow those fabled roses of Provins. Then he remembered he was supposed to be looking for a portrait of Titus Penhallow. Well, it had to be the young man with the wavy straw-colored hair, gray eyes, and dark eyelashes and brows.

"I say, Miss Kent, you're as alike as—"

The time-honored phrase *two peas in a pod* remained unspoken. Actually, it would not have been too much to say that it stuck in his throat, as Anthony now saw that while he had been perusing the mantel, Miss Kent had taken the last sandwich, and was now busily engaged in chewing.

Piqued, Anthony glanced pointedly at the empty sandwich platter. It would be ungallant in him to openly accuse her of guile, subterfuge, or outright thievery. Still, he had Miss Kent's measure now, and the next time they had tea together he would know what to do.

He watched as Miss Kent popped the last bit of sandwich in her mouth, chewed, swallowed, and dabbed at those Provins-pink lips of hers with a napkin.

Yes indeed, he was looking forward to besting her.

Their guests had left, and Jane, comfortably full, felt a little guilty about taking the last sandwich. On the other hand, the Duke *had* taken the last biscuit, so maybe that made it fair. Or was it possible there was some sort of unwritten rule about dukes getting more food than other people? Well, too bad, she thought defiantly. And felt rather sorry she hadn't eaten more butter-cakes.

Great-grandmother Henrietta, sitting bolt upright as she always seemed to do, said with a sniff:

"What a ramshackle person Anthony Farr is."

"Granny, why do you say that?" asked Livia. "I like him."

"I can't imagine why. He's simply *raffish*—hardly *my* idea of a proper duke. Did you observe the scuff on his boots? And his neckcloth! I daresay that you, Gabriel, would never leave your room, let alone the house, with yours tied in that shabby way."

"I do prefer a bit more precision for myself," said Cousin Gabriel, "but it doesn't mean I judge him based upon his sartorial preferences. Also, I believe he's an excellent landlord to his tenant farmers, and there's nobody I'd rather talk to about timber than Farr. Just last month he gave me some very useful suggestions for those yew groves that are getting overcrowded."

Great-grandmother waved her hand impatiently. "Yes, yes, that's all very well and good, but I object to his comportment. And his lack of dignity. And his obsession with his pigs."

Jane watched as onto Cousin Gabriel's face came a faint, amused smile. "You might well accuse me of the same obsession, Grandmama."

"Well, that's a different matter entirely," answered Great-grandmother loftily. "The Penhallow pigs are renowned throughout Somerset for their superior size and bone structure. Now, Jane," she went on, clearly done with dukes, timber, and things porcine, "I wanted to let you know that before you go off to your lessons tomorrow, Alice Simpkin, the Riverton seamstress, will come here to take your measurements and discuss various fabrics and trimmings. You're in urgent need of gowns, pelisses, hats, shoes, and so on."

Not for the first time since arriving at Surmont Hall, Jane felt rather like a character in a fairy tale. Herself the drab little ragamuffin. Arriving at a magnificent palace. And Great-grandmother the magician, casually waving a wand that would produce—hey presto!—new clothes. Jane tried to remember the last time she had had something new.

And couldn't.

She looked down at the ivory-colored silk brocade slippers Great-grandmother had loaned her. They were beautiful, but too tight. Only think of it. New shoes, which would fit. Happiness at the very thought filled Jane up like a balloon expanding with air, and for a few giddy moments she thought she might actually float up toward the ceiling.

"Thank you *very* much, Great-grandmother," she said, in her voice a lilt of pleasure. "And for taking me in like this. If you're sure it's not a horrible inconvenience?"

Silvery brows raised high, as if surprised, Great-grandmother said, "Of course not, my dear Jane. And naturally we've taken you in—you're family, and this is your home now. Your being here with us is, I know, exactly what Titus would have wanted."

"Family," Jane murmured, and smiled. What a beautiful word.

There was a tap on the open door. The Hall's butler, Crenshaw, said in his concise, measured tones that the headmaster of the village school—of which Henrietta Penhallow was patroness—awaited her in the Green Saloon. "Tell Mr. Lumley I'll be there directly, Crenshaw, thank you," said Great-grandmother, and rose to her feet in a brisk rustle of silken skirts.

Cousin Gabriel stood up as well. "And I'm to my study, to meet with my bailiff. I'll see you at dinner, ladies."

Jane watched as they left the room, then turned to Livia, admiring how neat and composed she looked in her simple, elegant gown of dark blue. Her vivid auburn hair was dressed in a high knot at the back of her head, with soft tendrils allowed to fall loose about her ears and frame her face. Jane wondered if her wavier hair would look as pretty like that.

"I've barely had a chance to talk with you, Jane, these past three days," Livia said with a kind smile. "I know you've needed to rest, and I've been so busy. How are you getting on?"

"Oh, ma'am, I hardly know. It feels like a dream. A good dream, but . . ."

"A little overwhelming?"

"A little," Jane admitted.

"I was overwhelmed too, when I first came here. I can't tell you how many times I got lost trying to get from one place to another! And I made so many mistakes and missteps."

Jane stared. How surprising. Livia seemed so easy in herself, and so accomplished. "Did you really, ma'am?"

"Oh, yes! Frequently, I assure you! But it got better, you know, over time. And please, won't you call me 'Livia'? There aren't that many years between us, after all."

"Livia it is, then," answered Jane, a little shyly.

"Good! That sounds much better." Livia smiled at her again, then went on in a more serious tone. "I've been thinking about what you said that first day, Jane, and how it must have been so hard having your great-grandmother Kent pass away, leaving you all alone."

"It *was* hard," Jane said, "but in her illness she suffered so much those last two years, especially as we began to run out of money, that in a way I couldn't help but be relieved for her. If that doesn't sound like an awful thing to say?"

"No, not at all."

"We did get along better toward the end, which made me glad. I'm afraid that I was rather a disappointment to her. She was very proud of her years in London, you see, and she tried so hard to bring me up in the same mold. She taught me how to speak properly, having once been a lady's maid to a well-educated banker's wife, and she also taught me to read and write, and to stand up straight, and *bathe*—that in itself made the other children see me as rather freakish." Jane gave a wry smile. "And she did her best to keep me close at home, which I hated. Although after my parents died, she *had* to let me go about the town, picking up and delivering the mending. And she even had to admit that I was good at it. I was clever at counting and making sure people didn't try to short the fee. Oh, how I loved my moments of freedom!" Then Jane sobered once more. "Looking back—and knowing what I do now—I think she was afraid I'd end up like Charity. She was always warning me against the village boys, saying I had to look higher. And how furious she was that her grandson Josiah married a mere blacksmith's daughter. Poor lady—life was so hard for her."

Livia nodded sympathetically. "But Jane, why exactly were you a disappointment to her?"

"Oh, because I hated sewing, and sitting quietly, and being *good*. I wanted to be running around with the other children, getting dirty in the mud and swinging from tree-limbs and chasing pigs. And I was always asking her things. I think I drove her half-mad with all my questions. Why is the sky blue? What are the stars made of? Why do some trees lose their leaves in the autumn? Where do babies come from? If it isn't true that toad-powder tea will cure the bloody flux, why did Great-grandfather write it in a pamphlet? What happened to make our poor king go mad? Are there really pixies in the forest? And boggarts, lurking in the dark and just waiting to bite one's ankles? And so on."

"You know, you're reminding me of something Granny once said about Titus," Livia remarked thoughtfully. "That he was a great one for asking questions, too. And he never liked doing what he was told, either."

"Did she say it like it was a bad thing?" asked Jane, a bit anxiously.

Livia laughed. "No, she said these were qualities Titus got from *her*. Apparently Granny was rather a renegade in her youth as well."

Jane leaned back against the sofa, in her mind picturing Great-grandmother Henrietta as she was now—so dignified, ramrod-straight, elegant, and exacting. "I must say, that's hard to believe."

"Isn't it? But that's what she says, and always smiles in a mysterious way and refuses to tell us anything else. She looks exactly like the *Mona Lisa* when she does that—full of fascinating secrets from her past."

Jane found herself wondering precisely what those secrets might be, and looked to the mantelpiece where, next to Grandfather Titus' portrait, was a small painting of Richard Penhallow—Great-grandmother's long-dead husband. Titus' father; Cousin Gabriel's grandfather. And *her* great-grandfather. Richard wore a long frock-coat, with white frilled sleeves extending from below the wide cuffs, a gorgeously embroidered waistcoat, close-fitting knee-breeches, white stockings, and black buckled shoes. His hair was worn long, and on his attractive face was a small, mischievous smile.

He looked quite like a person she would want to know, Jane thought. Was there something to do with Richard, perhaps, that had sparked Great-grandmother's mysterious smile?

Also, who was Mona Lisa? Someone else from the neighborhood to whom Jane would soon be introduced? And why did *she* have a mysterious smile? Was it really because of secrets in her past? Most people had those. Jane had some of her own, in fact, and a few of them actually did make her smile sometimes . . .

She broke out of her reverie when Livia stood up and said in her kind way:

"Well, Jane, I must go off to the kitchen and talk with Cook, and I want to stop by my poultry-yard for a few minutes, and go up to the nursery after that. Are you tired, or would you like to come with me?"

"Oh, I'm not tired anymore! And I'd love to come with you. If you truly don't mind?"

Livia flashed a warm smile. "I'd love it. It's wonderful having you here, Jane."

"Really, Livia?"

"Oh yes. I don't know how it is, but somehow it seems like you've always been part of the family. You fit in so well. And Gabriel just told me yesterday how your being here is such a nice boost for Granny. She gets a little melancholy sometimes, you know, about all her children being gone."

"Well, it's wonderful for me too," said Jane, blinking away sudden tears, feeling less like a grubby little sparrow and more like a nice clean swan, and then she rose to her feet, reaching out impulsively to hug Livia. "I never had a sister, but now I feel like I do."

Livia hugged her back, then pulled away to smile again at Jane. "It's the same with me. I'm so glad you found us. Now! Shall we be on our way, before we both turn into watering-pots?"

Jane smiled too, happiness making her feel all light and floaty again. "I'm ready."

"Good! And there's an excellent chance that Cook will have some more of those delicious York biscuits. In case we need something to tide us over till dinner."

"Oh, do let's ask," said Jane, and went away with Livia, cheerfully disregarding the fact that her feet, in those charming borrowed slippers, pinched her toes quite dreadfully.

"I say, Father, the most ripping thing happened today."

Anthony was stretched out on top of the covers of Wakefield's bed, both of them propped up on pillows. Flickering light from a three-branched candelabrum played over Wakefield's still-damp hair, which Nurse had, after Wakefield's bath, parted on the side and vigorously combed flat as she always did, giving Wakefield the appearance of a very small businessman. Who happened to be wearing a white ruffled nightshirt. The bedclothes were tucked up around his armpits, and snuggled against him was the little pug Snuffles, who was curled up in a ball and snoring in a quiet, peaceful way which Anthony found very soothing. He said:

"Do tell."

"On the way home from the vicarage, just as we passed the lodge-house, Higson ran over a toad."

"Did he?"

"Yes, and Father, the toad was absolutely *flat*. I had Higson pull up so I could get down from the cart and look."

"Did you pick it up?"

"Well, I would have, but Higson told me not to, or I'd get warts."

"I once found a dead toad over by the lake when I was just your age."

"Did you pick it up, Father?"

"Of course. I didn't have a groom breathing down my neck."

"Did you get warts?"

"No."

"I *told* Higson he was wrong," said Wakefield bitterly.

"Instead of warts I developed the most spectacular rash. My entire right hand and arm was a blistering scarlet for a fortnight."

Bitterness evolved instantly into admiration. "I say, Father, how splendid."

"Yes, in the sense that I had complete control over Nurse the entire time. I only had to threaten to touch her with the afflicted limb and she fled the room."

"I knew I should have picked up that toad."

"Unfortunately, my arm felt like it was on fire."

"Oh."

"Yes, altogether a mixed bag. So do keep it in mind the next time you see a dead toad."

Wakefield looked thoughtful, then said, "Father, will

you talk to Higson about letting me take the reins again? He's being very ibstoperous about it."

"Do you mean obstreperous?"

"Yes, that's what I said. Just because I ran us off the road last week. The cart *did* turn over, but the pony wasn't hurt, and that's what matters. We weren't hurt either. Oh, Father, you should have seen Higson. He rolled into the ditch just like a ball."

"Maybe that's why he's reluctant to have you drive the pony-cart again."

"I didn't do it on purpose, you know. Higson broke wind and I was laughing so hard that I wasn't paying attention."

"An entirely reasonable distraction, old chap, but when you're holding the reins it's all your responsibility."

"Yes, Father. Did you overturn carts when you were little?"

"Several times."

"Did it make you a better driver?"

"Yes."

"I'll do better, Father, I promise."

"I know you will. I'll talk to Higson."

Wakefield smiled beatifically, which made him look for the moment more like a cherub in a Renaissance painting than a businessman. "*Thank* you, Father! Can I drive the pony-cart to lessons tomorrow?"

"Yes. By the way, you're to have a new schoolfellow."

"I am? Who is it?"

"A young lady named Miss Kent."

"A *lady*, Father?"

"Yes, she's a relation of the Penhallows. I met her today over at the Hall."

"Oh, Father, she's not like Mrs. Penhallow, is she?"

"Which one?"

"The older one, with the white hair. She was very nasty to me at the *fête* last year."

"Was she? Why?"

"Well, I was rolling a hoop past the cheese stall, minding my own business, and—"

"Did you roll the hoop into her?"

"I say, Father, that's an awful onsanuation."

"Do you mean insinuation?"

"Yes, that's what I said."

There was a brief silence, modulated by the soft, pleasant sounds of Snuffles snoring.

"I did roll the hoop into her, but not very hard."

"Ah."

"I apologized, Father, but she only said that I was a menace to society. Which I'm *not*."

"No, not yet, at any rate."

"I'll tell you what, though, she was so nasty it made me feel like I *wanted* to be a menace to society."

"I know the feeling."

"Would you mind terribly, Father, if I became one when I grow up? A pirate, for example, or a highwayman?"

"It's hard to say. Perhaps we can revisit the subject when you're a bit older."

Wakefield nodded, then put out his hand to stroke Snuffles' soft little head. "So what's she like, Father?"

"Who?"

"The lady who's going to have lessons with Mr. Pressley and me."

"Miss Kent? I'm not sure. We hardly spoke."

"Does she seem like the type of person who would call you a menace to society if you rolled a hoop into her just a little?"

"I don't know, my boy. You might want to refrain from rolling hoops in her presence till you know her better."

"I will," promised Wakefield. "I say, I hope she's not going to turn out to be another boring grownup. Will you read to me now, Father?"

"What would you like tonight?"

"*Tales from Shakespeare*, please."

Anthony reached onto Wakefield's bedside table and pulled the Shakespeare book from among the stack, and opened it. "We're up to *Romeo and Juliet.*"

"What's that one about?"

"It's a sad love story."

"A love story? Ugh. Something *good*, Father."

"How about *Hamlet*?"

"Is there sword-fighting?"

"Yes, and a ghost, too. Also graves and a skull."

"That's better. Is there hugging and kissing in it?"

"A little, but it turns out badly."

"Oh, that's all right then. Read that, Father, please."

And Anthony, secretly glad to not be reading about a sad love story, turned the pages of *Romeo and Juliet* and started in on the unromantic *Hamlet*.

Chapter 4

Jane had been ushered into the vicarage by the dour housekeeper Mrs. McKenzie, and into a large, orderly study lined with bookshelves. There she met Mr. Pressley the vicar, who, she was extremely relieved to see, was very different from the Nantwich schoolmaster, being a pleasant, soft-spoken man of about Cousin Gabriel's age, or perhaps a few years younger. She also met the Duke's son Wakefield, tall for his eight years, wiry and fine-boned, with neatly trimmed hair the same light-brown color as the Duke's, though his eyes were brown and not the deep blue of his father.

"Miss Kent," said the vicar, "may I introduce to you Master Wakefield Farr, the Marquis of Rutherford?"

"How do you do?" said Jane.

"Very well, thank you," answered the little boy. "I say, you're rather old for lessons, aren't you?"

"Master Wakefield," said Mr. Pressley, gentle reproof in his voice, but Jane smiled at him and answered:

"Yes, I am. You see, I had no chance to go to school before."

"Why not?"

"There was no money."

"And there's money now?"

"It seems that way."

"That's jolly."

"Yes, it is. I'm very lucky."

"Are you glad to be having lessons?"

"Oh yes. There's so much to know, isn't there? For example, I want to learn more about Henry Tudor and all his wives."

"I know a lot already," said the little boy matter-of-factly. "Miss Trevelyan's writing a book about the fourth one, Anne of Cloves. The other day she read some of it out loud to Miss Humphrey and me."

"I just met them yesterday," said Jane, of course tactfully bypassing Wakefield's misnomer as she was hardly in a position to feel superior. "They seemed very nice."

"Oh, they're splendid. My aunt Margaret doesn't like Miss Humphrey, though. Because of her flowers."

Here the vicar intervened. "I would have called earlier at the Hall, Miss Kent, but Mrs. Penhallow indicated that you were fatigued after your long journey."

"Yes, I was. I spent most of the first three days in bed."

"That's nothing," Wakefield put in. "Father was once in bed for three years."

"Was he?" Jane said. "Why?"

"He fell out of a tree and hurt his back."

"Oh, that's dreadful."

"He said it was rather restful, actually."

Mr. Pressley intervened again, saying that perhaps they ought to begin, and in his gentle, pleasant way asked about Jane's educational background and interests while Wakefield labored over some sums, sitting at a large rectangular table and swinging his legs back and forth. Without in the least making Jane feel inadequate or ashamed of her ignorance, Mr. Pressley gave her some books to take home and read, and Wakefield submitted his ink-blotched paper for Mr. Pressley to review, and after that the three of them had an interesting conversation about Tudor history, the origins of the British Royal Navy, and the ethical implications of Queen Elizabeth's tacit approval of piracy.

"I told Father I might be a pirate when I grow up," remarked Wakefield.

"You're to be a duke, Master Wakefield," the vicar reminded him.

"When Father gets married again and has more children, I'll let them be dukes."

Mr. Pressley looked startled. "I wasn't aware that His Grace had entered into matrimonial arrangements."

"He will. Aunt Margaret will make him. And then I won't be the only sixcessor."

"I believe, Master Wakefield, you mean successor."

"Yes, that's what I said."

Mrs. McKenzie poked her head into the room to dourly announce the arrival of Mr. Attfield, the churchwarden, who had come on urgent parish business, and Mr. Pressley apologetically said he was afraid lessons would have to end sooner than usual.

"That's all right," said Wakefield. "Miss Kent and I don't mind, do we, Miss Kent?"

In point of fact Jane's brain did feel rather full, but it hardly seemed appropriate to join in with Wakefield's youthful glee. Fortunately Mr. Pressley then got up and said, "I'll see you both tomorrow," and so she and Wakefield got up too and made their way out of the vicarage and onto the front portico, where the light carriage which had conveyed her from the Hall stood waiting, as well as a dashing little pony-cart. Jane eyed it wistfully.

"I say, Miss Kent, would you like to come home with me and meet the Duchess?"

"There's a duchess?" Jane said, surprised. How could the Duke be planning on marrying when he already had a wife?

"Oh yes. Fat as anything, too. You should see the way she eats blancmange. It's the funniest thing in the world."

Jane found herself thinking about what she had told Livia yesterday. How, as a girl, she had hated being good. Apparently there was still plenty left of that girl within her, because with all her heart she now wanted to see an actual duchess eating blancmange. Great-grandmother Kent had talked a lot about duchesses, including the beautiful (and scandalous) Georgiana Cavendish, the Duchess of Devonshire, and also Catherine Wellesley, the Duchess of Wellington (who had married shockingly above her station). "Can we go in your pony-cart? I've always wanted to ride in one."

"If you don't mind squeezing in with Higson and me. You're awfully skinny, which is good—you won't take up much room."

"Well, if you and Higson don't mind, I don't mind either."

"Capital! I'm an excellent driver. Do you want to sit next to me? Normally I don't like being near girls, but you're not bad."

"That's one of the nicest compliments I've ever had," said Jane, sincerely. "Thank you. By the way, am I supposed to call you 'Your Grace'? Or 'My Lord'?"

"'Your Grace' is for Father, and 'My Lord' is for me, but since we're already friends I think you should call me 'Wakefield.'"

"Then I will. And won't you call me 'Jane,' rather than 'Miss Kent'?"

"All right. Come on, Jane, I'll introduce you to Higson."

Jane met Higson, who politely tipped his black beaver hat and assured her she'd get driven back from Hastings at her convenience, and so she told the Surmont Hall groom to go directly on home, with a message letting the family know where she was, and gave him the books the vicar had loaned her as well.

Wakefield managed to keep the pony-cart pretty much within the lane as they made their way from the vicarage toward the Radcliffe estate, though there was one close call when he got so caught up in telling her the exciting plot of a play called *Hamlet* that they nearly veered into an oak tree. Jane heard Higson muttering under his breath but, to his credit, he let Wakefield bring the cart back onto the lane without snatching at the reins as Jane was sure he longed to do.

They traveled past some large stubbled fields, in their quiet winter fallow, and shortly arrived at a handsome old brick lodge-house (near which Wakefield, with ghoulish enthusiasm, pointed out to Jane a spectacularly flat dead toad); they passed through the tall open gates and into a beautiful grove of mature trees on both sides of the winding road. By and by they came around a long gentle curve and in the distance Jane could see a great palatial house, not unlike Surmont Hall, but as they drew closer Wakefield turned off onto a smaller lane which soon brought into view a wide, long lake, very blue and serene, and then they came to a curious lump of a building, quite tumbledown and all covered over with dank-looking moss and vines.

"Wakefield, what *is* that?" she asked.

"Oh, that's our ruin."

"Your ruin?"

"Yes, isn't it jolly?"

"Yes indeed! But—what is a ruin, exactly?"

"Don't you know about ruins?"

"Well, I've seen plenty of rotting old houses back in Nantwich—that's where I'm from—but nobody called them ruins."

Wakefield tugged at the reins to bring the pony to a halt. "They should have, Jane, because that's what a ruin is. Aunt Margaret had it built last year."

"She had it built?"

"Yes, she says they're very fishinable, and that all the best people have them. Father didn't want it. He said it was a complete waste of money, especially when we have a perfectly good Greek temple we could let go to rot."

"You have a Greek temple?"

"Yes. You'll be able to see it when we go round the bend up there. Oh, and McTavish was so angry about having to put all those vines on Aunt Margaret's ruin that he gave notice."

"Who is McTavish?"

"Our head gardener. Father doubled his pay to keep him on. He says that aside from Miss Humphrey, there's nobody better at pumpkins than McTavish. Do you want to get a closer look?"

"I should say I do."

"All right, let's get down here. I say, Higson, you can take the cart back to the stables."

"Very good, Master Wakefield."

Jane and Wakefield climbed down from the seat and together went toward the ruin.

"Doesn't it smell awful, Jane?" said Wakefield approvingly.

"Oh yes, it's ghastly," Jane agreed. "Is that on purpose, or accidentally?"

"That's a very good question. We'll have to ask Aunt Margaret. Don't you wish we could go inside?"

"Yes, very much. This seems exactly the sort of place the ghost of Hamlet's father would be."

"Wouldn't he just!" said Wakefield, much struck. "But Father says to keep out, because he's not at all sure the roof will hold."

"That's very good advice, I think. Especially since one would probably carry out that bad smell, which would take *several* baths to get rid of."

"I shouldn't like that at all. One bath a day is enough. Come on, I'll show you where the temple is."

They walked in a leisurely way along the meandering path, which was rather rough and muddy, and Jane was glad she had decided to wear her old half-boots today, instead of the uncomfortable slippers which would already have been ruined by now. But both her pale-green gown, and the warm cherry-colored pelisse Livia had lent her, had hems which covered most of the boots, and thus Jane felt she had achieved the best of both worlds.

She took in a deep breath of crisp, cold air, aware, suddenly, that she felt very happy. She had been measured head to toe by Miss Simpkin the seamstress, and Great-grandmother had ordered a great many things on her behalf; she had learned some interesting things today, ridden in a pony-cart, seen a ruin, was on her way to meet a duchess, and—best of all—made a new friend.

"Wakefield," she said, "I'm very glad you invited me."

He was busy kicking a rock along the road in front of him. "It's jolly that you came, Jane. One does long for company sometimes."

"Yes, one does," answered Jane feelingly. "Do you have many playmates?"

"No, not really. There are some boys my age about—servants' children, you know—but Aunt Margaret doesn't want me playing with them."

"Oh."

"She says I'd have plenty of chums if I went off to Eton."

"That's a boarding school, isn't it?"

"Yes, in Windsor. It's rather a long way away, and I don't want to."

"Why not?"

"I like being at home."

Jane nodded. "It's a lovely home. I mean—the estate, and everything."

"Yes, it is. Look, there's the temple."

They had come around a curve in the path which had wound upwards on an easy gradient and now offered an excellent view across the lake to where stood a giant white building fronted by several massive columns, with a large triangular bit on the top, and practically reeking of antiquity.

"My goodness," said Jane, awestruck. "Did your aunt Margaret have that built too?"

"No, my great-great-grandfather Osbert did. Father and I like to ride over there sometimes and he tells me all about the Greek gods, because he says that's the perfect place to do it in. Ares is my favorite—he's the god of war, you know, and he's always getting into the most terrible scrapes. Who's your favorite, Jane?"

"I don't know yet. I still have to learn about them."

"You might choose Athena. She had gray eyes, like yours."

"What is she the goddess of?"

"Wisdom, peace, and war. Also, she was born straight out of her father's head, already wearing armor and carrying a spear."

"Dear me."

"Yes, isn't that capital? Father says Zeus—the father—must have had a frightful headache."

"One would think so."

"Aunt Margaret gets headaches sometimes. She has to go lie down for hours."

"I'm sorry to hear that."

"Yes, but then she's out of the way for a while."

Jane didn't know what to say to this brutally candid remark, and Wakefield cheerfully went on:

"Come on, I'll show you the Duchess. She lives over there."

He set off toward a small, charming brick house with a yard to the front which was enclosed by a stone balustrade four or five feet high. Jane followed, gaping in amazement. "The Duchess lives there?" she asked. Why, she wondered, didn't the Duke's wife live in that palatial old manor house with the rest of the family?

Had she stumbled across some dark, terrible mystery?

"Well, of course she does," said Wakefield, and Jane, catching up with him, saw that the front yard was filled with clean, fresh straw, and that against the brick wall of the little house lay an enormous pink pig, dozing peacefully.

They came to the balustrade and stood looking down at the pig. Was it a pet of the Duchess? thought Jane. It would certainly be an unusual sort of pet, but, on the other hand, Great-grandmother Kent had talked quite a lot about the eccentric Duchess of York, who was known, among other things, for populating her country estate with more than a hundred dogs along with monkeys, exotic birds, and kangaroos.

"There she is," said Wakefield. "Isn't she splendid?"

"To be sure she is," answered Jane, but glanced around, puzzled.

"What are you looking for, Jane?"

"I was wondering where the Duchess is."

"She's right there," said Wakefield, in the tone of one trying to politely ignore the fact that one's companion isn't very bright, and gestured toward the pig. "That's the Duchess."

Jane looked at Wakefield, who seemed quite in earnest, and then at the pig again. "You mean—the pig's name is Duchess?"

"Yes. Why do you look so surprised, Jane? I say, your eyes are as round as a plate."

Jane burst out laughing. Wakefield gazed up at her, looking surprised himself, and she managed to say, rather breathlessly, "Oh, Wakefield, I thought you meant to introduce me to your mother the Duchess."

"I haven't any mother."

Jane sobered at once. "Oh dear, I *am* sorry. I hope I haven't offended you, or hurt your feelings?" she said anxiously.

"Oh no. I'm used to not having a mother. She died when I was three, you see, and I don't remember her at all."

"Still, I'm very sorry, Wakefield."

"It's all right. Would you like to give the Duchess a scratch?"

"Would—would *she* like that?" answered Jane cautiously.

"Oh, she loves it. Duchess!" called Wakefield, and the pig woke up with a grunt and lifted its big head to glance inquiringly their way. Wakefield picked up a large stick that lay against the base of the balustrade and waved it enticingly. "Scratch?"

The Duchess heaved herself upright and came waddling over to her side of the balustrade. Goodness, Jane thought, she must weigh three times what I do. Or more. Wakefield wielded one end of the stick to scratch at that wide, hairy pink back, and the Duchess looked so contented that Jane had to laugh again.

"Now you try, Jane." Wakefield gave her the stick and

Jane, tentatively at first, scratched the Duchess, then more firmly as she gained confidence.

"This is rather fun," she said to Wakefield.

"Isn't it?"

"Here now, what's going on?" someone said roughly, and Jane froze. A sturdy middle-aged man in tweeds and with a big round red face came stamping toward them, eyeing Jane with both suspicion and hostility. Quickly Jane gave the stick back to Wakefield, feeling guilty, as if caught in some kind of horrible wrongdoing.

"Hullo, Johns. This is my friend Jane from Surmont Hall. She wanted to meet the Duchess."

"From the Hall?" repeated Johns ominously, and Jane remembered Great-grandmother Henrietta yesterday asking the Duke, although in a noticeably ironic way, about the dispute between their pigmen. "I don't let no people from the Hall near the Duchess."

"Oh, Johns, don't be redonculous," said Wakefield. "Jane's a good 'un."

The Duchess gave a loud grunt, which Jane took to be a flattering show of support, but Johns only glared at her more fiercely. "I'll thank you to step aside, miss, and that right quick."

Jane wasn't sure whether to cower, slink away, stand her ground, or, possibly, take the stick back from Wakefield and brandish it defensively, but then she heard pleasant crunching sounds and looked beyond Johns to see the Duke loping toward them on his long booted legs, dry winter leaves flattening beneath his boot-soles. He was wearing a long woolen greatcoat and a tall dark hat, which made him look incredibly elongated, and with him were three dogs—no, four, one was tiny—all trotting companionably more or less at his side, although to be precise the tiny one, a pug with a sweet squashed-looking face, was galloping valiantly along in a way that struck Jane as one of the most adorable things she had ever seen.

The Duke drew near, and Wakefield called out:

"Oh, Father, Johns is acting like Jane's a spy sent over from the Hall. Do make him stop."

"Like who's a spy?"

"Jane," Wakefield said. "Miss Kent here."

"Ah. Johns, stand down. You besmirch the noble name of Hastings."

"Besmirch, guv'nor?" said Johns, taken aback. "Well, I *never*."

"Besmirch," repeated the Duke firmly, and Jane was relieved when Johns moved aside and went to kick moodily at some bits of straw that had escaped the Duchess' pen. The Duke went on:

"How do you do, Miss Kent?"

"Very well, thank you," Jane said, then added punctiliously: "Your Grace."

"Father, I brought Jane over to meet the Duchess, and she scratched her back. I say, what's that you've got?"

"Blancmange." The Duke was carrying a china bowl which he held out for Jane and Wakefield's inspection. Inside was a molded, creamy-white confection which jiggled in a humorous, yet appetizing way, and Jane suddenly realized that she was hungry.

"How *ripping*," said Wakefield. "Jane, would you like to give it to the Duchess?"

"I'd love to."

The Duke looked at her, on his long thin face an expression of pleased surprise, as if discovering in her unsuspected depths of character. "Are you a pig person, Miss Kent?"

He said it in a way that was so clearly complimentary that Jane found herself smiling up at him. His eyes really were a striking shade of blue. They reminded her of the deep serene color of the lake which lay beyond the Duchess' charming little house. "Maybe so. Your Grace."

"You should call him 'Anthony,' Jane, as we're all friends now. Give Jane the bowl, Father, and I'll tell her what to do."

The Duke passed to Jane the china bowl, and Wakefield continued:

"Do you see the trough over there, Jane, against the balustrade? Put the blancmange in it. If your aim is good, you can toss it from here, or you can go round the corner and just drop it in."

Guessing that she would sink even further in the dubious esteem of Johns the pigman if she ending up flinging the blancmange into that nice clean straw, Jane said, "I'd better go round the corner." She did, and carefully tilted the bowl so the blancmange could slide out and fall directly into the long rectangular trough. It cracked in half and already Wakefield was laughing.

"Isn't blancmange funny, Jane? Father, isn't it funny?"

"Hilarious," agreed the Duke, and they all watched as the Duchess ambled over to the trough and sank her snout into the soft creamy confection, which soon bedecked her entire face and gave her a delightful resemblance to Father Christmas.

Jane burst out laughing again and Wakefield, giving her a glance of approval, said, "I knew you'd like it, Jane. Do you want to meet our dogs now?"

"Yes, please," she said, and so Wakefield introduced her to the biggest one, Breen, then Joe, Sam, and Snuffles the pug, all of whom seemed equally happy to be introduced to *her*. "May I pick up Snuffles?" she asked Wakefield, who graciously gave his consent, and so she lifted up the tiny pug and gave a joyful laugh when it settled at once into the crook of her arm. "How sweet he is! I always wanted a dog, but my great-grandmother Kent was afraid of them. A dog bit her when she was a girl, and she never lost her fear."

"Aunt Margaret's cat bit me last week," said Wakefield. "I was only trying to play with it."

"In fairness, my boy, your aunt Margaret told you not to."

"Yes, but Father, the poor thing always looks so millencocky, and I thought I'd try to cheer it up."

"Do you mean melancholy?"

"Yes, that's what I said. It wasn't worth it, though. It absolutely *sank* its fangs into my hand, do you remember, Father? Aunt Margaret said she'd never heard anybody scream so loud in her life, and that I probably broke both her eardrums. Which I don't think is true, because the other day I was trying to sneak past the drawing-room and she found me out right away. I say, is it time for luncheon? I'm starving. Jane, do you want to have luncheon with us? Cook told me there would be roast beef and macaroni today."

Jane looked at the Duke. She wanted to say yes, but it was really up to him.

And she saw that he was looking back at her.

Actually, he was staring, and with a rather flatteringly fascinated expression on his face, too.

Anthony was seeing Miss Jane Kent with fresh eyes.

Anybody who jumped at the chance to slide blancmange into the Duchess' trough was someone he wanted to know better.

Also, she clearly liked dogs, which was another major

point in her favor, *and* she was wearing boots just right for a tramp in the outdoors, a choice so wise and practical that he would have liked to—say—wring her hand by way of signifying his approval.

He would not, therefore, be so petty as to carry a grudge against her for taking that last sandwich yesterday; he would be magnanimous and let it go. Plus he had noticed that when she smiled, a charming dimple appeared in each cheek. There was something so appealing about dimples. He said:

"Do join us, Miss Kent."

She smiled again, and there they were—those dimples.

He smiled back. Yes, very appealing.

"Thank you. I'd like that. Your Grace."

"You both sound very stuffy," said Wakefield critically. "Come on, let's go. Jane, you'd better put Snuffles down. He likes to go about with the other dogs, and I don't want him thinking he's not as good as they are, just because his legs don't work properly."

"That's very thoughtful of you, Wakefield," Jane said, and gently put Snuffles onto the ground. He immediately scampered off to try and take hold of Joe's tail in his mouth.

The three of them, leaving behind a still-downcast Johns to rake out the interior of the Duchess' pen, walked toward the Hastings manor house. As Wakefield, who had positioned himself in the middle of their trio, told him all about today's lessons, Jane's agreeable interest in the ruin, her resemblance to the Greek goddess Athena, and how well he had driven the pony-cart, Anthony listened attentively, but he also cast a few sideways glances at Miss Kent.

He wondered why he hadn't observed yesterday that she had a nice face.

He liked how her big gray eyes were framed by dark curling lashes, and how her nose turned up, just a little and in a delightful way, at its tip. And how her chin was a bit pointed, giving her profile a look of subtle determination. Of course, he already had seen that her mouth was beautifully formed, pink as a rose in bloom, and very soft and tender.

Oh, and those dimples, too.

She was smiling at something Wakefield had just said, and so there was at this exact moment a dimple in the cheek that he could see from this angle.

What *was* it about dimples, that made them so attractive?

They had passed the stables, to which all the dogs were diverted, then had come onto the graveled sweep, and were now approaching the wide marble steps of the house. Wakefield went on chattily:

"Father, Jane told Mr. Pressley and me how before she had no money to go to school, but now she does. Isn't that jolly? Also, she just spent practically three days in bed, and I told her how you were in bed for three years. Do you remember the time I had the influenza and had to stay in bed for a whole fortnight?"

"The memory," said Anthony, "is seared into my brain. You're an awful patient, old chap."

"Yes, but Father, I felt terrible *and* I was bored. That's a foul kimbonition."

"Do you mean combination?"

"Yes, that's what I said. Oh, hullo, Bunch. Is luncheon ready? We're all starving."

"Indeed it is, Master Wakefield," said Bunch, who stood waiting in the Great Hall after a footman had opened the door to admit them.

"Well, that's splendid. Bunch, this is Jane from Surmont Hall. Jane, this is Bunch, our butler. He buttles like anything."

"Thank you, Master Wakefield," Bunch said, then bowed politely to Miss Kent and received her pelisse and bonnet which he passed along to one of the footmen. "Lady Margaret awaits you in the family dining-parlor," he said, and so they proceeded there at once, where they found Margaret sitting in her usual place at the foot of the table, looking all too funereal in her customary black, and Anthony introduced her to Miss Kent while a footman swiftly set an additional place.

"How do you do, ma'am?" said Miss Kent, and Margaret replied:

"How do you do? Do sit down before the soup gets any colder than it already is."

Conversation did not improve from there.

"I understand, Miss Kent, that you're newly arrived at Surmont Hall."

Miss Kent paused with her spoon lifted halfway to her mouth. "Yes, ma'am, that's right."

"You are from Nantwich?"

"Yes, ma'am."

"That's near Liverpool, is it not?"

"Yes, ma'am."

"A low, vulgar city by all accounts. I daresay Nantwich is not much different. You're a relation of the Penhallows?"

"Yes, ma'am. Mrs. Henrietta Penhallow is my great-grandmother."

"I believe, Miss Kent, the connection is somewhat irregular?"

"Irregular?" piped up Wakefield. "What do you mean, Aunt Margaret?"

Anthony saw that Miss Kent, who had flushed a rather

charming pink color, took advantage of Wakefield's questions to finally bring her soup spoon to her mouth, and then, looking very determined, she began to spread a great deal of butter on a roll. What did Margaret mean by that remark, anyway? Irregular connection. It sounded like some sort of plumbing problem.

Margaret was frowning at Wakefield, a sudden red flush on *her* cheeks, giving Anthony the distinct impression that, in her rapid-fire interrogation of Miss Kent, she had forgotten Wakefield was even there. Repressively Margaret said to him:

"Nobody was addressing you."

Wakefield shrugged and went back to his soup.

"Are you planning a long stay here in Somerset, Miss Kent?" Margaret continued.

Miss Kent paused again, this time with her buttered roll halfway to her mouth. At this rate, Anthony thought, she'd never be able to eat her meal, and with a sudden rush of gallantry he hastily interrupted:

"I say, Meg, have you seen my riding gloves? Can't find them anywhere."

Margaret gave him a frigid glance. "If you had bothered this morning to look at the suit of armor in the Great Hall, you may have seen the gloves tucked into the face-plate."

"Well, that's excellent." He had, actually, bothered, and had all along thought the face-plate a rather useful place in which to stow his gloves, and an amusing one to boot, but went on with an air of inquiring innocence: "So are they still there?"

"Of course not. I had one of the footmen remove them, and convey them to your room."

"Ah. Thank you." Damn it, thought Anthony, *this* subject's pretty well thrashed out already, and Jane's only halfway through her roll. Now what? He cast about in his mind, lit on something that would be akin to tossing a firecracker into a flaming pit of hell, and said, with deceptive casualness:

"I heard a rumor that Miss Humphrey's planning to show delphiniums at the *fête* this year."

This conversational gambit proved to be, Anthony would soon congratulate himself, a masterstroke, as Margaret promptly launched into a passionate (and seemingly endless) monologue about the relative merits of delphiniums versus irises, thus enabling everyone else to enjoy their luncheon without further impediment until, almond custard having been served and Margaret pausing to draw breath, Wakefield said, as he scraped his bowl clean with his spoon:

"Aunt Margaret, Jane and I were wondering if the ruin has a bad smell on purpose, or if it's by accident."

"Don't scrape about with your spoon; it's unsuitable behavior for a marquis," said Margaret coldly. "And are you referring to Miss Kent?"

"Yes."

"That is how you should address her as well."

Jane was nodding her thanks at the footman who had just given her a second helping of custard, but quickly said:

"Oh, ma'am, I told Wakefield to call me that."

"Indeed?"

"Yes," put in Wakefield, "because Jane and I are schoolfellows, Aunt Margaret, and also because we're great friends already. She gave the Duchess some blancmange, and she likes Snuffles, too. Yes, please, Marner," he said to the footman, who had come to stand next to him with the custard bowl, and watched with approbation as Marner gave him a large additional serving, then went on:

"So Jane and I were wondering about the smell, Aunt Margaret, because it's atrushish."

Even more coldly Margaret answered, "Are you attempting to say 'atrocious'?"

"Yes, that *is* what I said. It's not that we don't like the bad smell," Wakefield said kindly, "because we do. We just wanted to know if you had it done on purpose."

"A marquis," responded Margaret, "ought not to discuss olfactory matters at table."

"Well, I wasn't, Aunt Margaret, I was talking about bad smells."

Anthony laughed, and accepted from Marner his own second helping of custard. He said to Wakefield, "'Olfactory' means having to do with scents and smells and things like that."

"Oh, it does? Bad smells?"

"Any sort of smells."

"So are the stables an olfactory, then? Because there are a lot of smells made in there."

"I say, that's clever usage. But 'olfactory' is an adjective, not a noun."

"That's good to know, Father, thank you," said Wakefield, and scraped his spoon against the side of his bowl in order to capture a delicious blob of custard that clung there. "Jane, would you like to play billiards after luncheon? It's all right if you tear the cloth a bit with the stick, I do it all the time. Accidentally, you know."

"I daresay," said Margaret, "*Miss Kent* will be wanted back at the Hall."

At this Jane looked up from her bowl and at Margaret, who sat to her left. Her big gray eyes, which had been twinkling with humor just a few moments ago, were thoughtful now. "Yes, I suppose I shall be. I'm sorry, Wakefield. Another time?"

"All right, Jane," replied Wakefield, and Margaret said, between tight lips, "*Miss Kent*," and Anthony, who had been planning to spend a quiet, peaceful hour in his library delving once again into Dinkle's *Advanced Concepts in Piggery*, said, rather to his own surprise:

"Miss Kent, may I drive you home?"

Chapter 5

"It's very nice of you to take me back to the Hall." Jane and the Duke were sitting side by side in the high front seat of his curricle, an even more dashing vehicle than the pony-cart, and as they bowled along the curving road which led between the two estates, it felt a little like they were flying. Jane was enjoying herself very much. She added: "Your Grace."

"I was glad to, Miss Kent."

"Thank you also for luncheon. It was delicious. Especially the macaroni."

"Yes, I liked that, too."

"I hope you don't mind that I took the last of it."

"No, not at all."

Jane stole a glance at the Duke's profile. He handled the reins with easy grace, but his face, which had been cheerful when he'd tendered his offer to take her back to the Hall, was now gloomy beneath the brim of his tall dark hat, and his voice was flat and even a trifle grim.

The change had occurred just as Wakefield had been finishing his custard. Lady Margaret—in a sudden shift of *her* mood—had brightly announced that in all the excitement of having an unexpected guest for luncheon, not, of course, that it was in any way a trouble, or an inconvenience, or unwelcome, she had quite forgotten to share the news that an express had just arrived this morning with the gratifying intelligence that her dear friend the Countess of Silsbury, accompanied by her delightful daughter, Lady Felicia, would soon be arriving at Hastings for a lovely long visit. A very, very long visit. Possibly longer than anyone could even anticipate.

And that was when all the light went out of the Duke's expression. He had only said to Lady Margaret, in a voice so dry that all human emotion seemed leached from it, *I thought the Countess was merely an acquaintance.*

Lady Margaret had airily waved her hand, saying, *No doubt you mistook me. The Countess is a dear friend—why, she's practically family. I'm sure she and dear Lady Felicia will feel right at home here.*

Jane now remembered Wakefield saying earlier today, *When Father gets married again and has more children, I'll let them be dukes*, and the vicar looking startled, saying, *I wasn't aware that His Grace had entered into matrimonial arrangements*, and Wakefield replying with casual certainty, *He will. Aunt Margaret will make him. And then I won't be the only sixcessor.*

Jane glanced again at the Duke. She wondered if this Lady Felicia was his intended. He certainly didn't seem happy about it. Or, at the very least, he didn't seem to relish the prospect of having Lady Felicia and her mother come to stay. For the Duke's sake, she hoped Lady Felicia liked pigs. And that Lady Felicia was a nice person, who would be good to Wakefield.

They barreled past an enormous open field dotted with cattle, beyond which lay innumerable rolling hills, in quiet shades of wintry gray and brown, stretching out into the distance, and then into a wooded area, where the shadows were deep and tranquil, the silence tempered only by the sounds of horses' hooves and jingling harness. It was cooler here in the woods, and Jane was thankful for her warm pelisse.

She looked down at the hems of her gown and pelisse.

Pale green and cherry red, and shabby old dark boots peeping out from underneath.

In the Great Hall at Hastings, where Jane had put on the pelisse and her bonnet, she had seen how Lady Margaret was eyeing her from head to toe. And then she had sweetly said:

What a delightful color combination, Miss Kent. Red and green. One sees that so rarely. Really, you're quite an original.

As she had been tying the ribbons of her bonnet—a light blue bonnet, borrowed from Livia, which, incidentally, didn't match anything she had on—Jane had pondered Lady Margaret's remark. How interesting to veil an insult through words which, on their surface, were flattering, and through a tone of common courtesy. Was that how a duke's sister did things?

Back in Nantwich, nobody bothered trying to craftily disguise their barbs. It was all people shouting at each other things like *you bloody lobcock* and *eh, go on, you're nothing but a bewattled trug* and *say that to my face, you damned gaspy chub* and so on and so forth.

Jane had finished the neat bow under her chin, tugged it tight, and merely said, *Thank you, ma'am*, and laughed inside herself to see Lady Margaret look so nonplussed.

One didn't grow up in Nantwich without developing a bit of a tough hide.

The curricle emerged from the cool dark woodland and now, in pale sunshine again, they were passing more open fields to either side, in which sheep both grazed on what was left of autumn grasses and fed themselves from wooden racks filled with hay.

Grandfather Titus had been right in his letter to Charity: it was very beautiful here in Somerset, thought Jane, even in winter. In Nantwich winter meant dirty snow heaped up high in the streets, a cold so damp and penetrating one never really felt warm, thin watery soup, and chilblains.

She looked down at the pretty wool gloves Livia had lent her. They didn't fit her well, but oh, they were *warm*. Happily she wiggled her fingers, just a bit. No chilblains for *her* this year.

"I'm sorry."

Jane gave a little jump. "I beg your pardon? Your Grace."

"I said that I'm sorry."

"What for?"

"For my sister's asking you all those personal questions at luncheon."

"It's all right. Your Grace."

"I really don't think it is."

"Well, I wouldn't let it bother you."

"It does. Margaret shouldn't have been so damned nosy." The Duke gave a deep sigh. "She can be very difficult sometimes. Actually, most of the time."

"It's hard for people who have lost someone dear to them. It can make them very emotional, don't you think? Who was it that your sister is mourning?"

"Her husband."

"Oh, I'm sorry."

"He died over ten years ago."

"Oh," Jane said. "What a very long time to be in mourning. How hard for Lady Margaret. She must have loved him very much. Your Grace."

The Duke made no reply. Skillfully he brought the

horses around a great wide curve, and they came to a neat, well-kept old stone and brick building on their left—the Surmont Hall lodge-house.

Its caretaker, Mr. Allard, smiling, waved them through, and they continued on the broad winding path, past further groves of trees, and toward the Hall which soon came into view, a massive, looming house with multiple wings built on in a variety of architectural styles, plainly displaying a long span of centuries.

Livia had shown Jane a handsome old bedchamber in which Henry the Seventh was supposed to have stayed in 1487, though apparently this was in question according to Great-grandmother Henrietta, whose view was that the resident Penhallows would never have allowed such an impertinent upstart to stay with them.

Earlier today Mr. Pressley had said that Henry the Seventh, who had founded the House of Tudor, was widely viewed as a hero for wresting the crown away from King Richard the Third, also widely viewed as a villain who had had his own young nephews—rightful heirs to the throne—secretly murdered in the Tower of London where they had been imprisoned.

Wakefield had commented that his father always wondered if the story about the nephews was only Tudor pripigandia, and Mr. Pressley had said, *I believe, Master Wakefield, you mean propaganda*, and Wakefield (of course) had replied, *Yes, that's what I said.*

Jane smiled a little, thinking of this, and how through Wakefield she was enlarging her vocabulary very nicely, and what a charming young person he was, and suddenly the Duke said:

"You have dimples."

Jane turned her head to look at him, and he added:

"Two of them."

"Yes. Your Grace."

"One in each cheek."

"Yes."

The Duke's deep blue eyes were fixed on her face, and for a few crazy seconds Jane, vividly aware of how close they were sitting together, thought that he was going to kiss her.

Her heart gave a violent lurch within her chest and several things flashed through her head.

One was that she wouldn't mind if he did.

Yesterday he had seemed so ordinary-looking to her, but that was probably because she had been expecting him to come parading into the Hall's drawing-room swathed in velvet and ermine, and maybe with a scepter and glittering coronet, too.

Today she had realized that even though he was a duke, he was still a person like anybody else, and that she liked his great untidy mane of tawny hair, and how he walked with a sort of easy lope on those long legs of his, and that he had a very attractive mouth, with a narrow upper lip offset by a fuller lower lip which was a combination she found extremely enticing.

Another thing Jane thought was that the Duke's sister Lady Margaret would probably not want Jane to kiss him.

Also, remembering what Great-grandmother Henrietta had said yesterday about the Duke, and how disparaging she had been, *she* probably wouldn't want Jane kissing him either.

Nor would Great-grandmother Kent, who had forever been exhorting Jane to keep away from the boys—the men—who only wanted one thing. She had been extremely vague about what that one thing was, but as Jane had gotten older she had figured out what Great-grandmother meant.

Into Jane's mind now streaked an image of Lady Felicia

and her mother the Countess—though really, there was no need to picture them traveling in a giant pumpkin-carriage attended by lizard-footmen and a rat-coachman—who might even now be on their way toward Hastings. It was just a guess, but they, too, probably wouldn't want the Duke to be kissing Jane.

It was therefore impossible to escape the conclusion that there were quite a few people, alive *and* dead, who were likely opposed to the idea.

A person who was good would reject this wild kissing idea out of hand.

But she was, evidently, a person who might not be *that* good.

Because her heart was thumping hard within her, and her gaze was going back and forth between the Duke's fascinating blue eyes and his equally fascinating mouth.

Finally, she was wondering if they could kiss while the curricle was still moving so swiftly. He seemed to be such a capable driver that he probably could manage it, but it would still be an unfortunate means by which to get into a terrible accident and, say, die that way.

Maybe the Duke was thinking the same thing—or maybe he wasn't thinking at all about kissing her—because he turned his head away from her and shortly brought his team to an easy, graceful halt on the graveled sweep in front of the Hall.

Well, *damn.*

The massive door of dark knotted wood opened and a footman came down the steps and to Jane's side of the curricle, ready to help her down.

She said, "Thank you again. Your Grace."

"You're welcome, Miss Kent." His expression was still rather grave, but as Jane gathered up her skirts he added abruptly:

"Just a moment."

"Yes?"

"Do come play billiards with Wakefield if you like. Anytime."

"Really?"

"Yes."

"I may rip the cloth. Your Grace."

"You should see the gash I put in it last week."

"Did you make the shot?"

"Yes, but my glory was dimmed, obviously."

Jane smiled. "Well, I'd love to try it sometime. Thank you very much. Your Grace."

"You look just like a daisy when you smile."

His voice was a little husky, and the blue of his eyes had deepened in a very attractive way. Jane felt her heart give another excited jolt in her chest. She answered, with as much composure as she could muster:

"A daisy?"

"Yes."

"How lovely. I like daisies."

"So do I. But you probably guessed that already."

Jane nodded. She was feeling a little breathless now, and said with less composure, "It was just a guess."

"It was a good guess."

"Thank you. Your Grace."

"Dimples," he said, even more huskily.

"I—yes."

"And daisies."

"Daisies? Your Grace."

"Yes. And boots."

"I—I beg your pardon. Did you say 'boots'?"

"Yes, boots."

"Boots?"

"Your boots. Very practical. And fetching."

"Do you think so?"

"Yes. Very. I'd like to—well, never mind," the Duke said hurriedly.

"You'd like to what? Your Grace."

"I—uh—well, perhaps you ought to go in, Miss Kent. The wind's gotten up, and I don't want you to get chilled."

"That's very kind of you." Jane would have liked to press him further as to exactly what it was he wanted to do in regards to her boots, because she had no idea what he was talking about, but it was such an intriguing remark and his eyes had gone such a delicious dark blue and he sounded so delightfully intense, as if he were hungry, possibly even ravenous.

But now probably wasn't the best moment, with the footman standing nearby, and also she spotted Great-grandmother Henrietta standing in the tall doorway on the porch, and even from here Jane could see that Great-grandmother's silvery eyebrows had shot up high in her face, which made Jane suddenly feel all guilty and exposed somehow, so she went on just as hurriedly:

"Well—goodbye."

"Goodbye, Miss Kent."

Jane clasped the outstretched hand of the footman, thanking him, and got down from the curricle, then went quickly to the steps and up onto the porch where Great-grandmother was waiting.

From behind her she heard the wheels of the Duke's curricle crunching on gravel, but she didn't turn around to look as he drove away, and instead she followed Great-grandmother inside, still feeling rather breathless and discombobulated and also warm all over and despite feeling rather guilty, nonetheless wondering when she would see the Duke again and what might happen the next time they were alone together.

As soon as he got home Anthony went looking for Margaret.

He found her in one of the guest bedchambers with her head deep inside an armoire.

"What the *devil*, Meg."

Margaret emerged from the armoire, put her hands on her hips, and frowned at him. "I beg your pardon?"

"What the devil do you think you're doing?"

"If it's any of your concern, Anthony, I'm inspecting the room to ensure it will be ready for Lady Felicia."

This reply did nothing to improve his mood. "I mean, what the devil do you mean by harping at Miss Kent like that at luncheon?"

"Do stop saying 'devil'—it makes you sound positively satanic."

"I feel satanic. You bombarded her with prying questions. How do you know so much about her, anyway? You never met her before today."

"It's common knowledge," answered Margaret coolly, but her shoulders went up as she spoke. A defensive gesture. He pounced.

"By Jove, you were gossiping with the servants, weren't you? And *you* a viscountess. *And* a duke's daughter. How low the mighty have sunk."

A bull's-eye on that one, Anthony saw, as Margaret turned as red as a tomato. But her chin went high, high into the air, and she snapped:

"If you have nothing better to do than harangue me, Anthony, I suggest you betake yourself elsewhere. Go scratch that nasty pig of yours."

"Evidently Miss Kent already did, and made fine work of it, too. What the devil did you mean at luncheon by 'irregular connection'?"

"Stop saying 'devil,'" Margaret hissed at him, sounding rather satanic herself.

"Fine. What the hell did you mean by 'irregular connection'?"

"If you must know, your precious Miss Kent is illegitimate."

Anthony thought back to yesterday's tea at the Hall. "She said Titus Penhallow was her grandfather."

"He was, but he never married Miss Kent's grandmother. Which means she's not a real Penhallow at all. Anybody could tell just by looking at those cheap, ghastly boots she had on."

"That's more than a little hypocritical, coming from someone who just a month ago told me not to judge a book by its cover. Remember? When I objected to the fact that Miss D'Arblay—the charming young lady who, as you'll recall, preceded Miss Preston-Carnaby—went traipsing about the place in a leopard-skin cape, shoes made from African ostriches, and a hat festooned with half a dozen dead birds on top."

Margaret scowled. "How was I to know that her chief pastime was trying to shoot squirrels?"

"You mean her sole occupation in life, don't you? You're lucky she didn't put a bullet-hole in that cat of yours, just for fun."

"I had been informed, by reliable sources, that Miss D'Arblay was a highly eligible candidate."

"For what? President of the Society to Exterminate Squirrels?"

"We were," said Margaret coldly, "discussing Miss Kent."

"Yes, we were. Allow me to point out that no matter her background, Miss Kent's clearly been welcomed with open arms at the Hall, so what business is it of yours?"

Margaret sniffed. "I daresay you think it all a very romantic tale. The ragged little waif plucked out of the gutter and set loose among Polite Society. For all we know, she might have been selling herself on the streets of Nantwich. And did you see how *tentative* she was about using the correct utensils at luncheon? And how much she ate? I wouldn't be surprised if she tucked a few rolls into her pockets."

Anthony looked wonderingly at his sister. She stood very stiff and rigid in her black gown, arms akimbo and her reddened face a rictus of cold disdain. They were only ten or so feet apart, but it could have just as well been miles. "Have you forgotten, Meg, that William of Normandy, the illustrious Conqueror whom the Farrs supposedly accompanied to England, was a bastard?"

"Not *supposedly*. There are *documents*."

"Which we all hope are genuine. However, it *is* an established fact that our country's own Charles the Second had a great many side-slips, and that there are countless members of the nobility who are related to them. Confucius was illegitimate, and so was Leonardo da Vinci. And let's not forget the paternal grandfather of Anne of Cleves, Duke Johann the Second, who had sixty-three bastards, thereby earning himself the immemorial sobriquet 'the Childmaker.' One wonders, given how busy he was procreating, how he had the time to rule over his duchy."

"Who are *you* to be mocking procreation, you sorry excuse for a duke?"

Margaret's upper lip was curled away from her teeth as she issued this remark, and involuntarily Anthony said:

"Good God, Meg, you look just like Father when you do that."

"When I do what?"

"When you sneer like that. One of Father's favorite facial expressions, as I recall."

"At least *he* had the proper sense of duty! *He* knew his own worth! *He* managed to produce two sons!"

"Oh yes, Father was always keenly awake to the obligations of his rank," responded Anthony dryly. "He married you off to Skiffy without even letting you have that Season you wanted so badly, and got poor old Terence engaged to Selina not long after that. And then when Terence died, Father roped me into the betrothal the minute I turned twenty-one, deaf to each and every one of my protestations of horror, in which I made it clear that the only thing Selina and I had in common was a mutual loathing of the other. Very fixed in purpose, was Father. How he used to berate Mother for her inability to provide additional heirs. And how *she* used to berate him for his—ah—incompetencies in the marital bed. Yes, quite the happy family, we Farrs."

"And what, pray, is your point? Beyond indulging in maudlin reminiscence, of course."

And there it was, Margaret's upper lip receding again. Anthony couldn't help but recall Nurse warning him—when, as a little boy, he had been frowning up at her for some reason or another—that if he wasn't careful, his face would freeze like that forever. He felt for a brief moment the tempting, but of course unducal impulse to say exactly that to Margaret, but managed to suppress it, and she went on:

"Of course you have no point. You never do. You live in your own little dream-world of pigs and pumpkins, and—"

"Don't forget books, as long as you're cataloguing all *my* incompetencies. Also, my obsession with drainage trenches."

"It would take more time than I presently have to enumerate everything that's wrong with you, Anthony, but do allow me to thank you for your riveting discourse on illegitimacy through the ages. I'm sure Miss Kent would find it equally illuminating."

He looked thoughtfully at her. "You know, old girl, sometimes you're simply *mean.*"

"And *you're* just the sort of coarse, raffish person who likes to consort with pigmen and bastards. You're a horrible, horrible duke, and I have no doubt that if Father could see you now, he'd be ashamed to call you his son."

Anthony felt his mouth twist in a wry half-smile. "He said that himself often enough while he was alive, Meg, so you can rest easy on that point. Well—I believe I'll follow up on your earlier suggestion and betake myself elsewhere. Unless there's anything else you need to say?"

"Yes. Do something about that hair of yours before Lady Felicia arrives. You look like an inmate of Bedlam."

Anthony turned and left the room, and began making his way toward his library and the welcome interval of peace Dinkle would impart, however brief. He passed Margaret's big tabby cat in one of the corridors, stretched out on a console table between a pair of priceless Ming Dynasty dragons which were carved in intricate detail out of translucent jade.

Wakefield's right, thought Anthony. That's one sad-looking cat.

The family were seated at dinner, and for some time Cousin Gabriel, Livia, and Great-grandmother Henrietta had been talking about ongoing renovations within the Hall, crop rotation, the critical value of drainage trenches (especially during winter flooding), progress in the building of new tenant-farmer cottages, proposed landscaping in the spring, an unusual explosion in the local deer population, and a needed expansion to the village school.

As she ate, careful to mimic Livia's table manners, Jane thought to herself how clever and proficient her new family was. And how busy, and engaged, and occupied. Dinner had begun with Great-grandmother inquiring after her lessons today, and she was able to say, truthfully, that she had enjoyed it, and learned some interesting things about the Tudors and the founding of the British Navy, and then Great-grandmother had mentioned that the wife of Gabriel's cousin Hugo, Katherine Penhallow, had had two books published on the subject of British maritime history, an accomplishment Jane thought very impressive. She had asked about Hugo, too, and it turned out he was a master shipbuilder, with a glowing reputation not just here in England but beyond.

The Penhallows were so good at so many things.

Jane accepted another slice of broiled chicken, and as she ate it, wondered what *she* was good at.

She thought back to her years in Nantwich.

Well, she was good at surviving.

That counted for something, didn't it?

Yes. Oh yes, it did.

Later, alone in her room, dressed for bed in a voluminous white nightgown—another loan from kind Livia—Jane stood in front of the long pier-glass and raised up the hem to look at her legs.

Was it her imagination, or were they already fattening up? Her knees seemed less knobby, for one thing.

This was a gratifying development.

She looked with new pleasure at her ankles.

Yes, *definitely* less skinny.

Into her mind came, all at once, the intriguing exchange she had had with the Duke earlier today.

Boots.

Boots?

Your boots. Very practical. And fetching.

Do you think so?

Yes. Very. I'd like to—well, never mind.

Jane hoped she would find out what he meant.

She let the hem of the nightgown drop, then looked with wonderment around her elegant bedchamber for what was probably the thousandth time, contrasting it with the tiny cramped attic room she had for all her life before this shared with the Kent family's old crates and trunks. She pinched her arm, not too hard, but just to still make sure all this was real, and after that, having received a small but reassuring amount of pain, went over to the high four-poster bed, clambered in, pulled up the covers, let herself wallow luxuriously amidst the clean smooth sheets for a few moments, then picked up from the side-table one of the books the vicar had lent her. *The History of England from the Earliest Times to the Death of George II.*

She was especially curious to read about Henry the Seventh and Richard the Third. Was it really possible Richard had been the victim of Tudor propaganda? That he had been painted so dark merely in order to further their own ends? If so, that was quite underhanded of the Tudors. She would have to ask the Duke more about it the next time she saw him.

She wondered again when that would be.

It was so nice of him to repeat Wakefield's invitation to come and play billiards, wasn't it? And to be bothered about his sister asking a lot of personal questions. It was only natural, of course, that people would be curious about her. In a way, arriving as she had here at the Hall, she was a little bit like the goddess Athena, emerging so unexpectedly from her father's head. What a curious story. Jane's story was a curious one, too, despite her having been born in the usual fashion.

Not long after she had arrived at Surmont Hall, Great-grandmother Henrietta had mused aloud about telling everyone that Titus *had* married Charity. At first Jane had thought this would be a good idea—that it was the easy, uncomplicated way which would smooth over any potentially troubling waters.

Then she had envisioned herself among the neighborhood people.

And she had realized she would always, *always*, be uneasily wondering if perhaps some of the servants, already aware of her background, had gossiped and so spread the word around the county like wildfire. (Not that she would blame them if they had; it *was* an interesting bit of news.) Which would put Jane in the position of being a liar. And not just herself: Great-grandmother, Cousin Gabriel, and Livia would be lying, too, on her behalf.

That had decided her.

So she had politely but firmly refused to go along with Great-grandmother's plan, and, notwithstanding the heavy sadness which immediately blanketed her at the thought, she had offered to go away if being here was an embarrassment to her new family.

Great-grandmother had looked so stricken she'd almost felt sorry for saying it, but it had felt important to stick to her guns.

She wasn't going to ask anyone, no matter how well-intentioned, to live a lie.

Besides, lies, she had noticed, had a way of coming back to haunt one.

Like the time she had snatched a sausage at the market, from the open-air grill, when she had thought the proprietor wasn't looking. He *had* been, Great-grandmother Kent had been informed, Jane had denied it, but then Great-grandmother had grabbed at her burnt hands and sniffed them, and thus she had been unmasked. And slapped, and then had to endure long tedious hours of recrimination.

Although the sausage had tasted very good, on the whole, it hadn't been worth it.

So, regarding her background, she wasn't going to stand on various rooftops shouting it out to passersby, but neither was she going to deny what was true.

Back in Nantwich, Great-grandmother would sometimes stare broodingly at Jane, and talk at length about how the sins of the fathers would be carried on the shoulders of those who came after, blackening their souls. At the time Jane hadn't understood what she had meant, but now she did.

It wasn't *her* fault that Charity and Titus hadn't had a chance to get married.

Nor was it *their* fault, either.

What did matter was that they had loved each other.

Jane thought about something else she'd found in that old chapbook along with Titus' letter to Charity.

On one of the pages in between which the letter had been placed all those years ago, somebody—it had to have been Charity—had drawn a little heart, and inside she had written *CK & TP. Forever.*

It was heartbreaking, but beautiful, too. Jane liked to think that Charity and Titus had, after death, found each other again—found their happily ever after.

Love really was all that mattered.

Although, of course, having enough to eat and wearing clean gowns that were long enough and not being cold all the time were nice, too.

Thoughtfully Jane set aside the history book and reached under the covers to feel her ankles again. Yes, hurray, there really was a bit more flesh. And goodness, the skin there was delightfully sensitive. She was giving herself goose-bumps.

What *had* the Duke wanted to do with her boots?

And how charming of him to like those dilapidated old things.

Beneath the covers Jane felt at her knees. Oh yes, better. She slid her hands up along the equally sensitive skin of her thighs, up along the sharp protuberance of her hip-bones, to her rib-cage, her small soft breasts, and the tender circles of her nipples. It felt good, touching herself, but it was also true that it was good when somebody else was doing the touching.

The Duke, Jane remembered, had lovely big strong-looking hands, with long fingers, broad at the base and tapering toward the ends and flattened out a little, a feature that was very appealing to her.

So appealing, in fact, that she was getting warm all over again.

Abruptly she found herself wondering about his wife, the late Duchess, and what she had been like. Had the Duke loved her so much that he was reluctant to marry again? And was that why Lady Margaret—if what Wakefield had said was accurate—had to force him to remarry?

Jane thought about today's luncheon at Hastings.

The food had been delicious, but Lady Margaret (who certainly had a lot to say on the subject of flowers) had eyes so cold they reminded Jane of stones one would find at the bottom of a river.

Icy, icy cold.

Jane brought her hands away from herself, tugged down the hem of her nightgown, and reached again for the history book.

Then she remembered something else she was good at, besides surviving.

Apparently she was good at scratching pigs.

Jane smiled, warming up again as she thought of the Duke. She thought of dimples. And daisies. And her boots.

She would, she decided, wear them again tomorrow to the vicarage.

Chapter 6

To Jane's disappointment, Wakefield didn't come for lessons the next day. Mr. Pressley explained that the Duke had sent a note round saying that Wakefield was a trifle under the weather. Jane hoped it wasn't anything serious, and settled into a mathematics lesson, which was more fun than she had thought it would be, followed by an interesting interval looking at various maps of Somerset and talking about the history and geography of the area. Mr. Pressley told her that there were all kinds of old caves about, thought to have been occupied by ancient peoples thousands of years ago, and that the Somerset moors, though very rich and fertile, had a tendency toward brackishness and required constant drainage to permit farming and grazing.

Jane had a lot of questions, and as Mr. Pressley was anxious to make up for the shortening of yesterday's lessons, their time together ran quite late.

When Jane got back to Surmont Hall, luncheon was over, but the kitchen staff were very nice about making up a plate for her which she enjoyed while reading another book Mr. Pressley had lent her, poems by William Wordsworth.

Her favorite so far was "I Wandered Lonely as a Cloud"—she especially liked how Mr. Wordsworth compared a vast field of daffodils to the night sky, *Continuous as the stars that shine / And twinkle on the milky way.*

It was surprising, and lovely, how in just a few brief lines, he managed to harmoniously connect these two very different things.

Words were amazing, weren't they?

And how delightful that someone with the last name of Wordsworth had become a poet.

Also, how delightful that the talented Katherine Penhallow—to whom she was now linked by family connection—was a writer. *Pen* and *hallow*. Perfect!

Kent, mused Jane, meant something about knowing.

Well, the way things were going with her lessons, there was a possibility she might actually live up to her own surname.

After luncheon, Jane went looking for company.

Great-grandmother would be napping, she knew, and when she went up to the nursery, the children's nanny, speaking in a soft whisper, told Jane that all the children were napping too.

She went back downstairs and talked to the Hall's butler Crenshaw, and learned that Cousin Gabriel was out somewhere on the estate looking at apple orchards, and that Livia had taken a pony-cart to visit some of the tenant-farmer families.

So Jane put on her pelisse and bonnet again, and went outside for a long walk in the gardens to the back of the house, then amused herself meandering through the maze which, she had been informed, dated back to Elizabethan times.

I wandered lonely as a cloud.

It occurred to her that if she could ride a horse, or

drive a pony-cart like Livia, she could go visiting people. Wakefield, say, or Miss Humphrey and Miss Trevelyan. Or go into the village. At dinner she asked if this might be a possibility.

"By all means, my dear," said Great-grandmother. "Riding is a highly desirable activity for any lady of Quality, as well as a suitable form of exercise for a young person. You'll need a riding-habit, however. I can certainly ask Miss Simpkin to have one made up for you as soon as possible."

"Jane, you can have mine," Livia said. "I never wear it."

"Oh, Livia, are you sure? Then I could begin sooner."

"I've never been much of a rider, though there was a time Gabriel tried very hard to teach me." Livia flashed a saucy smile at Cousin Gabriel. "I'll dig up the habit after dinner, and start on the adjustments tonight."

Jane watched that subtle, but unmistakable warmth come into Cousin Gabriel's dark eyes as he smiled across the table at his wife. It must be nice, she thought, with a sudden aching twist inside her, to have somebody who smiled at one like that, and every day, too.

A person could get used to that.

She felt her mind drifting backward into the past, then with a great effort of will brought it back to the here and now, where she abruptly found herself thinking of a pair of deep-blue eyes, a thin sensitive face, the most delicious hands in the world . . .

Jane, Jane, stop daydreaming, she told herself, but noticed that it took quite a lot of effort to make this vividly tempting image fade away, and then it took her a few seconds to remember that they were talking about horses and a riding-habit and a kind offer of assistance. She said, with a quick rush of gratitude:

"Thank you very much, Livia, for altering it for me. Is

there a horse I might borrow, Cousin Gabriel? And could one of the grooms teach me?"

"We've horses aplenty, Jane. And if Livia can do her magic by tomorrow, I've got time in the morning. Titania's been wanting lessons, too."

How interesting her life had become, Jane thought. Academic lessons with an eight-year-old, and riding lessons with a four-year-old. It was a good thing she actually liked being around children. And she certainly was making up for lost time, thanks to these generous relations of hers. She smiled at him. "Thank you, Cousin Gabriel."

So the next day, Saturday, she and Titania learned how to sit a horse, and how to walk it and gently signal it to stop, and Jane felt extremely dashing in the bottle-green habit Livia had quickly altered, with its exquisite black embroidery on the cuffs and hem, and once again her old boots were proving to be just the right footwear for the occasion. She thought of all the times in Nantwich when she had longingly watched people riding, and how marvelous it was to—amazingly—be doing it herself.

One felt rather agreeably high up, sitting on a horse. She could hardly wait to learn how to canter and gallop.

On Sunday the family went to church. Jane was glad to see the Duke was there, and Wakefield too, and less glad, but fatalistic, about seeing Lady Margaret, clad once again in dismal black.

Mr. Pressley, without sounding at all pompous or bombastic, gave a thoughtful (and not too long) sermon on the topic of humility, and Jane learned that both Great-grandmother and Cousin Gabriel had very nice singing voices, and also that it was exceedingly pleasant to be sitting in exactly the right spot to be able to look at the back of the Duke's head.

There was an interlude, when Mr. Attfield the churchwarden was talking at length and rather boringly about raising funds to refurbish the transept, which Jane used to good purpose by gazing at the Duke's hair and finally realizing that its color reminded her of a lion—if the advertisement for Binty's Miracle Syrup which she had seen on a shop window in Nantwich had been a good representation of one.

Of course it was none of her business, but she did hope the Duke would keep his hair long like that. Somehow it seemed to suit him so beautifully.

It was strange, but as the service proceeded, Anthony had the curious feeling of being watched with a particular intensity.

He would have turned around to see if he was correct, but as Margaret had countless times instructed Wakefield to stop twisting about on the hard uncomfortable seat, he decided that he ought to be—in this small matter at least—a worthy role model for his son.

However, when the service was over and Anthony could very properly rise from his seat in the frontmost pew, he did turn around, and the first thing he noticed was that Jane was here in the church, too. He hadn't seen her since Thursday, when he had driven her back to the Hall and made a complete ass of himself by talking about daisies and dimples and so on.

He stared.

By God, she *did* look like a daisy.

Also, over her wavy flaxen hair she had on the same light blue bonnet, tied underneath her chin in a neat little bow, the color of which reminded him of a summer sky and also gave her eyes the soft deep shimmer of a stream running high.

Those fascinating eyes came to meet his, and she smiled. Those *dimples.* Anthony felt his brain immediately go to mush. A surprisingly pleasant sensation, accompanied by an equally pleasant feeling of heat caroming throughout his body. The aisle between the rows of pews was crowded with people and for a few crazy seconds Anthony wanted to leap up and over the dozen or so pews which separated him from Jane.

And then she turned away when Miss Trevelyan came up to greet her, so reluctantly he abandoned the idea which, although it would have been quite a lot of fun to try, was entirely devoid of dignity and clearly subducal.

He moved into the aisle, where he was promptly buttonholed by the garrulous Mr. Attfield, and managed to escape only after he had promised to make a generous donation to the transept fund.

He made it past two more rows of pews and Miss Humphrey said hullo, and so of course he had to stop and exchange a few courteous words with her (careful to avoid the painful subject of pumpkins), and after that Mr. Lumley the schoolmaster wanted to talk to him about the expansion to the Riverton school, and naturally he offered to donate to that as well, and when finally he got to the front steps of the church where he spoke with Mr. Pressley for a minute or so, he was deeply, and possibly even excessively, thankful to perceive that the Penhallow family had not rushed off to their carriage but were instead standing by the lych-gate talking with some other members of the congregation.

Penhallow had his youngest, the baby boy, held up against his chest, and Livia was holding their sleeping toddler; their oldest, a girl, was talking to Wakefield who was eyeing her as one would confront an unsettling visitor from another planet. Jane, Anthony saw, stood a little apart, watching the two of them with that engaging twinkle in her eyes.

As he got closer he heard the little girl saying something about a fairy who liked to ride horses and go fishing and fight battles, and Wakefield said scornfully:

"Fairies aren't real."

"Yes, they *are*," retorted the little girl, pushing him hard in the chest with both hands, and Wakefield staggered back.

"Titania," said Penhallow, with quiet authority in his voice, and the little girl looked up at him unhappily, but subsided.

"Hullo," Anthony said, and Wakefield came to stand next to him.

"I say, Father, she *pushed* me."

"I saw."

"Not bad for a girl," Wakefield went on, with a certain respect in his voice. "Jane, did you see that? I nearly fell over." He went over to where she was standing. "Has she tried to push *you*?"

"Not so far."

"Well, watch out."

"I will," she promised gravely. "Good morning. Your Grace."

"Good morning, Miss Kent." Now that Anthony was in closer proximity to her, his brain not only failed to return to its usual state of semi-coherence, his body had yet to cool to its normal temperature. He was burning up inside himself, he was more than a little agitated, his mouth had suddenly gone dry, and altogether he felt, in fact, as if he'd come down with the influenza which two years ago had felled Wakefield, but in an extremely nice way. Which of course made no sense, but these were the thoughts one had when one's brain had dissolved. "Lovely daisy, isn't it? That is—I mean—lovely *day*."

"Very," Jane agreed, smiling up at him, but without mockery at his embarrassing slip of the tongue, and with such sweetness that Anthony was reminded of chocolate so delicious, so rich, that it took superhuman strength to not eat a great deal of it all at once.

"You two still sound stuffy," said Wakefield disapprovingly. "I say, Jane, did you miss me at lessons on Friday?"

"I certainly did. I hope you're fully recovered from whatever was ailing you?"

"Oh, yes. I had undajisting, you know."

Anthony said to him, "Do you mean indigestion?"

"Yes, that's what I said. Cook made apple puffs with whipped cream, Jane, and I had four of them."

"Oh, those do sound good," said Jane. "But I'm sorry they made you unwell."

"Three would have been all right. It was the fourth one that did it. Afterwards my stomach stuck out amazingly. It was funny at first, but then it hurt quite a lot. Jane, what did Aunt Margaret mean at luncheon when she said you're an unrigular connection? It sounds like something she'd say about Snuffles' legs. Is there something wrong with *your* legs? You don't limp a bit."

"Wake," said Anthony.

"What?"

"You're getting rather personal."

"Yes, but Father, Jane and I are *friends*."

"True. But there are still some things you ought not to ask."

Wakefield looked up at Jane. "Did I say something wrong? I'm awfully sorry."

"It's all right. And no, there's nothing wrong with my legs."

"I say, I *am* glad. Oh, look, there's Miss Trevelyan. I want to ask her something."

Wakefield trotted off, and Anthony looked again at Jane, wanting to say something—anything—that would make her smile again. Did she like jokes? he wondered. He was horrible at telling them, because he could never remember the clincher at the end, and also he loathed puns of all kinds and could barely tolerate riddles. Although Wakefield had just recently, with eyes alight with merriment, told him a decent one about a man who wore his stockings the wrong side outwards. Why? Because there was a hole on the other side.

Would Jane find it amusing?

But then Anthony saw that she was gazing up at him with an expression he couldn't readily decipher. A kind of intense inquiry, as if she were bracing herself for something, but with a certain steady resolution, too. As one did when bad news was possibly coming but one knew one was strong enough to handle it.

"What is it?" he asked, taking a long step closer to her.

"Did Lady Margaret tell you?"

"About your—ah—irregular connection?"

"Yes. Did she?"

"Yes."

"About Titus Penhallow and my grandmother not being married?"

"Yes."

"I don't care, really, who knows it, but—does it change how you think of me? Your Grace."

This question, quietly spoken, made Anthony want to do two things, both equally impossible.

One, he would have liked to throttle his own sister for rudely—*meanly*—raising the issue at luncheon the other day.

Two, he wished he could wrap Jane up closely in his arms and do whatever it took to erase the look of rather painful inquiry in her beautiful gray eyes.

He wondered if a good long kiss would help.

It would certainly help *him*.

But, of course, it was Jane he wanted to help. So he stayed where he was and answered, with perfect truth:

"No."

"Really?"

"Yes." He saw, with pleasure, how Jane's dark brows, which had been drawn together in a questioning sort of way, relaxed, and her lovely mouth, which had looked tense, softened into something very nearly approaching a smile.

"Well, I'm glad. Your Grace."

"I'm glad you're glad."

"So am I."

"Yes," said Anthony, devolving into happy inarticulateness, "I'm very glad."

"I too. Your Grace."

Then they both fell silent, and Anthony wondered again about the stockings riddle, decided against it, and finally said, "I'm *very* glad."

And there it was.

Her smile.

Complete with dimples.

Heat surged through him, and Anthony was aware that he was sweating heavily, as if he had been helping out in the fields with the hay threshing, a vigorous activity which he enjoyed very much. (Of which Margaret—naturally—disapproved as being undukish.)

Jane said, "How is the Duchess?"

"Oh, she's very well, thank you. Johns says she's gained some weight in the past week."

"Is that good?"

"Very good. She's won the Fattest Pig award at the *fête* three years in a row."

"How splendid," said Jane warmly. "Congratulations. Your Grace."

"Thank you very much."

"Speaking of gaining weight, I'm a little fatter myself."

This seemed like exactly the sort of remark which allowed one to stare at one's companion as much as one liked. Although he wished she weren't all bundled up in a pelisse. Or wearing anything at all, really. Another delightful wave of sweat broke over him, but he answered cautiously. "You sound pleased."

"Oh, I am. I've still got a long way to go, though."

"How so?"

"I didn't have much to eat for the past couple of years, you see, so I've gotten far too thin."

"I say, that's dreadful. Why didn't you?"

"Money problems."

"Back in Nantwich?"

"Yes, that's right."

Anthony looked at Jane with both concern and respect. She spoke so calmly and forthrightly about what had to have been an incredibly difficult situation. He'd had plenty of problems—he *currently* had plenty of problems—but never had he lacked enough to eat. "You had no one to help you, Miss Kent?"

"It was just my great-grandmother Kent and me, and she was very ill."

"There was no one else?"

"No."

With great sincerity he answered, "I'm glad you came here, then."

"Me too. Your Grace."

"I'm *very* glad," he said, devolving again. Sudden inspiration struck him and he fished into the pocket of his greatcoat. He pulled out his hand and held it out, palm up, to Jane. On it were several small black disks embossed with an image of a castle. "Care for a Pomfret cake?"

"Is that licorice?"

"Yes."

"Oh, I'd love one."

"Have as many as you like. Wait just a moment—do you object to dog hair?"

"Well—not to *eat* it, of course."

"Of course not." He blew on his palm and the dog hairs dispersed, like fluffy seedlets from a dandelion, and he had to suppress a sudden childish desire to make a wish. "There, that's better."

Jane took one of the little cakes and nibbled at it. "It's delicious. Thank you very much. Won't you share them with me?"

He took one also. Jane had another one, and then another one after that, and he had not the least desire in the world to eat any more, which was funny, as he was very fond of Pomfret cakes. He watched with total contentment as she ate the last three.

"Thank you. Your Grace."

"You're welcome. My contribution to the cause."

"The cause?"

"The amelioration of thinness."

Jane laughed. "That's a lovely way to put it."

"Yes, rather elegant, don't you think? By the way, don't let anybody talk you into taking castor oil."

"Castor oil?"

"Yes, to help you fatten up. It's foul."

"That's good to know. I'd rather just eat things, anyway."

"I too."

She looked curiously at him. "Did someone give you castor oil?"

"Yes, my nurse did when I was a boy."

"I'm sorry."

"All in the past, thankfully."

"Was that when . . ."

"When what?"

"Now *I'm* getting rather personal, I'm afraid. Your Grace."

"Get as personal as you like," Anthony said, then vehemently hoped, with a fresh wave of sweat, that he hadn't sounded as if he were issuing some sort of carnal invitation.

As much as he would have liked to.

Although not, naturally, in some ghastly insinuating sort of manner that practically required one to leer or twirl one's mustache. Suddenly he was extremely glad he didn't have a mustache. Side-whiskers, yes, but never a beard or mustache, as they essentially seemed (based on his own observations) to be hairy devices in which to trap particles of food, and then one had to force oneself to neither stare nor snicker unducally. Which, unfortunately, he had done just last month during dinner with the D'Arblay family, whose patriarch had sported a monumental quantity of facial hair that not only gave him a stunning resemblance to Methuselah, but also had all too rapidly been embellished with breadcrumbs, buttered rice, bits of trout, and savory pudding.

It was the pudding that had sent Anthony over the edge, because it had not remained firmly lodged in Mr. D'Arblay's beard, but had, rather, slowly descended, as might a climber carefully slide down a treacherous length of rockface. And so he, Anthony, had audibly, noisily, and lengthily snickered.

After dinner Margaret had threatened to rip off one of his arms and beat him with the bloody stump.

And then feed the stump to the Duchess.

To which he had said, with calm confidence, that he trusted the Duchess to know better than to eat her own master's arm.

So angry had Margaret been at this remark that she had stormed out of his library and slammed the door with such force that the doorknob had fallen out.

"Well," Jane now said, snapping him back to attention, "I was wondering if you had to take castor oil when you were in bed for three years."

"No, luckily Dr. Fotherham had charge of me then, not Nurse, and he ran roughshod over her. Which cheered me a good deal."

"Was she terrible to you?"

"No, but she fussed over me till I nearly went mad with it."

Jane nodded. "My great-grandmother Kent was the same way. She meant well, but I always felt so—so hounded."

"Yes, exactly." How splendid, thought Anthony, with a sudden mysterious ache near the region of his heart, to be *understood.* And for a moment—just for a moment—he felt so sad that he wished Jane would put her arms around him.

"How old were you when it happened?"

"When what happened?"

"When you fell out of the tree."

"I was eleven."

"Oh, that's so very young. What did you do all those years in bed? Wakefield said you found it restful, but . . ."

On Jane's face was a look of such kind sympathy that the curious ache in his heart got rather worse.

"I mean, having hurt your back so terribly, you must have been in a lot of pain."

"It wasn't so bad." A lie, and he was fairly sure Jane knew it, but she didn't say anything, only looked up at him so kindly, and after a few seconds he went on:

"It *was* restful, really, because I didn't have to go back to Eton, which I was glad of as I was unhappy there, and while I was lying around in my room nobody paid much attention to me, which was another pleasant change, and I could read all day if I liked. Bunch—you met him the other day, he's our butler, but he was a hall-boy back then—he brought me books from the library, anything I wanted, which was awfully nice of him, as he risked getting caught ferrying them about for me."

"Why wasn't he supposed to be doing that?"

"Outside the scope of his regular duties."

"Oh."

"Yes, the butler back then ran a tight ship. How I despised him."

"Why?"

"He was a terrible bully. The things Bunch told me—well, I won't regale you with anecdotes, but suffice to say they'd curl your hair—not that your hair needs it," Anthony added hastily, looking with admiration at the wavy locks perceptible beneath the crown of her charming hat. "At any rate, the first thing I did when I became duke was to send Parslow off into pensioned oblivion, and gave Bunch his job."

"How very nice of you. Your Grace."

"Oh, Bunch is splendid at it. Happiest day of my life, frankly. Aside from Wakefield's birth. My God, but Margaret was furious." He saw that Jane was looking at him as if puzzled. "Not because of Wakefield's birth," he explained. "For promoting Bunch."

"But why?"

"Because Bunch was a second footman back then, and it violated protocol to promote him all those levels up."

"Oh."

"Yes, and according to Margaret it's been—ducally speaking—downhill ever since."

"Oh," Jane said again, and all at once Anthony felt an odd prickling at the back of his neck, as one might dimly sense impending doom, and so he looked around to see that from one direction Margaret was approaching, and from the opposite direction old Mrs. Penhallow was coming their way.

Neither had on her face an expression of warm cordiality.

Quite the opposite, really, and Anthony thought of two great icebergs inexorably colliding. Woe betide any flotsam and jetsam in their way, too. Not that it was a metaphor for Jane—it was, of course, himself to which he was referring. No, Jane would be more like some kind of beautiful aquatic creature. But what? A dolphin, because of her gray eyes? Dolphins were marvelous animals, weren't they? So sleek and intelligent, and wonderful swimmers. Probably never had to worry about dodging oncoming projectiles.

Or did they?

Because of sharks, for example?

"My dear Jane, it's time to go home," said Mrs. Penhallow, just as Margaret said:

"Where is Wakefield? I've been looking for him everywhere."

These two imposing icebergs—no, he meant ladies—greeted each with frigid politeness, but Anthony would have sworn that a strange look flashed between them, almost one of surprise, as if they had simultaneously discovered something. Then Jane was borne away by Mrs.

Penhallow, and Anthony went off in search of Wakefield, finding him within mere seconds chatting with Miss Trevelyan over by the front steps. Which made him wonder why Margaret had, apparently, so much difficulty locating him.

It was almost as if she was being deceitful.

He pondered this unpleasant notion for a few moments, then moved on in his mind to the infinitely more interesting subject of Jane.

A subject which, he suddenly realized, he could dwell upon for a surprisingly long time.

"Great-grandmother," said Jane, as the family was being conveyed home in their comfortable and spacious barouche, "did you know the Duke's wife?"

"Lady Selina? No, my dear, she died very soon after Gabriel, Livia, and I came from Bath to the Hall. Both Gabriel and I had been away for quite a long time, and for many months we were preoccupied with setting things to right." Great-grandmother looked at Jane with a keenness that made her feel rather uncomfortable, and went on, "Why do you ask?"

Jane had been thinking about what the Duke had said regarding the happiest moment in his life. About Wakefield's birth. Which was a wonderful thing to say. But she had been surprised to hear him say that Bunch's promotion took second place. And not—well—his wedding day.

Not that she wanted to put words into his mouth, naturally, but it was just that she had been expecting him to mention it.

Then Jane found she didn't really want to ask any more questions, at least not with Great-grandmother looking at her like that, as if there was something strange, or unseemly, or wrong about her curiosity, and so she was rather glad when baby Daniel woke up and began making loud babbling noises which were delightful and also seemed to somehow entirely fill the interior of the barouche, making further conversation a bit difficult.

Jane looked out the window and thought some more about the Duke.

When just a little while ago Wakefield had brought up the subject of her unrigular—irregular—connection to the Penhallows, she had been surprised to notice that while she ultimately didn't really care if Lady Margaret knew about it and thought her just another low, vulgar Nantwich sort of person, she *did* care if the Duke knew it and he thought less of her.

Somehow it mattered to her.

She had been hoping he wasn't like his sister Margaret. That he was different in his character and outlook on the world.

Which, it seemed, he was.

The fact was, really, that somehow, *he* had begun to matter to her. Not as a duke, but as a person. As a *man*. (A rather delicious man, too.)

Also, he had looked so very sad when he was talking about having to be in bed for all those painful years that she had wanted, more than anything, to try and comfort him. Maybe even put her arms around him.

She wondered what that would feel like.

He was lean, but he looked strong, too, so it would probably feel wonderful to hug him.

His hard firm strength against her own body.

He would have lovely muscles in his arms and shoulders, and prominent collar-bones, marvelous for trailing her fingers over, and possibly licking, very slowly and deliberately. A hard-planed chest. Maybe some tawny hair there, too. Or dark hair, like his eyelashes and eyebrows?

Perhaps there would be a swirl of it, lower, as she moved her hands down his body, along his ribs, to his flat stomach, and below . . .

The barouche gave a little jolt as it passed over a rut in the road, and suddenly Jane realized that she had moved beyond the idea of giving the Duke a comforting hug.

She was fantasizing about him naked.

Caressing him.

Her fingers on his warm flesh.

Well, and why not?

He was a very attractive man.

A very, *very* attractive man.

Jane didn't pull her gaze away from the window, but felt her cheeks heating up in a warm spreading flush.

Here in this new world of hers, she supposed, one ought not to engage in such activities—maybe even such thoughts—outside the bonds of matrimony.

She resisted the urge to glance across the seat at Great-grandmother Henrietta. To see if she still happened to be looking at her so keenly. Was there something wrong in thinking so much about the Duke?

Jane wondered, yet again, about her goodness.

Or her lack of it.

Maybe she wasn't very good at being good.

But why did it feel so . . . good?

Chapter 7

After church Anthony and Wakefield went to commune with the Duchess for a while, admiring her superb pink corpulence, and after that Wakefield wanted to hang around the stables, grooming his pony and brushing all the dogs and in general getting underfoot, so Anthony went for a long solitary stroll in the lime-walk, beneath bare interlinked branches that would, in summer, fill out densely with beautiful green heart-shaped leaves. It was curious, he mused, how his thoughts were full of Jane: her face, her eyes, her smile . . .

Finally he went into the house, stuck his gloves into the face-plate of the suit of armor which had belonged to one or another of his disturbingly savage ancestors, looked around for Bunch and shortly found him in his butler's pantry, eyeing a long line of silverware laid out on a sideboard.

"What ho, Bunch."

"Good afternoon, Your Grace."

"What are you doing?"

"Counting the silver again, Your Grace."

"Again?" Anthony dropped into a chair at the foot of the large oak table, and comfortably stretched out his legs underneath it. "Why again?"

"It pains me to say it, Your Grace, but I have reason

to believe the Preston-Carnabys departed with several pieces in their luggage."

"Ha," said Anthony. "Can't say I'm surprised."

"Indeed, Your Grace?"

"Oh yes. The mother in particular. Had a shifty look about her, don't you think?"

"I really couldn't say, Your Grace."

"You mean you *wouldn't*, Bunch. Most tactful person I know. Did they take the best silver? For all I know Margaret might send the Bow Street Runners after them."

"Acting on what I might, perhaps, describe as a kind of professional instinct, Your Grace, I took the liberty of instructing the staff to utilize the third best silver during the Preston-Carnabys' visit. Fortunately it bears a remarkable resemblance to the family's premier silver, and is easily replaceable."

"Not only are you tactful, Bunch, you're also the cleverest person I know. Well, by all means order however much additional silver you think we need. Are you hungry? Let's have some sandwiches and ale."

Bunch declined the invitation, having, he said, recently enjoyed luncheon with staff, but passed along the order to the kitchen, and before long sustenance had arrived and Anthony managed to coax him into sitting down at the table with him.

Halfway through his first sandwich Anthony paused, took a long drink of crisp ale, then put his glass down and gave a great sigh.

"Your Grace?" said Bunch, looking at him with the same friendly inscrutability that had marked their earliest exchanges. Even back then Anthony had seen that Bunch was perfect butler material. One never, ever knew what Bunch was thinking. But one always felt that Bunch was on one's side.

It was a very comforting feeling.

"Bunch," Anthony said, "ever had to do things you didn't want to, but felt you should?"

"Yes indeed, Your Grace."

"Did you do them anyway?"

"Yes, Your Grace. Duty being what it is."

"Yes, duty," said Anthony, rolling these three syllables around in his mouth as if they tasted bad, then had another swallow of ale. He sighed again. "Do you ever wonder what things would be like if poor old Terence hadn't kicked the bucket? He'd be the Duke, not me."

"That is so, Your Grace."

"He'd have done a much better job at it. Lord, do you remember the way he'd walk into a room? As if he owned it, and the rest of us his lowly vassals."

"He certainly had presence, Your Grace."

"That's one way to put it. On the other hand, if he *had* been the Duke, there wouldn't have been Wakefield, and that would be a great loss."

"Indeed so, Your Grace."

"Wake's splendid, isn't he?"

"He is indeed, Your Grace."

"But damn it, Bunch—*duty*."

"Yes, Your Grace."

Moodily Anthony finished his sandwich and then had another. "Bunch, will you do something for me?"

"Of course, Your Grace."

"Could you send someone to the village first thing tomorrow? There's something I want there."

"Certainly, Your Grace. What is it?"

Anthony told him what it was, feeling—inexplicably and against all odds—just a tiny, tiny bit better.

On Monday morning Miss Simpkin returned to the Hall, bringing with her the items Great-grandmother had ordered. Sitting on the edge of the pink flowery sofa in the Rose Saloon, Jane looked at everything with delight and awe as Miss Simpkin unpacked them from her baskets and laid them out on the opposite sofa.

Four new gowns, two bonnets, three pairs of gloves, ditto stockings, two pairs of slippers, a shawl and a pelisse, some chemises and a frilly nightgown, petticoats and stays, a warm dressing-gown, two dainty reticules, and (set neatly on the carpet) a new pair of half-boots made of gleaming dark leather which the Riverton shoemaker had crafted to the exact specifications Miss Simpkin had relayed to him.

"They're all so beautiful," Jane breathed, practically itching to try everything on all at once, which was obviously not possible or even desirable as one would smother in all that clothing and also distort their lovely and exquisitely crafted proportions. "Thank you, Miss Simpkin! And thank you, Great-grandmother!"

Sitting upright in an armchair, neat as wax in an elegant gown of pale violet ornamented with a soft white fichu, Great-grandmother smiled at her. "You're most welcome, my dear," she answered, then began to order additional items from Miss Simpkin, who made a list in her little notebook.

More of everything!

More gowns, bonnets, gloves, wraps, underthings, shoes!

Jane listened in bewilderment, but politely waited until Great-grandmother had finished. Then she said, "But surely, Great-grandmother, this is enough. This is all I could ever want or need."

Great-grandmother laughed, but kindly. "My dear, this is only the beginning—these are merely the basics, to tide you over."

The basics?

Jane swept her eyes again over all her beautiful new things.

Back in Nantwich she might have literally sold her eyeteeth for a fraction of this bounty.

"But Great-grandmother—"

"Now Jane, I trust you're not going to deny me the very great pleasure of seeing you properly outfitted."

Jane looked rather uncertainly at Great-grandmother, whose voice was both benevolent and oddly wistful, giving Jane the distinct impression that if she were to kick up a fuss, it might actually hurt Great-grandmother's feelings.

And that was something she most certainly didn't want to do.

Great-grandmother had already done so much for her.

So she said, with a rush of deepest gratitude, "Of course not, Great-grandmother. Thank you so very much."

Great-grandmother smiled at her, and Miss Simpkin went away with her baskets and her notebook, and then Jane helped Sally, the nice young servant who had been assigned to be her maid—an event Jane still had difficulty assimilating—carry everything up to her bedchamber.

Once that was done, Sally helped Jane dress in a light woolen day-gown of the softest, most delicious pink color which was, Jane was pleased to notice, already just a little tight around the waist.

She put on her new warm stockings, in a lovely cream color, and her equally lovely new half-boots with the delightful little fringe on either side of the silver-grommeted lace-holes, and after that the wonderfully warm pelisse in the prettiest silvery-gray wool, and the matching gray bonnet with the dashingly high poke, all lined in pink satin and with a row of tiny, pink, perfect artificial roses across the top.

And she went off to lessons feeling incredibly well-dressed.

"I say, Jane," said Wakefield, eyeing her closely, "you look different somehow."

"I'm wearing new clothes."

"Oh, is that it? Did you outgrow your old ones?"

"Not really. They're gifts from my great-grandmother."

"Not *my* idea of good gifts. Wouldn't you rather have something useful, like battledores and shuttlecocks? Or a bow and some arrows?"

"Those sound nice, too. It's just that I hadn't many clothes before."

"And now you do?"

"Oh yes, heaps."

"Well, that's jolly."

Jane smiled at him. "Yes, it is."

Mr. Pressley gave a gentle introductory clearing of the throat and changed the subject to the intricacies of English grammar, after which, rather to the relief of both Jane and Wakefield, they all moved on to current events, encompassing the powerful earthquake that had struck Aberdeen, Scotland, last August; the Spa Fields riots, just outside London, back in December; the brilliant success of Sir Humphry Davy's lamp in heightening safety for coal miners; and the daring British adventurers who recently had set out to explore the Congo River in Africa.

"I'd like to visit Africa," said Wakefield. "And see the wildybersts."

"Perhaps, Master Wakefield, you mean wildebeests."

"Yes, that's what I said. I read in a book that they can run awfully fast. And they're also known as ganoos."

"It's spelled G-N-U, Master Wakefield, but pronounced as 'new.'"

"What's the 'g' there for, then?"

"Dutch explorers called it *gnoe*," explained Mr. Pressley. "Which then became 'gnu' in English."

"It seems silly to keep on with the 'g,'" said Wakefield critically. "Why don't we just get rid of it?"

"A very good question, Master Wakefield, and one for which I don't have a good answer. Language isn't a logical thing."

When lessons were over, and Jane and Wakefield were standing on the front steps of the vicarage, Wakefield remarked, "I like Mr. Pressley, don't you, Jane?"

"Yes, I do too."

"He's not one of those grownups who acts like he knows everything. Because I don't think grownups do."

"No," replied Jane thoughtfully, "I don't believe they do either."

"They? Aren't you a grownup too, Jane? You *look* like one, at any rate."

Jane laughed. "Wakefield, you do ask the most delightful questions."

"Really? Aunt Margaret says I'm an awful nuisance with all the things I ask. She says children should be seen and not heard, and when I asked why, she said it just proved her point. Would you like to come over for luncheon? Father wanted me to tell you we're having macaroni again. He asked Cook to make it just in case you did."

"How very kind," said Jane, a little flutter of pleasure running through her, whether it was because it felt so good to receive a friendly invitation, or because she was hungry, or because she realized she was getting very fond of Wakefield, or because she would soon be seeing the Duke again: it was unclear to her at the moment. All she knew was that she was suffused with a light, happy, warm, floaty feeling that felt marvelous. She said to Wakefield, "That macaroni was so delicious. Yes, I'd love to come, thank you."

So Jane sent the Penhallow groom and carriage back to the Hall, and drove with Wakefield and Higson in the pony-cart over to Hastings. Wakefield even let her take the reins for a little while, which was a bit nerve-wracking but also extremely exciting, and Wakefield said that she would make a capital whip someday, a compliment which Jane, flattered, acknowledged happily.

When she and Wakefield went into the house, Jane handed over her bonnet and pelisse to a footman, thanking him and then glancing past his shoulder to see Bunch bowing politely to Wakefield.

She saw, now, as she hadn't the other day in the flurry of her arrival here at Hastings, that Bunch was very distinguished in his sober dark clothes, but also so intensely subtle, so unobtrusive in his manner, that one had to look closely at him to realize that he was of middling height and middling weight, with a nondescript face and a little dab of a nose and eyes of a vague kind of hazel but within them a quick intelligence, a perceptiveness, that was extraordinary and also, somehow, quite comforting.

Jane remembered as well that as a young vulnerable servant Bunch had risked his own well-being to be of service to a pain-filled, bedridden boy.

Clearly Bunch was a special sort of person.

As she came closer she smiled and said warmly, "Good afternoon, Bunch. I hope you're well?"

"Indeed yes, Miss Kent, thank you. I trust the same is true for you?"

"Oh yes. Thank you, Bunch."

From behind Jane a footman opened the front door, bringing with it a rush of chilly air and—Jane saw as she turned about—also the Duke, in his long greatcoat and tall hat and black scuffed boots.

Their eyes met and they smiled at each other.

"I say, you're here," said the Duke, as if something wonderful had happened.

"Yes."

The Duke stripped off his gloves and gave them, along with his hat and greatcoat, to the footman, and strode forward. "I'm glad."

"So am I."

"I didn't know if you would."

"Wakefield invited me."

"Did he tell you about the macaroni?"

"Oh yes."

"I asked Cook to make extra."

"How very kind of you. Your Grace."

"Are you hungry?"

"Very."

"So am I. It's been ages since breakfast."

"It feels that way."

"I say, you look different somehow, Miss Kent."

"I have some new clothes. Your Grace."

"Oh, is that it? They're quite fetching."

"Thank you very much."

"Your gown is a delightful shade of pink. If you don't mind my saying so."

"I don't mind at all."

"Extremely delightful."

"Thank you. I like it, too."

"It suits you."

"That's so kind of you to say. Your Grace."

"Are those new boots as well?"

"Yes, they are." Jane lifted up the hem of her gown just an inch or two, so that he could have a better look. Great-grandmother Kent would have called her a Jezebel, but Jane did it anyway. Also, she would have liked to lift up the hem quite a bit higher, but now, of course, was neither the time nor the place. Rather to her regret.

"They're awfully smart," said the Duke.

"Thank you."

"Are they comfortable?"

"Oh yes. So far."

"I'm glad to hear it. Sometimes one has to break in new boots, and they hurt."

"Not with these."

"That's capital."

"Yes, isn't it?" Jane realized that she probably sounded like a blithering idiot but found that, one, she couldn't seem to stop, and two, she didn't really care, because the Duke sounded like one also, and three, she was feeling extremely happy.

"They look just right for a nice stroll in the outdoors."

"I agree."

"Perhaps we could do that after luncheon."

"I'd like that."

"If you're interested, there's a topiary to the back of the house."

"What's a topiary?"

"Shrubs which have been clipped, you know, into various shapes. Our head gardener McTavish is a whiz at it. Wait till you see his rendition of Aphrodite rising from her clamshell. It's ripping."

"Who is Aphrodite, and why is she rising from a clamshell?"

"She's the Greek goddess of love. She was born in the sea out of foam, then floats to land in a giant clamshell. So she must be getting up to go ashore."

"That's quite a story."

"Isn't it? One wonders why the clamshell didn't sink underneath her weight. But that's mythology for you. Full of loopholes."

Jane nodded. "Well, I'd love to see McTavish's Aphrodite."

"Splendid."

"I say," intervened Wakefield impatiently, "you're not the only ones who are hungry. Can't we go eat?"

The Duke blinked, looking a little as if he were emerging from a pleasant dream. "By all means," he said. "Is luncheon ready, Bunch?"

"Yes, Your Grace."

"Excellent. Lay on, Macduff."

As they began walking along the wide, high hallway to the family dining-parlor, Wakefield, who had placed himself between the Duke and herself, said, "Father, Jane might not know who that is. The only Shakespeare she knows is what I told her about *Hamlet*. Jane, shall I tell you who Macduff is?"

"Yes, please, Wakefield."

"He's the thane of Fife in *Macbeth*, and—Father, what's a thane again? I forget."

"A Scottish chieftain."

"Oh yes, I remember now. Father, if we were Scottish, would you be a thane?"

"I believe the term has died out in recent centuries."

"Oh. If it hadn't, and we *were* Scottish, Father, would we be wearing kilts right now?"

"Possibly," answered the Duke, and Jane immediately found herself picturing him wearing one. He would, she thought, look very dashing dressed like that. She wondered if he had hairy legs. Which would be delicious.

"Well, I'm glad we're not," Wakefield said, "because I wouldn't like to eat haggis. At any rate, Jane, Macduff kills Macbeth in the end, which is a good thing, because Macbeth's a rotter."

"Why is he a rotter?"

"Because in order to get what he wants, he does all sorts of terrible things."

"What does he want?"

"To become king."

"And what terrible things does he do?"

"He murders people."

"He *does* sound like a rotter. And it sounds like he gets what he deserves in the end. Oh, hullo, kitty." Jane paused as they came to a white marble statue of a severe-looking man's head and shoulders set atop a pillar, on either side of which was a very expensive-looking chair upholstered in elaborately embroidered, deep red fabric. On one of the chairs was curled up a large, morose-looking tabby cat. Jane reached out a hand to pet it, then stopped herself. "Is this the cat that bit you, Wakefield?"

"Yes, that's Aunt Margaret's cat."

Jane pulled her hand away, then realized that she was exactly the same height as the statue. It was rather disconcerting looking into his face, as he seemed to be frowning quite horribly at her, so she turned away and glanced up at the Duke. "Is this one of your relations?"

"Yes, isn't he terrifying? Old Myles Farr, the fourth duke. Or was he the fifth? I can never remember. Apparently Elizabeth Tudor disliked him so much she forbade him to ever come to court again."

"Why did she dislike him?"

"Anyone would," answered the Duke. "Just look at that phiz. Looks like he's been sucking lemons, don't you think? When I was a boy I would scuttle past the old blighter as if the hounds of hell were at my heels."

"I used to also," said Wakefield, "when I was little."

A proper adult, thought Jane, would probably feel obliged to say, *When you were little? But you're still little, you know.* And even if the adult said it kindly, with all the best will in the world, it would still come out sounding utterly patronizing. Jane was very glad she hadn't said it. She was glad that the Duke didn't either.

And so they passed into the family dining-parlor, where they saw that the chair at the foot of the table was empty. "Bunch," said the Duke, "where's Lady Margaret?"

"I believe she's in her room, Your Grace, recovering from a headache."

"More macaroni for us then," said Wakefield, with a cheerfully callous disregard for his aunt's suffering, and sat down at his place.

Of course Anthony would never have said it out loud, but it was an undeniable fact that luncheon was a lot more fun without Margaret. Nobody glowered, nobody made pointed negative remarks, and nobody looked at anyone else as if they suspected them of using the wrong fork or sneaking rolls into their pockets.

Rather, they had a delightful time speculating about King Richard the Third and whether or not he was the victim of nasty Tudor gossip-mongering, and Anthony told Jane and Wakefield about Perkin Warbeck, a young man who claimed to be the son of one of the princes who had disappeared while being held in the Tower, and how it had cost the reigning king, Henry the Seventh, over 13,000 pounds to put down Warbeck once and for all, which turned Henry into an even greater skinflint who already didn't like spending money on wood to keep his family's rooms warm.

Jane mentioned the bedchamber at the Hall that Henry might or might not have stayed in, which made them all wonder if he *had*, did he insist that a fire not be lit for him, or did he take advantage of his hosts' generosity and keep a fire blazing at all times, which would, really, have been rather disingenuous of him.

After that Wakefield wanted to talk some more about haggis, which they agreed was certainly a peculiar dish, although, in fairness, England's own jellied eels was a peculiar one too, and Jane told them about her great-grandfather's dubious pamphlet on the use of dried eels to make hair grow faster, a topic Wakefield found riveting, so she shared with them a few other equally dubious remedies having to do with pills made from cobwebs (to treat gout) and also the one about dipping bread in wine and putting the bread up one's nose (to improve a lagging memory and also cure stubborn pustules located anywhere above the waist), and Wakefield had to be dissuaded from trying that one at once using water rather than wine.

By then all the macaroni was gone, and most of everything else, too, and dessert was shortly brought in.

"Apple puffs!" exclaimed Wakefield joyfully.

"I asked Cook to make them again," said Anthony to Jane, "in case you did come over. After church yesterday you said they sounded good."

She smiled at him, and it occurred to Anthony to wonder when was the last time he had been so happy. He couldn't remember, so he repressed a sudden paradoxical impulse to feel incredibly sad, and simply smiled back as best he could.

"Thank you. How *very* thoughtful. Your Grace. Yes, please," Jane said to the footman who was at her side with the platter filled with apple puffs. She took two, along with a giant dollop of whipped cream, as did Wakefield, and he himself did the same.

Jane took a bite and said, "This is *delicious*," and Wakefield answered rather blurrily through a mouthful of whipped cream:

"Isn't it just!"

After that a contented silence filled the dining-parlor like bright sunshine, and Anthony found himself noticing, for the first time in years, the wallpaper above the wainscoting, which was a ghastly dark reddish-purple color, and thinking that maybe he would tell Bunch to have it papered over in something more cheerful.

"I feel like having another puff," observed Wakefield, "but it's as if my *mouth* wants it and not my stomach."

"I'm fairly sure I would explode if I had a third one," Jane said.

"In solidarity, I'll refrain from eating another one also," said Anthony. "We'll be the very picture of sensible moderation. Although, given how much macaroni we all consumed, it may be rather a stretch. Shall we take a turn about the topiary, and remove ourselves from further temptation?"

"Yes, let's," said Wakefield, and so he and Anthony went to put on their coats and Jane her pelisse as well as a bonnet Anthony had never seen her wearing before, with a high poke and a shimmering pink lining and also pink roses on the top which, distractingly, reminded him of her lovely mouth.

Together they went outside onto the back terrace and into the gardens and to the topiary, where they stood for a while looking at McTavish's masterfully clipped Aphrodite shrub. It was a little scraggly given that it was wintertime, but still rendered everything pretty well including Aphrodite's long tendrils of hair and also her breasts and hips and legs, and Anthony found himself wondering what Jane would look like with her hair unbound like that and—once again—without any clothes on either.

He wanted desperately to glance at Jane, who was standing next to him, to reinforce his breathtaking imaginary vision of her, but had an uneasy feeling that if he did, she would know exactly what he was picturing and would think much the worse of him for it. So he shifted on his feet, readjusted his hat, and said, a little too loudly:

"Shall we move on?"

They did, and went to view McTavish's long line of shrubs which he had crafted to look uncannily like pumpkins, and Anthony confided to Jane his hopes for this year's *fête*, and Jane wished him good luck and also recalled another one of her great-grandfather's pamphlets which said that ordinary household dust was the world's best fertilizer (when combined with a small amount of flat beer) and was also an excellent remedy for night terrors when put into a small pouch and worn around the neck at bedtime.

"That sounds silly," remarked Wakefield.

"You'd think so," agreed Jane, "but I remember Great-grandmother Kent saying it was one of their best sellers."

When they finished strolling around the topiary, Wakefield, by now rather bored, said:

"I say, let's go play billiards."

So they all went inside and to the billiards room, where Wakefield explained to Jane the rules and generously let her have first crack at it. Jane only tore the green baize a little bit, and Wakefield poked both Jane and Anthony in their respective backsides with his stick, just for fun, and then (accidentally) ripped a truly magnificent hole in the baize after that, and Anthony made quite a good shot in a corner pocket, and throughout all this they laughed a great deal, and when they had finished their fourth game, Jane glanced out the window, gave a little start, and said:

"Oh, it's getting so late! It will be dark soon. I should go."

"Must you, Jane?" said Wakefield. "I thought we could go down into the basement rooms and look for rats."

"That does sound delightful," Jane answered, "but I'm afraid I really should go home."

"There aren't any rats," Anthony said.

"Yes, but it's fun to look for them, Father. Also, there are odd things down there. Do you remember the time I found that big copper tub and got into it, then couldn't get out?"

"What I chiefly remember is the hours of panic when I couldn't find you."

"Were you *very* afraid for me, Father?"

"Yes."

"I was a little afraid, too."

"I know."

"I cried like anything when you came."

"Well, I cried also."

"Aunt Margaret said that only girls are allowed to cry."

"What rot," said Anthony. "We men have feelings too."

"Yes, but she also said it was very poor form for a duke to cry."

"That may be true, but as I am, apparently, the worst duke in the world, I daresay it doesn't matter."

Jane said curiously, "Why are you the worst duke in the world?"

He shrugged. "Ask my sister."

"You'd better not, Jane," said Wakefield. "She'll talk your ears off."

"All right, I won't," replied Jane. "I'm fond of my ears."

Wakefield laughed. "That's funny, Jane. Do you like jokes, then?"

"Oh yes, very much."

"I do too. Here's one. A man is eating his salad, and he finds a button in it. So he says to the waiter, 'Look here, there's a button in my salad.' And the waiter says, 'Yes, but sir, it's part of the dressing.' Part of the *dressing*—isn't that funny, Jane?"

Jane laughed. "Very. Do you know the one about a man finding a fly in his soup?"

"I don't! How does it go?"

"Well, a man is having his soup, you see, and when he finds a fly in it he's very upset, and he makes a great fuss about it, and he says to his wife, 'Look, there's a fly.' 'Oh, you don't have to worry,' says the wife, 'it won't drink much.'"

"Ha! That's a good one, Jane."

"I'm glad you like it. I know some others—I can tell you them another time." She glanced again at the window, and Anthony promptly said:

"Miss Kent, may I drive you home?"

"If you're sure it's not a trouble?"

"Not at all," he said, and she smiled at him, and now, with the prospect of twenty minutes alone together, Anthony forgot all about being the worst duke in the world and instead felt his whole mind being blotted out by the glorious white light of happy anticipation. But not before he remembered to get something from his library and tuck it into the pocket of his greatcoat.

Chapter 8

They were barreling along on their way back to the Hall, and Jane said to the Duke, "It must have been terrible when Wakefield went missing like that."

"It was. He was only six at the time."

"Did he have any aftereffects? Like—well—night terrors?"

"Oh no, he had a good cry and was back to himself the next day. I was the one with the aftereffects. I noticed that I wanted to keep my eye on him all the time. So I had to be careful to not—what was the word we used yesterday? Yes, not to hound him, and make him feel confined. I was a roamer myself, you see, as a boy."

"Hastings seems like a nice place to roam."

"It is."

Jane nodded, thinking what a lovely caring father the Duke was. She also was noticing how very snug and cozy it felt, sharing the high front seat with him again. Their legs were practically touching. She wished they were. Would he notice if, very slowly and subtly, she slid his way? She pictured herself doing just that. Then, suddenly, she realized it was her turn to say something. What had they been talking about? Oh yes: Hastings. "It's a very nice place."

"Yes."

"For roaming, and so on."

"Yes, very good for roaming about," he said. "Also for pigs."

"Oh yes, I could see that."

"For topiaries, too. And for lime-walks."

"Oh, do you have a lime-walk?"

"Yes. It's splendid."

"Good for walking, I expect."

"Yes, very good for that."

"Do you go there often?"

"Frequently. For a walk."

"I like walking also."

"Do you, Miss Kent?"

"Oh, yes. Your Grace."

"A pleasant form of exercise."

"Yes, very. I did enjoy walking through the topiary today."

"I did also. McTavish is awfully clever, don't you think?"

"Yes. Imagine making art that keeps changing on one."

"I say, that's such an interesting perspective."

"Is it? Thank you."

"Well, when one paints a painting, for example, when one is finished, that's it. It doesn't change at all."

"Yes, very true." Jane found herself thinking that they were both blithering again, just a bit, and also about that somewhat scraggly Aphrodite in the topiary. She rather envied the shrub's lush curves. What, Jane wondered, would the Duke think of her naked with her hair loose like that?

Furthermore, what would he think of her for thinking things like that?

"By the way," said the Duke, and Jane looked at him a little nervously. Had he guessed what was on her mind?

"Yes?"

"I—uh—I have something for you."

"You do?"

"Yes." The Duke transferred one of the reins into his other hand, then reached into his greatcoat pocket and pulled from it a flattish, rectangular pasteboard box, which he gave to her.

She looked at him, surprise and pleasure intermingling in a rather intoxicating way, and then at the box. "Thank you very much! What is it?"

The corners of his mouth quirked ever so slightly. "Open it."

Carefully Jane put the box on her lap and lifted the lid. Inside were dark, square confections on a bed of crisp white paper. "Chocolates?"

"Chocolate conserves. Do you like chocolate?"

"I love chocolate. What a kind gift! Thank you so much."

"You're very welcome, Miss Kent. You see, there was—that is, there was something—uh—in our conversation yesterday, you know—well, you were so—I mean—that is, I—well, I just thought about getting you some chocolates."

He was stammering so adorably that Jane was a little sorry when he stopped. She said:

"They look absolutely delicious. How very, very kind of you. Your Grace."

"Have one."

"I think I will." Jane pulled off one of her gloves, picked up a conserve, and put it in her mouth. It was dense, sweet, moist. Melting on her tongue in a glorious burst of flavor and sensual texture. "Oh, it's wonderful! Won't you have one too?"

"Thank you, but it might be difficult. Gloves, driving, and so on."

Jane had an idea, and knew that if she thought about it for any length of time, her concerns about her goodness (or lack thereof) might overcome her. So she picked up another one of the conserves and held it close to the Duke's extremely attractive mouth. "Here. Your Grace."

He flashed a surprised look at her, his lips parted, and Jane popped the chocolate between them.

"Thank you very much," he said, a trifle thickly.

"You're welcome." Jane watched as onto the Duke's face came an expression of blissful enjoyment. *O to be savored like that.* Imagine, being envious of a little chocolate square. But there it was. He swallowed and she said, "May I give you another one?"

"I don't think I could stand it."

"What? Why not?"

"Oh, Jane." The Duke slowed his team and gently brought his curricle to a halt on the side of the deserted road. Afternoon had begun to wane, drifting slowly toward twilight, and overhead, the sky was a vast canopy of deepening violet. A flock of dark chattering birds arced up, down, and past them, leaving sudden soft silence in their wake.

The Duke turned to her, and Jane suddenly felt breathless. It wasn't just her too-tight gown, either. She said, a little shakily:

"Why couldn't you stand it?"

"I couldn't stand not doing this." As gently as he had slowed his horses, he took her hand, the one without a glove on it, raised it to his mouth, and pressed his lips to her palm.

His flesh on her flesh.

Warm, and probably tasting of chocolate.

Pure pleasure streaked through Jane like lightning and she inhaled sharply, her eyes fixed on the Duke's mouth—

his large and perfectly straight nose—the lionlike mane of his hair—

He lifted his head and looked into her face, a questioning expression on his own, and Jane saw that his deep blue eyes had darkened in that delightful way they had on their previous ride together.

"I—uh—I hope you don't mind that I did that, Miss Kent."

"No." Her voice was still breathless and shaky. "Not at all. You can—you can do it again if you like."

"Really?"

"Yes."

"I *would* like to," he said, and kissed her palm again. Jane shuddered as pleasure swept through her again. She could even feel her toes curling inside her boots.

"I say, Miss Kent, are you cold?"

"Quite the opposite. Your Grace."

"So you're *not* cold."

"No. I'm feeling very warm, actually."

"Oh, that's good."

"Yes, it is. Are *you* cold?"

"No, I'm fine."

"I'm glad to hear it. Your Grace."

"Actually, Miss Kent, now that you mention it, I'm—uh—feeling rather warm myself."

"In a good way?"

"Rather."

"Oh, that's nice." Jane smiled. They were definitely blithering again. They sounded like idiots, and she couldn't have cared less. Because she was sitting so close to the Duke, and he had kissed her palm, and was still holding her hand, and she felt like a twig merrily burning up in a fire.

"Dimples," said the Duke.

"Yes," she answered, breathless.

"They're marvelous."

"Thank you."

"Exceedingly marvelous."

"Thank you again."

"There's just something about dimples."

"Is there?"

"Oh yes. Absolutely, Miss Kent."

"I'm glad you think so. Your Grace."

"I certainly do."

"Thank you so much."

"You're very welcome. Well, I suppose we—uh—that is, we ought to be—wouldn't want you to be—I mean, you were right, it *is* getting dark, and—and I should be—I should be getting you home, shouldn't I?"

He was stammering adorably again, and Jane felt her temperature go up several additional degrees. Another idea came to her and she didn't waste any time wondering if it meant she was good or bad. She said:

"I think we ought to kiss each other."

He looked surprised. And then so happy that her own heart gave a leap of joy within her.

"Do you really, Miss Kent?"

"Yes. Your Grace."

"Then let's do that. If you're sure?"

"I'm very sure."

"I say, how *ripping*."

With one gloved hand still holding the reins, the Duke raised his other gloved hand to his mouth, took the tip of one finger between his teeth, tugged his hand free, and in a very dashing way spat out his glove and let it drop down into the well at their feet. Then that newly bare hand was warmly cupping her cheek, and the Duke brought his face closer to her own, and then his incredibly attractive mouth was on hers, and Jane, her lips eagerly parting, felt her bones melt away into wonderful nothingness as white-hot sensation took hold of her.

Oh, he *did* taste of chocolate, and maybe also of apple, and possibly even the cinnamon that was in the puffs at dessert, but most strongly of chocolate, rich, sweet, decadent, and he was altogether so delicious that Jane wanted to eat him up like another dessert.

The best dessert in the world.

She slid the tip of her tongue along the inside of his upper lip where, she knew, the flesh was sensitive, exquisitely receptive, and felt the Duke jerk in response.

So Jane did it again.

And *he* did it again. That reactive little judder.

There was something so very pleasurable about giving him pleasure.

It made her greedy for more.

Ravenous, even.

Jane kissed that enticing upper lip of his.

It would not be going too far to say that she fastened on it, like a bee upon a flower. Moistly. Juicily. First she sucked upon it, slow and sweet, and then without any warning at all she nipped with her teeth.

And the Duke juddered again.

"Jane," he said, low, husky, against her mouth. "Jane."

"Yes?"

"I'm going to—I want to—if *you* do—I mean, may I?"

She didn't know what he wanted to do, but was confident it was going to be something nice. "Yes."

And then the Duke kissed her upper lip, quite like she had kissed his.

Saliva from his mouth, shared with her.

Nectar, and she the happy bee.

A greedy, happy bee.

Chocolate, apple, cinnamon.

Delicious.

Vaguely Jane heard herself making a soft, humming sort of noise deep in her throat.

Really, almost like the sound a happy little bee might make.

She wondered, equally vaguely, but hopefully, if he was going to nip at her upper lip as she had done to him. Which she wouldn't mind one bit.

But instead, he slowly, slowly—*tortuously* slowly—deepened the kiss, his tongue against hers, wet, stroking, filling her, pulling back, filling her again, in a lovely pulsing rhythm that sent blazing warmth surging everywhere within her—oh, everywhere—and Jane didn't feel any disappointment at all that he hadn't bitten her as she had been hoping.

She *was* disappointed, however, when after a while he broke the kiss, because it was far too soon, in her opinion, to stop kissing. He drew back a little, and she saw that he was looking at her again with that same questioning expression.

"I say, was that all right?"

"More than all right." She smiled, then wondered if the sight of her dimples would galvanize him into kissing her again. Unfortunately he only said:

"Really?"

"Yes."

"You liked it?" he asked.

"So very much."

"I say, I'm glad."

"I am, too. Your Grace. Do you want to do it again?"

"Really?"

"Yes indeed."

He grinned, looking suddenly and adorably boyish. "Capital."

And he did kiss her again, and Jane didn't have to be

jealous of that little chocolate conserve anymore, because he deepened the kiss immediately and hungrily, and she felt wholly savored, and this time he *did* nip at her upper lip, and Jane gave a noisy gasp of enjoyment, and would have bitten *his* lip again, except that the Duke abruptly pulled away from her and straightened his tall dark hat which had gone charmingly askew.

"People," he explained, jerking his chin toward the road ahead, and sure enough, mere seconds after Jane had straightened her own hat and reluctantly scooted a few inches away from him, jammed her glove back on, put the lid back onto the conserve box, and tried with all her might to project the air of one who hasn't just been passionately kissing the person sitting next to her, from around the bend came a sleek black barouche drawn by a team of four horses.

It passed them in the gathering twilight and Jane got a brief glimpse inside, of two—no, three people, two women and a man, who evinced no curiosity whatsoever in the curricle drawn up alongside the road or its occupants. Which in a way was a good thing, as she wouldn't have welcomed their scrutiny, but on the other hand, Jane thought with a pointless yet rising indignation, what if they had suffered an accident and needed help?

The very least they could have done was to stop and ask.

Whoever those people were, she disliked them.

The Duke picked up his glove and put it back on, then chirruped to his horses. They began to move and the curricle rolled back onto the road. Jane glanced at him and saw that he looked both happy and rather dazed.

They didn't talk, but it was one of those nice companionable silences where one didn't feel one had to grope awkwardly for something to say or wish anxiously for something else to happen as a distraction. In fact, it would have been fine with her if they stayed like this for a very long time, rolling along side by side, with her mouth feeling all savored and her body still sizzling with pleasure. *And* with a box of chocolate conserves on her lap.

But, reality being what it was, it only took ten minutes or so for them to get back to the Hall.

When the Duke brought the curricle to a halt on the carriage sweep, Jane said to him:

"Thank you—well, for everything. Your Grace."

He looked at her, a little shyly, she thought, but still with that delightful dazed expression on his face and an unmistakable light in his eyes. "Thank *you*. Miss Kent. Jane."

The front door opened, a footman hurried out, and just like that, their lovely interlude of solitude was over.

When Jane came into the Great Hall, there was Great-grandmother Henrietta, who looked into her face, and at the box she was carrying, and into her face again, and, blushing wildly, Jane had once more that uncomfortable, unpleasant, sinking feeling of guilt.

"The Duke drove you home again?" said Great-grandmother.

Jane nodded.

"How kind," Great-grandmother said, but in a tone of voice which strongly suggested to Jane that while it might indeed have been a kind gesture on the Duke's part, Great-grandmother nonetheless still didn't approve of it, not one tiny bit.

Whistling a little under his breath, Anthony nimbly swept past a big, lumbering carriage with a great deal of luggage strapped on top, and then, a few minutes later, the barouche that had, to his infinite chagrin, kept him from kissing Jane some more.

Kissing Jane.

Wasn't that something.

He felt hot all over just thinking about it.

And what a good kisser Jane was.

Anthony hoped he had kissed her as well as she had kissed him.

He thought that maybe, just maybe, he had.

Because she had kissed him back, and made that adorable humming sound, and also she had audibly gasped when he'd bitten her upper lip, but in a pleased-sounding way, clearly not in horror, as one did when, say, one came across an angry bear, and he had been fairly sure that she (Jane, not the bear) was going to nip him again—when that damned barouche had interrupted things.

When, he wondered, could he and Jane kiss again?

He wanted to try having his mouth be just above hers, teasing them both in the most terrible and wonderful way, until they couldn't stand it for another single second, and then plunge into each other like they had just a little while ago and which had been *amazing*.

Also, he would love to trail his tongue along the side of her neck, maybe both sides of her neck, and maybe even nip at the soft skin there with his teeth. He wondered if Jane would like that, and if she would gasp or hum again. Or bite him on the skin of *his* neck. Which he thought he would enjoy very much.

And while they were at it, he'd really like to touch her with his hands.

Everywhere.

Without her having any clothes on.

Actually, without *him* having any clothes on either.

He hoped she wouldn't mind that he had hairy legs.

And a fair amount of hair on his chest, too.

Plus rather prominent collar-bones, as he didn't have much fat on him anywhere.

Speaking of which, Anthony suddenly remembered Jane telling him yesterday after church, in a cheerful manner, that she was getting a little fatter. She looked perfect to him just as she was, but if that was something that made her happy, he was all for it.

He was extra glad, now, that he had given her the chocolates.

He made a mental note to ask Bunch to get some more sent over from the village first thing in the morning. Perhaps a larger box this time.

With any luck, Jane would come over to Hastings again tomorrow after lessons and he could give her the new box.

Also, it would be fun to play billiards some more. By their fourth game together she had made impressive progress.

Maybe they'd be able to steal away for a few quiet moments together, too.

Or even longer than that.

He could hardly wait.

Anthony's mood of exuberance and anticipation lasted until the precise moment when, having arrived home, stopped in to see Wakefield, and changed for dinner, he came downstairs and saw the front door swing open, and three people come inside, and Margaret, up and about again, go sailing forward to meet them and on her face a wide, welcoming smile which struck horrible dismay into Anthony's whole being.

For here—as he promptly learned—was none other than the Countess of Silsbury, her daughter Lady Felicia, and her son the Viscount Whitton. Whose barouche he had blithely passed, in happy ignorance of the fact that it had, in fact, been bound for Hastings with what no doubt was the express purpose of ruining what had been an epically splendid day.

"My dear Jane," said Great-grandmother Henrietta, "your gown doesn't fit you properly. I must confess I'm rather surprised at Miss Simpkin's poor workmanship. Usually it's quite exact."

The family had gone to the rococo drawing-room as it always did after dinner, and had grouped itself cozily around the leaping fire. Cousin Gabriel had an open book before him, and next to him, sharing a small sofa, was Livia, who had her head bent over some sewing, and Great-grandmother was seated closest to the fire in a wide, elaborately carved giltwood chair that to Jane looked a lot like a small throne.

"Actually, Great-grandmother, I'm afraid I'm the problem. I've expanded a bit since Miss Simpkin took my measurements. I've been eating rather a lot."

"It has not escaped my notice," said Great-grandmother, but kindly. "So adjustments will, therefore, need to be made."

"Yes indeed." Jane looked down with pleasure at the soft, moss-green silk of her gown. How pretty it was! Miss Simpkin had suggested white, or cream, or ivory as suitable colors for a young unmarried lady, but Great-grandmother had overridden her, saying that white would wash Jane out, and how right she had been. The green of this particular fabric set off Jane's pale hair to perfection, and gave her gray eyes almost a silvery brilliance. She wished the Duke could see her in it. But before she fell into a pleasant daydream, which included not only the Duke's admiration at seeing her in this beautiful evening-gown, but also him undoing all those little buttons in the back and sliding it off her and so on and so forth, Jane went on:

"I was thinking that I could try again to learn how to sew, and do it myself."

"A very worthy thought, my dear, but I wouldn't suggest attempting to learn on something so complex as an evening-gown. Sally can alter your gowns, and I'll send word to Miss Simpkin regarding your changed dimensions."

"Thank you, Great-grandmother," said Jane. "But I would like to at least try. Even though I was horrible at it before. Livia, do you by any chance have anything easy for me to practice on?"

Livia looked up and smiled at her. "I've been mending rips in Daniel's smocks. Would you like to try one of those?"

"Yes, that does sound easy," said Jane, but after half an hour of wrestling with the fine white cotton, knotting her thread ineffectually, unpicking seams, poking herself with the needle, and finally ruining the little smock entirely by bleeding on it, Jane found herself both hideously bored and forced to admit she was still terrible at sewing. Apologetically she passed everything back to Livia and then picked up her book of Wordsworth poems, but before she could open it Great-grandmother said:

"My dear, for the time being, do come straight home after lessons. Tomorrow the *friseur* will arrive from Bath, as he does every quarter, to attend to Livia's hair and my own. And yours, too, now. Accompanying him will be a dancing-master I've engaged on your behalf, Monsieur Voclaine—he'll be staying here at the Hall for at least a fortnight, and possibly more, until you've become adept in all the various dances. And, of course, you'll want to continue your riding lessons, if not with Gabriel then with whatever groom he designates for the task."

"Oh. Of course. Yes, I'll come straightaway," Jane promised, trying hard to inject into her voice a convincing enthusiasm. She did want to learn how to dance, and become a capable horsewoman, and if Great-grandmother wanted to have her hair tended to by this *friseur* from Bath, Jane had no objection and of course was really very grateful, but . . .

But how could she go to Hastings after lessons?

Anthony lay in his bed with his head resting on interlaced fingers and his elbows akimbo, staring up into the darkness. He would have liked to be thinking about Jane, and how intelligent and nice and kind and beautiful and fascinating and desirable she was, but instead his mind was filled with the horror of Margaret's visit here to his room just a little while ago. She had been so cheerful, so animated, that Anthony's already low spirits had sunk even further.

What a marvelous evening, she had said, she couldn't remember when she'd enjoyed herself so much, and wasn't it delightful that the Viscount came along? Such a marvelous young man, and as for Lady Felicia—delightful *and* marvelous. And their mother the Countess! Also delightful.

Then Margaret had gone on to say that she so much wanted this visit to be a success, and that perhaps it had been a mistake, with their previous guests, to keep their own little party *quite* so exclusive, and so she was going to immediately send out invitations for tea, dinner-parties, perhaps even a *soirée musicale* or a ball, thereby providing select members of the neighborhood an opportunity to meet the Merifields.

And of course providing the Merifields with an opportunity to observe just how delightful and marvelous life was here.

After that she had bustled away, full of energy and

enthusiasm—quite possibly bent upon waking up the housekeeper and writing lists together till their candles guttered away into nothingness—leaving Anthony with barely the fortitude to untie his own neckcloth.

Which reminded him of yet another example of his glaring nondukishness.

He had no valet.

And why?

Because he didn't want one.

Of course there was that nice young chap Evans who took care of his room, saw that his things were laundered and pressed and stowed away and all that, but as it happened, Anthony was not only able to put on his own clothes, he could also take them off. Unless, of course, his usual capacities had been sapped by Margaret's ghastly cheer.

Into Anthony's mind now floated unfond memories of Father's and Terence's valets. They might as well have been twins in their rigidly upright demeanors, their frigid mannerisms, and their fanatical determination to keep their masters' boots polished to an eye-shattering gleam.

Selina, Anthony recalled in another unfond memory, had been after him to get a valet.

His lack of one, she had said, reflected badly on *her.*

Other memories of Selina began to rise, unfurl themselves like malevolent ghosts, and crowd inside his brain.

None of them were good.

Restlessly Anthony unlaced his hands from behind his head and turned onto his side, shoving away a great hank of hair that had fallen into his eyes.

Five long years of wretchedness. And loneliness.

It had been the worst sort of loneliness, too—the kind that came from having to be around someone one didn't want to be around.

The kind that left one feeling empty and secretly, impossibly, alone.

Damn it to hell, Anthony thought, actual pain tearing at his heart, he didn't want to get married again.

He felt like an animal released from what had seemed like endless captivity.

Such an animal would never willingly return to its cage.

Damn it *all* to hell—*never.*

And nothing would, or could, make him change his mind.

Chapter 9

Mr. Pressley had wrapped up today's lessons with a very interesting talk about astronomy, and now Jane and Wakefield stood once again on the front steps of the vicarage.

The weather had turned much colder.

The sky was a low, heavy gray, the wind was up, and little flurries of snow occasionally spun down and swirled about, coming to rest on the ground in tiny, chilly white flakes that somehow gave the impression of being stubbornly determined to hang around making people's feet cold for a long, long time.

"I was going to invite you over, Jane, so we could go looking for rats today, but Aunt Margaret says I can't. Because we have people staying, you see."

Well, Jane thought, Wakefield had beat her to it and spared her the embarrassment of saying, as if she were Wakefield's age, *I would have liked to come over, but my great-grandmother says I can't.* Then she suddenly remembered how last week, at luncheon, Lady Margaret had brightly announced the imminent arrival of her dear friend the Countess of Silsbury and her daughter Lady Felicia.

Lady Felicia . . . who was the Duke's intended?

Lady Felicia . . . in the elegant barouche which yesterday had passed by her and the Duke?

For a moment Jane wanted to say, in the most casual way possible, *People staying? Oh, really? Who is it?*

But she took hold of herself, trying not to feel wretched at the thought of the Duke and Lady Felicia under the same roof, and said, "I understand. Another time soon, I hope. Would you like to hear another fly joke?"

"Yes, please."

"There's a man at a restaurant, very upset, and he calls the waiter over. 'Look,' he says, 'there's a fly in my soup!' 'Don't worry, sir,' the waiter says, 'that spider on your bread will soon get him.'"

Wakefield grinned, then winced. "Ow."

"What is it?" Jane quickly asked.

"My tooth just bothered me. Way in the back." Wakefield poked an exploratory and not entirely clean forefinger into his mouth.

"Oh dear. Have you told your father about it?"

"No, this is the first time it's happened. I'm all right, Jane. It went away." Wakefield withdrew his finger and squinted up at the sky. "I was hoping to look for Orion's Belt tonight, and show Snuffles the Dog Star too. But I don't think we'll be able to."

"No," Jane said, looking up at the sky as well. Vehemently she wished that it would snow so heavily that—if her guess about the visitors was correct—the Countess of Silsbury and Lady Felicia would go away. Which of course was a ridiculous thing to wish for, because they could hardly travel in a blizzard. If anything, it would make them stay *longer.*

So right away Jane wished for the sun to come out and warm things up.

And that was ridiculous too, as then they would probably want to stay on and enjoy the lovely weather.

Jane, she said sadly to herself, you're a blithering idiot.

"Well—goodbye," said Wakefield. "See you tomorrow, Jane."

"Goodbye," she answered, repressing a sudden urge to enfold him in a hug, as if tomorrow would take years to come and she would miss him all that time. She also had to repress a sudden urge to add:

And do give your father my regards.

Wistfully she watched Wakefield go over to the pony-cart and climb onto the front seat, where Higson gave him the reins, and then he jauntily waved his little whip in farewell.

Jane waved back.

Then she walked to the Penhallow carriage and got inside, and went back home to the Hall to get her hair cropped (just the ends, over which the *friseur* exclaimed in what Jane thought to be unreasonable horror about their frizzed state), have her very first lesson in dancing (a cotillion, which the dancing-master Monsieur Voclaine assured her was easy, but it wasn't, at least not to her), and also to hear Great-grandmother mention at dinner that she had received from Lady Margaret a veritable spree of invitations.

At this Jane looked up from her thick juicy slice of *boeuf à la Bourguignonne*, which she had been cutting into an appropriately sized mouthful with newfound confidence in her ability to navigate all the cutlery at her place setting. "What sort of invitations, Great-grandmother?"

"A dinner-party tomorrow, to welcome their guests the Countess of Silsbury, her son the Viscount Whitton, and her daughter Lady Felicia. A tea the following day. Then an evening-party followed by an informal little dance. Possibly some amateur theatricals, some hunting, perhaps a ball, but certainly a *soirée musicale*." Great-grandmother gave a grim little smile, and continued:

"Lady Margaret says, in an additional note to myself, that she would of course entirely understand if I should find the prospect of any or all of these events too fatiguing and would wish to decline, and also that if you, my dear Jane, so newly arrived from such a very different sphere, would also prefer to decline, rather than submit yourself to a series of difficult, even daunting experiences, naturally that too would be most understandable."

Livia's green eyes, usually so warm and friendly, were now flashing with indignation. "Why, how absolutely insulting!" she exclaimed, but Great-grandmother's grim smile only widened.

"I would have received these invitations with utter indifference, were it not for Lady Margaret's note. I too aged to participate? And Jane socially inept? Now, of course, I shall accept them all."

Cousin Gabriel smiled. "I see that your dander is up, Grandmama."

"A vulgar colloquialism, but an apt one. Clearly Lady Margaret has made the dangerous mistake of underestimating me. How thankful I am for your dancing lessons, Jane, and that you have the beginnings of an adequate wardrobe. We'll spend some time together going over the proper etiquette for such occasions." Great-grandmother took a sip of her wine, her expression now one of both determination and speculation. "So Lady Margaret is hosting the Merifields. I know the family, of course. Or at least I knew the present Earl's parents. Absurdly full of themselves. Their estate is in Shropshire and they claim it was a gift from a grateful Edward the Third in 1361, for services rendered to the Crown. Ha! A likely story."

She gave a contemptuous little sniff, and pensively Jane went back to her *boeuf à la Bourguignonne.*

So the visitors Wakefield had mentioned *were* the Countess of Silbury and Lady Felicia. And Lady Felicia's brother, too. What were they like? Was Lady Felicia pretty? Did the Duke think she was pretty? Did he want to kiss her palm? And more?

It was likely that at this very moment, over at Hastings, they were all sitting down at dinner as well.

Jane wondered how that was going.

She would have loved to be a fly on the wall.

Or even a fly in somebody's soup.

From his seat at the head of the table in the formal dining-room, Anthony looked down its long gleaming expanse—crowded with tall vases of Siberian irises, many-branched candelabra, a great deal of stemware, big baskets of hot-house fruit, and various other things that made it difficult to actually see one's tablemates—and he directed his gaze to the foot, somewhere in the far distance, at which Margaret sat.

It would not have been an exaggeration to say that she was sparkling with good cheer as animatedly she enumerated to her guests the various treats that lay in store for them. Her eyes glowed, she gestured emphatically, her voice rose and fell. She was like a human glass of champagne. Also, Anthony noticed in vague surprise, that while Margaret's gown was its normal stygian black, her shawl was actually a soft, pale gray.

Now *that* was odd.

It had been over a decade since she'd worn anything that wasn't black.

Were all her black shawls in the wash?

That would be entirely out of character for the exceedingly organized Margaret.

Yes, very odd indeed.

"—and I do hope you will all be sufficiently entertained," she concluded smilingly, glancing both to her left, where sat the Countess of Silsbury, and to her right, at the Viscount Whitton.

"I'm sure we shall be," answered the Countess, smiling too, and Lady Felicia, from her place to Anthony's left, added:

"It all sounds too divine! Really, it's just divine to be here. We're so terribly glad you invited us."

"I'm so sorry the Earl couldn't come as well," said Margaret. "How unfortunate to break both his legs in a riding accident."

"Yes, yes, very unfortunate," said the Countess, "very unfortunate indeed, and naturally the poor dear doesn't care to be confined at home, but of course we're all terribly thankful that it wasn't worse, because it easily could have been, you know. We still don't know how the extra plank got onto that particular jump. People can be so terribly careless, can't they? I scolded our groundsmen quite fiercely. And really, it was so fortunate that Charles happened to be at home just when it happened, because it meant he could accompany us here. Such a stroke of luck! He has so many, many other pressing engagements elsewhere, you know. Well! And so we're to enjoy a dinner-party tomorrow evening, Lady Margaret. That will be simply charming."

"Yes, absolutely divine," said Lady Felicia. "Don't you think so, Charles?" she said across the table to her brother, leaning sharply to the left in order to get a good view of him.

The Viscount made no reply, only lifting one broad

shoulder in its perfectly fitted dark jacket, and gave her a smoldering glance from what Anthony supposed might be described as fine dark eyes.

He wondered how Lord Whitton made them smolder like that.

Did he have to work at it, or did it come to him naturally?

And could *he* make *his* eyes smolder?

Anthony tried. He narrowed his eyes, just a bit, and imagined that his pupils were on fire.

"Charles thinks it's divine also," said Lady Felicia. "We simply adore dinner-parties, don't we, Mama? Oh, Your Grace, is there something in your eye? You're squinting quite dreadfully."

Anthony gave up on smoldering. "It's nothing," he said to Lady Felicia, who smiled and nodded.

"Well, we simply can't wait to meet all your charming neighbors."

"And to think," the Countess said, "they include the Penhallows! How too divine. *Such* a storied pedigree! Not quite as distinguished as ours, of course, but whose is? And, of course, they're so very, very wealthy. I had thought, once, that dear Felicia might—Gabriel Penhallow being so very eligible, and so very charming by all accounts—but of course Felicia was merely a schoolroom chit when he came back to England. And then he went and married a girl no one had ever heard of. How very bizarre. But of course terribly romantic."

"Too, too romantic," agreed Lady Felicia. "Divine, really."

The Countess nodded. "And speaking of divine, Lady Margaret, I'm simply *fascinated* by this charming tale of yours—that of a new Penhallow come to stay at Surmont Hall."

"Not a real Penhallow, to my mind," replied Margaret, "but certainly a relation of sorts."

"Yes, a little love-child, raised in poverty and obscurity! How very charming. Well, only think of the Duke of Clarence, and all his by-blows—quite fully accepted into Society. If Henrietta Penhallow has taken this girl in, it certainly signifies a great deal, and there are few people, if any, among the *ton* who will gainsay her. I daresay she'll dower the girl quite generously. Do you recall when the Duke of Devonshire outfitted his oldest daughter with a dowry of thirty thousand pounds? An astronomical sum, to be sure, but that would be nothing to Henrietta Penhallow."

Viscount Whitton leaned a little forward, and Anthony wondered if he was going to say something, or at least make his eyes smolder again, but he only reached for his wineglass, and Lady Felicia said:

"How simply divine. What a very charming tale."

Well, thought Anthony, this was certainly a divine and charming conversation. He wished it was over. He wished dinner was over. He wished this day was over. Actually, he wished the Merifields' visit was over. But then he remembered passing their carriage with all that luggage strapped on top.

The copious luggage of people who were probably planning on a long visit.

Repressing a sigh, he lifted a spoonful of soup to his mouth, checking first to make sure there wasn't a fly in it. He thought of Jane. And the enormous box of chocolate conserves looking very lonely upstairs in his library.

It was strange, but he was finding it difficult to think of yesterday and how much he had enjoyed kissing Jane.

It all seemed to have happened so long ago.

And now it felt rather like a dream, getting hazier and blurrier by the hour.

Anthony glanced around the table again. Margaret was smiling at the Viscount. The Countess was smiling at Lady Felicia. And Lady Felicia was smiling at *him*.

He supposed he ought to be admiring her luxuriant dark curls, her pale translucent complexion, her cherry-red lips.

He ought to be admiring her elegant figure, too, and how her gauzy low-cut white gown helped to highlight, even emphasize, just how elegant it was.

But all he thought of was a cage.

A cage with a door opened seductively wide.

A door that would clang shut behind him were he fool enough to step inside it.

And he a prisoner once more.

Looking back at Lady Felicia, Anthony politely made his own lips curve upward. It was a thoroughly false and exaggerated smile, and he hoped he didn't look like a clown in a circus performance. God, how he feared and hated clowns. How pleasant it was to be an adult and to be able to avoid circuses entirely, although in other respects being an adult was overrated. Then Anthony had another spoonful of soup (no flies), tried to think of Jane, thought of a cage instead, felt like getting up and going somewhere else, anywhere else, but made himself stay where he was, and docilely finish his soup, just as might a person whose ankles had been bound to the legs of his chair.

Jane stood in front of her mirror, looking with pleasure at her reflection.

She was wearing her fanciest gown from among her four new ones.

It was made of a brilliant deep-red velvet, its long sleeves slashed with a silvery frilled lace which also ornamented the cuffs, the modest neckline, and the hem which flared just a bit, so that it swirled in a delightful way about one's ankles as one walked. On her feet were soft silver slippers, all shiny and new, and Sally had dressed her hair high at the top of her head, with long wavy tendrils allowed to fall loose about her ears and frame her face. A delicate aigrette—made of tiny, sparkling rubies and diamonds and a single white feather—was tucked to one side of her center part, and around her neck was an equally delicate necklace, the mate to the aigrette, which Great-grandmother had just a little while given to her from out of her jewel-chest.

Jane's eyes had filled with tears of delight and gratitude, and Great-grandmother, clearly pleased by Jane's reaction, had nonetheless ordered her—kindly but firmly—not to cry, as naturally she wouldn't wish to arrive at Hastings with a red nose and a splotched complexion.

So Jane had managed to pull herself together.

With her eyes still fixed on her reflection in the mirror, she ran a hand down the bodice, along the curve of her breast, to her hip and thigh. The velvet was so deliciously soft and luxurious, she felt like petting it as she would a cat. (Not Lady Margaret's cat, of course.) Also, Sally had had to alter this gown quite a bit, which she had, bless her, done good-naturedly, as Jane now had yet more flesh everywhere.

If she kept it up, she thought with satisfaction, twisting left and right to see how she looked from different angles, soon she would actually have cleavage again.

And so, not long after this—accompanied by Great-grandmother, Cousin Gabriel, and Livia—Jane stepped into the Great Hall at Hastings feeling rather good about herself, and bolstered, too, by a long and informative session with Great-grandmother about etiquette, some of which seemed practical, some of which seemed silly, but there it was. Jane had committed it all to memory.

Lady Margaret came gliding forward to greet them, resplendent in a gown of pale blue satin and taffeta, and suddenly Jane remembered what Wakefield had told her earlier today after lessons were over.

You'll never guess what happened at breakfast, Jane. I was so surprised I dropped my spoon into my porridge.

Why? What were you surprised about?

Aunt Margaret was wearing a dress that wasn't black. I almost didn't know who she was.

Oh, really?

Yes, I've never not seen her wear black. It made me think of something out of A Midsummer's Dream Night. Or is it the other way around? I can't remember. I'll have to ask Father.

What is A Midsummer's Dream Night?

Oh, it's a play by Shakespeare. There are some muscheevious fairies, you see, Jane, and they put magic juice into people's eyes, and then the people start acting like they're not the same people at all.

In a good way, or a bad way?

A bad way. Because there's all this talk of hearts, and love, and it's absolutely foul and boring. And you'll never guess what was even more surprising.

What was it?

Aunt Margaret didn't even notice that I dropped my spoon in my porridge. So then I dropped my fork in, just to see what she would do.

Did she notice that?

No, she didn't, and then I started thinking about what that girl Titania Penhallow said about fairies. What if she's right, Jane? And maybe a fairy came in the night and put magic juice in Aunt Margaret's eyes.

Now, seeing Lady Margaret all wreathed in smiles, Jane found herself wondering if there might be something to Wakefield's theory. Lady Margaret actually looked happy.

The Duke, on the other hand, did not.

As she greeted him, it came to her that the expression on his face was like a book tightly shut. He was everything that was polite, but there was no light in his dark blue eyes, nor even a hint of a smile on that delightful mouth which just two days ago she had enjoyed kissing very much.

Her spirits instantly sank.

Then she met the Merifields.

The Countess was a pretty, exquisitely dressed middle-aged lady, wearing a spangled silk turban of astonishing height, and her son the Viscount, who looked to be around twenty-five or so, reminded Jane of an illustration she had recently seen in *Ackermann's* magazine, that of the famous poet Lord Byron.

The Viscount was similarly handsome—strikingly so, with his dark curly hair all perfectly arranged, and his dark flashing eyes, and also he looked very fine in his elegant dark evening-clothes which did little to conceal broad muscled shoulders, a trim torso, and powerful legs.

He bowed over Jane's extended hand very gracefully and gave her a long, long look from beneath sensuously heavy eyelids as he did.

"A great pleasure," he said, "to make your acquaintance, Miss Kent," and in his cultured aristocratic voice was a faintly caressing note which had Jane looking back at him in surprise before moving on to Lady Felicia.

Dazzling in white sarsenet and shimmering spider-gauze, in her dark curls a golden coronet of sparkling emeralds and dangling low on the white skin of her breast a long rope of matching emeralds, Lady Felicia smiled very affably at Jane.

"It's too divine to meet you, Miss Kent, I do hope we'll get to know each other better."

"I hope so too, Lady Felicia," answered Jane politely, and stepped aside as into the Great Hall came Miss Humphrey and Miss Trevelyan as well as Mr. Pressley whom they had conveyed to Hastings in their little carriage. She heard a soft hissing noise from somewhere above her head, and looked up to the staircase where she saw, between the balusters, Wakefield crouching on the steps and holding Snuffles.

As she smiled up at him, he lifted one of Snuffles' tiny paws to wave at her. She gave a little wave back, thought how adorable the two of them were, wished she could go up the stairs to better say hullo (and pet Snuffles), but then other people came in, introductions abounded, Jane focused hard on remembering Great-grandmother's etiquette pointers, and eventually they all proceeded to the drawing-room and shortly thereafter to a very large and grand dining-room.

Jane was placed between Mr. Pressley and Sir Gregory Stoke, a baronet who lived on the other side of Riverton, and who, it turned out, had a pig he was planning on entering into this year's Fattest Pig competition at the *fête*. From him, as course after course came and went, she learned a lot about his Doris (a Hampshire breed, extremely fond of vegetables and meat scraps, calm-tempered except when having her hooves inspected, distressingly subject to worms, but otherwise robust) and about the care and feeding of pigs in general.

Sir Gregory seemed very nice, but Jane was still rooting for the Duchess to win.

With Mr. Pressley she had an interesting conversation

about literature, and he told her about some of his favorite authors including Geoffrey Chaucer, Jonathan Swift, Daniel Defoe, Mary Wollstonecraft, and a newer writer, a Miss Austen, whose *Mansfield Park*, he said, was one of the finest, subtlest novels he had ever read. Kindly he promised to lend Jane his copies of Miss Austen's books if the Penhallow library didn't already have them, and suggested she begin with the charming *Pride and Prejudice.*

Occasionally, as the meal progressed, Jane was able to glance around the long table.

The Duke sat at the head, still looking grave and remote, on either side of him Lady Felicia (very cheerful and animated) and Great-grandmother Henrietta (pleasant but also a trifle satirical in her expression). At the foot of the table sat Lady Margaret (also very cheerful and animated), with the Viscount (Byronesquely moody and bored-looking) on her left and another gentleman from the neighborhood on her right (Jane couldn't see his face very well because of a giant vase of flowers that was in the way).

Once or twice she got that intense and curious feeling of being watched, and looked hopefully toward the Duke, but it wasn't him, and when she swept her gaze down the table she realized that the Viscount was staring at her with those flashing dark eyes of his.

Uneasily Jane wondered if her aigrette had gotten all lopsided, or if she had some of that delicious spinach, baked in a rich sauce of cheese and cream, visibly stuck between her teeth—a more likely scenario as she had partaken of it quite liberally.

But later, when dinner was over and the ladies had left the dining-room and she could slip away and look privately in a mirror, she saw that although there was just a *tiny* bit of spinach between her two front teeth, she otherwise looked entirely presentable.

With the nail-edge of her forefinger she was able to dislodge the spinach, then grinned at her reflection just to be sure. Goodness, she looked rather like a clown doing that. She let her face relax, and as she returned to the drawing-room where the ladies were congregating, she recalled the time a traveling circus had come to Nantwich. Some of its performers had, by way of advertisement, paraded along the mean little high street. There had been acrobats, and people on stilts waving flambeaux, and somebody riding a remarkable two-wheeled contraption, and a couple of clowns with their faces painted all white except for around their eyes and their mouths where they displayed a great false crimson smile.

Jane, probably nine or ten at the time, had loathed and feared these clowns in equal parts.

It was just as well there had been no money to attend the show.

Even now, if a circus came to Riverton, she would avoid it as she would a giant hole in the ground.

It was a comforting thought.

When Jane stepped into the drawing-room, she was hailed by Lady Felicia, who called out her name and patted the empty seat next to her on the sofa where she sat. "I've saved you a spot! Do come join us!"

With a reluctance she hoped she was concealing, Jane went to sit with Lady Felicia on the sofa, opposite Lady Margaret and the Countess; nearby, neat and elegant in amber-colored silk, was Miss Trevelyan, and further away, in groups of two and three, were Great-grandmother, Livia, Miss Humphrey, and some other neighborhood ladies.

"I was just telling Lady Margaret how much we enjoyed seeing her ruin today," said Lady Felicia smilingly. "So charming."

"Yes, I do love a good ruin," said her mother the Countess. "So terribly fashionable—all the very best people have them. I daresay Surmont Hall has one also, Miss Kent?"

"No, I don't believe so."

"Really? How terribly odd. Ours, you know, dates back at least a decade. Have you thought about having a hermit brought on?" she said to Lady Margaret. "It would add so much *tone*. If you do, consider your candidates closely. Our most recent one left after only a year. He said he was bored."

Miss Trevelyan gave a crack of laughter, which seemed to surprise the Countess who looked at her with eyebrows raised.

"Well, even without a hermit, it's a very charming ruin," said Lady Felicia. "I enjoyed our little tour so much, Lady Margaret. Your temple is simply divine. And I don't think I've ever seen such a charming succession house. Oh, and your gardener! I was quite charmed by his gruff manner. Perhaps he'd be interested in being a hermit on a part-time basis? He would look simply divine in that canvas sack we had *our* hermit wear—don't you think so, Mama?"

"Oh yes, very charming, my dear. And, of course, terribly authentic."

Lady Felicia smiled and nodded. "Hastings is such a charming, charming place, Lady Margaret. I quite dote on it, you know."

Jane watched as Lady Margaret smiled and nodded also, and then the Countess said:

"I understand you're a writer, Miss Trevelyan? Such a terribly unusual occupation for a female."

"I daresay it is, My Lady," answered Miss Trevelyan with perfect equanimity.

"What impelled you to take it up?"

"Aside from the need to earn my own living, you mean?"

"Ah! Necessity! A terribly harsh mistress, is it not? You didn't care for governessing, or teaching in a school?"

"I taught for a little while in Bath, and found it insupportably dull. It was Miss Humphrey who encouraged me to try my hand at what I really love, which is writing."

"How charming! And you're currently writing about the various Tudor queens?"

"Yes, that's right. Henry the Eighth's, to be precise."

"Jane Seymour was always my favorite," said Lady Felicia. "*She* knew how to be a proper wife. I liked Katherine of Aragon, too, because she was a real princess. And I always thought Anne of Cloves was just so *dull*."

"Yet she managed to not get her head chopped off," said Miss Trevelyan, "in a deeply distressing life-or-death situation far from her own country. She was much cleverer than people give her credit for. Only consider how she was able to outmaneuver both Henry *and* her political enemies, who would have very much liked to see her sent to the block. I've just finished her biography, by the way. It's off to my publisher, and I've started in on poor Catherine Howard."

"I don't feel sorry for *her*," Lady Felicia said. "She knew the rules, and was unchaste anyway. She got what she deserved."

Miss Trevelyan looked at her, amiably but with a certain quizzical look in her eyes. "What if the rules were unfair, Lady Felicia?"

"What do you mean?"

"The rules which dictated that men could take their pleasure freely both before and after marriage, whereas women had to operate by very different standards, and suffer the consequences if discovered. Not so very different from today's standards," Miss Trevelyan added thoughtfully.

There was a silence.

Jane said warmly, "I'm looking forward to reading your book, Miss Trevelyan," only she was halfway through the sentence when Lady Margaret said:

"I do hope the weather will be just a trifle warmer tomorrow."

"Yes, that would be most charming," agreed the Countess.

Lady Felicia said, "Do you ride, Miss Kent? We're going hunting."

"Only a little. I'm still learning."

Her dark eyes wide, Lady Felicia replied, "Still learning? Oh—I daresay that before—" She lowered her voice, as if mentioning something that ought not to be discussed in polite company. "—before you came here, you had no chance to learn. How very dreadful for you! Riding is such a charming pastime."

"Yes," said Jane, "very charming," and had to resist the urge to sarcastically thank Lady Margaret for broadcasting to yet more people the story of her background. She also had to resist a sudden and useless urge to mentally kick herself for having been so high-minded and refusing to lie about it, as well as *also* resisting the equally useless urge to speculate on how different her life might have been if Grandmother Charity *had* revealed the name of her baby's father . . .

. . . And if Great-grandmother Kent had somehow gotten in touch with Great-grandmother Henrietta . . .

. . . Who might have swept into Nantwich years ago and carried Jane away to Surmont Hall . . .

. . . Where she would have been raised in comfort and warmth and security, and educated, and taught how to dance and use the right fork, and then would never have to sit next to someone like the confident and beautiful Lady Felicia, being patronized and additionally having to repress awful, stupid, bitter, entirely unhelpful feelings of envy that were making her insides rather hurt.

And then Jane's fancy veered off in an even more painful direction.

If Titus and Charity *had* managed to get married, their baby would have been legitimate, and everything would have been *entirely* different, and . . .

. . . And Jane's father Josiah certainly wouldn't have married a blacksmith's daughter who lived in the middle of nowhere, and thus she, Jane, wouldn't even have been born.

For a few agonizing moments Jane actually felt angry at Titus and Charity.

After which she felt guilty, and sad for them, and also sad for herself.

Then she got her bearings again and fought her way free from her sudden funk, reminding herself that the past was the past and couldn't be changed, and that everything (both good and bad) had made her who she was today (which was, really, just fine); then she saw that Miss Trevelyan was looking at her, and ever so slightly she winked at Jane, and Jane immediately felt very glad to have Miss Trevelyan for a friend and also her insides felt better right away.

The conversation meandered on to the latest Court scandals, a topic which Jane found of little to no interest, so her mind wandered here and there while the others spoke. At one point she found herself gazing rather fixedly at Lady Felicia, and realized that she was trying to envision her as the Duke's wife, and made herself both look away and stop imagining something that bothered her.

Something that bothered her more than she liked to admit.

And so she had to fight her way out of another funk that threatened to envelop her.

After what felt like a very long boring time—as Jane couldn't have cared less what inane things the Prince Regent had said and done—the men came into the drawing-room, people rearranged themselves, and Jane was sorry that the Duke went to sit with Sir Gregory, and even sorrier that Viscount Whitton intercepted her as she was on her way toward Miss Humphrey and Miss Trevelyan, and so she felt more or less obliged to go sit with him on a sofa and be stared at with those eyes of his while he talked about his various Society friends, his racing horses, the London clubs to which he belonged, his favorite tailor, and where he bought his watch-fobs, none of these topics being at all spellbinding as far as she was concerned.

Still, he *was* interesting to look at, in the way one might gaze with mild curiosity at a well-executed painting or sculpture, and that was, at least, something to pass the time. He really was extraordinarily handsome. Almost unbelievably so. Jane supposed there were a lot of women who would want to do more than simply look at him.

Suddenly she remembered Miss Trevelyan saying, the first time she had met her:

You may inspire me to try my hand at a novel—it would make a splendid plot, you know. A lovely young woman, born to a life of humble obscurity, discovers at twenty she's actually a member of one of England's oldest and most distinguished families. Although it would hardly be innovative, would it? Been done to death, really. Also, it would probably be better if the young woman turned out to be a princess or a duchess or something along those lines—especially if there's some sort of dark, enigmatic hero, too, with a fine curling lip of disdain. I daresay the book would sell better that way.

The Viscount, Jane thought, would make a delightful character in a book like that, being so classically handsome, so perfectly coiffed, so beautifully dressed. Why, his dark evening-shoes were so shiny that she could literally see her own reflection in them. She knew this because once or twice, biting back a yawn, she had leaned forward in the hopes of disguising her clenched jaw and discovered their mirror-like effect, which was a helpful way to quickly check on her aigrette again.

At any rate, would he be the hero?

He looked like one, but into Jane's mind came the memory of Great-grandmother Kent saying sourly:

Handsome is as handsome does.

Hmmm. He would have to be rewritten, in order to make him less boring. Just then the Viscount broke off from whatever he was nattering on about (Jane had stopped listening some time ago) and softly said, for her ears alone:

"You are a very desirable woman, Miss Kent."

Now *this* was slightly more interesting. Jane perked up at once.

"Thank you ever so much," she said demurely. "How charming of you to say so."

"*You're* charming. I've never met a woman I wanted more."

"Really?"

"Yes. You've set my heart aflame, Miss Kent. I wasn't alive—*truly* alive—till I met you."

This was definitely more like it, Jane thought. He was sounding exactly like a hero in Miss Trevelyan's novel. "Do go on."

"Would that we were alone."

Jane batted her eyelashes. “That would be divine.”

“It would be heaven here on earth,” softly said the Viscount, his fine dark eyes, intensely looking into her own, suddenly reminding her of small bonfires, perfect for roasting chestnuts. Or warming up a potato. Which reminded her. When would the tea-tray arrive?

“You stare, Miss Kent.”

“I do beg your pardon. You have the most fascinating eyes.”

“You do.”

“No, you do,” Jane said, for argument’s sake.

“No—*you*. Pools of liquid silver. I would gladly sell my soul to fall into them. And stay there forever, subsumed in their incandescence.”

“How kind.”

“Desire for you runs through my veins like quicksilver, Miss Kent.”

He had said “silver” twice, so she felt comfortable murmuring, “So divine.”

“Dare I hope—dare I have the audacity to hope—that you feel the same way too?”

“A lady,” said Jane, “never tells.” She batted her eyelashes again.

He put a hand to his chest. “My heart beats for you and you alone, Miss Kent. May I share with you some poetry of mine?”

Poetry! Could this get any better? “Please do.”

The Viscount cleared his throat. “‘You are my lady, my love—Fluttering sweet like the dove—You are my one and only—Without you I am sad and lonely. I sigh, I repine—Lady, lady, please be mine.’”

Jane put a hand to *her* chest, as if overcome with emotion. “How very, very charming.”

“I composed it just now for you, Miss Kent.”

Jane strongly doubted it, and even though she hadn't read much poetry so far in her life, it was pretty clear that the Viscount was no Mr. Wordsworth (or even a Lord Byron). But she said, "Too, too divine." And she wondered how much longer they could go on talking like this. They both sounded like blithering idiots, but not in the lovely enjoyable way she and the Duke did when they were blithering. *That* had been sincere, because her mind had whirled to a slow delicious halt at the exact same time her body had quickened, and if she had to guess, he had been feeling that way also.

Whereas this . . .

It was hard to tell which was worse: if the Viscount was being insincere, or if this was really how he talked.

What on earth did he want from her?

Handsome is as handsome does.

The back of Jane's neck suddenly prickled, and she looked up and around to see that from halfway across the room, Lady Margaret was looking fixedly at her. For a crazy few seconds, she wondered if Lady Margaret was trying to envision her as the Viscount's wife.

Because Lady Margaret wasn't smiling and cheerful.

Rather, she looked as if something was bothering her.

Quite a lot.

Jane wanted to snicker at the very idea of being married to the Viscount, and having to listen to bad poetry for the rest of one's life, but then she remembered trying to envision Lady Felicia married to the Duke, and she didn't feel like snickering anymore.

Impulsively she looked for him.

There he was, at the far end of the drawing-room, sitting with Mr. Pressley and Cousin Gabriel, one long leg crossed over the other. His tawny hair was slightly disordered in the way she liked so much, and his neckcloth was tied with a little more precision than it usually was, but not *that* much, which for some strange reason made her glad, and his evening-shoes, while not actually scuffed, had only a marginal sort of shine to them, which she found more than sufficient, and altogether he was so entirely attractive that she felt like (to quote the Viscount) sighing *and* repining.

But why wasn't *he* looking at her?

He hadn't, really, all evening, and with all her heart Jane wondered why, and had to fight off yet another impulse to sink into a funk—a rather bad one.

Chapter 10

To Anthony's disgruntlement (a word that made him think of the Duchess in a bad mood), the weather continued cold, clear, and crisp—perfect hunting weather, in fact, and so here everyone was the next morning, gathering just past the house on the wide graveled sweep.

He himself did not hunt, had never hunted, would not hunt, never would hunt, and whatever other verb forms would make clear his firm intention in this regard, no matter how undukely it made him appear in the eyes of the world, and had been so doing since the age of fifteen when he—to the perpetually renewed and scornful outrage of his family—refused to participate.

There had been a moment of extreme awkwardness last night when Lady Felicia, in a carrying voice which encompassed most of the drawing-room, expressed her bubbly enthusiasm for Margaret's hunting plan, and he had stiffly told her that no doubt his sister had unintentionally misspoken, as there was no formal hunting per se at Hastings, only strict rules permitting the local folk to take what they needed in the way of game, leaving his own gamesmen to provide for the manor house, although the Merifields were, however, welcome to go fishing if they liked, as the Hastings rivers and streams were abundantly stocked, and despite this hospitable alternative Margaret had turned a really remarkable shade of scarlet, leaving him, for a minute or two, in genuine fear that she would go off in an apoplexy in front of all the guests, or, at the very least, stalk over to the wide double doors of the drawing-room and repeatedly slam them open and closed.

Somehow, though, she had managed to control herself, pasted on her face what looked to him in all honesty like a clownish smile, and so the moment passed off, after which Sir Gregory graciously offered to accommodate the Hastings party at his own estate, and luckily the tea-tray came in not long after that, although Anthony did happen to notice that Henrietta Penhallow was looking at him with that disconcertingly sardonic expression on her face, and so, to avoid it, he had strolled over to the mantelpiece with the intention of casually resting one arm alongside it, and possibly crossing one ankle over the other, to look even more dukishly debonair, but instead he accidentally knocked over his father's cherished stuffed owl, which tumbled to the floor, dislodging one of the horribly lifelike glass eyes, separating the owl from its mahogany base, and causing the beak to snap off.

Which, aside from his mortifying embarrassment, was actually rather satisfying, as he had hated that stuffed owl all his life.

Jane had come to help him pick up the pieces (the glass eye having rolled across the floor quite near to where she had been sitting), and it took everything he had not to devolve into being a complete ass again and call her by her first name and tell her how much he liked her gown and that he had missed her and also he had some more chocolates for her and maybe they could go upstairs and hide away in his library for a little while and eat chocolates and kiss each other.

And he would have liked to ask her why she had sat with Viscount Whitton for so long, enjoying what had looked like a very cozy *tête-à-tête*, but of course it was none of his business and it was a free country and she could sit with whoever she liked for however long she wanted, even if it was an incredibly handsome, suave, polished fellow with perfect hair and giant bulging muscles and shiny shoes.

No, instead, he had been a different sort of ass and had merely thanked her for her help, still sounding very stiff and formal. And she had looked at him wonderingly, and gone away, and he had felt so terrible that he had no appetite at all for tea, even though there were the most stupendous éclairs and also tiny cucumber sandwiches which he usually loved, and Lady Felicia had tried to press on him a cup of tea which she had made for him just the way he liked, with a lot of cream and sugar, having, she said, noticed his preference, which was awfully decent of her but still he wished she and her family would go away, and in fact he wished everyone would go away, and leave him alone, so that he could resume his quiet peaceful life once more, reading his beloved Dinkle with his feet up on his desk, being a father as best he knew how, taking care of the Hastings people as best he could, giving away his money to causes that seemed to need it, and hanging around the Duchess, dreaming of glory at this year's *fête*.

"Why don't you like to hunt, Father?" Wakefield said, jolting Anthony out of his brooding reverie.

They were standing on the marble steps at the front of the house, watching as the Hastings grooms led horses from the stables for Margaret (stunning in a bright red habit) and the Merifields to ride over to Sir Gregory's estate.

"It's not my idea of fun, my boy."

"Why not? You like riding."

"Yes, but I don't like careening after a fox. Hardly seems a fair match. If they could find a fox as large as a horse, I might consider it. Although it would be terrifying."

Wakefield nodded thoughtfully. "Will *I* have to hunt when I'm the Duke?"

"That's up to you."

"I don't think I will, and then Aunt Margaret can say *I'm* the worst duke in the world."

"Something to aspire to." Anthony reached into his greatcoat pocket and pulled from it a couple of small squarish confections. "Caramel?"

Wakefield took one, plucked off the dog hairs, and popped it into his mouth. Around it he said, "I say, Father, did you notice at breakfast that I put my fork, my spoon, *and* my knife into my porridge?"

"Yes, and I did wonder. Yesterday you only put your spoon and fork in."

"I'm kindicting an experiment, you see."

"Do you mean conducting?"

"Yes, that's what I said. Don't you want to know what my experiment is?"

"I really do."

"Well, I'm trying to see how many things I can put into my porridge before Aunt Margaret notices."

Anthony nodded. It *was* surprising that Margaret, who had an uncanny knack for spotting dust on a shelf that was higher than her own head, had failed to observe Wakefield's illicit deployment of utensils. He supposed he ought to tell Wakefield to stop doing it, but the truth was that Margaret's behavior was so baffling that he didn't feel like it. Also, it was rather fascinating to watch things sinking into porridge. It made him think of quicksand, and how as a boy he had longed to actually stumble across a pond of it and toss things in. To Wakefield he said, "What will you do tomorrow?"

"I was thinking the salt cellar next. Ow."

"What's the matter, old chap?"

Wakefield, who had winced, now fished into his mouth and withdrew the sodden caramel. "It's my tooth. When I bit down just now."

"It hurt?"

"Yes, but it went away." Wakefield put the caramel back into his mouth. "I say, Father, are you going to marry her?"

"Who?" Anthony said, a little more sharply than he intended, because for a single, wild, insane, exhilarating moment he had thought of Jane before swiftly recalling that he never, ever wanted to marry anyone at all, never again in his whole entire life, even if he lived to be a hundred, or two hundred, or a thousand, and really, in point of fact, when it came right down to it, he didn't want to care about somebody in a way that made one think for the briefest second that one actually might want to marry that person, because that made one feel uncomfortable and wretched and full of memories from one's earlier experience being married which had been, in a word, hell on earth.

Wait—that was three words.

Which had been *hellish.*

Suddenly he realized that Wakefield was looking up at him curiously, perhaps having heard the rather odd note in his voice, and then Wakefield tilted his head toward the Merifield party.

"Her. Lady Thingummy."

"Lady Felicia?"

"Yes."

"What about her?"

"Are you going to marry her?"

"No."

Wakefield nodded, and Anthony couldn't resist asking, "Did she say you're a horrid little boy?"

"No, she said that I'm terribly charming."

Anthony also couldn't resist asking, "Did she say I'm a neglectful father?"

"No, she said that you're terribly charming."

"Does she want to pack you off to Eton?"

"No, she said she's sure I'm getting a charming education from Mr. Pressley."

"So, no half-crown then?"

"No."

"Too bad, my boy."

"Well, that's life, isn't it, Father? Sometimes you're the carriage-wheel, and sometimes you're the toad."

"I say, Wake, that's awfully clever. And all too true."

"Higson said it."

"I had no idea he was so philosophical."

"Oh, he's very pholisiphical, Father. Yesterday he said that life is like a dish of apricots."

"How so?"

"Because apricots are his favorite fruit."

Anthony thought this over. "Is there more?"

"There might have been, but I had a little trouble with the reins just then and so we forgot all about it."

"Did you run the cart off the road?"

"No."

"That's good."

"Yes, but it was a near thing, Father, and Higson went

absolutely *white*, so I stopped the cart for a little while until he stopped looking like a circus clown."

"That was thoughtful of you, old chap."

"It was the least I could do. Aren't clowns awful, Father?"

"Very."

"If I decide to be a menace to society when I grow up, I might become one."

"Well, that would be perfect."

"Much better than being a pirate or a highwayman, don't you think?"

"Absolutely."

"I think so too. Look, Lady Thingummy's waving goodbye at you."

Anthony glanced over to where Lady Felicia, on a spirited bay, was gaily flourishing her riding crop. He raised a hand in brief farewell and watched with secret, but unabashed gladness as she, along with Margaret, the Countess, and Viscount Whitton, rode away.

For a few hours, at least, he could pretend that his life was his own again.

"Here's Higson, Father," said Wakefield, and hopped down a couple of steps toward the pony-cart.

"Wait," Anthony said, and Wakefield paused, turning around to look up at him inquiringly.

"Yes, Father?"

"Is your tooth all right?"

"Yes, it's fine."

"Good. I'll see you after lessons."

"All right, Father. Do you know what's for luncheon today?"

"No."

"Can I invite Jane over?"

Anthony felt his stupid heart leap within him, and

sternly told it to sit down and shut up. "If you like," he said, as if it was a matter of complete indifference, which it wasn't, as part of him hoped she would come, and another part of him hoped she wouldn't, and he wished both parts would also sit down and shut up, because it was all just too awful and difficult.

Wakefield hopped away and Anthony watched him climb into the pony-cart and have the reins handed to him by the stoic, long-suffering Higson.

The pony briskly trotted off toward the vicarage, and for a minute or two Anthony stood there on the steps thinking about a dish of apricots and its possible philosophical value, then gave it up and went inside and upstairs to his library where he permitted himself a soothing half-hour with Dinkle (reading up on gum disease in pigs, a grisly but important topic), then labored messily over the accounts for an hour or so, and received his bailiff to talk at length about timber, spring crops, the puzzling apple blight, sheep-shearing, and, inevitably, drainage trenches.

Next he wrote some cheques, and looked through his books for one on fruit plagues, but the only one he had wasn't very informative, and after that he went downstairs to talk with Bunch for a little while, and also told him to give Higson a substantial raise.

Then he went back outside, collected all the dogs, and together they strolled over to the pig-cote where he found a spectacularly disfigured Johns (by way of a nose which looked like a squashed turnip), who told him with ill-concealed pride that last night in a Riverton tavern he and Cremwell had gotten into a fistfight which had left him, Johns, with a bloody nose but Cremwell with a bloody nose *and* a black eye.

"Oh, for God's sake, Johns."

"Aye, but guv'nor, he told everybody the Duchess's got the *gleets.* So I said, 'It's *you* that's got the gleets, my lad, *and* the shanker, *and* the crinkums to boot. And I'll bet your mam does too.' And he got all glimflashy."

"Well, of course he did. Johns, this has got to stop. How can you take care of the Duchess if Cremwell gets the best of you next time?"

"He wouldn't," answered Johns, offended.

"He might. He's no bugaboo, you know. And then I'll have to get somebody else to take over. Like Tebbinson, for example," he added with deliberate provocation.

"Tebbinson!" Johns was now both offended and horrified. "That grinagog! Guv'nor, you *wouldn't.*"

"If you're laid up in bed with broken bones I'd have no choice."

To this Johns made no reply, but Anthony could see him thinking it over, and, reasonably satisfied, he leaned both elbows on the balustrade and watched the Duchess at her trough, happily making her way through a large pile of leftover gruel, cooked pumpkin, and lentils, this last giving him considerable pleasure to observe as he disliked lentils, and the more of them the Duchess consumed, the fewer there would be in the world, even if only temporarily.

Then his eye was caught by a little shimmer high up in the doorway to the pig-cote's interior, and he saw a rather nice spiderweb glistening in the sunlight, so expertly and intricately constructed that for a moment or two he thought he actually saw a word woven in there.

Was there a J?

And possibly an A?

He squinted at it.

And . . . could that be an N, followed by a squiggly, scraggly E?

Of course not.

Dismissing this fanciful thought from his mind, Anthony walked back to the house in time to see the pony-cart return, with all parties intact, this being, he saw at once, a party without Jane, and he hardly knew whether to be glad or sorry, but may have been both, and then he and Wakefield went inside to have a leisurely luncheon together, during which Wakefield told him all about the annoying math problems Mr. Pressley had set him to do, and about the interesting discussion they had had about the French Revolution, and also that Jane had said that while she couldn't come over to luncheon, she appreciated the invitation very much, and she had mentioned that she would be coming over later on today for tea, along with the other Penhallows.

Anthony, therefore, used the rest of the afternoon to productively tamp down any lingering and troublesome yearnings he might have had for Jane, and so when tea-time rolled around and their guests had arrived, he was pleased to find himself perfectly, thoroughly, and entirely immune to her admittedly formidable and devastating charms.

Jane had not been at all sure she really wanted to go to tea today at Hastings, given that last night's experience there had been, to put it mildly, a mixed bag, but Great-grandmother had been adamant.

And give Lady Margaret the satisfaction of our absence? she had scoffingly declared, in her sharp blue eyes a martial gleam. *I think not.*

In the end, Livia had begged off, because little Lucy had seemed unusually querulous earlier, and Cousin Gabriel wanted to stay home to help Livia, he said, and spend time with all the children, so ultimately it was just herself and Great-grandmother who sallied forth.

And now here they were in the Hastings drawing-room with the Duke and Lady Margaret (elegant in green silk), the three Merifields, Miss Trevelyan and Miss Humphrey, Mr. Pressley, and Sir Gregory and his wife Lady Stoke, a pleasant, shy, monosyllabic lady who seemed a little overawed by the company in which she found herself.

Lady Felicia, the Countess, Lady Margaret, and Sir Gregory were animatedly sharing boring anecdotes about their day spent hunting, which had apparently been both divine and charming, Great-grandmother was satirical, the Viscount was staring at her again, the Duke was not only not staring, he wasn't even looking at her at all, and so Jane, feeling very grumpy, and maybe even rather heartsore, decided she might as well enjoy her tea and scones and sandwiches if nothing else, and occupied herself with that pretty well for some time.

Eventually Lady Felicia and the Countess began talking about last year's London Season, all the people with whom they had spent time, the various activities they had enjoyed, and how charming and divine it all had been.

"You simply must go this spring," the Countess said, glancing between the Duke and Lady Margaret with a kind of coy urgency. "It won't really be a Season without you."

"That would be delightful," answered Lady Margaret, looking, to Jane's surprise, just a little wistful. "The Farr townhouse has been empty for too long."

"Then it's settled!" The Countess beamed at them both.

"My sister is of course welcome to go," the Duke said, "but I most certainly won't."

"But Your Grace, whyever not?" exclaimed Lady Felicia. "I simply *adore* London! Don't you?"

"I detest it."

"But why? The shops—the parties—the parks—the theatre—Almack's—oh, *everything*!"

The Duke only shrugged, and Lady Felicia ventured:

"But . . . you've been to London, haven't you, Your Grace?"

"No."

"Then how can you detest it?"

"I detest the idea of it."

"Oh, Your Grace, you *must* go. Truly! It's absolutely divine, I do assure you!"

"I mustn't," returned the Duke, "and I won't."

His implacability was plain to see, and Lady Felicia looked rather helplessly at her mother, who quickly said:

"Felicia, my dear, perhaps you'd favor us with a song?"

"That would be delightful," put in Lady Margaret, who didn't look wistful anymore, but rather had the appearance of a volcano attempting to repress its own eruption.

Lady Felicia rose to her feet and went to the pianoforte, where she played "Robin Adair" very skillfully, and sang with equal skill in a sure, pleasing soprano, and after that, when urged, played and sang "Greensleeves" and "The Last Rose of Summer."

Watching and listening, Jane had to suppress an unwelcome impulse to feel envious again. Also she forced herself, as objectively as possible, to acknowledge what a pretty picture Lady Felicia made in her charming—yes, it really *was*—white gown, with her dark and perfectly arranged curls glimmering in the candle-light as she sat very straight at the pianoforte, her bejeweled fingers moving confidently across the keyboard.

But even so, the Duke wasn't looking at her, either.

If Lady Felicia was meant to be the Duke's intended, it didn't seem to be going all that well.

The Duke looked aloof. Impossibly self-contained.

Jane suddenly found herself thinking of something she, Wakefield, and Mr. Pressley had talked about today at lessons—the Bastille. The immense Parisian fortress and prison which had figured so importantly during the French Revolution.

Somehow the Duke was reminding her of the Bastille.

It was unpleasant, disconcerting, *and* painful to see him like this, so Jane stopped looking at him as well. She got up and, avoiding the Viscount, went over to sit next to Lady Stoke, and after a few minutes of labored conversation she hit upon a topic—poetry—which had Lady Stoke's shyness melting away into something approaching vivacity, and they had a very nice chat about Wordsworth, Coleridge, Shelley, and Keats, and Jane got to tell her how much she liked "I Wandered Lonely as a Cloud," and felt she had made a new friend when Lady Stoke immediately quoted, in her soft voice, all four stanzas.

All things considered, though, Jane wasn't sorry when tea was over and she and Great-grandmother could go home. She had started reading *Pride and Prejudice*, which she had indeed found in the Hall's library, as well as Katherine Penhallow's first book on maritime history, which wasn't necessarily a subject of innate interest to her, but was so well written, and so beautifully illustrated, that Jane enjoyed it more than she thought she would. It was rather a relief to sit by the fire in the rococo drawing-room, toast her feet a little in its warmth, and lose herself in a book.

Once or twice she glanced up to see that Great-grandmother was looking at her, on her handsome face a thoughtful expression, but when Jane asked her what she was thinking, Great-grandmother only smiled faintly and refused to say.

Chapter 11

Another day, another one of Margaret's ghastly events.

Yesterday was the tea.

Today, an evening-party and a dance.

And Margaret was still talking about a *soirée musicale*, some theatricals, perhaps a formal ball, more rides and walks, and even—good God, imagine the damned *humidity*—a breakfast in the conservatory which airily she described as *un charmant petit pique-nique faux en plein air*, as if saying it in French would somehow make it less horrific.

Gloomily Anthony eyed himself in his long pier-glass.

He loathed wearing evening-clothes, yet here he was, dressed up like an actor in a play he didn't want to be in.

Evans, hovering hopefully in the background, said: "Is there anything I can do to be of assistance, Your Grace?"

Anthony knew that Evans was itching to retie his neckcloth into something more elaborate and buff his dark shoes to a glossier finish, but only replied, "Thank you, but no."

He thought he heard Evans sigh, very, very quietly, hardened himself against it, looked at himself some more in his dark trousers, his dark waistcoat and jacket, his disinterestedly tied white neckcloth which twenty minutes ago had been crisp, his tumble of hair which he had halfheartedly pushed back from his face, and then he sighed too.

He looked bad enough standing still, but he would look infinitely worse when dancing.

Because he was horrible at it.

He could never remember the steps, the twists, the turns, the foot going here, the head turned there, hands clasping and unclasping, the bowing and the scraping, and all of that.

If he were a betting man, which he wasn't, as he considered gambling to be a complete and utter waste of time and money, he'd place a very large wager that Viscount Whitton was a dazzlingly good dancer.

And no doubt he would win the wager, but it would be a hollow triumph nonetheless.

Anthony sighed again and went to Wakefield's room, where he read to him from *Tales from Shakespeare*—they were deep into the dark and twisty *Merchant of Venice*—and inquired after his tooth, which Wakefield admitted was bothering him just a little tiny bit more, but only when he had bitten into some toasted almonds Cook had let him have, and after that Anthony kissed him goodnight, promised to look in on him later, and made his way downstairs in search of Bunch, whom he found in the drawing-room supervising the shifting of furniture in preparation for dancing, and asked him to send to Bath for the family dentist Mr. Rowland first thing in the morning, and to request that he come posthaste.

Then he went to the Great Hall, where Margaret and the Merifields stood chatting and loitering about in their finery as they waited for the guests to arrive—although to be precise the Viscount, suave and perfect in his evening-clothes, did very little chatting but a great deal of smoldering—and so Anthony passed the time leaning against a wall with his arms crossed over his chest, suppressing random thoughts of Jane, replying monosyllabically (and possibly even curtly) to Lady Felicia's lively attempts to draw him out, trying not to be envious of the Viscount, suppressing yet more thoughts of Jane, and also wondering how soon Mr. Rowland could get here.

If it hadn't been for the surprise arrival of a ball-gown from Miss Simpkin, made of a shimmering dusty-rose pink silk and so beautiful that it was literally impossible to not fly upstairs to her bedroom and try it on at once, Jane might well have manufactured an excuse not to go back to Hastings yet again.

All day she had been feeling—as had little Lucy yesterday—unusually querulous.

But when she saw herself in the rose-pink gown, and had time to admire more fully the cunning curlicued line of deep pink embroidery around the hem and the gently puffed sleeves and the rather low neckline, *and* to see that she really did have a bit of cleavage again, well, that decided her.

Because she looked very good.

Jane didn't think she was a vain person, and she certainly wouldn't have said that she was the best-looking woman in the world or anything like that, but it did seem fair to acknowledge that the shimmering pink fabric offered a lovely contrast to her pale hair, and gave her eyes an interesting glow, and that her figure looked very nice in it.

If the Duke didn't look at her in *this*, there was no hope.

No hope for him.

Jane was rather nervous about the dancing, but she had been practicing hard with Monsieur Voclaine, and Cousin Gabriel had promised to dance the first two dances with her, so that she could gain confidence, and as many dances as she liked after that, just in case she needed him.

Also, Titania had wanted to see her in her new gown, so Jane went to the nursery when her hair was dressed and she had on her beautiful necklace and aigrette, and it had been very flattering to be firmly pronounced as looking exactly like a fairy princess who could ride horses and go fishing and fight battles.

So, for the third day in a row, Jane went off to Hastings, feeling a little bit like a battle of some kind lay ahead of her.

It was lovely to see all her new friends, less lovely to be among Lady Margaret and the Merifields, and not lovely at all to see that the Duke was avoiding her eye.

Avoiding *her.*

Even in her beautiful dress.

It hurt her feelings.

Quite a lot.

Still, she mingled valiantly, doing her best to stay out of the respective orbits of the Merifields, but was nonetheless caught unawares when Lady Felicia came up behind her, because although one could try to be vigilant, one still didn't have eyes in the back of one's head.

"Dear Miss Kent," said Lady Felicia, "won't you come upstairs with me for a few moments, before the dancing begins, and assist me with my hair?"

Lady Felicia's hair looked perfect to Jane, but she felt it would be churlish to refuse, and so they swept upstairs side by side and to Lady Felicia's bedchamber. Once inside, with the door shut behind them, Jane said:

"What can I do to help you?"

Lady Felicia sank onto the little stool of the dressing-table, but with her back to the mirror, which made Jane suspect that she had been lured up here on false pretenses, especially when she noticed that Lady Felicia's eyes were darkly glittering in a way she had never seen in her before.

"Miss Kent, have you ever been so bored that you felt you were going to die?"

So, it wasn't about the hair. No exchange of girlish confidences either, not with the way Lady Felicia was glittering like that. Jane thought about her question. She had certainly been bored listening to yesterday's hunting anecdotes, for example, and last Sunday at church, when Mr. Attfield the churchwarden had droned on and on, but not so badly that she would have preferred to be dead. "Why do you ask, Lady Felicia?"

"Because I hate it here. I hate the country, I hate this place! There's nothing to do—it's the dullest place in the world. My God! I wish we had never come."

Jane looked at her in astonishment, and Lady Felicia went on:

"I hope you don't mind my telling you. But Mama won't listen, and of course I can't talk to Charles, because he doesn't care in the least about me, and I had to tell *someone*."

"I—I had no idea you felt that way," Jane said.

"Well, of course you wouldn't! Because everything must be *charming*, and *divine*, and *wonderful*! And I've got to make the Duke marry me, Mama says, or we'll be ruined. More ruined than we already are, that is."

Feeling rather stunned, Jane sat on the edge of the big luxurious bed. "You're ruined?"

"Yes, because Papa has gambled it all away. His inheritance—all of Mama's income—whatever can be mortgaged on the estate—my dowry. Everything. These emeralds are only paste." Lady Felicia gave a bitter laugh and flicked a contemptuous finger at the beautiful necklace which lay sparkling on her white breast. "I was engaged to be married, you know, last Season. But he shied away before it could be announced. He didn't want to marry a pauper, no matter how grand my title."

"I'm—I'm so sorry, Lady Felicia."

"And now I've got to try and make this awful duke fall in love with me. Ugh."

Even though the Duke had hurt her feelings very badly, Jane still said, "He's not *that* awful, surely."

"Oh yes, he is. He's the worst duke in the world! Haven't you seen those terrible boots of his? All he cares about is this place, and that dreadful son of his, and those dull farmers, and—and that stupid pig, and *apple blights*!" Lady Felicia gave another caustic laugh. "And he's *old*, and boring, and dreadful to look at, and when we're married we'll never, ever go to London, and I'll for sure die of boredom, stuck here in this hideous, dreary, awful *dunghill*."

Jane found herself leaning a little backwards, as if Lady Felicia's harsh words came at her like a forceful gust of wind.

"But the Duke is terribly rich," Lady Felicia went on, lip curled in derision, "and titled, and when Lady Margaret sent her letter inviting us here, Mama said it was the greatest stroke of luck there ever was. And I've been trying, and *trying*, to get him to propose, but he's a great stupid block and I can barely stand to be near him."

Jane leaned back a little more.

On the one hand, she felt a certain amount of sympathy for Lady Felicia, because it was obviously very difficult to be in her position.

On the other hand, the Duke was *not* a great stupid

block, he was very intelligent and very handsome and very easy to stand next to and not at all boring and certainly not old, and Wakefield was wonderful, not the least bit dreadful, and although Hastings did have dunghills, that was to be expected here in the countryside and it absolutely wasn't a dunghill in and of itself, and the Duchess wasn't stupid, she really was a terrific pig, and—

Well, she could go on and on, with her own forceful gust of words if she chose to say them out loud.

But *should* she?

Even though she hated the idea of the Duke being tricked into marrying Lady Felicia, was it really any of her business?

Lamely she said, "I'm sorry you're so unhappy."

Lady Felicia shrugged. "I'll be happier when I'm rich again. And I can kick that awful Lady Margaret out of the house, and send that dreadful child off to Eton where he belongs. Thank you for listening, Miss Kent. I can trust in your discretion, can't I?"

"What?" said Jane, still rather lamely, because her mind was going in all kinds of directions at once.

"You won't tell anyone what I've said, will you? You must promise. Or Mama will *kill* me. Or Charles will. Maybe in a hunting accident."

Lady Felicia spoke in such a serious voice that Jane wondered if she meant it in an all too literal way. And yet Lady Felicia was also—obviously—a fluid dissembler. Now *here* was a terrible sort of puzzle. Jane could feel her brow knitting as she tried to sort through it, but Lady Felicia then repeated earnestly, "Promise me, Miss Kent. Please."

"I promise," Jane said, though uneasily.

"Thank you. Shall we go downstairs?"

This time Jane trailed behind Lady Felicia, and when

they got to the drawing-room the musicians had just begun to play. Cousin Gabriel came for her, and Jane had to concentrate on the steps, which gave her the opportunity to not watch the Duke dancing with Lady Felicia, but still, in the back of her mind she kept hearing Lady Felicia's bitter, angry voice saying all those terrible things. And it didn't go away, even when she danced next with Mr. Pressley, who not only was an excellent dancer, he kindly coached her through some of the more complicated movements; or when Sir Gregory claimed her hand after that, laughingly cutting off Viscount Whitton by claiming the privilege of age over youth; or when they had finished their quadrille and Jane thanked him, very sincerely, and felt rather strongly that she needed just a little bit of time to herself, to try and stop the endless and distressing loop of invective running through her brain.

So she slipped out of the drawing-room.

Where to next?

She thought about it.

Why not the billiards room, where she and the Duke and Wakefield had once had such a merry time?

Anthony had fetched for Lady Felicia, at her request, a goblet of cool lemonade, and as he handed it to her she said, smiling, "Thank you *so* much, Your Grace."

"You're welcome."

"What a charming little dance this is! And what a divine dancer you are. I'm enjoying this all so, so much. You have such charming neighbors—I'm so glad to be getting to know them all better. There's something so *real* about country folk, don't you think? I truly do believe the rustic life is far superior to any other."

Well, this was quite a turnaround, given Lady Felicia's

earlier remarks about London. For a moment Anthony wanted to point this out, and possibly in a sarcastic way, but then he only gave a slight bow, remembering how, when he was a little boy, he had overheard Mr. Pressley's equally learned predecessor, Mr. Markson, say, *Discretion is the better part of valor.* Which had seemed like an incomprehensible aphorism back then, but somehow seemed to make more sense in adulthood.

"And so tomorrow we're all to try our hands at some theatricals! How charming that will be! What play should we do? Something romantic, don't you think? Oh, I do hope that you and I will have a chance to perform together, Your Grace. Wouldn't that be wonderful?"

Anthony gave another slight bow.

"I'm already planning my pieces for the *soirée musicale.* Do you sing, Your Grace? It would be divine if you could accompany me. Or perhaps you could turn the pages. That would be *such* a help. You really do have the best pianoforte I've ever played upon. Hastings is so very, very charming. I wish I could stay here *forever.*"

He gave yet another slight bow.

"I'm so fond of Lady Margaret. And dear little Wakefield! Isn't he the most charming boy in all the world? I quite dote on him."

He would have bowed again, even if it made his back start to hurt, but luckily one of the neighborhood sprigs approached just then, and begged for the favor of Lady Felicia's hand in the cotillion that was forming, and so, with a last smile and blushing glance, off she went, and Anthony seized the opportunity to quietly leave the drawing-room and go upstairs to peek in on Wakefield, who, he was very glad to see, was sleeping peacefully, one small hand flung up beside his head, and with Snuffles curled up next to him in a tiny ball, softly snoring.

Wakefield looked so sweet and vulnerable that Anthony gazed at him for a long time, worrying about his tooth all over again, and it took a tremendous effort of will to keep himself from going over to the bed and kissing him on the top of his head and telling him that he loved him very, very much.

But he didn't want to disturb his sleep, and so quietly Anthony closed the door and went away.

Slowly Jane paced around the billiards table, trailing her hand along the smooth polished rail and thinking hard.

Lady Felicia had extracted a promise from her, but still she felt a powerful anxiety on the Duke's behalf. On Wakefield's behalf. She even managed to worry a little bit about Lady Margaret.

Could she possibly drop a warning hint—without betraying her word?

Maybe she could write a letter.

Dear Your Grace—

Is that how one would begin? It sounded a little odd somehow.

Dear Duke—

That was how Great-grandmother addressed him—"Duke," and not with the "dear," because Great-grandmother didn't seem to like him very much, if at all—but would it be appropriate for *her* to start her letter this way?

Oh, Jane, she chided herself, does it really matter?

Your Grace—

This salutation sounded a little curt, but seemed safe enough.

Your Grace,
It has come to my attention that there may be a possibility that someone within your sphere is, perhaps, not the most straightforward in their—

"Their" was bad grammar. However, all Jane could ethically do was to hint, so the vagueness might actually be helpful.

Your Grace,
It has come to my attention that there may be a possibility that someone within your sphere is, perhaps, not the most straightforward in their dealings with you. I confess to some concern as to their intentions, both in the near future and later on. Far be it from me to interfere in matters that do not involve me, yet it is my sincere hope that—

That what?

—THAT YOU REALIZE WHAT IS REALLY GOING ON, AND THAT YOU DON'T MARRY LADY FELICIA, BECAUSE I'M NOT AT ALL SURE ABOUT HER, EXCEPT THAT I DO KNOW SHE'S DEVIOUS, AND ALSO YOU SHOULD START LOOKING AT ME AGAIN, BECAUSE . . .

Jane realized that she was shouting at the Duke in all-capital letters. In an imaginary note which she didn't even know how to finish. Well, this wasn't going well.

"You're avoiding me."

Quickly Jane swung around. Viscount Whitton stood in the doorway leaning against the jamb, all muscled and exquisite in evening-clothes, gazing at her with those dark, lambent, sensuously heavy-lidded eyes.

"And you," she said, "are interrupting me."

"Interrupting you at what?"

"Thinking."

"Of me, I hope."

"Not really."

"Miss Kent," said the Viscount, caressingly, "you're killing me."

More talk of killing! What a curious (and possibly bloodthirsty) family these Merifields were.

The Viscount came into the room and closed the door behind him. Softly he said, "Can't you see how much I want you?"

Jane was a little ashamed to notice that she was actually glad for the distraction, so that she could stop worrying about the Duke. "I'm afraid I can't."

"Let me show you then."

"How would you do it?"

The Viscount came closer, gazing into her eyes with such focused intensity that she found herself thinking of how raptors paralyze their prey before pouncing on them. Or did she mean snakes? Not that snakes pounced, of course. Although—maybe there *were* snakes which pounced and she just didn't know about them. There was a great deal she didn't know about wildlife. Maybe Mr. Pressley could help her with that.

Also, did the Viscount routinely stare like this in order to get what he wanted? He looked, frankly, a trifle catatonic. But perhaps it was a technique that worked well on some women. He certainly gave the impression of someone who was used to having his own way. A sweet, musky scent filled her nostrils and suddenly Jane realized that the Viscount was wearing cologne.

She wrinkled her nose a little.

She didn't care for it.

It was heavy. Cloying. Artificial.

The Viscount said, softly and deliberately, "I'd like to lift you up onto that table, Miss Kent, and lay you down upon it. I want to pull up your pretty gown, and draw your legs apart, and—"

"Why should *I* have to be on my back?" interrupted Jane. "That would be uncomfortable. I think *you* should be on your back."

"What?"

Jane resisted the urge to snicker. She had thrown him off his stride. "A true gentleman," she said in a prim sort of way, "would offer to be in the least comfortable position."

"I—what?"

"I could perch on the rail, I suppose, but if you were vigorous I might fall backwards, and that would be uncomfortable too."

"Miss Kent, I—"

"Really, I'm not sure a billiards table is the best idea. What about standing up?"

"Well, I—"

"Also, what if someone came in and found us? Then we'd have to get married, I suppose. Isn't that how things work in your circle?"

"But—but that's exactly what I do want, Miss Kent."

"You do?"

"Yes, I want to marry you."

"Why?" She was a little sorry to see that the Viscount clearly felt himself to be on firm ground again. He was confident, suave, polished. Just like his shoes.

"Because you enchant me. Entrance me. My heart throbs for you."

It wasn't only his heart that was throbbing for her, evidently, if he wanted to have her on top of a billiards table. "Really."

"Yes. And consider—you'd be a viscountess. *And* the future Countess. The pater, you know, nearly got himself killed in a—er—accident. So maybe sooner rather than later. Won't you allow me to announce our engagement tonight? You'd make me the happiest man in the world."

Goodness, he really meant it. Or at least the part about wanting to marry her. Abruptly, into Jane's mind came again Lady Felicia's bitter voice.

And I've got to make the Duke marry me, Mama says, or we'll be ruined. More ruined than we already are, that is.

She looked speculatively up into the Viscount's face. "Do you want to marry me for my money? Because I haven't any, you know."

Plainly caught off-guard again, he said, less suavely, "But your great-grandmother—everybody knows she's as rich as Croesus. Surely she's going to dower you generously."

Jane didn't know who Croesus was, nor did she have any idea about a possible dowry, but she said, lying through her teeth and in a conspicuously self-pitying way, "Oh, she won't. She doesn't mind getting me some new clothes, but that's where she draws the line, she says."

"But—your jewels."

"A loan," said Jane promptly and mendaciously.

"But surely—"

"To be perfectly honest with you, I'm not at all certain she's going to let me keep on staying at the Hall. For one thing, I'm costing her an arm and leg with all the food I eat, and also I'm absolutely useless at sewing. Who knows? I might end up living in Lady Margaret's ruin. Although I shouldn't like to wear a canvas sack," she went on musingly. "It would be drafty, don't you think? Still, in summertime that might be nice."

A crimson flush of blood was mantling his perfect face. "You're mocking me."

For the very first time, the Viscount, red and upset and angry, seemed to Jane to be an actual human being. It was a decided improvement. Although she still didn't want in the least to marry him. She gave a small, unapologetic shrug, and he took a step closer.

"You damned little spitfire," he said. "You vixen. How in the hell do you know about all those positions? My God, I want you."

"Standing up or on the table?" Jane said, sweetly inquiring, and he took another step closer, so that they were practically touching, and the heavy, cloying smell of his cologne was making her nose all stuffed up.

"I'm going to kiss you, Miss Kent, until you're breathless. I'm going to kiss you until you scream for mercy, and beg for more. I'm going to kiss you like you've never been kissed before."

"I wouldn't do that if I were you."

"Oh, but I am," the Viscount said, very silky and deliberate, his eyes burning into her own.

"Really, I don't think you should."

"I'm going to."

"Don't."

"You know you want it," he said silkily, and put his hands on her shoulders and leaned down, his mouth coming closer . . . closer . . .

Just before their lips touched, Jane neatly brought her knee up and into his groin.

The Viscount let out an undignified squawk, his knees buckled, and he lurched away from her, his handsome face gone white and twisted into a grimace of shock and pain.

"You—you *kicked* me," he said in a strangled, high-pitched voice.

"I told you not to do it."

"You *kicked* me," he repeated, as if he was having trouble assimilating the fact.

"It's probably more accurate to say that I *kneed* you," said Jane thoughtfully. "I daresay I should spell it out for you, too, just to make sure you don't confuse it with N-E-E-D and get your hopes up again. It's K-N-E—"

"I know how it's spelled," he snarled, but still rather weakly. He staggered to the nearest armchair and flopped into it, legs sprawled out without any suavity at all, and glared up at her. "How *dare* you, you little—"

"If you call me a damned little spitfire or a vixen, I may do it again."

The Viscount blanched and sank deeper into his chair. "You, Miss Kent, are no lady."

"And you aren't much of a gentleman, if you can't hear when a woman says no."

"I suppose you learned how to attack men back in that uncivilized little muckheap you came from."

"Nantwich."

"Whatever."

"And if you mean by 'how to attack men' that I learned to defend myself, you're quite right. Nantwich girls are tough, you see."

"Yes, I certainly do see," he said, but unpleasantly.

Jane continued to look thoughtfully at him. "If you really want to get married, you may be overlooking someone who is, perhaps, genuinely interested in you."

"Oh, you mean the revolting Margaret, who follows me

around like a hungry old dog? No, thank you. I'd sooner go jump in that lake of theirs. And *you*—you impudent little nobody—could have had me if you'd only played your cards right."

Jane shrugged again. "Well, this certainly has been charming, and possibly even divine, but if you'll excuse me, I'll be leaving you now."

"Good," said the Viscount, still quite unpleasantly. "Goodbye and good riddance."

For a moment Jane wondered if he might like to know that his formerly perfect hair was somewhat disordered. Personally she thought it looked better that way. But neither the information nor the compliment was likely to be received with any gratitude, and so she merely began strolling toward the door.

Anthony had just come downstairs when his eye was caught by a gleam of yellow far along the corridor, in the opposite direction from the drawing-room, and he paused, squinting.

It was Margaret in her sunny yellow evening-gown.

For some reason she had left her own party, and was standing in front of the closed door to the billiards room, statue-like in her immobility.

What the devil, he thought, and began walking toward her.

He was some ten paces away when the door opened and Jane came out, almost bumping right into Margaret.

"Oh, excuse me, Lady Margaret," she said, looking rather uneasy. "Have you—have you been here long?"

"Long enough," said Margaret stonily, and stepped aside.

Jane moved past her and into the corridor, then saw him and looked even more uneasy as she began walking his way.

What the devil *and* what the hell, Anthony thought. "Hullo," he said when she came close.

"Hullo. Your Grace."

"Everything all right?"

She stopped and looked up at him, so lovely and beautiful and beguiling and desirable in her rose-pink gown that he nearly keeled over with a sudden renewed surge of longing and also with despair.

"Well," Jane said, "I'm not so sure about that."

"What do you mean?"

"Oh, Christ, an *audience*," somebody said from further down the corridor, sounding very irritable, and Anthony glanced past Jane to see that Viscount Whitton had emerged from the billiards room. He saw at once that while the Viscount was still smoldering like anything, he was also noticeably ruffled in his appearance.

What the devil *and* what the hell *and* what the devil.

Plus, what the *hell*.

Had the Viscount been making love to Jane?

And had Jane been doing the same to *him*?

Anthony looked again at Jane, his despair instantly multiplying by a factor of ten. Or maybe a hundred. She was still neat as a pin, although that was hardly conclusive, and he would have given a great deal to know why she seemed so uneasy. Was *he* making her edgy? Or was it due to being, well, *discovered* by Margaret? And why did Margaret look so miserable?

God, what a scene.

The Viscount stood frowning and frozen just past the doorway, Margaret was stiff as a board just a few feet away with her head turned toward the opposite wall, Jane stood stock-still, and altogether Anthony's earlier sensation of being an unwilling actor in a play returned in full force, only now it was worse because it felt as if he was an actor who had completely blanked on his lines. He had no idea what was going on, except that everyone, himself included, seemed very uncomfortable.

He took a step closer to Jane, and whispered:

"I say, has that fellow been bothering you?"

"No."

"Oh." It would have been easier if she had said yes, because then he could go and—do what? Say nasty things to the Viscount? Kick him out of the house? Challenge him to pistols at dawn?

All of these were appealing options, but unfortunately without basis in grounded fact. More wretched than ever, Anthony ran a hand through his hair, suppressed an impulse to clutch at it, and blurted out to Jane in a low voice:

"Has he been kissing you?"

Jane's expression abruptly changed. Her big gray eyes went cold like a wintry sky, and her lips pressed together. Then she answered, in an equally low voice, but fiercely:

"Why should you care?"

She had never talked to him that way before, and Anthony immediately felt himself devolve into hopeless confusion. "I—uh—well, I—I mean, that is—"

"Also, what right do you even have to ask me that?"

"I—none—but I—I was just—"

"Just interfering where you shouldn't, you mean."

"Jane, I—I didn't intend—uh—it was just that I was worried about you—"

"It's *yourself* you should be worried about. You infuriating man."

"What? Why? About what? Oh, Jane, I'm awfully sorry if—if I've offended you—"

"Never mind," she whispered fiercely. "Just—never mind."

Then she walked around and past him, and he stood there in the corridor with his hands hanging loose and empty at his sides, feeling helpless and unhappy and bewildered, and quite entirely full to the brim with despair.

Chapter 12

It was Monday morning, and Jane and Wakefield were sitting across from each other at the large rectangular table in the vicarage study, both of them working on some math problems. In his seat at the head of the table, Mr. Pressley was silently reading essays that they had written about the English astronomer John Flamsteed, who in 1675 was appointed the very first Astronomer Royal, and ended up cataloging over three thousand stars, a very impressive achievement for the time.

Soft white winter sunlight poured agreeably into the study, the fire in the hearth crackled in a cheery way, and Jane should have been pleased that she was making excellent progress in the art and science of long division, but her mood was not good and had been not good since Friday evening's party and dance.

Every day, every waking hour, she had been bracing herself for news from Hastings. About the Duke's betrothal to Lady Felicia.

To add to her anxiety, nobody from Hastings had shown up at church yesterday morning, and Jane had had a hard time concentrating on Mr. Pressley's succinct, insightful sermon on the topic of forgiveness.

Instead she had been busy imagining the Duke and Lady Felicia kissing and hugging and so on (it was the *so on* part that was bothering her the most), and also feeling terrible to be entertaining such thoughts while in church. She had hoped that God, unlike herself, was paying attention to the sermon and was Himself in a forgiving mood.

Jane now figured out what the remainder would be if one divided 5,487 by 23, and was just about to write it out neatly when Mrs. McKenzie poked her head into the study to dourly announce that a parishioner had arrived in dire need of counsel, and could Mr. Pressley please come?

"Of course," answered Mr. Pressley, getting up at once. "Carry on," he said to Jane and Wakefield. "I'll be back directly."

As soon as the sound of his footsteps had faded away, Wakefield set aside his pencil and said:

"I say, Jane, the most tremendous things have been happening."

Jane put her pencil down too. Of course it was wrong to gossip but she was going to do it anyway, because she was dying for news, and hopefully God was still in a forgiving mood. "Really?"

"Yes. First of all, on Saturday morning Aunt Margaret was wearing black again. I asked her why, but she told me to be quiet and eat my breakfast. And then I got ready to drop my spoon into my porridge."

"Why?"

"Because I had been kindicting an experiment."

"Oh, I see. What kind of experiment?"

"Do you remember how I told you last week about Aunt Margaret suddenly not wearing black *and* not noticing me dropping my spoon into my porridge? *Or* my fork?"

"Oh yes, I do remember."

"So my experiment was to see how many things I could drop in my porridge before she noticed."

"Ah."

"But I had only just picked up my spoon when Aunt Margaret told me to not even *think* about it. Which means that if a fairy *did* put magic juice into Aunt Margaret's eyes, it wore out."

Jane nodded, and Wakefield went on:

"It also means my experiment is over, I suppose. But I'm not sure what I proved. I still don't think fairies are real. Also on Saturday, Lady Thingummy kept trying to get Father to go for a ride or a walk, or to show her round the conservatory, but he wouldn't."

"Do you mean Lady Felicia?"

"Yes, that's right. And I *think* Lady Thingummy's mother was angry with her, because when nobody else was looking I saw her sticking her elbow into Lady Thingummy's side. As if she wanted her to do something but she wasn't. *And* that Viscount What's-his-name was walking in a very funny way. I laughed when I saw it, because he was *waddling*, Jane."

"Dear me."

"Yes, and also on Saturday Aunt Margaret had a headache for the rest of the day and stayed up in her room. And yesterday too. Father and I got up early and went for a ride, and when we got back my tooth was hurting again, so he had Nurse give me a little bit of lidium and I went to lie down with Snuffles, and Father stayed with me the whole time. That's why we didn't go to church."

Jane looked with concern at him. He did seem a little peaky. "She gave you laudanum, Wakefield?"

"Yes, that's what I said."

"Are you feeling better now?"

"Oh yes. But Father's sent for the dentist," said Wakefield gloomily. "Some chap from Bath. Father says he's nice, but how nice can it be when somebody's messing about in your mouth?" He brooded for a few moments, then brightened again. "But I haven't told you the *most* tremendous thing yet, Jane. At breakfast today, an express came for Lady Thingummy from her husband."

"Do you mean Lady Silsbury? The Countess?"

"Yes. Why isn't he a count, instead of an earl? Or why isn't she a—an earlesse?"

"That's a good question. I'm afraid I have no idea."

"We'll have to ask Mr. Pressley. At any rate, Lady Thingummy screamed while she was reading the letter, and Marner was so surprised he dropped a dish of scrambled eggs."

"Oh! I hope nobody was angry with him."

"No, Father said the Duchess would love them. Don't you want to know what was in the letter, Jane?"

"Yes indeed. Was it—was it terrible news?"

"Not a bit of it. It turns out Earl What's-his-name—did you know he had two broken legs, by the way?"

"No."

"Yes, he broke them in a hunting accident, and had to lie around at home supposedly, until they got better. But while Lady Thingummy and Viscount What's-his-name and the other Lady Thingummy were here, he snuck off to London and made a bet at his club about which fly would land on somebody's head and he won thirty thousand pounds."

Jane stared at Wakefield. "My goodness."

"Yes, and here's what's even tremendouser. Lady Thingummy—the old one—said, 'Thank *God*,' and she took her napkin from her lap and dropped it right into her porridge. You should have seen how it sank, Jane. It was *ripping*. I was going to try it myself, even though I was pretty sure Aunt Margaret would notice, but then Lady Thingummy—the old one—got up and she said, 'Well, we're off then,' and then the other Lady Thingummy got up, and Viscount What's-his-name did too, and they were all smiling so much that they looked like *clowns*. I got up too and went to stand behind Father's chair, just in case."

"Just in case what?"

"In case they started juggling or something like that."

"Did they?" Jane asked. Because after hearing that somebody actually won thirty thousand pounds betting on a fly, anything seemed possible.

"No, they only went upstairs to have their things packed. Half an hour later they were gone."

"Gone?"

"Yes. And all their baggage, too. I know it was half an hour because I asked Bunch how long it took, and Bunch is always right. I say, Jane, your eyes are all round again, like the time you thought the Duchess was my mother."

"It's just that I'm so surprised."

"I was too. But isn't it jolly? They were awfully dull. Didn't *you* think so?"

"Well, I didn't know them very well," Jane prevaricated, though secretly she not only agreed with Wakefield that it was jolly that they had left, she was also glad, glad to the heights and depths of her soul, and also the width, that the Duke was not engaged to the devious Lady Felicia, and, moreover, that Wakefield wasn't in danger of being shipped off to boarding school against his will, and she even found it within her to be glad that Lady Margaret wasn't in danger of being shipped off somewhere as well. Though Jane also wondered if

Lady Margaret was unhappy about the Viscount going away.

Waddling away.

Jane grinned inside herself.

"Ow," Wakefield suddenly said, clapping a hand to his cheek.

"Oh, dear, is it your tooth again?"

"Yes."

"Is it bad?"

"Yes."

Jane looked at him with fresh concern. His sweet, fine-boned face was abruptly pinched with pain. She hated to see him like this. "Do you feel like you need a little more laudanum?"

"Yes, but I haven't finished my math problems."

"Don't worry about that. I think you should go home, Wakefield. What do you say?"

"I do want to be at home," he admitted, and she answered at once:

"Come on then."

They went to the front hall and got his jacket, and Jane helped him put it on, and together they walked outside and to the pony-cart where Higson sat patiently waiting. Wakefield didn't protest when she insisted on giving him a boost up, and if she needed any further confirmation that he really felt unwell, she had it when Higson made as if to hand him the reins and Wakefield replied:

"No, thank you, Higson, I don't want to drive right now."

"Higson," said Jane, "as soon as you get home, will you make sure the Duke knows that Wakefield needs him?"

"And Snuffles, too," added Wakefield.

"To be sure I will, miss," said Higson, and Jane saw how concerned *he* was too, and was satisfied that the

Duke would know posthaste. She stepped back and said, "Goodbye. Dear Wakefield, I'll be thinking of you."

"Goodbye, Jane."

They drove off at a spanking pace, and Jane went back inside to the study. Mr. Pressley still hadn't returned, which made her think that the poor parishioner, whoever it was, really was in dire straits. But if anyone could help, it would be Mr. Pressley, for whom she had come to feel an ever-increasing respect and admiration; he conducted himself with such calm, quiet dignity and kindness.

Jane picked up her pencil and immersed herself in long division again, though in the back of her mind was a continual, niggling worry about Wakefield.

When she returned home to the Hall, she had a hearty luncheon and was about to go meet Monsieur Voclaine in the ballroom for another lesson, but was intercepted by Great-grandmother, who—with a sardonic kind of satisfaction—showed her a note from Lady Margaret, who had written, in curt, but stiffly correct language, that due to circumstances beyond her control, the upcoming ball at Hastings, as well as the theatrical performance, the *soirée musicale*, and the *petit pique-nique faux on plein air* were all cancelled.

"It's just as well," said Great-grandmother. "Breakfast in a conservatory! Only imagine the humidity. I do wonder what poor Lady Margaret could have been thinking."

Jane could have told her, or at least offered up a guess, but she didn't, and gave back the note to Great-grandmother, then went on to her lesson, which had her grappling all over again with the annoyingly complex intricacies of the cotillion, which turned out to be an excellent way to divert her thoughts from the Duke.

Mr. Rowland, as resplendent as Anthony remembered him with his fluffy ginger hair and whiskers and even the same vivid peacock-blue waistcoat, arrived early on Tuesday, and Margaret brought him up straightaway to Wakefield's room. Anthony sat next to Wakefield, who lay in his bed, a little drowsy with laudanum but rigid and wary for all that, with Snuffles, previously tucked into the curve of Wakefield's armpit, now struggling to his tiny feet and eyeing the newcomer with hostility.

"Wakefield," Margaret said, "this is Mr. Rowland, our dentist, and I want you to do everything he says."

"I *won't*," answered Wakefield, reaching out for Anthony; and Anthony enfolded that small hand in his own larger one.

"You most certainly will," said Margaret, but the words were barely out of her mouth before Mr. Rowland said:

"How do you do, Your Grace. And, more importantly," he added, his voice friendly and gentle, "how do *you* do, My Lord?"

"Terrible," answered Wakefield, and Snuffles barked as loud as he could, which was surprisingly noisy given his diminutive size.

"Oh, that nasty dog," said Margaret in disapproval. "I'll have it taken out right away, Mr. Rowland."

"By no means, Lady Margaret," replied Mr. Rowland, with a nice mixture of deference and firmness. "He's very right to protect his master. What a delightful little creature he is—I had a pug myself when I was a boy. How he snored! My Lord, may I sit next to you and your father?"

"No. Go away."

"Wakefield!" Margaret was scandalized. "Mr. Rowland has come all the way from Bath just to see you. You're to be quiet and do what you're told."

"*You* go away," said Wakefield, his voice trembling, and Anthony said:

"That might be best, Meg."

He could see that she was about to protest, but then Mr. Rowland added, in his gentle, tactful way:

"You needn't worry, Lady Margaret. We'll take very good care of His Lordship, I promise you."

Margaret scowled, but left the room, although she could have, if she wanted to, closed the door more quietly than she did.

Mr. Rowland's eyes were twinkling ever so slightly as he said, "Now, My Lord, it's just we men, which is bound to be much more comfortable, don't you think? Are you sure I can't sit next to you, just for a bit? I won't do anything without asking you first."

"I suppose so," said Wakefield ungraciously, and, not at all put out by his patient's hostile tone, Mr. Rowland went to wash his hands very thoroughly in the basin on top of the dresser before coming to sit down on the side of the bed.

"What's your dog's name, My Lord?"

"Snuffles."

"Ah, that's excellent. I named *my* pug Rolypoly. 'Roly' for short, of course. Is Snuffles a good snorer?"

"Oh yes, he snores like anything. It's capital," answered Wakefield, with just a little more animation.

"Yes indeed. It always sent me right off to sleep. Does Snuffles try to eat moths and butterflies? Roly did, though there was only the one time I ever saw him catch one. I wish I could tell you what his face looked like with the moth in his mouth! He spat it out and ran away, and I laughed so hard I actually retched."

Thanks to this engaging anecdote, Wakefield's suspicions softened sufficiently to both allow Mr. Rowland to pet Snuffles for a little while, and also to let him (after he went and washed his hands again) examine the afflicted tooth, though the whole entire time he held on to Anthony's hand very tightly, and Anthony wished it was *his* tooth that was bad, and would have cheerfully changed places with Wakefield in a heartbeat.

The family were gathered in the Little Drawing-room, and Crenshaw had just announced that dinner was ready, when there came the sounds of boot-heels, firm and quick, in the hallway, along with other, lighter footsteps moving even more quickly.

James the footman came in—actually, he rather burst into the drawing-room, clearly nipping in ahead of someone else—and just barely had time to say, "His Grace the Duke of Radcliffe," before the Duke himself came striding in.

Jane saw at once that this wasn't the aloof, impossibly distant, somewhat more carefully dressed duke she had recently seen at Hastings. His tawny mane of hair was in wild confusion, his neckcloth was awry, and his boots were just as scuffed as ever. Even though Jane was very conflicted in her thinking (and feeling) about him, still she immediately thought to herself how very and delightfully handsome he was. And then his dark-blue eyes sought hers directly and held them.

"Good evening, Duke," said Great-grandmother, with a kind of barbed sweetness. "What a surprise. Have you come to join us for dinner? We'll have another place set for you."

"Good evening, ma'am," said the Duke, then nodded at Livia and Cousin Gabriel. "How do you do. I apologize for coming at such an hour, but I've brought a note for Miss Kent, and to beg a great favor from her."

He advanced into the room and pulled from his great-coat pocket a letter, slightly crumpled and also dotted with dog hairs, which he gave to Jane.

She opened it right away.

Dear Jane,

My bad Tooth must come out tomorrow and it's all very foul. But it would be a little less foul if you could come and keep me Company. The Dentist chap isn't bad but I am still Afraid although please don't tell anybody I said so.

Your friend
Wakefield

Jane looked up at the Duke. "Of course I'll come! Oh, poor Wakefield! What time do you want me there?"

The Duke's face relaxed just a little. "That's splendid, Jane. I can't thank you enough. Can you come first thing? Around eight or so?"

"Yes, certainly."

"Your Grace, is Wakefield ill?" asked Livia. "Can we help at all?"

He turned to her. "Thank you. He's got an infected tooth that's to be pulled tomorrow morning. It's not a permanent one, which is the silver lining, but it's still going to be miserable for the poor fellow."

"I take it," said Great-grandmother, "that Wakefield has asked for Jane?"

The Duke nodded. "Yes."

"My dear Jane, are you quite certain you wish to attend? It's sure to be an unpleasant procedure. I remember when your grandfather Titus, in fact, had an extraction as a child. I like to think I'm made of sterner stuff, but in truth I had to leave the room and ask for smelling-salts."

Jane saw that the Duke's face had tightened with anxiety again but he said, looking at her with a kind of painful gallantry:

"It *will* be unpleasant. If you'd prefer not to come after all, I'll of course understand."

"My great-grandmother Kent had several teeth pulled," Jane said, "so I know what it's like. And I expect your dentist is a great deal better than the man who did the pulling back in Nantwich. I'll be there. Your Grace."

"Thank you, Jane," he said, with so much gratitude that she forgave him for being such an ass lately, and smiled up at him.

"Shall I have a place set for you, Duke?" interposed Great-grandmother. "Otherwise I'm afraid our dinner may be a trifle spoilt."

"No—thank you, ma'am. I'll be off. My apologies again for disrupting your dinner hour. See you tomorrow, Jane."

"Goodbye," she said, "and please send Wakefield my love," then watched him nod again and leave the drawing-room with those long loping strides of his. It really was quite a charming way to walk, all fluid and athletic. Honestly, if he *had* been wearing an immense ermine-trimmed dukish sort of cloak, it would ripple behind him in a very delightful way.

Suddenly Jane noticed how incredibly empty the room seemed without the Duke, and she also noticed that in her heart she seemed to feel a similar sudden emptiness in his absence. Startled, she stared at the doorway through which he had passed. Was it possible? Was it really possible that she was—

"Gabriel," said Livia, "I wonder if we ought to have a dentist in to look at the children."

"By all means," answered Cousin Gabriel. "Have you noticed any problems, my love?"

"No, I *think* they're fine, but how can one know for sure?"

"The Penhallows," Great-grandmother remarked, "are famed for the superiority of their teeth."

Livia laughed. "I remember your saying that, Granny, the first time we met. Do you recall that ghastly scene in the Orrs' garden? You accused me of being stubborn as a mule. And you didn't like my red hair, either. You said there hadn't been such a common shade in the line since Sir Everard Penhallow married into the York family three hundred years ago."

"What *I* remember most," Cousin Gabriel said, "was the outrageous act that preceded it."

Livia smiled and gave him a sparkling glance. "Outrageous indeed. Jane, surely your great-grandfather had a useful pamphlet about dental health?"

With a little start Jane emerged from her wondering daze. "Oh yes," she answered. "He suggested taking a mouthful of hay that had been soaked in vinegar during a full moon, then biting into it with one's left hand held over one's head to find out if one has abscesses."

She laughed, but saw that Great-grandmother apparently found no humor in it, but was instead looking at her quite pointedly, a thoughtful, even slightly troubled expression on her face.

And all during dinner, Jane noticed, Great-grandmother seemed to be in rather a bad mood, and she couldn't help but speculate—uneasily—if it had something to do with herself.

"Where's Jane, Father?" said Wakefield, for probably the tenth time that morning, and patiently Anthony replied:

"She'll be here, my boy, worry not."

"But what if she *doesn't* come?"

"She promised she would."

"What if she changes her mind?"

"I really don't think she will."

"Yes, but what if she gets in a horrible carriage accident on the way here?"

"Unlikely."

"Or what if the carriage is attacked by highwaymen?"

"Even more unlikely."

"What if she *does* get here, but Aunt Margaret won't let her come upstairs?"

This actually seemed remotely possible to Anthony, but he answered calmly:

"Bunch would come and let us know that Jane is here."

Wakefield nodded. "That's true." Pale and wan, he lay in his bed propped up on pillows, with the faithful Snuffles at his side, and Anthony, propped up next to him and stretched out on top of the covers, reached over to ruffle his light-brown hair just a little.

"Father, what if I scream?"

"Scream as much as you need to."

"Can I? Aunt Margaret said I must be a good little marquis and not make a peep."

"Rubbish."

"Really? Father, have *you* ever screamed?"

"Oh yes, quite a bit. After I fell out of that tree, you know, and when they had to move me to bring me inside."

"Did somebody tell you to stop?"

"Yes, my father did, and my mother, too. So did my brother and your aunt Margaret. Entirely unhelpful commentary, I might add. But Wake, you'll have laudanum, remember, and that will help a lot with the pain."

"I hope so. Will Snuffles be scared if I scream?"

"That's a very good thought. Do you want Jane to hold him?"

"No, I want Jane to hold *me*. Could Bunch take care of Snuffles?"

"I'm sure he wouldn't mind."

"Let's do that then. I wouldn't want Snuffles to be scared. He's very sinsotive, you know."

"Do you mean sensitive?"

"Yes, that's what I said. I say, Father, someone's coming. Is it Jane?" Wakefield looked eagerly to the doorway, and Anthony did too, and a few moments later Margaret—dismal in her standard black and her expression reminding him of the nasty glowering lemon-sucking face of old Myles Farr the fourth (fifth?) duke—was ushering Jane into Wakefield's bedchamber.

"Jane, you're here!" exclaimed Wakefield joyfully.

Clad in the same soft, pink woolen gown she had worn that unforgettable day when she had come over to Hastings with Wakefield after lessons and they all had had such a merry time at luncheon together, and also walking through the topiary and playing billiards, after which he had driven her home and given her chocolates and blithered like anything and kissed her (and been kissed), Jane smiled warmly at Wakefield, and came to stand at the side of the bed. "Of course I'm here."

"I was afraid you wouldn't be."

"Wild horses couldn't keep me away."

Snuffles came staggering amidst the bedclothes to greet Jane, his funny little curly tail wagging vigorously, and Jane bent down to pet him fondly.

"Jane," said Wakefield, "I might scream."

"No, you won't," put in Margaret. "You're going to be a proper patient and be quiet."

"*You* be quiet! *You're* not the one getting a tooth

pulled! Father, make her go away!" Wakefield's voice was suddenly shrill and he had gone dead-white.

"How dare you talk to me that way." Margaret, on the other hand, was a bright furious red.

"Meg, you'd better go," Anthony said, doing his best to keep his voice calm even though he wanted to take Margaret by the scruff of her neck and shove her out the door. "You're upsetting Wake, and it's the last thing he needs."

"It's my right to be here!" she retorted angrily. "I'm *family*. Not this—this stranger!" She pronounced "stranger" as one might utter a filthy expletive, and Wakefield said shrilly:

"Jane's not a *stranger*! Jane's my *friend*! Go away, go *away*!" And he burst into noisy tears, just as Mr. Rowland came into the room. He looked with concern at Wakefield, who had buried his face in Anthony's shoulder, and said:

"My Lord, what's wrong? Are you in very great pain?"

Before Wakefield could answer, Margaret snapped:

"Never mind. I can see when I'm not wanted. You can send for me if I'm needed. Though I'm sure you'll all be happy to exclude me." She shot a deeply venomous glance at Jane and stalked out of the room.

There was a silence.

As Anthony stroked Wakefield's hair and tried not to hate Margaret, Snuffles valiantly came climbing up his chest to reach Wakefield and lick his ear, which made Wakefield giggle, instantly lightening the mood in the room, and Anthony said:

"Jane, may I introduce you to Mr. Rowland, our dentist? Mr. Rowland, this is our friend Miss Kent, who's going to stay during the procedure."

"Well, that's splendid," said Mr. Rowland. "And that's what *you* want, My Lord?"

"Oh yes," answered Wakefield, lifting his head from Anthony's shoulder. "I told Jane I might scream. Jane, you won't mind, will you?"

"Of course I won't," she said stoutly, and Anthony, looking at her across the expanse of the bed, felt so much gratitude and admiration that he would have sworn that around her strong beautiful self was an actual nimbus of grace, glowingly full of life.

Jane didn't need smelling salts, or feel as if she had to leave the room during Wakefield's extraction, but it *was* extremely distressing to see Wakefield's suffering.

Fortunately Mr. Rowland was quick and kind and deft, and the Duke himself was nothing less than a reassuring tower of strength, holding Wakefield's hand and talking calmly and lovingly throughout, and Wakefield, who kept his eyes squeezed shut, never saw that his father's face was white as snow and that he was sweating heavily.

As for herself, she was, as Wakefield had requested, snuggled up next to him on the bed with one arm curved beneath his back and the hand of her other arm clasping his smaller one. She kept herself soft and easy, and added her own reassuring murmurs during the intervals when the Duke briefly fell silent to draw a deep breath or to wipe his face on the shoulder of his jacket.

When it was all over, and the tooth had been removed intact, and Wakefield's cheek was stuffed with soft cotton, Mr. Rowland said heartily:

"Well done, My Lord, well done. You did beautifully."

Wakefield opened his eyes to half-slits and weakly said around the cotton: "Yes, but I screamed."

"I don't mean to offend you, My Lord, or hurt your feelings, but you didn't even get close to the volume of several of my adult patients. Indeed, there was that one gentleman in Bath who made so much noise that part of the ceiling fell down."

Wakefield gave a ghost of a laugh, and Mr. Rowland took a bit of clean cotton and very gently wiped away the tears on Wakefield's face.

"Now, My Lord, I'm going to give you a little more laudanum so that you can rest and sleep. Shall we have Snuffles brought back in?"

"Yes, please."

"I'll go get him," said Jane, but Wakefield whispered:

"Don't go, Jane. Father, can *you* get Snuffles?"

"Of course, my boy." The Duke gave Wakefield's hand a little squeeze, released it, and got up. He ran both his hands through his hair, which made him look more disheveled and handsome than ever, and gave Jane such a long look of both exhaustion and thankfulness that she seemed to feel it directly in the region of her heart. She gave him an encouraging little nod in return, and he went loping away to find Bunch, who earlier had solemnly received Snuffles from Wakefield, mentioned a nice little marrow-bone he had set aside for Snuffles in his pantry, and promised to look after him most carefully.

Mr. Rowland got up and began to prepare a dose of laudanum, and a few moments later a short, plump, elderly lady, dressed plainly in gray with a capacious ruffled cap atop her white hair, bustled into the room.

"Master Wakefield!" she exclaimed, hurrying over to the bedside. "How are we feeling? Oh my, our cheek *is* big and fat, isn't it? Your naughty, naughty father wouldn't let me come before, but I'm here now. How do you do, miss," she said, coldly, to Jane, then went on, beaming down at Wakefield, "A little castor oil is *just* the thing to set you aright, I've the bottle right here in my apron—"

"Nurse, go 'way," said Wakefield, feebly but angrily. "I don't want you."

"Not want me?" the old lady said, bridling. "Upon my soul! Of course you do, Master Wakefield. I'm sure you don't mean it. Nurse always knows best, doesn't she? Now, we'll just have a nice spoonful of castor oil, and—"

"Jane, make her go 'way," Wakefield said, pleading, and Jane, knowing she lacked the authority to order Nurse around, looked with equal pleading at Mr. Rowland. He promptly said:

"Yes, yes, it's very kind of you, Mrs.—Niddy, isn't it?—but castor oil isn't quite what I would suggest at this moment. Now, as I'm sure you would agree, His Lordship needs absolute quiet in order to rest and recover, and I'm also sure, knowing you have only his best interests in mind, the last thing in the world you want would be to see him deprived of it. Thank you very much for stopping by."

Jane watched with deep appreciation as throughout this short, tactful speech, Mr. Rowland managed to nimbly shepherd Nurse out of the room and close the door in her face in such a way that it seemed as if she was doing *him* a good turn.

"Jane," whispered Wakefield, "he's a good 'un, isn't he?"

She smiled down at him. "Yes, he is. How are you feeling, dear Wakefield?"

"Tired. And rather awful."

"Do you have a lot of pain?"

"It's not so bad. It's just that blood tastes terrible."

She nodded. "Once, when I was a girl, I was running along the high street in Nantwich, and I tripped and fell and banged my cheek against a rock. My gum was bleeding quite a lot, and I'll always remember the taste of it."

"Did you scream, Jane?"

"Oh my goodness, yes. And I cried, too."

"Well," Wakefield said, "if you *and* Father screamed when you were little, I suppose it's all right that I did."

"You were splendid, dear Wakefield."

"Was I really?"

"Oh yes. I'm very, very proud of you." She dropped a light kiss on top of his head, and he smiled, just a little.

"That felt nice, Jane."

Mr. Rowland came back to the bed and gave Wakefield some laudanum on a spoon, and then the Duke returned with Snuffles in the crook of his arm, and Snuffles was so incredibly glad to see Wakefield that Jane had to blink back tears watching their happy reunion.

"Father, Nurse came," said Wakefield, over Snuffles' joyful whimpers.

"Yes, I saw her in the corridor," answered the Duke, a little grimly, as he sat down next to Wakefield, "with the telltale bulge of a bottle in her apron. She nipped in, didn't she? And against my direct orders. I'm afraid I wasn't very friendly toward her just now."

"Did you scream at her, Father?"

"No, of course not. But I *was* rather severe."

"I wish I'd seen it."

"You will," returned the Duke, "if she tries to come in again."

Wakefield nodded. "Father," he said drowsily, "Jane kissed me."

"Did she?"

"Yes, and I liked it. It was very kimfitting."

"Do you mean comforting?"

"Yes, that's what I said. Jane, you're not going to go 'way, are you, while I'm sleeping?"

Jane looked inquiringly at the Duke, and he nodded at once. She said, “No, I’ll stay as long as you like.”

“Good,” murmured Wakefield, and very shortly was fast asleep, with Snuffles settled into a furry ball at his side, gently and serenely snoring.

Chapter 13

From his chair next to Wakefield's bed, Anthony glanced across the room to the three big windows facing out onto the back gardens and topiary.

After a few hours of intermittent snow-flurries, the great gray canopy of the sky had gradually cleared to muted sunshine, and now afternoon had just begun to fade into the soft pewter, blue, and violet shades of early winter twilight.

Soon, he thought, the stars would start to show themselves.

And he also thought for a few moments about a book he had recently been reading, on the invention and development of the modern telescope.

How fascinating—indeed, how wondrous—to get a better glimpse at the infinite mysteries of the cosmos.

Then Anthony looked back to the bed, where Wakefield lay sleeping. Snuffles was next to him, and next to Snuffles was Jane, napping.

She lay on her side facing Wakefield, resting her cheek on one hand and the other hand stretched out toward Wakefield as if to make sure he was still there.

Her pale flaxen hair had come loose from its casual

knot low at the back of the head, and two or three long wavy tendrils splayed across the shoulder of her pink gown and onto her breast.

In repose she looked a little younger, a little less resolute than she usually did, and somebody who didn't know her, gazing at her from a chair only four or five feet away, would be entirely unaware that when she smiled, the most enchanting dimples appeared on either cheek, as if by magic, and that her big dark-lashed gray eyes would dance in a very appealing way.

But *he* did.

He did, and it made him glad to know it.

It made him glad, and happy, and full of a mysterious yearning which surprised him in its intensity.

Then Anthony leaned back in his chair, stretched out his legs, and wearily let his head drop back against the padded top-rail.

What a day it had been.

As the hours had passed, Wakefield had drifted in and out of sleep, Mr. Rowland had flitted in and out to cast an appraising eye on things in between seeing to anybody else at Hastings who wanted to consult with him, both Margaret and Nurse had stayed away (whether wisely or petulantly remained unclear), and Bunch had come and gone with offers of refreshment and to himself bear Snuffles away and outside before promptly returning him to Wakefield.

Breen, Joe, and Sam, he reported on one visit, had been begging most abjectly for admittance into the house, Wakefield had said that Snuffles would very much like having them near, and so now, on the hearthrug before the fire, the three big dogs lay sleeping in a blurry interconnected heap and positively radiating contentment.

For a few moments it all seemed so natural and so

normal—Wakefield, Jane, the dogs, and himself—that it suddenly was rather shocking.

Anthony looked again at Jane, as if seeing her anew.

He remembered how, last week, on the day of that ghastly tea, he had applied himself diligently to *not* wanting Jane here. To deliberately, arduously, and successfully shut himself off from her. He had spoken to her quite dukishly, he supposed—exactly as if she didn't matter to him at all.

Even so, and although she had rather snapped at him on the night of the dinner-party and dance, and gazed up at him with so much coldness that it seemed to freeze his very soul, when Wakefield had asked for her, ungrudgingly had she come.

Which said something quite marvelous about Jane.

Anthony knew he would have gotten through Wakefield's ordeal on his own if he had had to. But Jane being here had made all the difference in the world—not just for him but, more importantly, for Wakefield also. How Wake had clung to her!

And as the day wore on, Anthony had felt something within himself.

He was . . .

It took him a while to find the words. They didn't come easily.

He was . . . opening up to Jane again.

Opening up to her like . . .

Several analogies presented themselves, one after the other.

Things that opened.

Flower-buds, eyes, bottles, books . . .

Doors and windows . . .

Gates, drawbridges, sluices, oysters . . .

Oysters? Anthony slid a little lower in his chair.

Comparing himself to an oyster was rather undignified, but still apt.

Because, dammit, they *did* open.

He smiled a little, picturing himself as the world's largest oyster.

His Slipperiness the Duke of Oyster.

Swanning about the ocean floor in a seaweed cape and a crown glittering with diamonds and pearls from a pirate's treasure chest, loftily ordering all the mussels and eels and lobsters about.

The image sprang vividly into his mind.

Especially the bit about the pirate's treasure chest.

As a boy he had dreamed of diving deep into the sea . . .

. . . Finding a glorious pirate shipwreck . . .

. . . Swimming in and among the ghostly wreckage . . .

Suddenly he really *was* an oyster, he could feel the pulse of the ocean's cool tide against his face—shell?—and underneath his feet (did oysters *have* feet? He did, somehow) was the shifting surface of the sandy floor.

A seahorse bobbed up to him, bowing low, and from atop a nearby rock an octopus—a friend of his?—cheerily waved all its tentacles. A large swirling crowd of tiny sardines shimmered up, dipping their little heads in unison, and spun themselves away, and with a great leap of his oyster heart he saw a beautiful gray dolphin, all sleek, supple grace and power, swimming near, smiling at him. He lifted a hand—yes, he had a hand, possibly two of them—in greeting. And then a shadow fell, a big black moving shadow, something large and ominous was swimming overhead—a shark?—blocking the light, and—

Anthony started awake and his dream fell away.

He brought himself upright in his armchair and saw that Bunch was standing in the doorway, holding a silver salver, and behind him, Anthony could see, were a couple of footmen. The dogs on the hearthrug stirred, and Wakefield did too, murmuring:

"Jane?"

"I'm here," said Jane, awake again. She reached out to pat his shoulder, and then she sat up, smoothing her hair away from her face.

Bunch came into the room with his salver, and behind him followed the footmen, each bearing a tall vase. One was filled with big white cheerful-looking daisies and the other with gorgeous pink roses de Provins.

"The flowers are for you, Master Wakefield," said Bunch. "And here are some letters which accompanied them."

"Father, you read them," said Wakefield. "My eyes are still sleeping."

Bunch held out the salver, and Anthony took the letters and opened them. "The daisies are from Miss Humphrey and Miss Trevelyan, who send their love. And the roses are from Surmont Hall. Livia—Mrs. Penhallow, I mean—sends best wishes for a speedy recovery, from everyone at the Hall."

Wakefield nodded drowsily, and Bunch said:

"A letter for you also, Miss Kent."

"Thank you, Bunch."

Anthony watched as Jane, sitting on the bed with her legs neatly tucked beneath her, took it from the salver, opened it, and silently read.

"Who's it from, Jane?" asked Wakefield.

"It's from my great-grandmother. She wants to know when I'm coming home." Jane glanced to the windows, which were filled with the deepening shadows of sunset.

"Can't you stay, Jane?" Wakefield struggled up on his pillows, then shoved the covers away with a hasty gesture. "Oh, I'm *hot*."

Anthony reached to the side-table next to Wakefield's bed, picked up the glass of barley-water, and went to sit by him. "Would you like a sip, my boy?"

Wakefield turned his head away, to where Jane sat. "No. Jane, you'll stay, won't you?"

She put her hand on his forehead. "You *are* a trifle warm. Won't you have just a little barley-water? It's very refreshing."

"I will if you promise to stay."

Anthony almost chided Wakefield for stooping to blackmail, but saw how flushed he was; his voice had gotten distressingly shrill. Then he realized that Jane was looking to him, her dark brows raised inquiringly, and once again he nodded thankfully.

"I'll stay," she said.

So Wakefield let Anthony give him some barley-water. At Bunch's direction the footmen put the vases onto the dresser, and then Bunch said, with a tactfully lowered voice:

"May I inquire about dinner arrangements, Your Grace?"

"Jane's staying, and—"

"It's mean to talk about dinner," interrupted Wakefield, "when I can't have any. Because I can't *chew.* And my mouth still tastes funny."

"Cook has prepared for you some jellies, Master Wakefield."

"What kind?"

"Your favorite, Master Wakefield—raspberry, with just a hint of lemon. Should you care for something more on the savory side, she has also prepared a beef jelly which, I believe, you have upon occasion found appetizing."

"I want macaroni," said Wakefield sulkily.

"Tomorrow, my boy, I should think," Anthony said. "In

the meantime, Cook's jellies are the best in Somerset, you know, and quite possibly in the whole of England."

"I'll have some, Wakefield," said Jane, "if you don't mind sharing them with me."

"Do you like jellies?" he asked her.

"Oh, I love them. Back in Nantwich they were a great treat, you see. And when I was a girl I used to put the spoon up to my lips and *inhale* the jelly between my teeth, which always annoyed Great-grandmother Kent."

"That's what I do, if Aunt Margaret isn't watching."

"If I'm not watching what?" Unnoticed by everyone with the possible exception of the superhumanly eagle-eyed Bunch, Margaret had come to stand in the doorway, and now she took a few steps inside and stood frowning over at Wakefield.

"Nothing," muttered Wakefield, sulky again.

Margaret turned to Jane. "As it's getting dark, Miss Kent, I've had your carriage brought round to the front."

"She's staying," put in Wakefield.

"You're not to impose on Miss Kent any longer, Wakefield. I'm sure she has any number of duties awaiting her attention at the Hall, and that her family will be glad to have her home for dinner. Do try to stop being so selfish."

"I'm not selfish, *you're* selfish!" Wakefield burst out, and Anthony immediately felt a hideous and depressing sense of *déjà vu*.

"Wake," he said, "calm down. And Meg, you might want to do the same. He's a little feverish, and—"

As if on cue, Mr. Rowland came into the room and looked around with gingery eyebrows raised.

"Pardon me, Your Grace—you say that His Lordship has a fever?"

"Yes, Mr. Rowland," Jane said, "he *is* rather warm.

Wakefield, you're shivering. Won't you get under the covers again?"

"All right, Jane," he replied, "I'm most awfully cold," and he let Jane pull the bedclothes snugly up around him.

Mr. Rowland went over to Wakefield and felt his forehead also. "Yes, you're quite right, Miss Kent. It's not unexpected, and people typically feel worse when evening comes on."

"He'll need to be bled, obviously," said Margaret. "I'll send for Dr. Fotherham."

Wakefield shrank closer to Jane. "I *won't* be bled! I *need* all my blood."

Mr. Rowland turned to Margaret. "You are, of course, welcome to send for your physician, Your Ladyship, and naturally I would be glad of his opinion. However, I strongly advise against bleeding, especially with a person so young."

"When I was a child," said Margaret, fixing him with a steely gaze, "we were always bled when we had fevers. Dr. Fotherham's predecessor was a great proponent of it, and my parents thought *most* highly of him."

Mr. Rowland merely gave a slight, pleasant, noncommittal bow, and Anthony said, trying to keep his voice equally neutral:

"Meg, you know Dr. Fotherham doesn't bleed people."

"What I know," returned Margaret, turning her steely gaze his way, "is that you are shockingly indifferent to the welfare of your only child and heir."

Anthony stood up. "Now see here, Meg, that's uncalled for."

"Father's *not* undiffering!" cried Wakefield. "*You're* undiffering! Go away, you—you old *crow*!"

"Wake, that's enough," said Anthony, but Margaret had stiffened angrily.

"Very well, I will." She spun on her heel and marched out of the room, and Anthony, stricken with hideous *déjà vu* all over again, had to resist an urge to go over and slam the door behind her, just for dramatic effect. But he gathered himself and said:

"Jane, would you like to write a note, and have it sent back to the Hall with your carriage?"

Jane nodded, and he went on, "Bunch, send for Dr. Fotherham, please. I'd like for him to have a look at Wakefield. Jane and I will have our dinner in here. Have a table and chairs brought in, will you, along with Wake's jellies, and some lemonade as well. At some point the dogs will need to be fed and taken out. Mr. Rowland, Bunch will see to your own dinner arrangements."

A small agreeable bustle ensued, and Anthony, sitting down again next to Wakefield and holding his warm and rather sweaty little hand in his, thought for a moment of black-clad Margaret eating her own dinner somewhere in the house all by herself, and found he could summon within himself not a single tiny scrap of pity.

"I say, Jane, it's most awfully good of you to stay the night."

"I don't mind at all."

"Well, thank you again. Also, I feel that I should apologize."

"What for?"

"First of all, for Margaret, for being so beastly. Second, for Wake's kicking up a fuss and insisting you sleep in his room, and crying about not having dessert, and for being so—well—temperamental."

"Oh, it's not his fault," Jane said. "People naturally feel dreadful after an extraction, I think. Why, I remember how my great-grandmother Kent cried all day after one of hers. Which was shocking, as I had never, ever seen her cry before, not even when my parents died. There's something about losing a part of yourself, perhaps, and of course there's a certain amount of violence to the whole thing which is miserable."

The Duke nodded, and together they gently veered to the left and paced along another length of the Hastings ballroom. Footmen had lit candles in just half a dozen or so of the many wall-sconces, and the enormous, high-ceilinged room was filled with a soft, dim, cozy glow. Overhead, the crystal drops in the great central chandelier twinkled ever so faintly with the reflected lights of the candles. It was rather magical, Jane thought. And how exceedingly marvelous to have a little time alone with the Duke. She supposed that Lady Margaret was off sulking somewhere, rather than attempting to play the chaperone's role, and briefly Jane took a moment to wonder if either of her great-grandmothers would approve of the situation.

Probably not.

Jane, you're a bad, bad girl, she said to herself, then mentally she gave a defiant shrug.

Her *behavior* might not be ideal, but she herself wasn't bad. For example, she wasn't trying to sneakily trick the Duke into marrying her (as Lady Felicia had), and she wasn't attempting to seduce someone against their will (like Viscount Whitton had), and she didn't go about glowering icily at other people who were only trying to help a scared little boy (which Lady Margaret had done just this morning).

No, she, Jane, was all right.

And besides, it felt good to be walking.

About two hours ago, Dr. Fotherham—stocky, grizzled, exuding an air of unflappable competence—had arrived, examined Wakefield, agreed with Mr. Rowland that some feverishness was not unexpected, vehemently spurned the very idea of bleeding (much to Wakefield's relief), suggested a soothing saline draught if Wakefield felt like drinking it, asked to be sent for again if the fever did happen to worsen, and otherwise recommended further bed-rest until Wakefield's usual energy returned.

After that, dinner had been brought in, and also a trundle bed for later; the housekeeper had discreetly produced for her a warm nightgown and a flannel wrapper, and after they had eaten (and the Duke had been correct, the jellies *were* delicious), Bunch had come in to sit with Wakefield for a while so that she and the Duke could go stretch their legs.

When they had left, Bunch was sitting in the chair next to Wakefield's bed reading out loud from a volume of fairy tales, Wakefield having no taste for anything heavier at the moment, and Jane had secretly marveled at how Bunch performed this kind service with his usual self-assured, pleasant graciousness, as if it was something he did every day.

So here she and the Duke were, walking round and round. He had adapted his long stride and she had slightly lengthened her own, so they kept pace together quite easily.

They veered again to the left, passing a long row of chairs draped in Holland covers.

Jane said, "This is such a beautiful room. When was the last time you had a dance in here?"

"Oh, a couple of years ago. Margaret had a costume ball for yet another one of her so-called friends with a highly eligible daughter."

She gave him a sidelong glance. There were a lot of questions she wanted to ask, but she decided to go with a simple one. "What was your costume?"

"I regret to say," the Duke replied, "and more than I can properly express, that I allowed myself to be coerced into going as Augustus."

"Who?"

"Augustus. The first emperor of the Roman Empire."

"Oh, I see. What did you wear?"

"A toga."

"What is that?"

"It's a great long piece of cloth that one drapes all around and about oneself, and over a tunic. A horrible nuisance, really. Mine kept threatening to come undone, which made me look more like a fool than ever. A highly nervous fool."

"I'll bet you looked quite dashing. You're so tall and you have nice shoulders."

"They're nice? Do you really think so, Jane?"

"Oh yes. Was the ball a success?"

"I suppose it depends on who you ask. The aforementioned young lady came as Marie Antoinette, wearing an extremely tall wig, and when she brushed up too close to one of the sconces, her wig caught on fire and so one of the other guests flung a pitcher of orgeat over her head to put it out, which worked, but it also made the floor very sticky. Three or four ladies lost their slippers walking over it, and seemed to feel their dignity suffered as a result. Also, someone came dressed as Ivan the Great, got very drunk, and started doing Russian squat-kicks. He knocked over at least two people that I know of, along with a side-table filled with champagne glasses, which made for quite the noisy mess. Several people," the Duke added, "started clapping, and Marie Antoinette's mother—who, if memory serves, was dressed as Cleopatra—went into hysterics and had to be carried to her room on an improvised stretcher."

"Is there more, or are these just the highlights?"

"Well, it also rained so heavily that nobody could go wandering out back into the gardens. Although one couple did try when it briefly let up, and came across McTavish starting to cover the Aphrodite shrub, so that it wouldn't shed too many leaves in the downpour. Apparently the chap made some kind of disparaging remark, and McTavish was so angry that he loosed upon them a Scottish curse."

"Dear me. Did you ever find out what the curse was?"

"I did ask McTavish later, but he was still so furious that I quailed and slunk away, before he could loose a curse upon *me*. Besides, he was holding the most fearsome pair of shears."

Jane smiled. "So would you say the ball was a failure or a success?"

"Margaret, of course, was livid about the whole thing, especially when her houseguests actually fled in the night, but as I managed to escape being wrangled into issuing a proposal, I'd call it an unabashed success. Do you really think my shoulders are nice?"

"Yes, I do," answered Jane, noticing that she was feeling very light and happy and floaty, as if her bones had gotten all deliciously hollow, and also that she really wasn't the least bit guilty about being alone with the Duke and making intimate personal remarks about his appearance—specifically his lovely, *lovely* shoulders.

The Duke said: "They're not as big and wide as Viscount Whitton's."

"No. But that doesn't mean his are better, you know."

"Quite a fine-looking fellow, though, don't you think?"

"I suppose some people might find him so."

"Did you, Jane?"

Jane looked up at the Duke. Both his voice and his

expression were very earnest. Together the two of them veered again to the left. "Not especially."

"Really? It's just that—well, I noticed that he seemed to stare at you quite a bit, and you talked to him for ages at the dinner-party, and also, that night of the dance, I saw you coming out of the billiards room, and then he followed right behind you—I say, am I being infuriating again?"

He spoke so humbly that Jane was touched. "No."

"Well, that's good. Do you mind—do you mind if I ask again? If he was kissing you? It's been rather torturing me."

"No, he didn't kiss me. He tried to, though."

"But you said he wasn't bothering you."

"Oh, he wasn't. First I told him no, and when he didn't listen, I simply brought my knee up, you know, to a rather vulnerable area of his, and that helped to make my point."

"Jane," said the Duke, in a tone of deepest respect.

"Your Grace."

"Did you really?"

"Yes."

"By Jove, that's *capital*."

"Thank you."

"That explains why he was walking so oddly the next day."

"I daresay it does."

"I'm sorry to say that I snickered behind his back."

"I would have, too."

"Would you, Jane?"

"Yes. He deserved it."

"Maybe so. Weren't you frightened when he came at you, though? He has all those muscles."

"Oh no, it was rather amusing. *He* was rather amusing. Didn't you think so?"

"You found him amusing?"

"Yes indeed. Because he thought so much of himself. And wasn't it funny, the way he hung about so morosely, and made it seem as if his eyes were aflame?"

"I tried to do that," confessed the Duke.

"Tried to do what?"

"To make my eyes do that."

"And did you?"

"No, apparently not. I just looked demented."

"Well, I wouldn't worry about it," Jane said. "I like the way your eyes darken sometimes."

"Do they?"

"Yes."

"And you like the way they look when they do that?"

"Oh yes. Also, they're a lovely deep shade of blue." They veered again, passing another long row of covered chairs.

"That's such a nice thing to say. I like your eyes, too."

The Duke said this so shyly and humbly that Jane slipped her arm through his. "Thank you. Your Grace."

There was a silence, tempered only and in a very pleasing way by the regular cadence of their matching footsteps. After a while, the Duke said:

"I say, this feels very companionable."

"Walking arm-in-arm?"

"Yes. I wanted to," he added, "but I didn't know if you would also."

"You could have asked."

"I was afraid you might still be angry with me."

"Did I seem that way?" Jane said, surprised.

"No, not at all. But I did wonder."

"Well, I *was* upset with you that night. I'm sorry if I snarled at you."

"There's no need to apologize. I was being a sapskull,

as, I fear, I all too often am. But why did you say I ought to be worrying about myself?"

Jane considered how to thoughtfully and judiciously answer him without betraying Lady Felicia's confidence, though she was noticing that her brain seemed to be moving a little more slowly now that she was in physical contact with the Duke. It was an extremely nice sensation, and she could practically feel her blood, rushing eagerly through her veins, heating up, possibly even coming to a nice vigorous boil, sending delicious mind-dissolving tingles everywhere. She nearly started to purr, then caught herself just in time.

"I say, Jane."

"Yes?"

"I was just wondering what your answer was going to be."

Jane tried to pull herself together, but as she didn't truly wish to, because it felt quite marvelous to be warming up like this, she didn't make much progress. "About what?"

"About why I should be worrying about myself."

"Oh. Well, perhaps the danger has passed."

"Really?"

"Yes, possibly."

"You're being rather cryptic, Jane."

"Am I?" she said dreamily, not really caring, and brought herself just a little bit closer to him.

"Yes, but I'll take you at your word. So," the Duke went on, "I needn't worry about myself anymore, you're not angry with me, you don't think the Viscount's shoulders are better than mine, and you like the color of my eyes, and the way they sometimes darken. Have I got it all correctly?"

He sounded so much like an earnest schoolboy wanting to be sure he'd learned a lesson well, Jane smiled up at him and inched yet closer. Her skirts were brushing up against his long legs. "Yes."

"Good."

Another silence fell between them. It was a comfortable silence, but to Jane it also felt as if it was simmering with motes of heat, invisible, magical, intoxicating. She loved the feel of her hand around his forearm. It was all bony and strong, with a satisfying hint of muscle, and without being disagreeably bulky. The only thing that would make it better would be if she could feel the warm bare skin of his arm. Was it nice and hairy?

They veered, gently and unhurriedly, a few times. Then:

"Jane."

"Yes?"

"May I ask you something?"

"Certainly."

"Did you happen to finish the box of conserves I gave you last week?"

"Yes, I finished it the same day."

"Did you? You didn't feel sick or anything from eating all that chocolate?"

"Oh no, I felt wonderful."

"I'm glad."

"Thank you again. They were delicious."

"You've very welcome. I—uh—I got another box of conserves for you."

"You did? How very, very kind of you."

"It was twice as big as the first one I gave you."

"Was?" She looked up at him curiously.

"Yes, well—uh—the thing of it is, I was in such a bad mood that I—well, I—you see, I ate most of them myself. I'm most dreadfully sorry. Also, I'm not even sure why I'm telling you this. I'm sorry."

"It's the thought that counts."

"Although maybe not with chocolate."

She smiled. "Maybe not."

"Would—would you mind if I got you another box?"

"I wouldn't mind at all."

"That's very gracious of you."

"Not at all. It's nice to have something to look forward to."

"Yes, it is. Jane, would it be all right if I asked you something else?"

"By all means."

"Well, I don't mean to sound self-centered, but I was just wondering when it was that you saw my eyes darkening. Nobody's ever said that to me before, you see. Do you happen to remember?"

"Oh yes," Jane answered, more dreamily than ever. She was very warm and tingly everywhere and she felt very, very good. "It's when you've been kissing me."

"Oh—ah—really?"

"Yes."

The Duke stopped, and Jane did too. She stood looking up into his face, admiring it all over again. His deep-blue eyes, she was pleased to see, were darkening like anything. He said:

"I wonder if—uh . . ."

"Yes?"

"I was just wondering—if—if you wouldn't mind if we did it again."

"Kissing?"

"Yes."

"No."

"*No* you do mind, or *no* you wouldn't mind?"

"I mean I think we should."

"Kiss?" he said earnestly.

"Yes."

"You're—you're not going to deploy your knee on me?"

"Absolutely not."

"Oh, that's good."

"Yes, it is." Jane smiled up at him, thinking how delightful it was to know that they were going to be kissing soon.

As she herself had just said, it was nice to have something to look forward to.

Chapter 14

For a fleeting moment Anthony thought about the incredibly handsome Viscount Whitton and his perfect hair and his enormously broad shoulders and all those muscles of his and he felt horribly inferior, but in the very next moment he remembered that Jane had said how nice *his* shoulders were, and also he remembered how the Viscount had walked around on Saturday, which briefly made him want to snicker again, but as he looked down into Jane's face and noticed how she was smiling at him, looking very much like the most beautiful daisy that had ever existed, everything else in the world seemed to fade away into a wonderful nothingness and if anybody were to wander by and ask him how he was feeling he would have said, truthfully, that he felt marvelous and excited and full of joy and lust, although at the same time he hoped with all his being that nobody *would* wander by, because it would be a grievous interruption of this magical time with Jane.

Anthony smiled back at her.

He was remembering how, after that time they had kissed before, he had thought about trying to have his mouth be just above hers, teasing them both in the most terrible and wonderful way, until they couldn't stand it for another single second.

And he had wanted to trail his tongue along the side of her neck, and maybe nip at the soft, sensitive skin there. *If* that was something she would like, of course.

Also, he remembered thinking that he would like it very much if she did the same to him.

Too, he had wanted to touch her with his hands. Everywhere.

Now he wanted all those things, and as soon as possible.

He was aware that he longed to plunge eagerly at her. Into her. Without calmness or restraint.

But would that display a dreadful lack of finesse?

She had said that it was all right for them to kiss again, and suddenly he had no idea how to go about it.

Especially when he was nearly shaking with his desire for her.

Should he slowly take one of her hands, and take just a small step closer?

Or maybe he should reach for both of her hands?

Alternatively, would it be better if they weren't holding hands, and if he simply drew near to her?

He could put his hands on Jane's shoulders, not in a domineering possessive way, naturally, but lightly and caressingly. Besides, he would love to touch her anywhere he could. The round knob of her shoulder, the sweet protuberant bone on her delicate wrist, the warm nape of her neck, the curve of her breast, the flare of her hip, the length of her leg . . .

All of this rushed through his mind in a rapturous kaleidoscopic sort of way, then Anthony suddenly realized that he was staring at her lovely, tender, rose-pink mouth. He swallowed, hard.

"I say, Jane."

"Yes?"

"I really do want to kiss you in the worst way."

Her eyes danced. "I doubt it will be in the worst way. Based on how it was before."

"Oh, really? Well, that's reassuring. The thing of it is, Jane, I'm—I'm—uh—it's just that I—well, I—that is—"

"Do stop blithering," she said, but kindly, and took a firm, sure step forward so that their bodies met, and lifted herself up a bit on her toes while at the same time she slid her arms about his neck, and then without hesitation she brought her mouth against his own, plunging against him and into him with her warm, soft, wet tongue.

Kissing him without calmness or restraint.

And yet, somehow, with finesse.

By Jove, Jane was an *amazing* kisser.

One must, Anthony thought, a little dazedly, rise to the occasion.

So he wrapped his arms tightly around her, noticing at once that there was more to her than he had observed upon first meeting her, she had in fact the most delicious soft yielding breasts, and some flesh to gently pad her ribs, and after that interesting discovery he met her tongue with his own, as would a thirsty traveler in the desert find a spring of lifesaving water, and when in a little while hers gracefully and invitingly gave way, he plunged eagerly into *her* mouth.

Jane gave a low hum of what distinctly sounded like pleasure, which made Anthony yet more joyful and lustful.

They kissed and kissed and kissed.

Was it a single long kiss, or a lot of individual ones, demarcated, as it were, by how they slanted their heads, by how they deepened into each other and teasingly withdrew, over and over, like a sweet carnal dance?

He didn't know and he didn't care.

Except, as a side note, that maybe, just maybe, this was a kind of dance he *could* do.

A heady thought indeed.

At some point Anthony nipped at Jane's upper lip with his teeth, which felt marvelous, and at some other point she did the same to him, which felt equally marvelous, and when it got to the stage where they were both quite breathless from being mouth to mouth for an extended period of time, he lifted his head and drew a great deal of air into his lungs and after that he slid his tongue down and along the soft skin of her neck.

Jane hummed again.

So he did it two more times.

She hummed, and Anthony thought of daisies, and bees, and some lines from the Cavalier poet Thomas Carew: *But the warm sun thaws the benumbed earth / And makes it tender; gives a sacred birth / To the dead swallow; wakes in hollow tree / The drowsy cuckoo, and the humble-bee.*

"Jane," he said, "I'd like to bite you just a little right now. Where I've been—uh—licking you."

"Oh, would you?" Her voice was slow and dreamy, and she was still rather breathless. "That sounds nice."

"Yes, but it might leave a mark, wouldn't it? A conspicuous one. Would you want that?"

She lifted shining gray eyes to his. "How thoughtful of you to ask. I *could* cover it with a fichu, or a shawl, but then I'd probably feel like you did with the toga, and worry about it slipping off."

"Well then, I won't bite you," he said gallantly but regretfully. "Good Lord, I sound just like a vampire, don't I?"

Jane laughed. "If you are one, my great-grandfather Kent has a wonderful remedy to cure you."

"Does it involve vinegar? Or household dust? Cobwebs, perhaps?"

"No, you would need to go outside in the dead of night, and bury your best shoes underneath an elderberry tree."

"Would it *have* to be my best shoes?"

"Oh yes, because anything less than that might turn you into an actual bat."

"I see. How did that pamphlet sell?"

"Very well, Great-grandmother said. Several of the neighborhood cobblers carried it in their shops."

Anthony laughed. "Jane, your great-grandfather sounds like a dreadful rogue."

"Yes, I think he was," she agreed. "Great-grandmother said he always wanted to write novels, but there was no money in it. By the way, I have an idea."

With this last sentence her voice had gone all soft and honeyed again, and Anthony immediately forgot about vampires, bats, pamphlets, failed novelists, and enterprising London cobblers.

"Do tell," he said, his own voice getting rather husky.

Jane reached up to the bodice of her pink gown, to where it covered her heart, and without hurry she pulled down the fabric to reveal a swell of breast, white skin, a delicate constellation of freckles.

"Try biting me here."

Lust surged through him with such vehemence and joy that Anthony had to take a moment to steady himself. Forget smoldering eyes, he thought, his whole *self* was smoldering. On fire. *Alight.*

"Jane," he said, "that's a splendid idea."

She smiled. "Thank you. Are you going to do it?"

"Yes."

"When?"

"As soon as I get a little self-control back."

"Oh, do you feel out of control?"

"I rather do."

"Well, that's nice."

"Is it?"

"Oh yes. You're not worrying about my knee, are you?"

"No. I'm worried that I'm going to pounce on you too ravenously."

"That's nice, too."

"Really, Jane?"

"Yes."

Thus encouraged, but nonetheless exerting himself to be slow, slow and deliberate, to savor every delicious moment as it came and went, Anthony put his hands on Jane's ribcage with a kind of awe, his fingers sensitive to every rise and fall of bone and flesh. He could still hardly believe she was letting him touch her. Hold her like this. As if she actually enjoyed it. Then—*slow, slow*—he leaned down, and kissed the soft little swell of her breast.

He heard her sharply indrawn breath, and glanced up into her face.

"All well, Jane?"

"Oh yes. Can you do that again?"

"You liked it?"

"My God, yes."

"I say, I'm glad. Yes, I can do that again. Of course." And so he did. He could feel the strong quick thump of her heart. Was it really possible that he, with his mouth and his hands, had made it beat faster? If so, how absolutely *tremendous*. "Again?"

"Yes, please."

He kissed that sweet swell, then, trying hard not to rush in his driving eagerness, he dipped his tongue beneath the embroidered neckline of her bodice and heard—*felt*—that indrawn breath again. A wild jolt of hopeful pleasure shot through him, and Anthony felt so fiery hot that somewhere in the back of his mind, he was surprised not to smell smoke issuing from his person.

Slowly he slid his tongue down again, then up along the slope of soft flesh, to her fingers where they grasped the fabric of her bodice to open herself to him. He kissed them, too, dipping his tongue between the delicate web of flesh between her fingers while thinking of the tantalizing juncture between her legs, too, in a kind of allusive caress, and Jane started humming again, low and soft and deep in her throat. He wondered if she was having the same thought.

He also noticed that his legs felt a little shaky with his hot, hot desire, and vehemently he wished they could lie down together, body to body and mouth to mouth, stripped of all their clothes and Jane's glorious pale hair tumbling free.

Anthony paused, so entirely taken by this vision of them that he had to remind himself to breathe.

Jane said, softly, "All well?"

Her voice brought him out of his dazzled trance and he said, "Oh yes," against her breast and suddenly remembered that he was supposed to be biting her, just a little, here on this soft, sensitive part of her, leaving his mark, but secretly, a kind of erotic knowledge that only they two would share.

So he did it.

Jane gave a gasp and her fingers let go of her bodice and buried themselves in his hair.

The little red marks disappeared beneath the pink fabric. Secret now, but imprinted, indelibly, in his mind. Anthony straightened and Jane's hands slid from his hair and along the sides of his face and jaw, then to the lapels of his dark jacket which she gripped hard. He looked down into her face, which was rosy and flushed, and she looked up into his face which, he guessed, might also be flushed with the hot blood of lust and pleasure and hope and joy.

He felt wonderful and also, at the same time, rather vulnerable. They had shown each other something quite intimate about themselves. And into his memory came the cynical, cautionary line from Alexander Pope: *A little learning is a dangerous thing . . .*

With quick effort Anthony turned his mind away from it. Rather awkwardly he said to Jane, "Was—was my biting you all right?"

"*More* than all right." Those lovely gray eyes were shining up at him again.

"That's splendid."

"I want to bite *you*."

"You—you do?"

"Yes indeed."

"Really, Jane?"

"Yes. But only if you'd like it, too."

"I—I would."

So powerful a rush of desire rocked him that he was glad he didn't topple over from it, as although that would have been a kind of compliment to Jane's powers of enchantment it would also be incredibly mortifying, and in addition one sometimes fell unconscious when dropping to the floor, a scenario entirely to be avoided, especially since it would delay or even abrogate the opportunity to be bitten by her. "I—well—uh—I'd—yes, I would like that. Please. And thank you."

"Where?"

"On—on my neck also. If you really don't mind?"

She smiled, and Anthony thought of Aphrodite. Not in shrub form, and of course he meant no disrespect to McTavish's undoubted skill with those fearsome shears, but rather he was thinking of Aphrodite's eternal and intangible essence: alluring, seductive, captivating.

"I don't mind in the least," Jane said. "But there's just one thing."

"Oh? What is it?"

"Your neckcloth is in the way."

"Oh—ah—yes."

"May I?" Lightly she moved her hands between his lapels to the white linen cloth which, with his usual disinterest, he had earlier today tied in some kind of haphazard arrangement. Anthony swallowed.

"Yes. Of course."

With swift dexterity Jane untied the neckcloth and slid it away from around his nape, letting it drop in a coil of fabric onto the floor. Anthony was startled by how electrifyingly exposed he felt. How—again—both wonderful and vulnerable. She ran her fingers inside the collar of his shirt and along the bare skin of his throat, and Anthony felt goose-bumps shiver up and down his arms.

"Mmmmm," Jane said softly, sounding exactly like a person who had just tasted something delicious. Like, say, an éclair, or a freshly baked apple puff smothered in whipped cream. Or a chocolate conserve. Then she trailed her fingers down and lower, to the open vee of his shirt, along the hard ridge of his collar-bone, and then to the whorl of springy hair beneath that.

"You have hair on your chest," she said.

"Yes."

"I wondered if you did."

Anthony stared down at her in amazement. "You—you did?"

"Oh yes. And I wondered whether it would be dark, like your eyelashes and eyebrows, or lighter, like your hair."

Anthony swallowed again. "Well, now you know." *A little learning is a dangerous thing . . .*

"Yes, now I know that it's dark. Not as dark as your eyelashes and eyebrows. Soft. Wonderful." Jane leaned forward and kissed him on his chest, right between the vee of his shirt, and Anthony had to suppress the urge to startle like a horse, so exciting, even shocking, was the sensation of her mouth there. It was also exciting, *and* shocking, to learn that Jane had spent any time at all thinking about his chest and wondering about it. She kissed him there again, lingeringly, and all at once Anthony remembered something.

"I say, Jane."

She lifted her head. "Yes?"

"It's—it's possible that I smell rather bad. I—I was sweating, you know, when Wakefield was having his extraction. And—and also I've been sweating here in the ballroom, with all the—the kissing, you know, and whatnot."

Jane put the side of her face against his chest, shocking him again, and breathed in deeply. "You smell delightful."

"I—I do?"

"Oh yes. Earthy and masculine and delightful."

Anthony listened hard for any traces of sarcasm or irony in Jane's voice. But there was none, or at least he, in his uneasiness, couldn't detect any. "Really?"

"Yes. Very. Can you lean down just a little, so I can reach your neck?"

He did, wondering if she was going to lick his neck as he had done to hers, or kiss it as she had kissed his chest. Either would be fine. Or both would. Repeatedly. But she surprised him—again—by immediately nipping at the tender skin along the side, sending through him another electrifying surge of pleasure heightened by the little tantalizing shimmer of pain. Anthony caught his breath.

"Jane."

"Yes?"

"That was marvelous."

"I'm so glad you liked it."

"I certainly did. By the way, have my eyes darkened?"

"Yes indeed."

"And you really like it when they do?"

"Oh yes. Very much."

"Well, that's splendid. Thank you. Would you do it again?"

"Bite you?"

"Yes, please."

"Of course."

And she did, and now *he* felt like humming.

Actually, he felt like doing more than humming. That earlier wish came back, more forcefully than ever: the wish, the longing, the powerful urge to lie down with Jane, to strip away all their clothes, to do more than kiss and lick and nip.

So much more . . .

But then, unfortunately, practical considerations snaked their way into his fevered mind.

Forced their way in, the sneaky little bastards.

Practical consideration the first: they couldn't do it here in the ballroom.

For one thing, they might easily be discovered. Also, *where* would they? The hard, polished, gleaming floor was their only option. Of course, out of courtesy and concern for her comfort he would offer to be on the bottom, although he was a little unsure of the actual logistics of such a position.

No, wait—there were chairs.

A chair could work. Couldn't it? He'd never tried it himself, but it seemed like a real possibility. He could sit on one, and Jane could, well, sit on *him*.

Would she like that?

Even if she did, he remembered to his sorrow, they could still be found out. Practical consideration the second.

Thoughts whipped through his brain, lightning-fast.

They could, if she agreed to it, slip upstairs to his bedchamber, where he had a large, even vast, and very comfortable bed.

They would have privacy there.

The walls were thick as anything and impressively noise-muffling. Once Wakefield, trying to reach a book on the top shelf of his bookcase, had climbed up onto the lower shelves and toppled over the bookcase with (as he later described it) a tremendous thump, sending books crashing and scattering everywhere, and he, fortunately, leaping out of harm's way. Anthony, in his room across the hall, hadn't heard a thing.

But—speaking of upstairs, and practical consideration the third—they'd been here in the ballroom for a long time. Bunch had therefore been with Wakefield for the same amount of time. Wouldn't it be selfish to go sneaking away to his bedchamber?

Especially since he would want to spend all night with Jane.

Or, perhaps, they could share a quick interlude together?

No, that would somehow be worse.

Inconsiderate, possibly.

As if he merely wanted to use Jane for his own pleasure.

When what he really wanted was hours and hours and hours together . . . for their *mutual* pleasure.

Which was, he was coming to see, unlikely.

Even impossible.

Practical considerations abounded. Multiplying like unwanted rabbits.

Besides, he hated the idea of sneaking around. As if they were doing something not only illicit, but wrong.

And *wasn't* it wrong?

They weren't married, and of course they never would be, as naturally he would never, ever allow himself to be dragged (quite possibly literally kicking and screaming) into the marital trap again. Once burned, twice shy and all that. *Plus*, he would never, ever want to take advantage of Jane.

Kissing her like this hadn't been taking advantage of her, had it?

A draft of cool air had come slithering down the back of his neck, chilling him all over, and Anthony was at the same time realizing that if someone did happen to come in, a footman or a maidservant, or even Margaret, prowling about like a cat, he or she or they would see him standing here with Jane without his neckcloth on and that would not be in the least bit a good thing.

He or she or they, seeing him and Jane like this, might jump to all kinds of conclusions.

The very idea of which made him, Anthony, feel all exposed and chilly and guilty and uneasy and selfish and miserable and, even worse, as if he had been unceremoniously dropped into the Arctic Sea. Lust and longing and desire were quenched as if they had not been—minutes ago—roaring through him like the triumphantly freed waters of a broken dam.

So Anthony took a step back. He reached down to pick up his neckcloth. As he wrapped it around his neck and began to tie it he said, "Well, I—I daresay we should be going back upstairs."

"Yes, of course."

"It must be getting quite late."

"Yes."

He made himself look at Jane.

The rosy flush in her cheeks had faded away, as had the

bright glowing shine in her eyes. But she met him look for look, steadily, and her voice was even and pleasant. Anthony forced himself to not lower his gaze, to the bodice of her pink gown, to the place where, concealed, was the mark of his teeth upon her breast.

He finished tying his neckcloth. The good thing about the way he usually tied it, he supposed, was that when he did it hastily and without a mirror and also filled with remorse and guilt and ambivalence and even an odd sort of relief, it would probably look about the same and no one could possibly suspect that he had allowed Jane to take it off and leave the sweet mark of *her* teeth beneath it.

"Shall we?" he said, gesturing awkwardly toward the doorway.

"Yes."

And so they left the ballroom and went upstairs, where they found Wakefield sound asleep, with Snuffles right next to him, the sole source of illumination in the room the three-branched candelabra on the bedside table, and Bunch still sitting in the same chair, only he had set aside the book of fairy tales and was deep into *Tales from Shakespeare*.

Before Jane settled in for the night, the Duke showed her where his bedroom was—just across the hall from Wakefield's—and Bunch asked her to ring at any point should she need him. Jane thanked them both, then went back into Wakefield's room where, behind the screen Bunch had thoughtfully instructed a footman to bring in for her, she changed into her borrowed nightgown and braided her hair into a plait.

Once she had checked on Wakefield again, gotten into the trundle bed, and pulled the covers up around her shoulders, she lay awake thinking about the day, and especially about strolling around the ballroom with the Duke and what had happened in there.

Things had started off nicely, continued on to glorious, then shifted into awkwardness as the Duke's mood abruptly changed.

Jane remembered how, on the day of the tea here with the Merifields, she had observed this same shift in him. He'd reminded her, forbiddingly, of the Bastille. Aloof and inaccessible.

But now she was thinking more of a concertina, that curious musical instrument with the bellows which expanded and contracted. Once, back in Nantwich, she had seen a German musician playing one on the high street, and she had joined the little crowd around him to watch. How interesting to see the concertina stretch in and out in the musician's deft hands.

The Duke seemed rather like this.

Expanding and contracting.

Opening himself up and then backing away.

It was hard to know where she stood with him.

Jane thought again about his late wife Lady Selina. Had the Duke loved her so much that it was impossible for him to develop a new attachment?

Just tonight he had said about the costume ball: *As I managed to escape being wrangled into issuing a proposal, I'd call it an unabashed success.*

It was a puzzle, Jane thought.

But how to solve it?

She could hardly sidle up to the Duke and say, *Lovely weather we're having, and by the way, are you in love with a dead woman?*

Such things were not unknown. Great-grandmother Kent, for example, had mourned the loss of her husband, that rapscallion pamphleteer, to the very end of her days. She had had, Jane recalled, a couple of suitors while in Nantwich, all of whom she had roundly spurned, saying that her heart was buried deep in the grave.

To further complicate the questions swirling in Jane's mind, she couldn't quite picture herself saying to the Duke: *Also, while we're on the subject of your possibly still being in love with your late wife, I was wondering why you seem to run rather hot and cold in your relations with me.*

Actually, when she thought about it for a while, she *could* picture herself asking about the hot-and-cold concertina issue.

What might hold her back, she realized, was that maybe she didn't want to know the answer.

In a situation like this, a person might, perhaps, be justified in guarding her own heart rather carefully. Being wary. No matter how much that person liked another person, or how much that person (the one guarding her heart) enjoyed kissing that other person (the one to be guarded against) and would have very much liked to kiss that other person for a lot longer and engage in further intimacies, because that other person was marvelously attractive and intelligent and sensitive and generous and with such an engaging sense of humor and also had the most delicious mouth as well as gorgeous collar-bones and an amazingly strong, hard-planed chest with wonderful springy hair on it, along with (as he had tonight, though not always) a heady scent of sweat and stables and a faint tang of chocolate about him, all of which basically made that person (herself, of course) feel drunk with desire.

Jane sighed, then turned from her side onto her back.

She lay there for a while, thinking and puzzling, occasionally imagining herself in a lovely cozy bed with the

Duke and firmly suppressing these enticing images, after which she tried to corral herself into counting pretend sheep jumping over a stile, but somehow the sheep kept turning into pigs, enormous pink hairy pigs, and Johns the pigman with his big red round face came stumping up to wave a stick in her face and tell her to go away, and Great-grandmother Henrietta was tugging at her arm and telling her it was time to leave, and Lady Margaret was tugging at her *other* arm and agreeing with Great-grandmother, and Grandfather Titus suddenly appeared, a mischievous smile sparkling in his gray eyes, laughing impudently at Great-grandmother and Lady Margaret and Johns, then looking at Jane and telling her that duchesses ought to eat more blancmange, which was how Jane dimly realized that she was dreaming, and made herself wake up so that she could sit up in her trundle bed, let her eyes adjust to the darkness, and ensure that Wakefield was still sleeping peacefully.

He was, and she drifted back into sleep, but sat up several times in the night to check on him. As dawn approached, Wakefield became restless, muttering as he tossed and turned, and when Jane got up and went around to the side of his bed, she could see that he was flushed again.

Gently she put a hand on his forehead. The heat from yesterday had returned, and rather more strongly than it had been before.

"Jane?"

"I'm here, dear Wakefield."

"I don't feel so good."

"I think you're a little feverish again. Can I give you something to drink?"

"Is there lemonade?"

"Yes. It's still nice and cool."

"Yes, please."

Jane helped Wakefield sit up, and gave him some lemonade which thirstily he drank. Then he lay back against his pillows, his face pinched again with discomfort. He said:

"The hole in my mouth hurts."

"A little, or a lot?"

"A lot."

Jane stroked a lock of fine brown hair off his forehead. "You may need some more laudanum, and something for your fever. I'm going to get your father. I'll be right back."

She put on the flannel wrapper the housekeeper had given her and went to knock on the Duke's door across the hall.

Perhaps he had been sleeping lightly too, for he promptly opened the door wearing only buckskins and a loose white shirt, his hair all tousled and the shadow of new dark beard on his face.

She said, "Wakefield slept well last night, but he's a little worse this morning," and he flashed her a look of such concern intermingled with gratitude that she had to sternly remind herself to be careful, no matter how delightful he looked in just trousers and a shirt (which showed a fair amount of his chest) and with marvelously untidy hair and so on. It was a good thing, she thought, that Nantwich girls could not only be tough, they could also be wary when necessary. And now, she reminded herself even more sternly, was the perfect time to be *extremely* tough and wary.

Together she and the Duke went into Wakefield's room, and a minute or two later he was ringing for Bunch who shortly appeared as calm and precise and immaculate as ever, and at the Duke's instructions went away to send for Dr. Fotherham again.

Not long after that Mrs. Niddy, as if she had been keeping her eye on the hallway traffic, came trotting in, her apron bulging with what looked to be a variety of bottles and medicaments (and Jane would not have been in the least surprised if among these items was a well-worn copy of *Four Hundred Practical Aspects of Vinegar As Used to Reduce Corpulence, Purify the Humours, Improve the Complexion, and Attract a Most Desirable Spouse*, or some other of Great-grandfather Kent's diverse array of pamphlets, though to the best of her knowledge he had never written anything about castor oil). Wakefield, hot and flushed and miserable, shrieked at the sight of Nurse, and the Duke—colder and sterner than Jane had ever seen him before—told her to leave the room at once.

"But Master Anthony," Nurse began to protest, "I'm sure I'm only here to *help*," and the Duke merely repeated:

"At once, if you please."

In his voice was such implacable authority that Nurse dipped a deep, cowed curtsy and trotted off through the doorway, whatever she had stowed in her apron clinking and clanking in a rather agitated manner. Before these mysterious, even ominous sounds had faded away Wakefield said:

"Oh, Father, that was *ripping*."

The Duke was frowning at the doorway and didn't answer.

"Father."

After a moment the Duke turned to look at his son. "Yes?"

"I was just saying how ripping that was."

"Routing Nurse?"

"Yes. It was awfully dukish of you, Father."

The Duke only shrugged, as if skeptical, and poured

out more lemonade to offer to Wakefield. When Bunch returned to inquire about breakfast, the Duke said:

"It's time for a change, I think, Bunch. Nurse is to be reassigned to other duties within the house—light ones, of course, given her age—or, if she prefers, she may wish to finally accept her pension and go to her family in Riverton. I'll tell her myself as soon as possible. Have you anyone on the staff who might be a suitable replacement?"

Wakefield issued a cheer, albeit a rather weak one, and Bunch said, after a moment of reflection:

"Martha Lawley, Your Grace, who is at present an under-housemaid, might—"

"I like Martha!" interrupted Wakefield eagerly. "She's always got a treat for Snuffles in her pocket. She's nice."

Bunch gave a courteous little bow. "I entirely agree, My Lord. She's also the eldest of six children, and thus has considerable experience overseeing the care of young people. However, Your Grace, it would be a significant elevation in status, representing a major disruption in the traditional hierarchical order, and I would be remiss if I failed to mention it."

The Duke replied, "You mean, Bunch, that my sister won't like it. Well, that's too bad. Can you instruct Martha as to her new duties, and hire a new under-housemaid? Also, can you have fresh lemonade and barley-water brought up? Wake, do you want a jelly, or some porridge?"

"No. The hole in my mouth hurts too much."

"I'm sorry, old chap. We'll have you right as a trivet as soon as we can. Coffee for me, Bunch, please. Jane, what would you like?"

"Coffee also, please."

"Would you like anything else?"

"No, thank you." Jane was hungry, but would wait

until she could eat without poor pinched Wakefield being forced to watch. She had gone to sit at the end of Wakefield's bed, and she looked curiously up at the Duke.

He had opened up to her again, just a little.

And she wondered—with both a giddy rush of anticipation *and* a cold uneasy sensation slithering up her spine—just how long it would last.

Chapter 15

Dr. Fotherham came promptly, and Mr. Rowland gracefully ceded further care of Wakefield to him, especially as he was to spend the day doing extractions and providing other tooth-related services for various people on the estate before returning to Bath later in the afternoon. Although Wakefield bore no grudge toward the kindly Mr. Rowland for inflicting misery and suffering upon him, he had known Dr. Fotherham all his life and found comfort in his familiar face and brisk, no-nonsense manner.

Judicious doses of laudanum were recommended, as well as saline draughts for fever and cool lavender compresses. Dr. Fotherham privately told Anthony that he was in no way alarmed, but that they should expect Wakefield to be cranky and restless for a day or two.

"Where's Lady Margaret?" he said, glancing down the empty hallway. "Usually she's a burr in my side, after me to bleed people and otherwise tell me my business. Not sick with one of her headaches, is she?"

"Actually," said Anthony, "I don't really know."

Dr. Fotherham looked a little surprised for a moment, but didn't comment further, only saying he would go downstairs to inquire, and Anthony went back into Wakefield's room. Jane, dressed in her pink gown again and her hair smoothed into a tidy knot at her nape, was sitting in the chair next to the bed sipping her coffee and telling Wakefield jokes.

Here in the bright sunlight of morning, with Dr. Fotherham's reassuring assessment, and two cups of hot fresh coffee in him, and Jane looking so lovely and composed, Anthony felt less awkward than he thought he would with the memory of last night—with its pleasures and temptations, its discoveries and revelations—so searingly vivid still, and with her bite-mark on his neck covered up by his neckcloth but exquisitely sensitive nonetheless.

He had wondered if Jane would be all cold and stiff this morning, or haughty and offended, or distant and angry, but she wasn't. She was pleasant and steady. Which was good, wasn't it?

"—so the man in the restaurant calls over the waiter, very upset, and he says, 'See here, my man, there's a caterpillar in my salad!' And the waiter says, 'Oh, don't worry, sir, there's no extra charge.'"

Wakefield, reinforced with laudanum and already more comfortable, laughed. "That's a good one, Jane."

"Another?" she asked.

"Yes, please."

"There's a man in a restaurant, absolutely furious, and he summons the waiter. 'Look!' he says, pointing at his salad. 'Do you see *that*? There's a small slug in there!' So the waiter says, 'I'm very sorry, sir, would you like me to get a bigger one?'"

Wakefield laughed again, and Jane sipped at her coffee, then said:

"Do you like riddles? I know a few of those, too."

"Oh yes, I do like riddles. Can you tell me some?"

"Of course. What animal do you look like when you take a bath?"

Wakefield thought. "I don't know."

"A little bear."

He took this in, then laughed. "A little *bare.* That's funny, Jane! Tell me another one."

"How do sailors get their clothes clean?"

"How?"

"They throw them overboard and then they're washed ashore."

Wakefield laughed again, and Jane said, "One more for now. If one horse is shut up in a stable, and another one is running loose down the road, which horse is singing 'Don't fence me in'?"

"The one running down the road."

"No, neither. Horses can't sing."

Wakefield grinned. "I say, Jane, that's clever."

Standing and watching them, and also noticing how Jane's pale wavy hair shone in the sunlight, and that her eyes were twinkling with humor in that very charming way she had, Anthony wondered if, perhaps, *some* puns weren't awful, when shared under certain circumstances, and maybe, just maybe, riddles weren't as ghastly as he always thought they were. Maybe he could even try telling a joke. Impulsively he said:

"Do either of you know the one about the student asking about yolk of eggs?"

Jane shook her head and Wakefield answered, "No. How does it go, Father?"

"Well, there's a student and a teacher, you see, and the student says to the teacher, 'Do you say "Yolk of eggs *is* white" or "Yolk of eggs *are* white"?' And the teacher says, "*Yolks* of eggs *are* white," and "*Yolk* of eggs *is* white." And then the student says . . ." Anthony paused. "Hold on a moment. I just had the clincher in my mind. And then the student says to the teacher, 'I'd say "*Yolk* of eggs *are* white." No, wait—that's not right. Damn it, I've forgotten it." He ran a hand through his hair, and saw that both Jane and Wakefield were looking up at him very kindly.

"Father, yolks of eggs aren't white, they're yellow."

"Yes, of course. Right you are, my boy. I've got it now. So the student says, 'I'd say "Yolk of egg is *yellow.*" ' "

"That's very good, Father," said Wakefield indulgently, and Jane's eyes twinkled more than ever.

"In my defense, I heard this joke when I was just about your age," Anthony said, without resentment at the fact that his eight-year-old son was patronizing him. "So really it's a miracle I remembered it at all."

"Higson told me a good one the other day," Wakefield said. "A man sends for the doctor, and when the doctor gets there, he sees that the man's ear is all torn and bloody. And the doctor says, 'What happened?' 'I bit myself,' the man says. And the doctor says, 'That's impossible! How could anyone bite themselves in the ear?' And the man says, 'I was standing on a chair.'"

He laughed, and so did Jane, and Anthony, who was filled with admiration for Wakefield's ability to tell a joke straight through from start to finish, did too. Also, he noticed with surprise and pleasure, he was filled with happiness, too, and that same rather shocking sense of naturalness. Of comfort and familiarity. The three of them hanging about together and having fun. Jane and Wakefield and himself . . .

"I'll have to tell it to Dr. Fotherham," said Wakefield, then suddenly yawned. "I say, I'm sleepy again."

He slid down low on his pillows again and dozed for a while, and Jane went downstairs for breakfast, and Anthony read some Dinkle but mostly thought about Jane and also his curious dream of being the Duke of Oyster, swanning about in the ocean. Then Jane came back upstairs and he went down for breakfast and ate a great deal and contentedly read the newspapers and didn't miss Margaret one iota, and after that he went to find Nurse, who was weeping in her rocking chair in the nursery, and he discovered through patient questioning that she had only been staying on because Margaret had been insisting, and that what she really wanted to do was to receive her pension and go live with her son George and his family in Riverton and have a little garden and play with her seven grandchildren and sit in the sun whenever she could. Thus they parted on excellent terms, and Anthony, hoping against hope that Nurse wouldn't force castor oil on her unsuspecting grandchildren, went back to Wakefield's room and found that Wakefield was awake and grumpy and rejecting the cool compress Jane was offering and in general was angry at the world again.

"His fever is up a bit, but not much," Jane told him, and turned to Wakefield. "Are you sure you won't let me put this on your forehead? It will feel quite soothing, I think."

"No," said Wakefield sulkily.

"Do you want me to tell you some more riddles and jokes?"

"No."

"Shall I read to you?"

"No."

"Would you like something to drink? Or a nice jelly?"

"No."

"Oh, poor Wakefield," said Jane, with such kindness and compassion that Wakefield burst into tears, and then let Jane sit next to him on the bed and hold him for a while, and finally agreed to let her smooth the compress on his forehead which he shortly admitted did feel rather nice. Then he asked Anthony to read some more from *The Merchant of Venice*, but got very upset at how Shylock was being treated, even though he had, of course, been wrong to ask for a pound of flesh, and said that Portia was a bully, lawyers were terrible, Antonio and Bassanio were stupid, and that it was the saddest and worst play ever written.

Anthony set aside *Tales from Shakespeare* and Jane began to tell them about the book she had been reading, which was called *Pride and Prejudice*, but Wakefield interrupted her to say that love stories were boring and also stupid, after which Anthony offered to play backgammon with him, a game which lasted only five minutes before Wakefield swept the counters off the board and cried again.

This time he let Anthony hold him, stopped crying to laugh when Snuffles tried to eat one of the counters, then cried some more and Jane picked up all the counters and put them away with the board.

With perfect timing Bunch came upstairs just then and mentioned, as if offhandedly, that Cook had made a cool, creamy, vanilla-flavored pudding which had set up to perfection, if anybody would care for some, and Jane said she'd love a dish, with whipped cream if there was any, and then Wakefield said he would too.

So he ate some of that, admitted that it tasted very good, found it just a little bit amusing when Jane got whipped cream on her nose, and nobody said anything when he let Snuffles lick his dish clean, even though it was strictly against the rules, and Anthony secretly thought that he would have liked to lick the whipped cream off Jane's nose, and, while he was at it, taste again the irresistible sweetness of her mouth.

It was early afternoon when Martha Lawley, a stocky, pleasant-faced young woman in her early twenties, came to the doorway of Wakefield's room where she dipped a little curtsy and said that Mr. Bunch had sent her to ask if she might sit with Master Wakefield for a little while, so that His Grace and Miss Kent could go downstairs and have their luncheon which would be ready in just a few minutes.

Wakefield was inclined to be resistant and surly about this plan, but softened when he saw how glad Snuffles was to see Martha, and that Martha not only had a treat for Snuffles in her pocket, she had also brought some lengths of string and offered to show him how to make a Jacob's Ladder, Kitty Whiskers, and a Cup and Saucer, a prospect so enchanting that he accepted at once, and even let her persuade him to have a nice long drink of saline draught.

Jane and the Duke therefore had a peaceful (and delicious) luncheon together in the dining-parlor, the one with the truly hideous dark-red wallpaper which she preferred to ignore, and he asked her a lot of questions about Nantwich and what it was like to grow up there and how it happened that a few years ago she ended up all alone with only a sick great-grandmother and what had inspired her to travel all the way here to Somerset, and after she had answered his questions he said, with unmistakable sincerity, that he was very impressed by her bravery, a compliment which Jane wasn't quite sure she deserved, but she appreciated it regardless, and after that they talked about astronomy and what the stars might be made of and how constellations got their names and why exactly it was that shooting stars were so captivating.

As they ate and talked, Jane could see that the Duke was *definitely* open to her again.

He was animated, there was light in his deep-blue eyes, he smiled, and was altogether so cheerful and engaging and fun to talk with that Jane had to forcefully remind herself again to be wary, just like the Nantwich girl she had been and obviously still was in many ways although considerably cleaner and better-dressed. And when the Duke proposed a walk when luncheon was over, but perhaps inside the house as there was a hideously cold ferocious wind whipping about today, Jane thought about saying no but found herself saying yes anyway, and was glad when he suggested they stroll up and down the portrait gallery rather than going again to the ballroom where she feared the temptation might be too great for her, because it was an undeniable fact that she was very much enjoying the Duke's company and was, despite all her best efforts, falling prey again to his dangerous attractiveness.

As they walked along the lengthy gallery, they paused before several of the paintings that most interested her.

Here was the Duke as a little boy, thin, solemn, his blue eyes enormous in his slender face and his abundant light-brown hair looking as if it had been violently combed into submission.

Here were his parents, the late Duke and Duchess, stiff, regal, proud, handsome, and richly dressed in gleaming silks, satins, and velvets.

And here was another boy, older, taller, broader, with darker hair and paler eyes, but with the same haughty air of the Duke and Duchess.

"That's Terence," explained the Duke. "My older brother. Should've gotten the title, you know, not me. He had all the requisite airs and graces."

"There's more to a duke than that, I hope."

The Duke shrugged, and Jane said:

"What happened to him?"

"He was attending the first annual cricket match between Eton and Harrow, and during the second inning he got so angry at Eton's wicket-keeper that he swore he was going to throttle him, then ran out onto the field and was hit in the head by a ball. Never regained consciousness."

"How terrible. I'm so sorry."

"Only a month before his wedding, too. So a few weeks after the funeral, when I turned twenty-one, I was betrothed to his fiancée Lady Selina."

Jane felt her eyes getting all round again. "You were betrothed to your dead brother's fiancée?"

"Yes. Here she is."

They paused before an enormous portrait of the Duke as a very young man, tall and straight, and a young woman in shimmering cloth-of-gold, seated stiff and upright in a gilded chair next to him. Her hair was brown with glints of gold in it, her eyes were brown, her complexion like porcelain, and she was remarkably pretty, though her expression, Jane mused secretly to herself, was off-putting, for she was gazing directly at the viewer as if she found what she saw entirely beneath her notice, or, possibly, repugnant.

"She's very beautiful," Jane said, truthfully.

The Duke didn't respond, only moved on to another painting. "And here's Wake as a baby."

Once again the Duke, a few years older, was standing, and the Duchess was sitting and looking at the viewer; adorable little Wakefield, held rather carelessly with one arm by the Duchess, was looking up at the Duke. And the Duke was looking down at his son, a faint smile curling his attractive mouth.

"Here's Margaret and Terence."

Enclosed by a heavy, elaborate frame, Lady Margaret and Terence, both very handsome and proud and appearing to be on the cusp of early adulthood, were standing outdoors, side by side, with the Hastings lake and Greek temple in the background.

"Why aren't you in the painting?" Jane asked.

"Oh, I was in bed then, because of my back, so they went ahead without me."

"That seems unfair."

"Even if I had been well, the prospect of untold hours in their company posing for a painting would have been highly unappealing."

"Oh. You didn't get along?"

"No, I was rather the odd man out, I suppose you could say. Very different in temperament, interests, and so on. Terence used to call me a changeling baby, and my father always said that it was only my strong resemblance to himself that kept him from accusing my mother of adultery and actually sending her off to a nunnery even though we're not Roman Catholics, and me to a distant relative of theirs in Wales somewhere. Although I might, in fact, have been happier there."

"Well, that's just awful." Jane saw that although the Duke was being stoic and matter-of-fact and not the least bit self-pitying, still her heart ached for him and without taking any time at all to consider the consequences, implications, *or* ramifications, rashly she reached up to put her arms around him, just as she had wanted to do that day after church when he had looked so sad talking about having to be in bed for all those painful years, and the next thing she knew he was saying "Jane," with wonderment and awe in his voice, and the next thing she knew after *that* was that they were kissing each other and she had completely forgotten about being careful or wary and instead was having a marvelous time with her mouth crushed against the Duke's in a highly delightful way and their bodies pressed so tightly together that she was sure he could feel every curve and plane of her body, because she certainly could feel his and they were, each and every one, *delicious*, except for the fact that their clothing was really getting in the way of full and utter deliciousness.

They broke apart only when they heard a distant footfall, which turned out to be a servant on the backstairs, but it did inspire fresh caution, and so, with a final shared smile, which made it abundantly clear to Jane that not only was the Duke open to her, she was equally (and recklessly) open to him, they made their way back to Wakefield's room and found him awake, but ready for more laudanum, and Martha sitting at his bedside with Snuffles on her lap, a clear sign of Wakefield's enthusiastic approval.

Accordingly Anthony gave Wakefield another dose of laudanum, and when he had swallowed it Wakefield announced:

"Martha says she doesn't believe in giving children castor oil."

Everyone looked at Martha, who reddened a little but said, "In my family we use it for a compress, or if our hands get all dried out, but we'd never take it off a spoon or nothing. Because it hurts your stomach something awful. Your Grace. Ma'am."

"Well then, Martha, you're obviously going to fit right in," answered the Duke, and Wakefield said triumphantly to her:

"I *told* you Father wouldn't mind."

A footman arrived and stood just past the open door. Mrs. Henrietta Penhallow had called, and could Miss Kent please come downstairs to the drawing-room as soon as was convenient?

This innocent question immediately provoked in Wakefield a loud angry outburst, which soon devolved into tears. Mrs. Penhallow had come to take Jane away, only Jane mustn't go, he didn't want her to go, couldn't she stay just for one more night, just until he could eat macaroni again?

"Wake," said the Duke, but Jane softly said to him, "If you don't mind having me, I'd be glad to stay for another night."

He lit up. "I say, that would be splendid. You really don't mind?"

"Not at all."

"Thank you," he said quietly, and Jane said to Wakefield:

"I'm staying."

He stopped crying and lit up too. "Oh, Jane, that's *capital*." Then he dimmed a little and said to the Duke, "Father, you'll go downstairs with Jane, won't you? Just in case Mrs. Penhallow tries to take her away?"

"I think," said the Duke, "that Jane is perfectly capable of conveying herself where and how she likes. But I'll go with her for moral support if she happens to need it."

"Well, that's jolly. Martha, have you noticed how soft Snuggles' ears are? He likes it if you pet them."

So Jane and the Duke left Wakefield's bedroom upon a scene of renewed calm, and together they began to make their way downstairs, and Jane noticed, with a sudden sharp sense of pleasure so intense that it was rather unnerving, how entirely comfortable and companionable it felt to be walking side by side with the Duke, each of them adjusting their stride just a tiny bit without even having to mention it, as if it were completely easy and natural and just how things should be.

Though he wasn't exactly proud of it, Anthony had gotten rather used to Margaret's absence, and so he was a little surprised to see her in the drawing-room. And he was more than a little surprised to see her and old Mrs. Penhallow seated rather cozily next to each other on a sofa, apparently engrossed in pleasant conversation.

It was like seeing formerly hostile generals from opposing camps engaging in an amicable parley.

He hadn't seen Margaret look this benign since before the Merifields came.

Actually, he hadn't seen her look this benign for a lot longer than that.

Uneasily he wondered if they had been talking about *him*, busily comparing notes as to his various flaws, shortcomings, faults, foibles, failings, inadequacies, deficiencies, limitations, and general subducalness.

His surprise turned to astonishment when Margaret greeted both himself *and* Jane with marked civility, and also when Mrs. Penhallow greeted *him* with a similar marked civility.

For a few moments of intense disorientation, Anthony wondered wildly if he were dreaming.

Showing no signs of disapproval or dismay, Mrs. Penhallow smiled at Jane, then asked after Wakefield, complimented the lofty dimensions of the room, remarked upon the chilly weather, mentioned the state of the roads, hoped Lady Margaret's justly renowned Siberian irises were doing well, and wondered when Jane was coming home.

"I'd like to stay one more night, Great-grandmother," answered Jane, and turned to Margaret. "I hope that's all right with you, ma'am."

"Of course," said Margaret graciously. "If there's anything you need, Miss Kent, I trust you'll let me know at once."

"That's very kind," Jane said. "Thank you."

Mrs. Penhallow didn't stay long, and Jane walked with

her to the front door to say goodbye. Bracing himself for the predictable storm of Margaret's wrath to break over his head, Anthony took the opportunity to let her know about Nurse's retirement and Martha Lawley's promotion to the post, and was not only surprised and astonished but also actively shocked when Margaret merely nodded and thanked him for letting her know.

"I say, Meg," he said, looking hard at her, "are you all right?"

"Yes, of course. And how are *you*?"

As this was quite possibly the first time in their whole entire lives together that she had asked him this, Anthony felt his jaw drop, and so precipitously that he was surprised it didn't catapult to the floor and pitch upwards so forcefully that his eyeballs shot out from their sockets and dangled by their stalks.

He said, "Oh, I'm fine."

"I'm pleased to hear it."

Jane came back into the drawing-room, but stood hesitating just past the doorway, and Margaret graciously said:

"Please do come in and sit down again, Miss Kent."

Jane did, and Margaret went on, "I'm afraid that we may have gotten off on the wrong foot together, Miss Kent. I was preoccupied, I daresay, with getting the house ready for guests, and then of course with guests here, I was so terribly distracted then as well. I'm so glad you'll be here for another night—it will give us a chance to talk together. I do so much hope we can start over again, and be friends."

Anthony actually put a hand underneath his jaw, to keep it from dropping again in his astonishment. But Jane, very composed, only said politely:

"Thank you, Lady Margaret. I hope so, too."

Then there was some remarkably affable (if very mundane) chitchat for a while, and Anthony found himself thinking how nice it would be if Jane and Margaret really did become friends. For one thing, Margaret might stop saying nasty things about irregular connections, people sneaking rolls into their pockets, and other, similar remarks which were not only unnecessary but depressing.

The rest of the day passed quite peacefully.

He and Jane spent time with Wakefield, talking about pigs and astronomy and Greek mythology and also how it could be possible that not everyone in the world liked dogs, and Jane told them a few amusing stories from her life back in Nantwich, and then he and Jane had dinner with Margaret, who was *still* being friendly, and they talked about this and that (still mundane, but actual conversation nonetheless), and then he and Jane went back upstairs and played backgammon with Wakefield and he, Anthony, read out loud from *The Tempest*, which had, in Wakefield's opinion, a ripping beginning as it started with a terrible storm at sea and a shipwreck.

Margaret even came in, wanting, she said, to see how Wakefield was and if Jane had everything she needed, and although Wakefield was clearly far from overjoyed to see her, at least he didn't shriek and collapse into tears, but only answered with a reasonable amount of calmness that he was feeling better and that he hoped to start chewing things again tomorrow and also go over to the stables and visit his pony who he was sure had been missing him a great deal, and after this brief exchange of civilities he asked Anthony to please keep reading, because he wanted to know what happened with Caliban whom he considered to be the most interesting character in the story by far.

Margaret stayed so long, seating herself in a chair by the fire and listening to *The Tempest* with her hands folded restfully in her lap, that there was absolutely no opportunity for him to take another stroll with Jane somewhere which might just have allowed them to kiss a bit. (Or a lot.)

This was a disappointment, but still Anthony went to bed that night feeling happy and peaceful.

Jane went to bed that night feeling thoughtful and uneasy.

For one thing, she didn't quite like how earlier today Great-grandmother had, as they had walked to the front door together, inquired as if casually about her sleeping arrangements, and seemed rather excessively relieved to hear that a trundle bed had been brought into Wakefield's room. Also, she had said she would have some exciting news to share when Jane came home, and when Jane asked what it was, Great-grandmother had only shook her head and smiled, saying playfully that she would wait to tell Jane at the Hall. Jane had felt a little like a horse in front of whom a carrot was being dangled just out of reach, and then felt awful for feeling that way when there was every probability that kind, generous, indulgent Great-grandmother had something pleasant in store for her.

And another thing: Jane didn't trust Lady Margaret's sudden turnaround into amicability.

It reminded her of the time Betts Johnson, a girl in the neighborhood with whom she had shared a powerful and bitter antipathy from age five onward, had, at the age of twelve, abruptly presented to Jane a face of sweetness and affability, offered to give her a roasted turkey leg, admired the color of Jane's hair and how it waved, and invited her to come home and see the new doll her mother had made for her. Jane, longing to make friends and greedy for the turkey leg and keen to see the doll, had eagerly gone with Betts who, as soon as they were in the shadowy little alley behind her house, whistled and thus summoned two of her cronies, and the three of them fell upon Jane and had beaten her to a pulp.

That was, in part, how Jane had learned to be a wary Nantwich girl.

And there was one more thing.

She had been hoping to find a few (or many) moments in which to kiss the Duke some more, but with Lady Margaret hanging about like she had, it had been impossible. When Wakefield tired of listening to *The Tempest* and admitted that he was ready for sleep, the adults had each gone their separate way for the night.

So Jane had retired to her comfortable little trundle bed feeling thoughtful, uneasy, *and* disappointed.

Chapter 16

The next day Wakefield woke up so much restored that he not only demanded breakfast right away, he happily devoured his soft scrambled eggs with three slices of crunchy buttered toast, and even though he hadn't yet eaten macaroni, he accepted with very reasonable good humor Jane's suggestion that it was time for her to go home.

"If I can eat toast, I can eat macaroni like anything," he said. "Thanks awfully for coming to stay, Jane. I'm sorry if I was beastly."

She smiled and kissed him on the top of his head. "You weren't at all. Goodbye, dear Wakefield."

"Goodbye," he said, and gave Snuffles a bit of buttery crust.

So Jane said goodbye as well to the Duke and Lady Margaret, who both thanked her profusely, and Jane, sitting in the Hastings carriage which was to take her back to Surmont Hall, watched as Lady Margaret's friendly face receded into the distance, then felt sorry she hadn't looked at the Duke instead.

Why did she feel as if she had lost an opportunity she would never get back?

It was a cold, unsettling feeling.

Jane leaned back against the soft velvet squabs, pulled her pelisse a little more tightly around her, and scolded herself for being silly. Her visit at Hastings had gone well, Wakefield was fine, she had been deliciously kissed by the Duke, and now she was going home.

Surely there was no reason to feel so uneasy.

No reason at all.

It seemed as if she had been gone from the Hall for a month, or more, rather than just two nights. She was received with such warm familiarity by Great-grandmother, Livia, Cousin Gabriel, and the children, too, that it helped take her mind off the puzzling questions of the Duke's concertina-like behavior and also his sister's sudden transmogrification into amiability. Jane was longing to ask Great-grandmother about her exciting news, but between taking a nice long bath and spending a lively hour in the nursery, and after that witnessing the arrival of all the other things Great-grandmother had ordered for her from Miss Simpkin (which had to be inspected and admired and, in the case of an absolutely stunning jade-green evening-gown with matching satin slippers, tried on at once), it wasn't until after dinner when she, Cousin Gabriel, and Livia were gathered in the rococo drawing-room that Great-grandmother finally made her announcement.

"I have decided, my dear Jane, that you and I are going to London for the Season."

"What?" said Jane, astonished, and saw that Livia and Cousin Gabriel were surprised as well, so clearly they hadn't been told the news either.

Great-grandmother was looking very pleased with herself. "Yes, you're going to make your Society *début*, my dear. We'll attend the Queen's Drawing-room, naturally, and as for vouchers for Almack's, I've written to

Sally Jersey—who says, of course, she's merely awaiting our arrival before coming to call with them at once. I've also written to Mrs. Dauntrey, of the Dauntrey Employment Agency, to hire staff for the Penhallow townhouse in Berkeley Square, and to my favorite Town modiste, Madame Hébert, as you'll require—despite the protestations I can already see you fomenting—a great many additions to your wardrobe."

Great-grandmother smiled at Jane (who, a little dazed to hear of all this bustle, couldn't help but think again that her dear kind relation truly wasn't one to let the grass grow under *her* feet), and then went on:

"That will be our first priority, and once you're properly outfitted I shall introduce you to all my acquaintance among the *ton*, and of course in addition to balls, dinner parties, Carlton House receptions, Venetian breakfasts, rides in the Park, et cetera, et cetera, we'll visit various galleries and museums, attend concerts and lectures, and do whatever else strikes our fancy."

Even more dazed, Jane suddenly found herself thinking of Great-grandmother Kent, who always said, in ringing tones of the deepest conviction, that the London Season was merely an excuse for all the country's worst and wickedest rogues, rakes, rascals, scoundrels, tarts, jezebels, hussies, sinners, reprobates, degenerates, libertines, wastrels, scapegraces, spendthrifts, dandies, harpies, idlers, loafers, strumpets, harlots, trollops, jades, coxcombs, popinjays, scandalmongers, fops, swells, drunkards, gamesters, wantons, slatterns, malingerers, layabouts, triflers, fribbles, philanderers, lawyers, French spies, freethinkers, seditionists, atheists, anarchists, adulterers, Americans, snuff-takers, coffee-drinkers, writers who had no business calling themselves that, disgraced politicians, and various other n'er-do-wells—under a very thin and glittering veneer of so-called respectability—to congregate in all their finery, which in the case of men meant obscenely tight pants and in the case of women, thin wispy transparent gowns with shockingly low necklines.

Which of course had made Jane wish with all her irrepressibly defiant heart to experience it herself, knowing all the time that it was to be forever denied her, given that there was a very good chance she was going to live out the rest of her life in Nantwich and quite likely in the most fearsome, abject, and pitiful poverty if she didn't get over her intense hatred of sewing, which she probably wouldn't, and the Lord only knew (as Great-grandmother Kent often said) what was going to become of her.

Jane took a deep breath, which made her chest expand against a bodice which, satisfyingly, would soon need to be let out again.

London!

The *Season*!

Oh, what fun!

She felt as if she had suddenly been plunged into a great busy beehive of excitement, although she had never in real life gotten that close to one, having (she hoped) a reasonable amount of common sense, nor was she so caught up in dazzled delight that she would really think that being thrust into an actual beehive would be pleasant.

All she meant was, this was a very exciting development and she could hardly wait to see if Great-grandmother Kent's assessment was in any way correct. Though, upon the briefest interval of reflection, it seemed unlikely that Great-grandmother Henrietta would deign to grace such a scandalous rogues' gallery with her lofty presence.

A conundrum which only made the prospect even more intriguing.

Even as Jane was pondering this, a memory rose.

A familiar voice:

I detest the idea of it.

The Duke, saying this to Lady Felicia about London.

Gamely Lady Felicia had insisted:

Oh, Your Grace, you must *go. Truly! It's absolutely divine, I do assure you!*

And he had replied, cool and implacable:

I mustn't, and I won't.

How long did a Season last? For how long would she be away from home, and the Duke?

And Wakefield, and Livia and Cousin Gabriel, and the children, and all her new friends, and Mr. Pressley, too, and his lessons and wonderful sermons?

And . . . what if while she was away, Lady Margaret produced the perfect candidate for the Duke? Someone so devastatingly clever and beautiful and accomplished and delightful and splendid and entrancing that she could finally overcome his longtime reluctance?

Don't be stupid, Jane, she told herself severely, you're not a guard dog to circle the Duke with your teeth bared.

Besides, if it took that kind of vigilance to keep the Duke from looking at another woman the way he sometimes looked at her, with his blue eyes both dark with passion and filled with light, then maybe there was no point to her concern.

"Grandmama," said Cousin Gabriel, jolting Jane out of her reverie. She saw that he was looking at Great-grandmother with an expression that was half quizzical, half amused, his dark brows raised. He went on:

"You're not going to engage in matchmaking again, are you?"

"I'm sure I don't know what you mean." In Great-grandmother's aristocratic voice was just a hint of haughtiness.

Livia laughed. "Oh, Granny, beware! The best laid plans, you know."

Jane glanced among the three of them, baffled, and Livia went on kindly:

"I'm sorry, Jane, we're being obscure! You see, when Gabriel was a single gentleman, Granny—who knows absolutely everyone in Polite Society—embarked on herculean feats of matchmaking, determined to find him the best and most perfect bride in the world, but to no avail. Poor Gabriel ended up with me."

Cousin Gabriel turned on her that subtle, loving smile. "Not poor. Lucky. Fortunate. *Incredibly* fortunate."

Livia smiled back at him, and Great-grandmother loftily waved her hand in the air, saying:

"If it should happen that Jane meets someone she likes very much, someone suitable, then naturally we would all be thrilled for her."

Someone suitable.

Jane rolled this phrase around in her mind. She had gleaned, even while only half listening to the Merifields' boring chatter about London, that the Season provided an opportunity for people (and by "people," they obviously meant "young women") to find a spouse. To contract an eligible—suitable—union.

To Jane the so-called Marriage Mart had sounded bizarre, frankly, and reminded her of Nantwich's biweekly livestock auction.

Still, people needed livestock, and lots of women wanted to get married, so maybe there was something useful and efficient to it after all.

But what about herself?

Did *she* want to be married?

There was a time, three years ago, when she had. (But she had made her choice, painful as it was, knowing she was doing the right thing.)

And now?

What did she want now?

Jane thought about the deep enduring love clearly shared between Livia and Cousin Gabriel. It was beautiful, and inspiring, to see—especially as Livia had told her how, at first, she and Gabriel positively disliked each other and didn't in the least want to be married. Too, Livia had mentioned Gabriel's cousin Hugo and his wife Katherine: how they had, after a similarly inauspicious beginning, fallen madly in love with each other. There was another Penhallow cousin, the one who lived far away to the north in the Scottish Highlands, who had been forced to marry because of an arcane and ancient decree, but apparently he and his wife had found unexpected happiness together.

Which just went to show, happy marriages *were* possible.

Mentally Jane tucked away this interesting nugget, and thought again about the phrase *someone suitable.*

For some reason it made her think of Betts Johnson, and how she, Jane, had naively let herself be lured away to that dark alley.

Well, like a proper Nantwich girl, she would be alert and wary and awake to danger and also for any opportunities that came her way. Not a big greasy delicious turkey leg waved in her face, of course—hopefully she'd moved beyond that sort of easy temptation.

She would look for opportunities for happiness.

All these thoughts flashed swiftly through Jane's head.

Great-grandmother went on smilingly, "Yes, thrilling indeed. As a cherished member of the Penhallow family, my dear Jane, you are to look as high as you please. And, naturally, you'll be dowered just as you ought."

For a fleeting moment Jane thought about the Viscount

Whitton and his dashed hopes in this regard. A brief urge to snicker came and went.

Cousin Gabriel said, "Jane, you know you can say no, don't you?"

"Say no?" Great-grandmother's blue eyes—suddenly anxious, even pleading—turned to Jane. "Oh, but my dear, you'll not deny me this opportunity? This very great joy of introducing you to the world, and letting everyone see how proud I am of you? If my darling Titus had lived—if your poor grandmother Charity had too—why, this would all be happening as a matter of course. It gives me so much happiness, thinking how Titus would have wanted this for you, and how I'm able to provide you with what you deserve. I can't give you back your childhood in Nantwich, with all your challenges and hardships—the deprivations and uncertainties—but I *can* give you a Season worthy of your bright beauty and good heart."

Great-grandmother's eyes were now shimmering with tears and her voice had gone all soft and shaky. Jane was entirely taken aback to see her usually doughty relation like this. Well! She'd be nothing less than an ingrate, a cruel selfish terrible ingrate, to refuse, and besides, that irrepressibly curious and defiant part of her really *did* want to go. Even though there was yet another part—which felt stubborn and fearful and also full of longing—which wanted to dig in its heels and stay here in order to ignominiously patrol around the Duke like a vigilant guard dog (though it was not a part of herself of which she felt at all proud).

While Great-grandmother was at Hastings yesterday, had she told Lady Margaret about the London plans, and *that* was why she'd gotten all strangely and suddenly amiable?

Because she, Jane, would be out of the way?

Jane Kent, with the irregular connection, with the low sordid background, who wasn't good enough for her brother the Duke?

Jane set her jaw, and said:

"When will we leave, Great-grandmother, and for how long will we be in London?"

Great-grandmother smiled, blinking away her tears. "Is that a yes, my dear?"

"Yes. Yes, it is."

Great-grandmother's smile broadened swiftly into cheerfulness. "Oh, how marvelous! I should like to leave in a fortnight. It will be a trifle early in the Season, but as Madame Hébert will be very busy with our numerous commissions, which will take some little while, I do believe the timing will work out nicely."

Two weeks! So soon. So very soon. Jane took this in. "And when will we come home?"

"It depends," answered Great-grandmother. "The Season ends in early July, but afterwards we might like to visit some friends of mine at their country estates, or go to Brighton, perhaps, and enjoy the sea for a while."

Jane nodded, as if this all sounded delightful, which it did on the one hand, while on the other hand, inside herself she was thinking that Lady Margaret could deftly produce *multiple* candidates while they were away, and also it seemed there was a strong likelihood that they would miss this year's *fête*, which meant she wouldn't be able to cheer on the Duchess in the Fattest Pig competition *or* root for the Hastings pumpkin to finally receive the first-place gilt cup.

Something she had really been looking forward to.

She needed a plan, Jane thought to herself. And a little time to think.

So she said nothing more, and that, apparently, was

that. Livia and Cousin Gabriel exchanged a look, then he picked up his book again and Livia went back to her sewing, and Great-grandmother spent a very animated hour describing to Jane in great detail all the many pleasures and diversions that awaited her.

Jane smiled and nodded.

Nodded and smiled.

Part of her was happy, part of her was uncertain.

Later, before going to her bedchamber for the night, she walked with her candle to the Picture Gallery, and stood for a while looking at a portrait of Grandfather Titus when he was just about her own age. He seemed to be looking directly back at her, in his gray eyes a merry, devil-may-care sparkle. *Hey ho!* she fancied him saying. *Love or nothing, my dear girl.*

Love or nothing.

And just like that, Jane immediately knew what she was going to do.

She was going to take a big risk.

It made her feel frightened and exhilarated both at once, as one might feel standing boldly on the edge of a high cliff.

Was she going to jump?

Love or nothing.

Yes, she was.

So fortified was Wakefield by his hearty breakfast that by midday he had been up and about again, and off to the stables to see his pony, polish some tack, and help the grooms muck out stalls, this last being an activity he enjoyed a great deal and always ended with him being absolutely filthy and reeking of manure, Margaret screeching, Nurse also screeching, Wakefield screeching back in self-defense, a bath during which there was more screeching as well as water being splashed on every available surface including the ceiling, and general unpleasant mayhem.

Anthony took a moment to drop a word in Martha Lawley's ear, and she promised to do her best to divert Wakefield up the backstairs and into a brief but comprehensive bath before anyone else was the wiser.

Thus reassured, Anthony went for a long stroll up and down the lime-walk, dreaming of summer and the tiny, white, sweet-smelling blossoms among which the bees danced and hummed. Dreaming, too, of Jane and her incendiary kisses. When could they meet again? And, hopefully, find some private time together?

As he paced, Anthony mused upon the difficulties in actively seeking a way to be alone with a woman (beyond the unexpected opportunity provided by one's child's tooth extraction, not that he ever wanted to repeat *that*).

This was certainly quite the reversal.

Usually he struggled to find ways to *not* be alone with a woman.

He remembered, with a chill of horror snaking down his spine, the panicky agony of practically being shoved into the conservatory with Miss Preston-Carnaby, and Lady Felicia's determined attempts to corner him in some shadowy place, and Miss D'Arblay's rabid urgings to go traipsing deep into the woods hunting squirrels together; and into his mind rose the alarmingly vast specter of all the other matrimonial candidates whom Margaret had over the years brought to Hastings.

He had dodged and hidden and evaded and skulked.

Now, however, he *wanted* to be alone with Jane.

But how?

He bent his mind to this knotty problem.

Could he have his own extraction, as an excuse to bring her back to Hastings for a couple of nights?

Unfortunately, all his teeth were in excellent condition, and as much as he longed to kiss Jane again, he drew the line at sacrificing a perfectly good tooth (and of course it would be impossible to persuade the scrupulously ethical Mr. Rowland to join him in this devious conspiracy).

Plus, one could hardly kiss well, or want to be kissed, having just had a tooth pulled.

He *could* ride over to Surmont Hall, on the pretext of talking to Penhallow about some question of estate management, and arrive just around tea-time. But having tea with Jane, especially under the sardonic eye of old Mrs. Penhallow, was hardly the same thing as—say—the two of them being deliciously alone in the Hastings ballroom.

By the time he finished his walk Anthony still had no answers, but all the same, it seemed like a good problem with which to wrestle, and his mood was sanguine.

This cheerful state of mind persisted all throughout the rest of Friday—especially since Martha proved to be as good as her word, and the day passed entirely without any screeching at all, at least within his own earshot—and lingered through Saturday morning, up until, Anthony having gone to visit the Duchess, Johns had come stumping over, looking so buoyant that Anthony was sure that he had gotten into the most gruesome fight with his nemesis Cremwell and royally bested him. Johns announced:

"Well, that's one less thing to worry about, guv'nor."

Anthony gave the Duchess a final scratch, smiling as she gave a loud grunt of satisfaction, then put down the big stick, resigned to hearing a macabre and painstakingly detailed account of every injury Johns had dealt the hapless Cremwell. "What is?"

"She'll be gone soon. Never did like her hanging about the Duchess. I always did say, you can never be too careful, and I'll tell you this, guv'nor, *I'll* be sleeping better at night once the coast is clear."

"Who will be gone soon?"

"That Miss Kent."

Anthony had been leaning his elbows on the balustrade, watching the Duchess meander over to her trough to poke around with her snout at the scattered remainders of an enormous breakfast, but now he abruptly straightened and stared down at Johns. "What do you mean?"

"That Miss Kent," explained Johns. "She's leaving."

"What? Why?"

"To London, guv'nor, for that there Season as they call it, which don't make no sense, do it? Give me spring, summer, autumn, and winter! 'Twas good enough for my pa, and *his* pa, too, so it's good enough for me and mine, I reckon! Anyroad, old Mrs. Penhallow's a-taking that Miss Kent to London, so she can get her leg-shackled to some high-and-mighty nob. Leastways, that's what the missus says."

"London? Leg-shackled? To a nob? How does Mrs. Johns know this?" In his shock and dismay Anthony felt as if *he'd* been in a gruesome fight and royally bested, and he put out a hand to the balustrade as if to steady himself against further blows.

"Why, her niece Abby's a kitchen-maid over at the Hall, guv'nor. Tells the missus all the news. That there young shaver Daniel's cut a new tooth, you see, and Mrs. Livia lost two of her best layers last week, and one of the footmen came down with the collywobbles, right bad he did, and—"

"When is Miss Kent leaving?" Anthony interrupted.

"A fortnight. Cheer up, guv'nor, there's no need to be Friday-faced! I'll keep good watch over the Duchess, see if I don't, these next two weeks, just in case that Miss Kent tries to—"

"Johns, you're being—" Anthony broke off just before he said "redonculous." He went on, "You're being absurd."

Johns bristled. "Oh, I am, am I? Now look here, guv'nor, do you want that first prize again this year or not?"

"You know I do," said Anthony, but before he could be drawn into a spirited verbal competition with Johns as to who wanted it more, and possibly a nasty debate about the probability of Jane actually sneaking over to the pig-cote and doing harm to the Duchess, he let go of the balustrade and said, "Give her some fresh straw, will you?" Then he gave a loud whistle for the dogs, turned on his heel, and walked quickly back toward the house, Breen, Joe, Sam, and Snuffles following him in an affable ragtag pack.

Having diverted them to the stables, he went inside and up to his library where he found that even Dinkle couldn't distract him from the reality that was not only staring him in the face, it was shoving a fist into his gut, meanly tweaking his entrails, putting its hands around his throat, pounding a mallet on his head, squeezing his lungs, and also—it being a reality rather like a malevolent many-armed octopus, able to inflict discomfort on multiple fronts at once—pressing down so hard on him he half-wondered if he would ever be able to get up from his chair.

Maybe it was just as well.

Eventually he would die, rot, get extremely smelly, and then turn to dust, which might actually be a relief.

Jane was leaving.

In two weeks.

For London.

For the Season.

During which old Mrs. Penhallow would exert herself in marrying Jane off.

And it was well-known in these parts, and possibly all over Somerset, and perhaps throughout the entirety of England, that Mrs. Henrietta Penhallow was a person who *got things done.*

Anthony could not have said just how long he sat there, immobile, stunned and hurting; it was only a shout—*"Jane!"*—from outside which galvanized him into pushing himself up from his seat to go to the windows that looked out to the front.

It was Wakefield who had joyfully shouted. There he was on the graveled sweep below, going to meet Jane, who was riding a small, neat bay, behind her trailing a groom who quickly dismounted to help Jane down from her horse.

Just as quickly Anthony stepped away from the window, not wanting to be seen.

He plunked himself back in his chair, ran his hands through his hair, got up again as if to go somewhere else, then went back to his desk, sat down, ran his hands through his hair a second time, plucked at his neckcloth, needlessly shuffled the papers on his desk, and desperately wondered how he should behave toward Jane.

Who was leaving.

Who was leaving *him.*

To go off to London and marry someone else.

Someone better than him, no doubt.

A high-and-mighty nob.

A viscount, an earl, another duke?

Maybe the best duke in the world.

Some urbane, polished fellow, sophisticated and graceful, all broad-shouldered and heavily muscled and perfectly dressed and with a crisp, beautifully tied neckcloth, who always knew exactly what to say on all occasions, and of course was also a marvelous dancer who loved to hunt and go to London parties where he transfixed everyone with his witty quips and smoldering eyes, quoted poetry, and basically did everything right.

Well, and what of it, old chap? said a voice in his head,

sounding an awful lot like his late brother Terence. Breezy, careless, self-assured, authoritative. Dukish. *You don't want to marry her anyway. Why should you care if she goes away?*

Anthony sat up straighter.

By Jove, it was true.

He didn't want to be married.

He *wasn't* going to be married.

He would *never* be married again.

Not only that, he had, in fact, been reasonably content with his life before Jane came, and when Jane left, he would go on being reasonably content. And that was enough for any man. What was the point of reaching for the stars? None. A silly endeavor (practically speaking as well as metaphorically). And so life would soon resume its accustomed course. He would be peaceful once more.

Anthony folded his hands together on top of his reshuffled papers, exactly as would a man who was satisfied with his life as it was. Who had fought back against the nasty, grasping octopus-reality coming at him with flailing tentacles. He could breathe, he could swallow, he could stand up as he liked.

He was fine.

Take that, you wretched octopus-reality, he said to himself, then suddenly remembered a dream he'd had earlier in the week. Himself as the Duke of Oyster, lording it over his fellow denizens of the deep. A seahorse, a crowd of sardines, an octopus who, he recalled, had seemed friendly at the time.

Good God, what an odd dream.

What on earth had brought it on?

He cast his mind back to the time and place.

Oh yes: it was the day of the extraction. In the soft burgeoning twilight Wakefield and Jane and Snuffles had been napping, and he had been sitting in the chair next to the bed, exhausted and half-asleep already.

He had felt himself—how had he put it?—opening up to Jane.

Like an oyster.

He had smiled a little, imagining himself as a giant oyster.

His Slipperiness the Duke of Oyster.

But what he had forgotten, that day, was that if an oyster could open up, it could close, too.

Tightly.

So that nothing—no one?—could get in.

Footsteps sounded from the hallway, and Anthony heard them with newfound serenity. He was a closed-up oyster, a door slammed shut, a drawbridge brought up. No one would ever know that on his throat were the marks of Jane's sweet love-bite; they were fading away, day by day.

Soon they would be gone.

There was nothing to panic about.

He was fine.

He was safe.

He was *fine*.

"What do you want to talk to Father about, Jane?" asked Wakefield, who had volunteered to show her to the Duke's library where, Bunch had informed them in the Great Hall, he was to be found. Now they were walking along a long hallway. "Can I be there, too?"

Jane paused, and looked down at him with an ache in her heart. Oh, she was going to miss him! "I need to talk with your father alone, dear Wakefield. But I'll talk with you afterwards. Where will you be?"

"In the billiards room. I made a capital hidey-hole.

Wait till you see it—you'll love it. I say, what's the matter, Jane? You don't have a bad tooth, do you? You look just like I felt when I did."

"Do I?"

"Yes, you looked very millencocky just now."

"Like your aunt Margaret's cat."

"Yes, that's right."

Wakefield had used that word on the day she had first gone with him to Hastings, met the Duchess, and been invited over for luncheon. How very long ago that seemed. Jane smiled a little, then sighed a little, too. "No, my teeth are fine. Thank you very much for asking."

"If your teeth are fine, why do you look so much like Aunt Margaret's cat?"

She leaned down to kiss the top of his head. "Wakefield, you *do* ask the best questions."

"You told me that already. Only last time you said they were delightful. Can you stay for luncheon? If we're lucky, we won't have to listen to Aunt Margaret talk about flowers like she did that other time. Wasn't it awfully dull? Why is it that grownups can be so boring? I don't mean you, Jane, or Father, but it does seem that a lot of them are. Will *I* be boring when I'm a grownup, do you suppose?"

Jane had to suppress the urge to kiss his head again. "Somehow, Wakefield, I don't think so."

"Well, I hope not. But what if I can't help it? What if I start talking about flowers, or the weather, or what the roads are like, or other stupid things like that, and I can't stop myself? Will you give me a secret signal, Jane? You could wink your eye, like this—" Wakefield demonstrated by squeezing one eyelid closed and distorting half his face. "Or you could do this." He twirled a finger in the air. "And then I'll know I'm being boring and shut up."

She would not—could not—bring herself to say, *I may*

be elsewhere when you're a grownup, dear Wakefield. So she only nodded. And together they went to an open doorway, standing on the threshold of a large, light-filled room which had two entire walls of sturdy mahogany shelving that were packed with books of all sizes, shapes, and colors. There was a pair of comfortable old leather armchairs set before the fireplace, in which a fire leaped and danced and crackled in a very cheerful way, and a large handsome desk of some dark scarred wood, crowded with papers, notes, books, pencils, letter-openers and paper-knives, pens, and a big inkwell. Also upon the surface of the desk were the Duke's feet in their familiar dark scuffed boots, crossed at the ankles, and the man himself with his chair tipped back and, apparently, deeply absorbed in a book.

"I say, Father, didn't you hear us coming?" said Wakefield, and the Duke gave quite a start.

"Oh, hullo," he said, removing his legs from his desk and setting aside his book. "I was just reading up on swine dysentery. Absolutely riveting. Do come in."

"Jane wants to talk to you alone, Father, and then she's going to talk with me in the billiards room. By the way, Jane rode here all by herself. If you'd looked out the window you would have seen her. She was riding like anything. Isn't that ripping?"

"Very," he said, but without much warmth. "Congratulations."

"You sound awfully stuffy, Father," said Wakefield critically. "Aren't you glad that Jane's learned how to ride? Now she can come over whenever she likes."

The Duke only nodded, and Wakefield said, "Now you *look* stuffy. What's the matter?"

"Nothing."

Wakefield stared hard at him, then shrugged. "If you say so. See you later, Jane."

"See you later," she said, and Wakefield began hopping away on one foot, and then she took a deep breath, wishing her heart would stop pounding like it would if one were standing on the edge of an extremely high cliff and about to do something bold and extreme and possibly very foolhardy.

Jane stepped inside the library, and, as firmly as possible, she closed the door behind her.

Chapter 17

Anthony was pleased to discover that he was quite unmoved by the fact that not only was Jane here, they were actually alone together. And even though she looked incredibly attractive in her dark-crimson riding dress, which made her gray eyes glow like a wintry moon, and also displayed to fine advantage her neat, elegant figure, he was able to register all this without any involuntary physiological responses (such as his mind dissolving, a wild thump of his heart, hot fire consuming him everywhere, an urge to leap up and rush over and take her in his arms, and so on).

Still, he wasn't sorry there was the wide expanse of his cluttered desk separating them.

Rather like a moat, really.

Which made him the castle, and Jane the unwelcome intruder to be repelled. He said:

"Won't you sit down?"

And he gestured at the two mahogany chairs set before his desk.

"Thank you." Jane sat down in one and took her time settling her skirts.

There was a silence, during which Anthony thought

about the best duke in the world, who without doubt would know right away what to say in a situation like this. And in a breezy, careless, self-assured, authoritative manner. So he said, with what was really remarkable aplomb:

"Dreadful thing, swine dysentery."

"I imagine so," Jane answered. "I do hope the Duchess isn't suffering from it."

"No, she's fine."

"Oh, that's good. Is she fatter?"

"Yes, she is."

"That's good, too."

"Yes, it is," he replied, and wondered if she was going to mention that *she* was a little fatter now also, just as she had that time after church and which had had him staring hungrily at her, wishing she wasn't wearing a pelisse (or anything at all), and breaking out in a sweat all over. But she didn't, and he was glad to observe that he was as cool as the proverbial cucumber. He felt a faint ripple of pride. How tremendously dukish of him. He went on, with fresh confidence:

"Nice weather we're having."

"Yes."

"Warmer out."

"Yes."

"Spring's on the way."

"Yes, I suppose it is."

"How were the roads?"

"Fine."

"That's good. Sometimes they're not."

"Well, today they are."

"That's good," he said.

"Yes," she said.

Anthony picked up a stack of papers, rustled them importantly, then put them down again. Thanks to him they were having a perfect conversation. He felt another ripple of pride. "Margaret's flowers are doing well."

"That's nice."

"Yes, isn't it?"

Jane nodded. "Yes."

"I'm sure Margaret would be delighted to show them to you."

"Another time, perhaps."

"No time like the present."

"Speaking of which," Jane said, "I came over to tell you something."

"Oh?" he replied, casually.

"Yes. Great-grandmother is taking me to London for the Season."

"Is she?"

"Yes. She just told me yesterday. We leave in a fortnight."

"Ah."

Jane was looking at him steadily, and he looked right back at her. The Duke of Oyster, closed up tight.

"Don't you want to know when I'm coming back?"

He shrugged. Dukishly. "If you'd care to tell me."

"Well, the answer is I don't know."

"Not much of an answer, really."

Jane said, "The question was more important than the answer."

"Was it? How so?"

She smoothed out a wrinkle in the dark-crimson skirt of her riding-gown, her brow furrowed, then looked up at him again. "I asked if you wanted to know when I'm coming back. And if the question wasn't that important to you, then there's probably no need to say much else."

"I suppose you're right. No point in belaboring things,

is there?" By God, more dukishness, Anthony thought jubilantly. He was really getting the hang of it at last. If his father were alive, he might actually be proud of him for once.

Jane stood up.

Without another word she went to the door and put her hand on the doorknob.

She stood there for a few moments, and then abruptly she turned around and came to stand in front of his desk. Her face was resolute, a little stern, and also quite daisy-like and beautiful.

Not that he cared, of course.

Idly he picked up a letter-opener and began to fiddle with it.

Just as would a duke who had better things to do, and was merely waiting for a troublesome visitor to leave but of course was too polite to say so.

His dark-blue eyes were dead.

She had seen it the moment she had first looked at him.

And his manner was aloof, cool, haughty.

Just as if he had never smiled at her, never laughed with her, never put his arms around her, never kissed her with unguarded passion and fervor.

As if they were little more than strangers to each other.

Feelings of both hurt and anger had driven her up from her chair, propelled her to the door, but she had managed, with a great effort of will, to push them aside for the moment.

Because she had something else to say.

Because she had looked at Grandfather Titus' portrait, fancied him declaring, *Love or nothing*, and she had made a promise to herself.

Come hell or high water, she was going to keep that promise.

She was going to jump.

Now, standing before the Duke's desk, Jane watched as he toyed with a shiny silver letter-opener. How crowded and cluttered his desk was, she thought irrelevantly, wondering if he was one of those people who didn't mind it and in fact worked very efficiently that way, or if he would benefit from a bit of help with his organizational skills.

Well, she would probably never find out.

She said, "I care a great deal for you, you know."

He was silent, his dead eyes on the letter-opener.

"In fact, I think—I *know*—I've fallen in love with you. That's why I thought you might like to know when I'm coming back."

Silence.

"I thought you had come to care for me too," Jane went on. Quietly. Steadily. "But I see now that I was wrong. That it doesn't matter to you when—or if—I return. Is it because you're still in love with your wife? I've been wondering about that."

Abruptly the Duke lifted his eyes—in them a flash of what looked like surprise—then lowered them again, to the letter-opener which he turned over and over with his long fingers, broad at the base and tapering toward the ends and flattened out a little, which she had found so very appealing. "Yes," he said coolly. "Yes, I am. I do apologize if my behavior has led you to believe that an attachment was being formed, or to expect an offer from me. It was very wrong of me, and I shan't repeat it in future."

And there they were. The cold hard facts. All neatly assembled at last, and leading nowhere. Jane looked for a while at the Duke, letting everything sink in. It was all over. She had said her piece, he had said his, and there wasn't much left to say—just one last thing.

No: two.

"I understand you perfectly," Jane said to him, doing her best to tamp down all the emotions flooding through her. She wanted to get through this with her pride intact. "Thank you for the clarity. By the way, I was looking through an old chapbook of my great-grandfather's last night. It's called *Four Hundred Practical Aspects of Vinegar As Used to Reduce Corpulence, Purify the Humours, Improve the Complexion, and Attract a Most Desirable Spouse.* And I came across a section which says one can cure apple blight by dousing the trees with a highly diluted solution of vinegar and distilled water. One does it every two weeks until the blight is gone. Well—that's all, I think."

"Is it? Thank you so much for stopping by, Miss Kent."

So it was "Miss Kent" now. Of course it was.

Jane turned to leave a second time, then remembered the other thing she wanted to say. "Is that box for me?"

"What box?"

She pointed to a large rectangular pasteboard box sitting on his desk, which matched exactly the one he had given to her when he was driving her home from Hastings and they had kissed for the first time, except that it was approximately four times as large. Just a few days ago, in the ballroom, where they had kissed some more, he had asked if he could give her another box of chocolate conserves, an even bigger one. She had said yes, and how nice it was to have something to look forward to.

She *had* been looking forward to receiving some more chocolates from him, and now that she thought about it, standing close to the Duke's desk, she could actually smell the sweet, delicious, unmistakable fragrance wafting up from the pasteboard box.

He said, "What about it?"

"Is it for me?"

"No," he answered, and Jane was so angry and hurt that she had to bite back the cruel hasty words:

You are *the worst duke in the world!*

Instead she pressed her lips together, also resisting the urge to snatch up the box and run, cackling maniacally, out of the library and down the hallway, as satisfying as it would have been. There was, after all, something to be said for a dignified exit.

"Goodbye then," she said. "Your Grace."

"Goodbye, Miss Kent."

And so she turned and went to the door, and this time didn't hesitate, but twisted the knob and left the room.

She didn't look back.

By Jove, that went well, thought Anthony to himself with satisfaction.

How convenient that Jane had unwittingly provided him with the perfect means by which to wrap things up, all nice and tidy.

Is it because you're still in love with your wife?

For a moment he had wanted to burst out laughing.

Because he had never loved Selina, nor she him.

But there was no need to tell Jane that.

So he had lied with an ease that really was impressive.

Yes, I am. I do apologize if my behavior has led you to believe that an attachment was being formed, or to expect an offer from me. It was very wrong of me, and I shan't repeat it in future.

What dukishness!

Well done, old chap, he said to himself. Well done.

Then he reached out a hand and lifted the lid of the big pasteboard box.

Is that box for me?

No.

Another splendid lie.

He picked up a conserve and ate it.

It was absolutely delicious.

He took two more conserves and stuffed them both into his mouth. While he was chewing, he wondered how long Jane was going to be in the house. She had said she was going to the billiards room to talk to Wakefield.

The billiards room, where the three of them had had such a marvelous time.

It seemed like a faded dream to him now.

Tenuous.

Inconsequential.

At any rate, he wasn't going anywhere till he knew for sure Jane was gone.

So he ate quite a few more conserves, only stopping when his hands got smeared with chocolate and his lips felt greasy and his stomach began to hurt, just a little.

But it didn't matter.

Because he was *extremely* safe and *exceedingly* fine.

Indeed he was; and these were absolutely, positively, his final words on the subject.

Taking a long, deep breath to steady herself, Jane paused on the threshold to the billiards room. The big table in the center was draped all over with an enormous linen tablecloth that puddled on the floor in dark green folds. She went to the table and knocked on the rail. "May I come in?"

There was a rustling sound, and then Wakefield lifted one edge of the tablecloth and poked his head out. "You'll have to crawl, Jane, but you won't mind that, will you?"

"Not a bit of it."

"Be careful not to tip over the lantern."

"I'll be careful."

"All right. Come on in."

"Thank you very much." Jane dropped down onto her knees, bent low, and made her way underneath the billiards table. Once she was completely inside Wakefield let go of the tablecloth, fully enclosing them. The sudden darkness was tempered by the cozy yellow glow of a small glass-topped lantern. Next to the lantern was an old leather canteen and a chipped plate filled with biscuits.

Jane sat with her legs tucked beneath her and her head a bit ducked to avoid the bottom of the table, and Wakefield sat across from her.

"I say, Jane, isn't this the best hidey-hole you've ever seen?"

"It certainly is. Thank you for letting me inside."

"You're welcome. I've been pretending I'm a spy who's been captured by the French navy and thrown into the hold and tortured most awfully. But I haven't given away any of my secrets, and I'm plotting my escape. Biscuit?" He picked up the plate and held it out to her.

"Yes, please." Jane took one and bit into it. "Thank you. It's delicious. Are those currants I'm tasting?"

"Yes, but I've been pretending they're weevils. And that the biscuits are moldy hardtack. Cook wanted me to use a nice plate, but Bunch found this old one instead. Isn't it jolly?"

"Oh yes, it's perfect. Just the sort of plate the French navy would give to a prisoner. What's in your canteen?"

"Just water, but I'm pretending it's old and stale. So that I can suffer bravely, you see."

She nodded. "How are your escape plans coming along?"

"Well, I was thinking I could pretend to be dead, and when the sailors take off my chains so that they can carry me up to the deck and throw me overboard, I'll surprise them and grab one of their swords and have the most ripping fight and beat them all."

"That sounds like a wonderful plan. What will you do after that?"

"I'll throw all the dead sailors overboard, so that *they'll* be eaten by the sharks and whales and octopuses, instead of me. Then I'll sail the ship back to England and the King will try to give me some medals but I'll say no."

"Why will you say no?"

"Because I'm not just brave and clever, I'm also very unprutendish."

If the Duke were here, Jane thought, he'd say, *Do you mean unpretentious?* And of course Wakefield would answer, *Yes, that's what I said.*

But the Duke wasn't here.

He was probably still in his library, waiting for her to go home. And maybe even eating the chocolates that were supposed to be for her.

"I say, Jane, you're looking like Aunt Margaret's cat again."

"Am I?"

"Yes, you are."

"Well, I do have something I want to tell you, Wakefield."

"Is it that you can't stay for luncheon?"

"Yes and no. You see, I'll be going away to London in a few weeks, and I wanted you to know that."

Wakefield peered at her in the cozy dimness. "Why are you going to London, Jane?"

"Because my great-grandmother wants to take me, and also because I'm curious to see it."

"I'd like to go, too. I told Father I want to see the Tower of London and the Egyptian Hall and also Astley's Amphitheatre, as long as there aren't any clowns. But he won't take me, because he hates London."

"Yes, I know."

"When are you coming back?"

"I'm not sure."

"Oh, Jane, you're not going to be away for a long time, are you? We still haven't gone into the basement to look for rats, and I wanted to show you the tree Father fell out of. Also, lessons are more fun with you there."

"I've enjoyed our lessons together very much," said Jane, guiltily dodging Wakefield's question. "And I'm going to miss you while I'm gone. Do you think I could write to you? Would you like that?"

Wakefield, who had been looking wistful, and also rather like Lady Margaret's dolorous cat, brightened. "I say, I *would*. Nobody ever writes to me. I always ask Bunch when I see him sorting through the post, but there's never anything for me."

"Well, now there will be."

"Do you promise, Jane?"

"Yes, I do."

"All right. I'll miss you most awfully, but getting letters will help. Can you use a lot of wax for the seal? It will make the letters look more important."

"It will, won't it? Yes, to be sure I can."

"That *will* be jolly. Would you like another biscuit?"

"Yes, please."

So she and Wakefield ate several pieces of moldy hardtack which was crawling with weevils and they drank some disgustingly stale water as they pretended to be celebrated English spies trapped in the dank ghastly cells of the Bastille, and Jane agreed to be the decoy (by acting as if she was choking on an old chicken bone), so that when the nasty guard opened the door to their cell to see if Jane was alive or dead (and with true French nastiness hoping that she was dead), Wakefield with amazing swiftness and strength bashed him into unconsciousness before he had time to make a sound and alert the other equally nasty guards, and then he and Jane slipped out of the hideous bowels of the fortress (taking a few moments, of course, to release all the *good* prisoners from captivity, Wakefield having had the good sense to extract the keys from the unconscious guard's belt), and then they emerged onto the streets of Paris with such splendid cunning and savoir faire that no one had the least idea they were enemy spies on the loose again.

After that Jane said, apologetically, that it was time for her to go home, and so she crawled out from underneath the table, kissed Wakefield on the top of his head again, thanked him once more for letting her play a small but crucial role in his dashing exploits, and went to the Great Hall where she received her warm pelisse, bonnet, and gloves from a footman.

She stood for a moment looking around her.

Here was exactly where she had stood that memorable day when she had arrived at Hastings with Wakefield after lessons and the Duke had come into the house and said, *I say, you're here*, with so much pleased wonderment in his voice that she had felt incredibly happy, and they had blithered away to each other in such a delightfully idiotic manner before going on to a delicious luncheon which included heaps of macaroni and also, for dessert, apple puffs with whipped cream which were so good that even now she could feel herself salivating a little just thinking about them.

It was a beautiful memory.

Then came another memory, more recent, and considerably less pleasant.

Is it because you're still in love with your wife?

Yes, I am. I do apologize if my behavior has led you to believe that an attachment was being formed, or to expect an offer from me. It was very wrong of me, and I shan't repeat it in future.

"Miss Kent?" a voice said gently, and Jane blinked, bringing herself once again into the present moment. *Don't look back*, she told herself with as much firmness as she could muster, *look to the future*. Then she realized that it was Bunch who had spoken. Bunch, who was looking at her with his inscrutable but somehow friendly hazel eyes.

"Yes, Bunch?"

"Your groom has brought your horse round to the front."

"Oh, he has? Thank you. Oh, Bunch—" she began to say, then realized just in the nick of time she was on the verge of blurting out, *Why is the Duke being so awful?* Instead she repeated silently to herself, *Don't look back, look ahead, don't be like Great-grandmother Kent who let the past define her, and bitterness poison her.* And she said out loud, "I'm going to London with my great-grandmother Henrietta."

"Indeed, Miss Kent? Will this be your first visit to the metropolis?"

Jane had a sneaking suspicion that Bunch already knew all about it but was too discreet to say so. She didn't mind. "Yes, it will be my first time. I'm looking forward to it, but—well, there are some people I'm going to miss."

"I quite understand, Miss Kent," answered Bunch politely, and again Jane was sure he knew exactly what she meant and really did understand.

Which somehow was very comforting.

She managed to smile at him and then put on her things and went outside, was helped up onto her horse by the Penhallow groom, and began riding back to the Hall. As they passed the handsome old brick lodge-house, Jane noticed that the extremely flat dead toad was still there.

It seemed so appropriate somehow.

All the way home she thought about what had just transpired at Hastings.

The Duke and his dead eyes and cool voice and haughty manner.

Nonetheless, she had said what was on her mind and in her heart.

I care a great deal for you, you know.

In fact, I think—I know*—I've fallen in love with you. That's why I thought you might like to know when I'm coming back.*

I thought you had come to care for me too. But I see now that I was wrong. That it doesn't matter to you when—or if—I return.

And he had rejected her in the bluntest of terms.

Leaving her full of love and longing and loss and also quite a bit of sadness and anger.

All these things would eventually fade away, like a bad dream.

Also, Jane thought, there was one good thing about beating one's head against a wall: it felt better when one stopped.

Still, she wished that she and Great-grandmother could leave not in two weeks, but tomorrow.

She was ready to be gone.

And to begin her future.

Her dukeless future.

Neither he nor Wakefield had much appetite for luncheon.

Even though he was, of course, absolutely fine, there was no denying that all those conserves were sitting in his stomach taking up a lot of room and feeling rather like a lead truncheon had somehow got lodged in there.

As for Wakefield, he had artlessly revealed that he and Jane had recently eaten a whole plate of biscuits while they were pretending to be daring spies who cleverly outwitted their beastly French gaolers. Then he went on, "Father, did Jane tell you she's going to London? Is that why she wanted to talk to you by herself? She told me underneath the billiards table, and I said I wanted to go to London, too."

Anthony shot a glance at Margaret who was sedately chewing, and to his surprise she didn't comment or even look up from her plate.

"Yes, she did tell me," he said to Wakefield. "Are you quite finished? I thought perhaps we could walk over to the lake and skip some stones."

"Oh yes, that would be jolly," answered Wakefield, instantly diverted. "I say, Father, will you show me that trick again? The one that has the stone bouncing like anything?"

"It's all in the wrist," said Anthony, relieved at having successfully changed the subject. He stood up, and Wakefield did, too.

So they went to the lake and skipped stones for a while,

then stopped by the pig-cote to say hullo to the Duchess (and to Johns, who had zealously assigned himself guard duty just in case Jane decided to sneak over and put calomel in the slops or do something else just as devious, at which point Wakefield told him he was talking rot and being redonculous), and after that they decided to walk over to Miss Humphrey and Miss Trevelyan's house where they were just in time to hear Miss Trevelyan read out loud from the latest chapter in her manuscript about Catherine Howard, which was rather sad and grisly, but afterwards they all cheered up when Miss Humphrey brought in a platter of freshly baked scones and some really good pears from her greenhouse, though to Anthony's surprise and sorrow he could only eat one of each, that odd and unpleasant truncheon being still lodged in his stomach, and he watched with no little bitterness as Wakefield, Miss Trevelyan, and Miss Humphrey indulged, even feasted, on the delicious scones and pears and also some piping hot India tea (which he thought would help resolve the truncheon but didn't, and made him worry, just a little, that it had taken up permanent and unwelcome residence within him).

By the time he and Wakefield got home, it was nearly dark, and there commenced the usual bustle of bathing and dinner and then bedtime. Having last night finished *The Tempest*, Wakefield asked for more Shakespeare.

"By all means." Stretched out in bed next to Wakefield, Anthony reached onto the bedside table and took *Tales from Shakespeare* from the top of the stack, opened it, and looked at the table of contents. His heart sank a little, but then he remembered that he was absolutely and perfectly fine. He was thus able to calmly say, "We've read everything except *Romeo and Juliet*."

"What's that one about? I forgot."

"It's about two people who fall in love despite opposition from both their families, get married anyway, and then they die."

"Both of them?"

"Yes."

"How do they die?"

"Romeo drinks poison, and Juliet stabs herself."

"I say, how jolly," Wakefield said approvingly, then added, "Why do they do it?"

"Because he thinks she's dead, when she's really not, and then she does it because she thinks *he's* dead. Only she's right—he is."

Wakefield took this in. "So they wouldn't have died if Romeo hadn't made a mistake?"

"Quite possibly."

"Does he try poking her with a stick or something like that, just to be sure?"

"No, he talks about how sad it is that she's dead. And then he drinks the poison."

"That was stupid of him. He should have made sure."

"In fairness, Juliet had taken a drug that made her *seem* like she was dead."

"But she wasn't, not really."

"That's right."

"I still think he should have tried poking her with a stick."

"It might have helped."

"Is Romeo supposed to be the hero of the story?"

"Yes."

"He sounds stupid."

"That's as may be, but there *is* a fair amount of sword-fighting, if that tempts you at all. Shall we give it a go?"

"No," said Wakefield firmly. "What's the point of reading a story if the hero is stupid?"

"I daresay you're right. What else, then?"

"Greek mythology, please."

So Anthony switched books and read a very exciting story about the obviously heroic Perseus who was given shoes that allowed him to fly and a hat that made him invisible, after which he beheaded the nasty snake-headed Medusa, got into a terrific fight with a sea-monster called Cetus, and accidentally killed his grandfather with a discus (thereby demonstrating that everyone is capable of making at least one honest mistake), all of which Wakefield enjoyed very much and also made him feel a bit more lenient toward the hapless Romeo.

"I say, I'd like some shoes that would let me fly," he said. "I'd go to London to see Jane, and also I could ride Old Snorter like anything. Instead of falling off I'd fall *up*." Then he gave a tremendous yawn. "Father, why were you so stuffy toward Jane when I brought her to your library?"

"Was I?"

"Yes, you were."

"I didn't realize I was being stuffy."

"You were being very stuffy."

"Was I really?"

"I just told you that you were," said Wakefield drowsily. He yawned again, then pulled the covers up snugly around his shoulders. "Goodnight, Father."

Anthony kissed him. "Goodnight, my boy. Sleep well." He got up, blew out the candles, and left Wakefield's room, softly closing the door behind him. He stood in the quiet hallway for a few moments, contemplating his newly peaceful life and how incredibly fine everything was, and then he went to his library, where he took the big pasteboard box that was sitting on his desk and dumped it in his trash bin. Then he took the bin and set it outside in the hallway, where its contents would be collected and taken away.

He wasn't sure when, or if, he'd ever feel like eating chocolate conserves again.

Chapter 18

Sitting at the mahogany writing-desk in her gorgeously decorated bedchamber in the Penhallow townhouse, Jane picked up a quill and dipped it into the inkwell. It was very late, and she was tired, but every day was so busy and filled with activity that she had little time for leisure. And she did want to write some letters.

1 June 1817

Dear Wakefield,

I hope this finds you well. How are your French lessons with Mr. Pressley coming along? Soon, I daresay, you will be able to impersonate a French spy like anything. As for me, I am keeping up with mathematics but not much else, I'm afraid. I find I like algebra a great deal, and I'm getting much better at long division. The other night, at a party, I met somebody who, as it turned out, is a mathematician and I enjoyed talking with him quite a lot. He told me (in terms that I could understand) about a recent study which develops the idea of infinite sums and trigonometric functions, and also about a lecture on mathematics and astronomy that's taking place next week and I hope very much to go.

I was sorry to hear in your latest letter that you had to disassemble your hidey-hole in the billiards room. It's too bad that a family of mice found all those biscuit crumbs so delicious and decided to take up residence there. And yes, I agree that it was very kind of Bunch to have them transported outside rather than letting your aunt Margaret's cat loose upon them. Also, I'm sorry your father wouldn't let you keep the mice in a nice cage, as that would indeed have been jolly. Still, I suppose they're happier being free to roam about.

Speaking of your aunt Margaret's cat, I was shocked to hear that it bit the ankle of one of your recent houseguests, and that the poor young lady needed Dr. Fotherham's services. I do hope she hasn't developed an infection or anything like that.

You asked if I had been to the Egyptian Hall yet. Yes, my great-grandmother and I went with a large party last Wednesday despite her concerns that it would prove to be a vulgar exhibition packed with all manner of equally vulgar people. It certainly was crowded, but there were a great many people from the most fashionable circles, so perhaps that assuaged some of her concerns.

I thought of you the whole time we were there. There were a lot of stuffed birds, a saddle which once belonged to the emperor of Mexico, some interesting models of Aztec temples, Napoleon's famous war-carriage, and something I think you would have liked very much—a giant serpent which was all coiled up with its head raised and its jaws open wide, into which was placed a life-size model of a well-dressed woman. So it looked as if she was being devoured by the serpent.

To own the truth it all looked very artificial to me, but while we were standing there staring at it, several women screamed and a man passed out, overcome, as he explained as soon as he regained consciousness, by the unspeakable horror of it all. (Great-grandmother said afterwards she was sure he was doing it just to get attention and show how refined his sensibilities were, when all he merely did was to make a cake out of himself.)

They were selling cards with illustrations of the serpent and the war-carriage, these being their most popular exhibits, so of course I got them for you. They are enclosed, and I'm sorry for the extra postage but I hope no one will object.

With great affection,
Your friend,
Jane

After letting the ink dry and putting the two cards on top of the first page, Jane folded up her letter and, mindful of her promise, sealed it with a really enormous blob of wax. Then she took another piece of paper and started writing again.

1 June 1817

Dear Livia,

Thank you very much for your letter, and with all the news from home. How exciting to hear that Daniel has said his first word! And how funny that it was "chicken," and that you and Cousin Gabriel laughed yourselves into stitches over it. I'm sure he'll be saying "Mama" and "Papa" very soon.

Also, I'm glad that Titania didn't mind falling off her horse into the mud. And that she got right back up onto her horse—good for her. She is such a determined little person, isn't she? I must confess I nearly fell off my horse the other day, because I caught a glimpse of Princess Charlotte and Prince Leopold in a carriage and was craning my neck so hard that I was nearly horizontal in my saddle. Luckily the Earl of Westenbury, with whom I was riding, noticed just in time and gallantly helped prop me up.

You asked how Great-grandmother's matchmaking endeavor has been going, and if it's driving me to distraction. It hasn't, really, I'm enjoying the Season a lot—and I have to say I am very impressed by her diligence. She is much esteemed, admired, and fawned over and we are invited everywhere: we go to breakfasts, teas, dinner-parties, assemblies, balls, Almack's, the theatre, for walks and for drives, et cetera, et cetera, and I have met so many eligible men that I must admit it's been rather difficult keeping their names, faces, and titles straight. (Which is quite a funny thing for a girl from Nantwich to be saying.) Some of them are very nice, and Great-grandmother—who's told me more than once she hopes I'll be betrothed before the Season ends—lets me know who she thinks might be a good choice for me.

I had wondered, of course, how my unconventional background might play into things here. Would I get funny looks, or little innuendoes, or cold shoulders, or rude remarks, and so on. Amazingly, none! Such is the power of Great-grandmother's personality, I daresay, that nobody has ever mentioned my background at all. Honestly, I wouldn't be surprised if people are afraid to even gossip behind my back, for fear that Great-grandmother will somehow find out and her wrath will descend upon them. She is quite the force of nature! I do love her.

Tomorrow she's taking me to meet Mr. Farris, the family's man of business, and to formally codify the terms of my dowry. I'm dreadfully uncomfortable by how much money she's spending on me, but every time I bring up the subject she gets so sad about Titus that I feel quite wretched.

I miss you all. Please give the children kisses from me.

Love,
Jane

P.S. I forgot to tell you before—I've seen the Merifields quite a few times. Lady Felicia is engaged and seems very happy. The Viscount does his best to ignore me, even though the Countess keeps trying to get him to talk and dance with me and so on. Poor man. It's terrible of me, I know, but I find it all quite humorous.

Jane sealed Livia's letter with considerably less wax, then began to write one more letter.

1 June 1817

Dear Miss Trevelyan,

I hope this finds you and Miss Humphrey well and enjoying the warmer weather. How is Miss

Humphrey's garden doing? And your writing? My great-grandmother and I are both well and enjoying London. I wanted to tell you that at an evening-party last week, the subject of the Tudor queens came up—somebody mentioned being related to Jane Seymour—and someone else said he had read your books about Katherine of Aragon and Anne Boleyn and enjoyed them very much. Imagine my sense of self-importance when I was able to say that not only do I know the author, but that I had first-hand knowledge of a third book coming soon, and that you were deep into the writing of the fourth! Several people said at once they would buy your books. So I do hope I've done a little to help with sales.

Sincerely yours,
Jane Kent

Having sealed this third and last letter, Jane yawned, stretched, and got up. She blew out her candles, took off her dressing-gown, and climbed gratefully into bed, where she lay for a few minutes pushing aside her sleepiness and thinking about her letter to Livia. Everything she had written was true, but she had deliberately not mentioned the fact that she had already received several offers (which Great-grandmother had refused on her behalf, this being fine with Jane, as she couldn't see herself coming to care for any of the men tendering them, all of whom Great-grandmother had dismissed as being, for one reason or another, not sufficiently deserving of the hand of her beloved great-granddaughter), nor had she said to Livia that she seemed to be living in a curious state of mind encompassing happiness and sadness both at once.

Happiness because she really *was* enjoying her Season.

The sadness, of course, was because of the Duke. She thought about him more often than she would have preferred, but she was doing her best to look forward, not back.

Well, *damn.* Even by thinking about how she was trying not to think about the Duke, she was . . . thinking about him again.

Yes, thinking about him, and how much she had enjoyed his company, and how incredibly attractive she found him, and . . .

Jane tugged up the hem of her nightgown, and slid a hand between her legs. She brought herself to pleasure's peak, rather quickly, and drew down her nightgown again, turning onto her side and staring into the darkness. It wasn't so bad, touching oneself, but one would rather be touched. Ardently, passionately, eagerly.

Love or nothing.

She wanted to love and be loved.

To share a bed—a life!—with somebody.

She thought about the men she'd met here in London. The Earl of Westenbury, for example. He was stunningly handsome, with beautiful manners, and was exceedingly well-dressed. But—not only did she not find him terribly interesting, she didn't feel he was genuinely interested in *her.* There were no real sparks between them.

What about his friend, Étienne de Montmorency, Society's darling? So rich, so urbane, so charming, and even better dressed than the Earl. No: there was something *insinuating* about him, and anyone who spent so much time hanging about the Prince Regent wasn't a person she could admire—the Regent being, in her opinion, lazy, licentious, and a terrible father who also wasn't doing a particularly good job of running the country while his poor father the King was so pitifully discomposed.

What about the Viscount Parfitt-Saxe? He was nice, and such a good dancer, and never seemed to mind that she was still fumbling her way through the cotillion.

Mr. Samuel Graham? He had a lovely dry sense of humor, and was a dog-lover, too.

Colonel Palmer? He told delightful stories about his travels around the world, and she liked his adventurous spirit.

The Archduke Karl Augustus? There was something so appealing about a man who wore a royal sash (diagonally from shoulder to waist) with such unselfconscious élan, plus he was a little shy, which she also found appealing.

Perhaps, Jane thought, *I ought to consider them more carefully.*

She could try. She *would* try.

Love or nothing.

"Did ye no' hear me, Yer Grace?"

Anthony started, and looked into McTavish's scrubby weather-beaten face, the expression of which conveyed a mixture of exasperation and concern.

He had not, in fact, heard what McTavish had just been saying to him, as he had been brooding over the look the oracular Mrs. Roger had given him the other day when he was in Riverton.

It had been a long, hard stare, and it would not be going too far to describe it as a glare. Or even a scowl. Why had she done that? He had jostled no passersby, kicked no dog (not that he ever would), insulted none of his fellows, and all he had been doing was riding along the high street minding his own business, which was primarily trying to repress thoughts of Jane.

Also while not listening to McTavish just now, he had been thinking with a kind of weary relief that when he got home their houseguests would finally be gone, Miss Evelina Allenton having received exactly zero offers of marriage from himself and additionally been declared by Dr. Fotherham fit and ready to travel after her traumatic experience of being attacked by Margaret's cat and having her ankle mauled.

So mortified had Margaret been that she had, in front of their guests, instructed Bunch to take the cat and have it drowned in the lake, and Anthony had watched aghast as Margaret scooped up her suddenly limp and boneless pet and thrust it at Bunch who had impassively received it at arm's length and left the drawing-room at his usual stately pace, as if he was used to someone giving him disgraced cats to carry away and put paid to however many lives they happened to have left.

While not possessing any real affection for the cat, Anthony had nonetheless been horrified by Margaret's vengeful spirit (especially since Miss Allenton had been taunting the cat with a morsel of bacon Anthony had no idea why she happened to have on hand), and all he could think to do by way of swiftly excusing himself from the room was to announce that he needed to answer nature's call, a coy and horrible euphemism which he had never in his life deployed before, but when a cat's life (or lives) was (were) at stake, even a miserable and grumpy feline which he had yet to hear purr in ten years of very distant acquaintance, there had been no time to concoct a better excuse.

Luckily, he had caught up with Bunch for a low-voiced confabulation just off the Great Hall and Margaret's cat had been secretly bundled off to Bunch's pantry, where it was to be confined until the Allentons had left, and when

Anthony had slipped into the pantry very early this morning hoping that Bunch had not been clawed, bitten, nipped, tripped, pounced upon, savaged, ravaged, shredded, hissed at or otherwise beleaguered, and possibly to the extent that he, Anthony, would have the misfortune of stumbling across Bunch's bloody and tattered corpse stretched out upon the floor, he had been astonished to see Bunch, still in his dignified dressing-gown and slippers, sitting at the head of the big oak table drinking a cup of tea with Margaret's cat curled up in his lap and looking so contented that Anthony had actually rubbed his fists in his eyes to make sure it was still the same cat.

It was, and it had been *purring.*

"Yer Grace," said McTavish again, rather loudly, and Anthony gave another start.

"What is it, McTavish?"

"Caterpillars."

"Caterpillars?"

"Aye. Caterpillars."

"What about them?"

"They're in the succession house, Yer Grace," said McTavish grimly. "And ye know wha' *that* means."

"Do I?" answered Anthony vaguely. Indifferently.

"If we dinna stop them, there'll be nae apricots come September."

Apricots? What had Wakefield told him about the surprisingly philosophical Higson's remark on the subject? It took him a few moments to recall it.

Life is like a dish of apricots.

It still made no sense, but rather than trying to puzzle it out again, Anthony only shrugged. "Oh well," he said to McTavish, who peered at him sharply, his great wild eyebrows drawing together with that same mixture of exasperation and concern, after which he gestured with a dramatic sweep of his burly arm and said:

"Look at *this* then."

Anthony duly looked at the long row of little pumpkins that stretched out to left and right beneath the cheerful summer sun. Vivid orange and nestled cozily among their green leafy vines, they were flourishing.

"We might just bring home the gilt cup this year, Yer Grace."

Anthony shrugged again.

McTavish drew a deep breath, let it out gustily, and said, "I was saving the best news fer last. The lassie's vinegar remedy is working. The blight on the apple trees is gone."

"Is it?"

"Aye."

"That's nice," said Anthony, but with so little enthusiasm that the exasperation left McTavish's face, and concern was all that remained.

"Ye ought tae go home, Yer Grace."

"Should I?"

"Aye."

"Why?"

"'Tis luncheon time."

"Is it really?"

"Aye. Go home, Yer Grace, and eat something. Ye look like one o' my scarecrows," McTavish said bluntly.

"Do I?"

"Aye, ye do. 'Tis nae a wholesome sight. Go home, man, go home."

"Very well," answered Anthony, and began drifting back toward the house. As he came near the lime-walk, he could smell the sweet scent of the tiny, white blossoms among which the bees danced and hummed. The trees were verdant and lush with their green heart-shaped leaves having returned in riotous abundance.

He passed by the lime-walk, unmoved, thinking vaguely

that it might be pleasant to be a scarecrow. Very little was asked of one; nobody paid much attention to one. One just hung about suspended on a pole, season after season, and eventually one quietly rotted away.

At luncheon Wakefield said, "Father, why aren't you eating?"

"I'm not hungry."

"You said that yesterday. And the day before that. And the day before that. And—"

"I take your point, my boy."

"Then why aren't you eating? Are you all right?"

Anthony glanced down at his untouched bowl of soup. There was no way it would fit in his stomach. Because of the truncheon. Then he remembered that he was fine. Absolutely, perfectly, entirely, utterly, completely, and totally fine. "Of course I'm all right."

Wakefield looked skeptical, but went back to his own bowl of soup, and Margaret said cheerfully:

"What a shame the Allentons had to leave so soon. I'll write to Georgiana Dibbs and let her know that she and her daughter Cassandra are welcome to come sooner if they like."

"More people coming to stay?" said Wakefield. "I'm tired of all these houseguests, Aunt Margaret."

"If I wanted to know your opinion on a subject which is none of your concern, Wakefield, I would have asked you."

"Yes, but Aunt Margaret, they're all awfully boring, you know."

"Nonsense. And stop slurping your soup. It's unsuitable behavior for a marquis."

"When I'm a duke I'll slurp my soup like anything."

"No, you won't."

"Yes, I will."

"You won't. Now be quiet and finish your soup."

So of course Wakefield slurped his soup, Margaret glared at him, and wearily Anthony intervened, by way of drawing her fire:

"Bunch has been taking care of your cat, Meg."

"What?" Margaret snapped. "I told him to—"

"I told him not to."

"And that was none of *your* concern. How dare you countermand my order?"

"What did you tell Bunch to do, Aunt Margaret?" asked Wakefield, deeply interested.

"Be quiet and *finish your soup.*"

Wakefield scowled, scraped his spoon against the side of the bowl, and loudly slurped some soup.

"Stop it at once, Wakefield."

"Stop it at once, Wakefield," said Wakefield, imitating her stringent tone exactly.

"Are you repeating my own words back to me?"

"Are you repeating my own words back to me?"

"Why, you rude and insolent little boy!"

"Why, you rude and insolent little boy!"

"Stop it."

"Stop it."

Margaret turned to him, glaring. "Anthony, are you going to permit this shocking display of disobedience to continue?"

"Anthony, are you going to permit this shocking display of disobedience to continue?" said Wakefield, glaring also.

Under other circumstances, Anthony might have had to repress an impulse to laugh, so comically precise was Wakefield's imitation of his aunt, but today he only said, tiredly, "Wake, do stop. And Meg, leave off, please."

"Leave off? I won't *leave off* when I'm being mocked by a rude and disobedient little boy! If you were a better father, you'd punish him as he deserves! If you were a duke in anything but name, you'd—"

"Oh my God, Meg, but you're exhausting," Anthony said, and slowly got up from his chair. "Come on, Wake, let's leave your aunt Margaret in peace."

"But Father, I'm still hungry."

"Bunch will have some sandwiches made for you."

Wakefield shoved back his chair and jumped nimbly to his feet. "Oh, that sounds jolly. Can I eat them underneath the billiards table?"

"No," said Anthony. "You'll eat them in Bunch's pantry, sitting at the table."

"All right, Father."

So listlessly did Anthony leave the family dining-parlor and walk along the corridor that Wakefield got impatient and skipped on ahead of him, leaving Anthony alone with his thoughts, which at the moment happened to be a recollection of what he had read (or, to be precise, what he hadn't read) this morning in the papers while not eating his eggs and toast and so on.

As was his new habit, he had furtively turned to the *London Gazette* first.

To scan the engagement announcements.

Always looking for the name of Jane Kent.

He had yet to see it.

So far.

Jane had been gone for weeks and weeks.

And maybe sometime soon he would see the announcement with her name in it.

Maybe even tomorrow.

"There it is," said Great-grandmother softly.

She and Jane stood side by side, looking at the tobacconist shop with its crowded window-front filled with pipes, snuffboxes in all shapes and sizes, fancy silver cases for the well-heeled connoisseur, shallow bowls for spitting into, and dozens of big glass jars filled with amber-colored tobacco.

Here, on busy, noisy Cheapside Street, was where Great-grandfather Kent had had his print-shop.

Here, most likely, was where Titus Penhallow and Charity Kent had met all those many years ago and fallen madly in love.

Jane stared at the window-front, imagining it filled with an enticing array of Great-grandfather's pamphlets and chapbooks promising health, success, good looks, and love along with dozens of solutions to life's problems large and small. She pictured a young, dashing Titus strolling by, stopping to read some of the titles, bursting out laughing, and going into the shop to buy some as a joke for his friends; behind the counter, helping out in the family business, was Charity.

The rest, as the saying went, was history.

Jane gave a deep, long sigh, feeling (yet more strongly) somewhere between happy and sad. Then she said, "Thank you very much for coming here, Great-grandmother."

"I wanted to see the shop too, my dear. Would you like to stay longer, or shall we be moving on?"

"I'm ready to go."

Together she and Great-grandmother went to the big elegant Penhallow barouche which was waiting for them in the street. A footman held open the door and helped them inside, and so they set off, arriving half an hour later in the quiet, stately offices of the Penhallow man of business Mr. Farris, an elderly, soberly dressed man who turned out to be equally quiet and stately. He had the paperwork ready for Great-grandmother to sign, which she did, then had Jane read it through so that she would thoroughly understand it, and just as Great-grandmother looked to be ready to get up and depart, he said in his precise way:

"Given that you've brought Miss Kent here, Mrs. Penhallow, I assumed that in addition to formalizing the terms of her dowry, you also wished to share with her the contents of your late son Titus Penhallow's will." He indicated a burgundy document folder set before him on his desk.

"Titus' will?" echoed Great-grandmother, and Jane saw that she had abruptly gone rather white. "I don't know anything about that."

"I spoke with you and your husband about it, Mrs. Penhallow, shortly after your son's death. It could be that in your shock and grief you retain no memory of it."

"Yes, that may be so," Great-grandmother answered, pale but steady. "I was distraught beyond words. May I see the will, please?" She reached out her hand and Mr. Farris gave her the document folder.

Great-grandmother read the will, then, silvery brows raised high, she looked to Mr. Farris. "My husband and I gave Titus a generous allowance—perhaps a too-generous one—and we know he lived extravagantly. I don't understand how he could have amassed and thus left nine thousand pounds to 'any progeny I might have,' as he put it."

Mr. Farris answered: "When he came to my office to dictate his will, Mrs. Penhallow, your son made mention of having recently been quite fortunate at cards."

Great-grandmother nodded. "He was a gamester, a proclivity my husband and I both hoped he would eventually outgrow." Then her look sharpened. "Exactly when did Titus come to you, Mr. Farris?"

"A fortnight before his untimely death, Mrs. Penhallow."

"Then—" Jane leaned forward and said to Great-grandmother, "Then perhaps he realized—or knew it was a possibility that—"

Great-grandmother nodded again. "That he would have progeny with Charity. Well, my dear Jane, it seems you have inherited a modest little sum from your grandfather."

Jane sat back in her chair, sudden tears welling in her eyes. There was no way to know if Titus had realized he was going to be a father, but that he had taken this decisive step to provide for his child (and thus his grandchild) made her feel all at once that her connection to him went deeper than the stunning resemblance between them. "Oh, Great-grandmother," she said softly, "how I wish I had known him."

Great-grandmother only nodded again, tears shimmering in her eyes as well. Then she gathered herself, thanked Mr. Farris, and rose to her feet as regally straight and proud as ever, and then she and Jane very shortly plunged back into the social whirl that filled their days and nights: a tea, a dinner, a ball.

It was while she was dancing with the Viscount Parfitt-Saxe that Jane found herself thinking at length about the nine thousand pounds that were hers and hers alone. To a girl growing up on practically nothing, making her increasingly cautious way along the mean streets of Nantwich, a sum like this wasn't modest, as Great-grandmother had described it, but astronomical.

She did some quick math in her head.

Nine thousand pounds invested in the five percents would yield an annual income of 450 pounds. A Nantwich girl could live like a queen on that.

It was, in short, an independence.

No matter what happened, she would never have to marry someone for their money.

It seemed unlikely that Great-grandmother would, say, throw her out of the house if she didn't become engaged over the next few months or years, but it was nice to think that—thanks to the prescient generosity of Grandfather Titus—she probably wouldn't be reduced to taking in mending to get by.

Because that, of course, would be a *disaster.*

"You smile, Miss Kent," said the Viscount. "And you are preoccupied this evening."

"Am I?"

"Yes. What are you thinking about?"

"Oh, sewing."

"Sewing?" He looked at her with a quizzical little smile. "Is there something you're working on at home?"

"Oh no, quite the opposite. I'm horrible at sewing."

"Are you?" Deftly he guided her through a complicated chassé, murmuring, "Step—feet together—step again. Well done, Miss Kent. You say you're horrible at sewing?"

"Yes, and also I find it very boring."

"Well, perhaps you'll change your mind."

"Unlikely."

"If you like, my mother could show you a few tricks. She's very fond of sewing and is quite skillful at it."

"Thank you, but I'm afraid it would be a waste of her time."

"I'm sure she wouldn't mind. In fact, the other day she said she was hoping to get to know you better."

"How kind," said Jane, bypassing the hint and also hoping it didn't mean the Viscount was gearing up for a proposal, as she was just now realizing that although she liked him well enough, and she really appreciated how much he was helping with her dancing, and with such lovely tact, too, there was within her absolutely no desire to fling herself against him, or to have him fling himself against her, or even a longing to spend a great deal of time in his company without anybody doing any flinging at all, all of which struck her as a bad sign for potential marital bliss.

Her heart, it seemed, was still stubbornly and pointlessly full with yearning for someone else.

Damn the Duke!

He was probably rejoicing in her absence, cherishing the loving memory of his late wife, eating a lot of chocolates, strolling up and down a lime-walk fragrant with the blooms she would never see *or* smell, and having the most marvelous time, all without her.

The very idea of it made her want to fling herself against him, not in passion but in anger, and take him by his neckcloth, and—

And rip it from around his neck, and nip him hard, then bolt up onto her tiptoes and press her mouth against his, and—

Shut up, Jane, she sternly told herself, *you're a blithering idiot.*

So focused was she on lecturing her unruly self that she missed a step, bumped into the Viscount, *still* felt nothing upon coming into full bodily contact with him, hastily apologized, secretly mourned that she might never get the hang of the cotillion, and began to feel unreasonably low in spirits. Not even the recollection of her nine thousand pounds, cozily sitting in the bank, cheered her up much, if at all.

Anthony kissed Wakefield goodnight and quietly left his room, crossing the hallway to his own bedchamber where he flopped onto his bed and lay there with his head resting on interlaced fingers and his elbows akimbo.

So charmed had Wakefield been by the startling transformation of Margaret's cat, which had actually curled sinuously and, more importantly, *pleasantly* around his ankles as he sat at the oak table in Bunch's pantry eating sandwiches, that he had asked for "Puss in Boots" for tonight's bedtime read.

After the story ended with the lowly miller's son becoming a wealthy marquis and marrying the beautiful princess, thanks to the dauntless efforts of his cat, there were two morals tacked on for the reader's edification.

One praised the importance of industry and cleverness in the attainment of one's goals, and the other emphasized the importance of wearing the right clothes in winning the heart of one's beloved.

Wakefield had not been interested in the morals, and instead had asked if it would be possible to have four small boots made for Aunt Margaret's cat, as that would be a ripping thing to see: an actual puss in boots. Anthony had agreed that it would be, but suggested that they not push their luck, given that it was only recently that the cat had sunk its extremely sharp teeth into someone's ankle and drawn a fair amount of blood.

Wakefield had acknowledged the disappointing, but genuine wisdom in this perspective, and so had nodded off to sleep.

But Anthony *was* interested in the morals—if he needed any further proof that he was, for better or for worse, an adult—and thought about them for a while.

Then he thought about some of the other fables and fairy tales he had been reading to Wakefield.

Things always wrapped up nicely in them: there was structure, order, form.

Just like his own life, really.

If somebody were to write it up as a fairy tale, it would go something like . . .

Once upon a time, there was a boy who was destined to be the second son. And he didn't mind it. But when he grew to adulthood, fate intervened and he became a duke. He was forced to marry a woman he despised, and who despised him, and so he fell into the slough of despair. Only the birth of a delightful little son brought light into the darkness. Then the woman died, which was dreadfully sad, but at least the duke could be alone once more.

No: not alone, but free.

. . . but at least the duke was free once more. Years later, fate intervened again and brought into his life another woman (who had the most beautiful gray eyes in the world) whom he rather liked. And who clearly liked him, too. But when the beautiful gray-eyed woman confessed her love for him, the duke turned her away, because he didn't want to be married ever again and thus imprisoned, a perfectly logical, reasonable, and understandable position which made complete and total sense. After that, an evil fairy very unkindly caused a truncheon to be placed into the duke's stomach, but he was fine anyway, and he lived happily ever after.

That seemed pretty accurate.

Anthony shifted on the bed.

God, he was tired.

Tired in every part of him.

He could feel his mind slowing, drifting into a curious state between sleep and wakefulness. He should, he supposed, get up and take off his clothes and clean his teeth and all that, but . . . he didn't.

Instead, for some strange reason, Anthony found himself remembering something Jane had once said about fences. And about freedom, by implication. Or was he reading too much into it?

It was the day after Wakefield's extraction. And also the day after he and Jane had strolled around the Hastings ballroom and kissed each other so delightfully and lengthily, and who knew what might have happened after that if he hadn't abruptly gotten uneasy about having his neckcloth removed and feeling rather exposed (in more ways than one), and put an end to all the kissing and caressing.

At any rate, he had gone into Wakefield's room the next morning and there was Jane, her pale wavy hair shining in the sunlight and her beautiful gray eyes twinkling in that very fetching way she had. She was sitting next to Wakefield's bed and sipping her coffee and telling jokes and riddles. And she had said:

If one horse is shut up in a stable, and another one is running loose down the road, which horse is singing "Don't fence me in"?

The one running down the road, Wakefield had answered.

No, neither. Horses can't sing.

Now Anthony wondered, rather dreamily, if he would prefer to be the horse safely shut up in a stable, or the one running loose down the road to an unknown destination.

And then—his mind drifting and slowing, lazily wheeling—he found himself also remembering how Wakefield had criticized Romeo for not making sure that Juliet was really dead, because if (according to Wakefield) he had been just a tiny bit more diligent, disaster might have been averted and (it therefore followed) Romeo and Juliet might have had a shot at their own happily ever after.

What's the point of reading a story if the hero is stupid?

Anthony thought about his own little story.

Surely the hero—the Duke—wasn't stupid.

He was being sensible and clear-headed.

Wasn't he?

Perhaps his actions could be better explained by some additional text.

So when the beautiful gray-eyed woman confesses her love for the Duke, this could come next:

But the Duke's heart still dwelt in the darkness from before. In bleak memory and in fear.

So, the hero was trapped in the past and afraid.

Honestly, it didn't suggest fineness at all.

But still, he wasn't stupid. Right?

Surely he, Anthony, wasn't being stupid.

He was being sensible and clear-headed.

Wasn't he?

He didn't know, because he had fallen deeply asleep, and was, at present, entirely dead to the world.

Chapter 19

It was shortly before the notorious hour of eleven, when Almack's closed its doors to any latecomers after that. Jane was dancing a quadrille with the Archduke Karl Augustus, during which they were having a halting conversation and she was also hoping her stomach wouldn't loudly rumble, as she was rather hungry and could only look forward to the meager refreshments the Patronesses annoyingly and inexplicably seemed to feel sufficient: cake without any icing at all, thin and not entirely fresh slices of bread and butter, and lemonade and tea.

A week had passed since the momentous trip to Mr. Farris' offices. The Viscount Parfitt-Saxe had indeed proposed and she herself had gently refused him, to the dismay of Great-grandmother who had reminded her that the Viscount would one day be the Earl of Tandermere, an old and distinguished holding in northern England, and although no earl could of course equal the Penhallows in standing and prestige, she had said, still it would have been a worthy match.

So Jane had guiltily felt she was letting Great-grandmother down.

And here she was with the Archduke.

Of whom Great-grandmother also approved.

Jane did a slow spin counterclockwise, rose up on her toes, dropped down again, then clasped the Archduke's gloved hand. He smiled at her and she smiled back.

Could she progress beyond mere liking?

Frankly, it was doubtful.

The Archduke's reticence, she had come to realize, was less about shyness and more about the fact that he really had very little conversation. Which didn't bode well for future marital happiness. One could only go so far admiring the elegant silken sash one's spouse wore about his person at all times while in public (a thought which made her wonder if he wore it to bed, too, and it certainly would get rumpled, disarranged, or even torn during intimate moments which would not be ideal).

Also she had realized, to her sorrow, that she had initially liked what she thought was shyness because it reminded her of the Duke.

Who sometimes had been so charmingly shy and self-effacing.

Jane removed her gloved hand from the Archduke's, dipped a little curtsy, and took three steps backward, leaving room for the couple next to them to advance. Her stomach did rumble, but luckily not loud enough for anyone else to hear, and she fell into thoughts of what she might scavenge from the kitchen when she and Great-grandmother got back to the townhouse.

Some leftover chicken if there was any. And some potatoes in their tangy mustard sauce. Oh, and a couple of those apple puffs which were good, though not as good as the ones she had had that wonderful day at Hastings—

Movement by the door caught her eye and Jane saw someone coming inside, mere moments before the doors would be implacably shut. It was a man she didn't know, dressed very fine in a black coat and breeches and dazzlingly white shirt and crisp neckcloth. Although—

How tall he was, and with hair of a familiar tawny color, combed flat and sleek—

Jane heard herself actually gasp, which would have been very theatrical of her if she was doing it for effect. But she wasn't. It was a gasp of genuine surprise and possibly also of astonishment as well as shock.

It was the Duke.

The Duke.

Her Duke.

No—not hers, of course.

What she meant was that the Duke of Radcliffe was here.

In other words, the Duke.

Here, in Almack's, in London.

Here.

In London, a place he hated.

Was it really possible?

These disjointed thoughts whirled through Jane's head like a storm.

Another couple paraded in front of her and she craned her neck to look around them.

Yes, it *was* the Duke.

He stood very straight and tall, gazing searchingly around the room.

Was he looking for *her*?

Now she could see that Lady Jersey, one of the most affable of the Patronesses, was hurrying up to greet him.

Jane also got a hasty glimpse of his elegant dark evening-shoes, polished to a high gleam.

And she gave another gasp, a smaller one, but a gasp nonetheless, even though she could hardly have expected him to arrive at Almack's wearing those familiar dark scuffed boots in which he looked so dashingly devil-may-care.

But to be wearing such impeccably shined shoes!

It seemed entirely out of character.

Yet another couple paraded past, then stopped, entirely blocking her view, and Jane nearly gnashed her teeth in frustration, but then it was her turn, along with the Arch-duke, to sally forth along the line, and she tried very hard to concentrate, but she put out her left foot incorrectly and ending up barreling right into Karl Augustus which was mortifying, but also produced the useful information that she didn't want to do any flinging with him, either.

She hastily apologized, tried harder to concentrate, and had to impatiently wait until the quadrille was over, which seemed to take four or five thousand years.

But it did eventually end, and Karl Augustus led her from the floor. Jane thanked him, adding politely, "I enjoyed our dance very much. Now if you'll excuse me, I've just seen someone from home whom I must say hello to."

She turned away and now *she* was the one searching the room with her eyes. Looking for that tall wiry form, that striking tawny hair.

But the Duke wasn't standing by the doorway anymore.

Had he . . . had he left?

Already?

Jane abruptly recalled their final conversation together. In his library at Hastings. His deep-blue eyes, dead; his manner, cold and haughty. He had been awful to her and hurt her feelings and it had made her furious.

Was she still angry at him?

Or was she angry all over again at him for coming here and then, possibly, going?

Just like a concertina, opening and closing.

Letting her in, shutting her out.

Well, she wasn't going to put up with that ever again.

Jane set her jaw, being careful, as she did so, *not* to gnash her teeth although she really would have liked to.

She looked around the crowded room one more time.

He wasn't there.

So, determinedly, she made her way toward the refreshments, and got herself a plate with the biggest piece of cake she could find.

"I'm delighted you could come, Your Grace," said Lady Jersey smilingly, and rather nervously Anthony replied:

"It was awfully kind of you to send me the vouchers, ma'am."

"But of course! Your father was a great friend of mine, you know. How you do resemble him! Poor dear Bunny."

"Bunny?"

Lady Jersey gave a little tinkling laugh. "My pet name for him. Such a sweet man."

Even more nervously Anthony answered, "Indeed," and for a few moments wondered wildly if Lady Jersey had mistaken him for someone else, as "sweet" was quite possibly the absolute last adjective in the whole of Samuel Johnson's authoritative *Dictionary of the English Language* he, Anthony, would have ever selected to describe his late father, but there was certainly no point in mentioning this, especially since the very reason he had applied to Lady Jersey for a voucher was because of a long-ago conversation between Margaret and Terence he had happened to have overheard, in which they both agreed there was a strong likelihood that Father was carrying on with Lady Jersey; and so he had hoped she might, if only for sentimental reasons, do him this favor and thereby obviate the need to go about importuning the other Patronesses for admittance to this much-vaunted and highly exclusive establishment.

Frankly the place seemed pretty drab and dismal, or at least that was his initial impression before Lady Jersey had rushed up and drawn him off to this private corridor before he'd had a chance to look for Jane some more. He *could* have called at the Penhallow townhouse, but thought it might be better to appear unexpectedly (and perhaps even heroically) in front of a great many other people and impress Jane with how dukish he looked with his subdued hair and intricately tied neckcloth (which had taken him nearly an hour to do up properly and now felt like it was throttling him) and up-to-the-minute evening-clothes and his shiny new shoes which (incidentally) hurt his feet, so that Jane would instantly forgive him for being such a terrible ass and maybe even let him kiss her then and there in front of everyone—a highly improbable scenario, given that it would no doubt create a hideous scandal and he would hardly want to embarrass Jane like that.

But a chap could dream, couldn't he?

"Yes, you *do* look so much like dear Bunny," said Lady Jersey with that same coyly glinting smile, and Anthony, breaking out into a sweat and hoping with all his heart that she wasn't—O God—*flirting* with him, wondered how in the name of all that was holy could he detach himself from this unnerving conversation and go back into the room with all of the other people, one of whom he wished very much would prove to be Jane.

He resisted the urge to pluck at his neckcloth, which was horribly starchy and stiff, but the impulse did result in a helpful flash of inspiration: What would the clever, resourceful Puss in Boots do in a situation like this?

Why, he'd smoothly extricate himself with a smile, that's what.

So Anthony made his lips curve upwards (hopefully not clownishly) and said with as much suavity as he could muster:

"Thank you again, ma'am. May I escort you back?" He held out his arm, and to his pleased surprise and secret triumph Lady Jersey slid her gloved hand around it, and he swept them away from the corridor and back among the lights and the music and, crucially, all the other people. He bowed and moved away with a sudden spring in his step.

Jane.

She *had* to be here.

Bunch had informed him that Almack's on a Wednesday night was *the* place for Polite Society to congregate.

So here he was, all dressed up as if he were the best duke in the world.

Oh, Jane, where are you? he thought, moving among the crowd.

There were so many people that he felt like an astronomer looking at a galaxy but seeking out one singular bright and perfect star.

Then he caught a glimpse of shining wavy flaxen hair and for a moment it felt as if his heart was going to jump out of his chest.

He strode toward that flaxen hair.

As he got closer, approaching from behind, he saw that it was part and parcel of a woman wearing a brilliant deep-blue gown which demurely revealed a voluptuously ripe figure.

Could it be . . . ?

"Miss Kent," Anthony said. "Jane?"

She swung around, and he saw with another violent

thump of his heart that it *was* Jane, that bright and perfect star, all beautiful and elegant and shapely and wonderful, with (he couldn't help but notice) the neckline of her deep-blue gown revealing some incredibly delicious and fascinating cleavage.

Happiness at finding her streaked through him and also desire which he tried to tamp down as it was completely impossible to do anything about it right now, and instead he stared down into her lovely familiar daisy-like face, wondered if he should quote poetry, or perhaps drawl with superb aplomb *Fancy meeting you here*, but instead he only managed to say, engulfed as he was with relief and happiness and desire:

"Hullo."

"Hullo. Your Grace," answered Jane a bit thickly. She swallowed, and he gleaned that she had been eating a piece of cake which (judging by the plate she held in one hand) was almost gone, and also he noticed that she had a small crumb nestling at the corner of her mouth which he would have liked to lick away, and he *also* observed that she was smiling at him but not very much and her big gray eyes had in them an expression which struck him as rather cool and wary.

After its joyful acrobatic leaps his heart now sank low, as if exhausted, and all he could think to say next was:

"There's a cake crumb on your face."

"Where?"

"At the corner of your mouth. On the left side."

She swiped it away with the tip of a finger. "Is it gone?"

"Yes."

"Thank you for telling me."

"You're welcome. How—how's that cake? Is it any good?"

"Not really. There's no icing."

"No icing? How beastly."

"Yes, it *is* beastly."

"Why are you eating it then?"

"Because I'm hungry."

"Ah. I say, Jane, it's marvelous to see you."

"Thank you," she repeated, but so politely and coolly that his heart plunged so low he could almost hear the pitiful *plop* as it hit the floor. He labored on:

"You look—you look marvelous."

"How kind."

"I mean it. I—uh—I—" He nearly ran both hands through his hair in his agitation and unease, remembering only in the nick of time that he wanted to appear dukish for once, and chaotically disordered hair wouldn't help his cause in the slightest. "I—uh—I'm wearing some new clothes."

"So I see."

"Puss in Boots," he blurted out, then nearly plopped onto the floor himself in his embarrassment.

Jane was looking up at him quizzically, which was, perhaps, better than cool wariness. "I beg your pardon?"

"Puss in Boots, you know. The—the moral—uh—one of them, I mean—was about wearing nice clothes in order to impress someone. Do—do you happen to know the story?"

"No."

"It's—it's an old fable about a very clever cat who helps his humble master become a marquis and get rich and marry a beautiful princess."

"I see. And the cat wears boots?"

"Yes, that's right."

"How many?"

"How many what?"

"How many boots does the cat wear? Two or four?"

"In the illustrations in Wakefield's book, he wears two.

Because when he goes on his quest to help his master, he's suddenly walking upright."

Jane nodded. "How *is* Wakefield?"

"He's very well, thank you. How is your great-grandmother?"

"She's well also. I trust your sister is too?"

"Well, yes and no."

Jane was looking up at him inquiringly now, which, Anthony thought with a surge of hopefulness, was even better than being looked at quizzically. "Is Lady Margaret unwell?" she asked.

"When I left Hastings she was in bed with one of her headaches. She didn't want me to go to London, you see, and she worked herself up into the most ghastly rage. I told her she was welcome to go too, but—well, that's when she slammed the door to my library so hard that she sprained her wrist."

"Dear me."

"Yes, and when Dr. Fotherham came to look at her wrist she insisted he bleed her."

"But he doesn't bleed people."

"Of course not. But Margaret worked herself up into another ghastly rage, and that's when her headache came on."

Jane took this in, and nodded again. "How is the Duchess?"

"Oh, she's splendid."

"I'm glad to hear it."

"Yes, she's fatter than ever."

"So am I."

"I noticed," said Anthony, shyly, and made himself not look away from her face and to that glorious and enticing cleavage again. "You do look splendid, Jane."

"Thank you."

"So did it work?"

"Did what work?"

"Did my—my hair and neckcloth and shoes and all that—did it impress you?"

Jane looked him over consideringly. "You've gotten very thin. Are *you* unwell?"

Anthony noticed that she hadn't directly answered his question, which was discouraging, but she *had* asked about how he was doing. "No, not really. It's just that I—I—uh—I haven't had much appetite lately."

"I'm sorry to hear that."

"It came on when you went away."

"Did it?"

"Yes, I—oh, Jane—Jane, I—"

"I believe this is our dance, Miss Kent," suddenly said a voice, which, Anthony saw, belonged to a good-looking fellow in evening-clothes which were just as fine as his own, plus his short and nicely clipped hair lay incredibly flat and sleek against his head.

Jane introduced him to Mr. Graham, whom he instantly envied and also loathed due to his having the privilege and honor of getting Jane all to himself via a dance together.

"Well," she said, "I must go. It's been delightful to see you again. Your Grace."

"Have you—" Anthony took a deep breath and went on bravely: "Have you any other dances free?"

"I'm afraid not."

She was still looking at him consideringly, he saw. As if assessing him somehow. Quickly he said, "May I—may I call on you at home?"

"Yes."

"I'll do that, then."

"You have the address?"

"Yes."

"How?"

"How what?"

"How did you get the address?"

"I asked Gabriel Penhallow for it before I left. May I call on you tomorrow?"

"Certainly," Jane said, and try as he might, Anthony could detect only common civility in her tone, and nothing particularly warm or friendly. And then Jane gave her plate to a passing servant and Mr. Graham took her away. A horrible chill went through Anthony, and the truncheon inside him seemed to immediately double in size. So far it could not be said that his quest was going particularly well. Although Jane had smiled at him, it had seemed rather perfunctory, nor had her beautiful eyes twinkled or sparkled one tiny bit.

Not a good sign.

He stared at Jane for a few minutes as she danced with that rotter Mr. Graham (who of course danced very well) and then, worried that he might be staring conspicuously and even dementedly, looked away from her, right into the sharp blue eyes of Mrs. Henrietta Penhallow, who from halfway across the room was staring at *him*.

She gave him a slight, sardonic nod, appearing to be not at all glad to see him, and he nodded back, in point of fact not particularly glad to see her either and be looked at so satirically, and after that he got himself a plate with some cake on it, but couldn't eat a mouthful, surveyed and rejected the hideously thin slices of bread and butter, tried a swallow of the bad and lukewarm tea, and then he left Almack's, wondering why people made such a fuss about it, and went home to the Farr townhouse in Grosvenor Square where Bunch was waiting up for him, and who listened with his usual inscrutable yet sympathetic demeanor as Anthony gloomily described for him precisely how his evening had gone.

On their ride home from Almack's Jane had mentioned, in a neutral voice, seeing the Duke there, and Great-grandmother had, with similar neutrality, acknowledged seeing him as well.

Nothing more had been said, but for the three days following, Great-grandmother somehow managed to ensure that they were busier than ever and never home during the usual hours for receiving callers.

Cards from their numerous visitors piled up, but none of them were from the Duke.

So much for him keeping his word, Jane thought bitterly.

Coming and going.

Open and shut.

That was just who the Duke was.

Jane was angry with herself for worrying over how thin he had gotten.

And for hoping to see his card among all the others.

And for thinking how very long these past three days had seemed.

She went to the window of her bedchamber and looked out. It was black with night out there, and also—exactly complementing her mood—raining.

Just *perfect.*

The hour was very late, and she was ready for bed, having changed into a nightgown and frothy silk wrapper, but instead of pulling back the covers and blowing out her candles, and finally putting an end to another bitterly disappointing day, she went to sit in one of the two chairs set before the fireplace, where a small cheerful fire still leaped and danced. She stared at the little flames and sternly ordered herself not to cry.

Don't look to the past, she reminded herself. *Look to the future.*

Love or nothing.

Look to the future.

Love or—

A sudden rattling noise against her window had Jane up and on her feet. What on earth?

She hurried to the casement window and looked out—and down—and to the courtyard in the front of the townhouse.

In the dim light of a gas-lamp alongside the street, she saw, below her on the paving stones which glimmered wetly, the Duke.

He was looking up at her from beneath the brim of his tall hat.

And he was holding something underneath his greatcoat, which made his chest look grotesquely bulky.

Jane couldn't help it.

She felt herself breaking into a smile.

Quickly she turned the latch on the window, opened it, and stepped out onto the narrow balcony enclosed by waist-high wrought-iron fencing. Luckily she was protected from the worst of the rain by the overhang above her. She leaned over the fencing and whispered loudly:

"What are you doing here? Your Grace."

"I've come to see you," the Duke whispered loudly back. "Can I come up?"

"Don't ring the bell, it will wake everyone up. I'll go downstairs and let you in."

"No, don't. I'm coming up."

"What? How?"

"Watch."

Jane did, fascinated.

First the Duke pulled out the bulky object from the shelter of his greatcoat. It was something in a rucksack which he hung around his neck by its rope cord. Then he went to the window on the ground level below her room, stepped up onto the ledge, and, taking full advantage of his great height and his long arms and legs, reached up with both hands to a length of horizontal stone above the window that jutted out a bit, just enough for him to take hold of it, thrust himself upwards with amazing strength and dexterity, and in a single fluid motion perch on the jutting stone and grab the bottom rail of the iron fence of the balcony outside the drawing-room, directly below Jane's own balcony.

His other hand came up to grasp the bottom rail, he drew himself upward and grasped the upper railing, one hand and then another, and after that he nimbly vaulted over the railing and onto the balcony.

Then he did it all again and with equal nimbleness vaulted up and over the railing and onto Jane's balcony.

He looked at Jane, and she looked at him. She *still* couldn't help it—she was smiling, and possibly even grinning. She said to him:

"Puss in Boots?"

"Yes, I'm enacting the other moral, about being resourceful. Also, of course, *Romeo and Juliet.*"

By great good fortune Jane had happened to recently see a production of this very play and so after a moment she gave a laugh and said, "The balcony scene!"

"Just so."

"You're a very good climber."

"Thank you. It's nice to know I still can."

"I was very impressed."

"Were you? Well, that's splendid, because I'm wearing

my regular clothes tonight, so I can't try to dazzle you with my stylish new evening-wear."

Jane looked down and saw with pleasure the familiar scuffed boots. "You'd better come inside before the Watch sees you and suspects you of foul deeds."

"That phrase always makes me think of chickens running amok," he said, and followed Jane inside her bedchamber. Quickly she closed the window and turned to look at him more closely.

"You're soaking."

"Just my coat is, really. And my hat."

"Give them to me."

He unslung the rucksack, which had a curious angular appearance, and carefully put it on the floor, then took off his greatcoat and hat; the coat she took to the tall pier-glass and draped it over one of the knobs in the frame. The hat she lay on top of her bureau. Then she gazed at him again.

His hair was a little wet from the rain and lay tumbled about his face in the way she liked so much. His face was too thin, and in those deep-blue eyes of his was a steady look of earnest supplication.

Jane felt her heart starting to melt like snow beneath the sun, but only let it melt into icy mush, not free-flowing water, because she was, like all good Nantwich girls, cautious when necessary. Taking refuge in a bit of hostess-like formality, she said to him:

"Won't you come sit by the fire, and get warm?"

"Thank you."

So they each sat in one of the chairs set before the fireplace, and Jane saw that he was looking at her like a man who was hungry not for food, but for something else. She tried hard to steel herself against it, which was difficult as she was, in fact, very happy that he was here (especially after climbing up to her room with such dashing and romantic panache), so she summoned up in her mind the pain and sorrow that had been dogging her all these many weeks in London, and especially during the past three days. "Why didn't you call like you said you would?"

"I did call. Seven times, all told. You were never home."

"Why didn't you leave a card?"

"I don't have cards. There was no time to have them printed up. Didn't your butler tell you I was here?"

"No," said Jane, a further dangerous rush of happiness swooping through her. He *had* called, he *had* kept his word.

"I was afraid he wouldn't. He looks like the most awful stickler."

"That's why my great-grandmother hired him."

"I can't say I'm surprised."

"Bunch is *much* better, in my opinion," Jane said. "Were those pebbles you tossed against my window?"

"Yes."

"You have good aim."

"Thank you. Years of practice skipping stones, I daresay."

"In the lake at Hastings?"

"Yes, that's right."

"I used to be quite good at skipping stones," she said reminiscently.

"Back in Nantwich?"

"Yes, there was a little river behind my house. How did you know which window was mine?"

"On one of my visits here I cunningly asked one of the footmen if the people whose rooms were to the front didn't mind all the noise from the street. And he said that Mrs. Penhallow did, and had hers to the back, but that it didn't bother you at all."

"That was clever of you."

"Thank you. I was getting rather desperate, you see."

Jane already knew the answer, but she asked the question anyway. Because she wanted to hear him say it. "Desperate about what?"

"Desperate about not seeing you."

Another rush of happiness swooped through her. "Great-grandmother keeps us very busy."

"As I learned to my increasing dismay. I say, Jane, I wanted to ask you—if you're—you're in love with anybody, or—or engaged, or anything like that. I've read the papers every day, horribly afraid that in the announcements I'd see your name."

The Duke had leaned forward, his big attractive hands loosely clasped between his knees, his eyes fixed on hers, his too-thin face tense and rather pale now in the flickering light of the fire.

"No," said Jane.

He took a breath. "You're not engaged?"

"No, I'm not."

He took another breath, a deeper one. "Are you in love with anybody?"

"Yes."

At this the Duke looked crushed and his hands tightened. But he said, steadily: "I see. I—I wish you very happy, Jane."

"Thank you. Don't you want to know who I'm in love with?"

"If you'd like to tell me," he said, and she could see the effort it took him to remain so steady and so generous. Her heart melted some more. There was still plenty to be cautious about, but that didn't stop her from saying:

"It's you. Your Grace."

"You're—you're in love with me? Still? After all this time?"

"Yes."

Jane watched the wonderment dawn in his eyes, and to her came a beautiful line from *Romeo and Juliet.* Only she changed it a little bit at the end.

What light through yonder window breaks? It is the east, and the Duke is the sun.

Chapter 20

Anthony stared at Jane, who looked so lovely and voluptuous and desirable in the ruffled diaphanous white thing she was wearing which he only now just realized was a wrapper worn over a nightgown, and with her pale hair in a loose plait he longed to undo, that he could hardly stand it.

Nonetheless, he tamped down the desire that crackled through him like a lightning strike, and focused on what she had just said.

Was it really possible?

That she still cared for him?

Even *loved* him, after he'd been so beastly to her?

"Jane," he breathed, and slid from his chair which was set so cozily next to hers and knelt before her, he being sufficiently tall to have them, satisfyingly, exactly face to face. He took her hands in his own and he said:

"I love you too. Oh, Jane, dearest Jane, won't you please marry me? I'll do my best to make you happy, now and forever."

She looked back at him, somehow managing to look both elated and resolute at the same time. She smiled and then she sighed and then she answered:

"Maybe."

"Maybe?"

"Maybe."

Anthony felt his brain launch into an extremely vigorous set of gymnastics.

Jane hadn't said "Yes," which was naturally the answer he had been hoping for, so that was a blow, quite a painful one, but on the other hand, she *did* love him, which was amazing, incredible, and wonderful, and also she hadn't said "No" to his proposal which would have been infinitely more terrible; so things could certainly be worse, and at the very least "Maybe" had a world of possibilities contained within it, and he knew Jane well enough to know that she wouldn't be saying "Maybe" unless she meant it and she had a good reason for saying it, but, regardless, no matter how one looked at it, she hadn't said "Yes" and it was hard to not get the answer he was urgently hoping for in every particle of his being.

Anthony told his brain to calm down and be reasonable, and very quietly he said to Jane:

"Is it because I'm the worst duke in the world?"

"You're not the worst duke in the world."

"My sister thinks so, and so does your great-grandmother, I suspect. The one thing they've ever agreed upon, in fact."

"Well, I think they're wrong."

"Really, Jane?"

"Yes, really."

"It's kind of you to say so. Actually, now that I think of it, there's something else I daresay they would agree upon. A corollary of sorts. They wouldn't like the idea of us being married."

"Because my great-grandmother thinks I'm too good for you, and your sister thinks you're too good for me?"

"That about sums it up."

"It doesn't matter what they think," Jane said. "What matters is what *we* think."

"That's exactly what I told Margaret when she started kicking up a fuss. And then I told her she can go suck an egg—a phrase I'm not proud of, but it was a rather heated conversation. And it did relay my sentiments pretty plainly. That's when she stormed out of my library and sprained her wrist. But what about you, Jane? Are you worried about your great-grandmother's disapproval?"

On Jane's lovely face was more resolution than ever. "I'd be very sorry to disappoint her, but I hope that my happiness would matter to her more than her notions of who would make a good husband for me."

"Like that fellow you were dancing with the other night?"

"I suppose so."

"He's an awfully good dancer."

"Yes, he is. But he isn't you."

At this Anthony felt his hopes getting themselves up, but he also felt in all honesty compelled to say:

"He's a much better dancer than I am."

"I'm not all that good myself. We could practice together."

With enormous courage Anthony said, "I'd like that."

She smiled at him, and his hopes irrepressibly went a bit higher, but then she said the words which all too often in life have a disturbing, even ominous ring.

"We need to talk."

With even more courage he replied, "Then let's talk."

"Yes, but you should let go of me. I can't concentrate very well when you're touching me."

"Oh, Jane, really? Because that's how I feel about you."

"Yes, it's true."

It was a highly pleasing and reciprocal answer, and,

suppressing an ardent wish to kiss each of Jane's beautiful, capable-looking hands, obediently Anthony released them instead, and went back to sit in the other chair.

He looked at Jane, and Jane looked at him.

Finally she said, "What made you change your mind?"

"I believe you mean to say, 'How did you manage to stop being such a fool?'"

She smiled just a little. "So how did you?"

"It was an arduous process, I'm sorry to say. I got more and more miserable, you see, after you went away. But I was stubborn, and frightened. Horribly frightened. And then, one night, I was thinking about something Wakefield had said, about Romeo being stupid, and what a bad hero he is, and also—well, you already know about Puss in Boots inspiring me. When I woke up the next morning the answer was there for me, as plain as day. I realized I didn't want to be the stupid hero in a sad love story. I wanted to be the brave hero in the story, even if I didn't know if it would have a happy ending or not. The next day Bunch and I set off for London."

Jane took this in, and nodded. Softly she said, "Why were you frightened?"

"My marriage to Selina was dreadful, and I was afraid of getting married again."

Her gray eyes went wide. "But you said you were still in love with her."

"It wasn't true. We loathed each other, she and I, and I was wretched beyond words. But you asked me about it, that day in my library, having somehow arrived at the idea that I loved her, and cravenly I seized upon it in the most horrible way as an excuse to push you away. I'm dreadfully sorry. I was a fool, a sapskull, an addlepate, a chucklehead, and every other species of stupidity." He added, filled with excruciating remorse: "I hope you can forgive me. Would it help if I got down onto my knees again, and literally groveled? I'd kiss the hem of your gown if you let me, too, but then I'd be most awfully tempted to kiss more of you."

"That does sound very nice," answered Jane, going a little pink, "but it would distract me, I'm afraid."

"Well, let me know if groveling at any point would help."

"I will. So you're not afraid to get married anymore?"

"To be clear, I'm not afraid anymore of marrying *you*. Will you tell me why you're saying 'Maybe,' even though you love me? I say, that *is* so marvelous to think about. Your loving me, I mean."

"I do. And I'm so, so glad you love me, too." Jane smiled at him, revealing to Anthony's deep delight those entrancing dimples, then went on: "Now that I understand about your first marriage, I have two reasons left. One has to do with my past in Nantwich. You already know that Titus Penhallow didn't marry Charity, my grandmother. And that I grew up poor, and lived rough."

"Yes. It doesn't matter to me, except that I hate thinking about how hard things were for you."

"That's very kind. Thank you. You should also know that three years ago, I met a boy—a young man—who was traveling with his family from Ireland to go to America. They had to stop in Nantwich for a while until his mother recovered from a difficult childbirth. Declan and I fell in love and planned to be married, and—we became lovers. I was going to go with him and his family to America, but Great-grandmother Kent got sick, terribly sick, and of course I couldn't leave her. She wouldn't have survived the journey. So I stayed, and Declan went on." Jane looked away, into the dancing flames of the fire, her expression for a moment distant and rather pensive. Then she gave herself a little shake, and turned her eyes back to him, resolute as ever. "I'm telling you this so that if you absolutely must have a virgin for your wife, you would know the truth and could change your mind. Your Grace."

"I do wish you'd stop calling me that," Anthony said, momentarily distracted.

"What should I call you?"

"'Anthony' would do nicely."

"All right, I will. Anthony."

"How delightful it sounds, coming from your lips. Jane, are you—are you still in love with Declan?"

"No. It's a chapter from my past. An important one, but it's a memory now, that's all. Beautiful and a little sad. Does it bother you?"

"Does what bother me?"

"That I'm not a virgin."

"No," Anthony said truthfully. "I'm just glad you're in love only with me." Then he added, shyly, "Would it bother you to know I've only been with Selina?"

"No." Jane was looking at him straightforwardly and also kindly. "I can't imagine it was pleasant making love with someone you didn't care for."

Anthony sighed. "No, it wasn't. It was a miserably brief and mechanical act in which we both did our duty and couldn't wait for it to be over. But it did bring forth Wakefield, and that was a great blessing."

"Yes," said Jane. "Do you think he would mind having me for a stepmother?"

"I think he'd love it," answered Anthony, perking up at once. But then he drooped slightly. "Are you ready to tell me your other reason for saying maybe?"

"Yes. This reason has to do with you."

"I knew it," said Anthony gloomily.

Jane leaned forward. Her expression was still both resolute and kind. "It has to do with your . . . inconsistency,

Anthony. I noticed, back in Somerset, that you seemed to run rather hot and cold toward me."

He leaned forward also, in his mind secretly cursing that slippery, inconstant Duke of Oyster. "But that was before, Jane," he replied, earnest, eager, urgent. "Before I got over my fears. And when I was letting Margaret torment me with an apparently infinite number of marital candidates. That's stopped, naturally, and so I told Margaret." He gave a sudden laugh. "Oh, Jane, you should have seen her face. She's never seen me put my foot down like that. And while I was at it, I also told her I'm going to have the wallpaper in the family dining-parlor done over. Margaret screeched something about it being well over a hundred years old and therefore worth preserving, but I put my other foot down and said I was tired of eating in a room that looks like a two-day-old bruise, and then her face turned the exact same shade of reddish-purple. What would you think of a nice cheerful yellow instead?"

"I think it would look very nice."

"Done." Then Anthony leaned forward even more. "Jane, I won't be like that anymore—running hot and cold on you. That's over."

"I hope so. That's why I think we should wait to see for certain."

"I'll prove myself to you, Jane. I will," he promised. "Would now be a good time to do some groveling?"

"That won't be necessary. But I do need for you to be sure. To be . . . there."

"I am. I will. I'm here."

Jane held out her hand, and he took it in his own, as one might receive something incredibly precious: reverently. Gratefully. She said: "Then we needn't say anything to anybody—aside from Great-grandmother, who ought to know—and we'll take our time."

"Yes. I'll wait forever if I have to."

She smiled. "It won't be forever."

"Does this mean we have a—a private understanding between us?"

"I suppose it does."

"Then may I give you something? A gift? It's in my greatcoat pocket."

"No, not yet," said Jane. "I'm afraid I'll like it so much that I'll lose my resolve."

Anthony smiled, and lifted her hand, and kissed it. "Then I'll wait on that, too."

"Thank you, Anthony. Would you kiss my hand again, please? That felt so nice."

He did, and Jane smiled at him some more, and Anthony couldn't help but feel his hopes getting up yet higher.

"Do you still hate London, Anthony?"

"I hate it less now that you're in it."

"That's quite a compliment. What have you been doing, in between coming to call here?"

"That kept me pretty well occupied, but I did go to Parliament and listen to some speeches. I've never heard such a lot of rubbish talked about the Corn Laws in my life. So I decided I'm going to take up my seat."

"You are? How wonderful."

"Yes, for the first time since old lemon-sucking Myles Farr the fourth—or possibly fifth—duke was summarily ejected from London by Queen Elizabeth. I daresay I'll get used to making fiery speeches, waving my arms about, and vehemently denouncing my opponents."

"You'll be splendid," said Jane warmly. "Does this mean you'll be staying on here in London?"

"If you don't mind."

"I'd love it."

"I say, I *am* glad. So do you like London?"

"Oh yes. I wouldn't want to live here all year round, but I've seen so many interesting things and met so many interesting people. My great-grandmother Kent said that Polite Society is entirely made up of rogues and degenerates, but I think she was exaggerating."

"Well, that's good to hear. Especially since I'd like to have Bunch go to Hastings and bring Wakefield back with him. He wanted to come with me, you know, and I promised to bring him another time."

"Oh, how delightful! I've missed him so much."

"And me also, Jane?" he asked, rather shyly.

"You also."

"I missed you like anything. I couldn't eat because of missing you, and because I have a—" Anthony broke off in surprise. "It's gone."

"What's gone?"

"The nasty truncheon-like feeling in my stomach, taking up all the room in there. By Jove, I'm ravenous."

"I've got some apples I squirreled away."

"Excellent. I've got something too." Anthony got up and went to his rucksack. He opened the drawstring closure and carefully withdrew a large pasteboard box which he brought over to Jane. "This is for you." And he saw with the most incredible burst of joy in his heart that she was looking up at him with her gray eyes twinkling in the way he loved so much.

"Is it what I think it is?"

"Yes. To make up for being such a dreadful, selfish, pompous ass that day we said goodbye."

"Thank you very much, Anthony." She took the box and put it on her lap, then pulled off the lid. "Oh, they look delicious."

"Is this gift weakening your resolve?"

"Just a little, but in a good way. Would you bring the apples over? They're on the table next to my bed."

So Anthony got the apples and sat down again next to Jane, and together they ate the apples and quite a few chocolates. Jane told him about some of the interesting people she had met, whom she thought he might enjoy meeting also, as well as about some places where they could go with Wakefield. Anthony told her all the local news, and topped it off with the miraculous transformation of Margaret's cat which had Jane exclaiming in wonder.

"Yes, it purrs like anything now," said Anthony. "And it seems to have struck up quite a friendship with Snuffles." He took a bite of apple, chewed, then suddenly said around it:

"Good Lord, I nearly forgot to tell you, Jane. Your great-grandfather's cure for apple blight worked."

"It did?" Jane beamed. "How marvelous."

"Yes, and McTavish is going to try it to get rid of caterpillars in the succession house. Doesn't it make you wonder if any other of your great-grandfather's remedies actually work?"

"I can think of something else that did."

Anthony took another bite of apple. "Really? What is it?"

"Do you remember the title of the chapbook I brought with me from Nantwich? It's called *Four Hundred Practical Aspects of Vinegar As Used to Reduce Corpulence, Purify the Humours, Improve the Complexion, and Attract a Most Desirable Spouse.*" She smiled. "Well, and here you are."

"Jane," he said, "that's a dangerous thing to say to a man when you're wearing such a charming frilly insubstantial thing and with a bed right nearby."

"Yes, it *is* tempting, isn't it?" she agreed, twinkling at him.

"So tempting, in fact, that I probably should go. Will I see you tomorrow?"

"Yes, you will. Could you come by around noon? I'll talk to Great-grandmother beforehand, but I think the three of us should talk together, too."

"I'll be there."

They stood up, and Jane got him his greatcoat and hat, which he put on, and together they walked to the casement window.

"It's still raining," she said. "Will you be able to climb down safely?"

"Yes. Jane, may I kiss you before I go?"

"I was hoping you would."

"Were you really?"

"Oh, yes." Jane tilted her beautiful daisy-like face up to him and Anthony didn't hesitate. He wrapped his arms around her and kissed her, and she brought her arms up and around him too, and kissed him back, and it felt at once entirely familiar and incredibly new, and also wonderful beyond words, and it took the most tremendous amount of will not to pick Jane up and carry her over to that tempting bed and help her off with all her clothes and rip off his own as well, and feast his eyes on every magnificent inch of her (for starters), but if she could have resolve, he decided, he would also.

Finally, reluctantly, he pulled away, and saw with immense satisfaction that Jane was glowing and rather breathless.

"Oh, *Anthony*," she said.

"Yes, Jane?"

"Parting is such sweet sorrow."

"It is, but we're not going to end up like poor old Romeo

and Juliet, that's for certain. Well, goodnight. I'll see you tomorrow. I say, that does sound ripping. 'Tomorrow.' Or, really, 'later on today,' which is even better."

"Yes, it is." Jane opened the window and he stepped out onto the balcony, turning once to quickly kiss her again, one more time, and then he slung a leg over the railing, nimbly climbed down, and landed on the pavement stones as neat as a cat.

He glanced up.

There was Jane, smiling down at him, and Anthony felt so happy and so hopeful that he floated back to the Farr townhouse as if on gossamer wings, not caring whether or not he was the worst duke, or only a terrible one, or maybe even, possibly, a mediocre one, because he knew that he was, regardless, the happiest and most hopeful and constant man in the world.

Jane told Great-grandmother the next morning that she and the Duke had come to an understanding. They weren't betrothed, but they might be. Only time would tell.

Great-grandmother was shocked, and then she was appalled, and then she was bitterly disappointed. She had, she said, wanted someone better for Jane—someone of a much higher caliber, someone of whom Titus would have approved.

Gently Jane replied that while she greatly appreciated Great-grandmother's ambitions on her behalf, it was, perhaps, worth remembering that Titus himself had pursued his own happiness, regardless of what anyone else might think or say, and wasn't it possible that he would have wanted his granddaughter to do the same? Besides, she added, if things worked out between herself and the Duke, she'd be living right next door, and wasn't that better than if she ended up married to someone who lived far to the north of England, or in Europe?

So persuasive was Jane that Henrietta—while not yet reconciled to the possibility of her darling great-granddaughter marrying the Duke—admitted that all this gadding about in search of a worthy match (and especially these past few days) had been a trifle fatiguing, and she would prefer a less hectic schedule that permitted her to take her daily afternoon nap which was always very restorative.

She also confessed to a grudging admiration of the Duke's daring and resourcefulness in climbing up to Jane's room, as it was, she said, something that her own dear Richard would have done. She refused to say more on the subject, but Jane did see in her eyes the tiniest spark of a nostalgic smile.

Thus when the Duke arrived promptly at noon, bearing very pretty bouquets for each of them, Great-grandmother received him with a guarded civility, and when eventually he told her about his intention to claim his seat in Parliament, and to try and knock some sense into people's heads (metaphorically speaking) about the Corn Laws, she was so much in agreement with him that when he rose to his feet to take his leave of them, she actually gave him her hand to kiss. He shot a startled look at Jane, but nonetheless bowed over Great-grandmother's hand with such courtly old-fashioned grace that later, when the two of them were alone again, Great-grandmother remarked, with elaborate casualness, that although she wished the Duke would tie his neckcloth more carefully, he did have about him a certain air of distinction, and she also recalled that Gabriel had had many positive things to say about the Duke including the fact that he was an excellent landlord to his tenant farmers, knew a great deal about timber management, held all the proper views on drainage trenches, and always donated generously to local causes.

Lady Margaret, Jane remarked back with equal casualness (and also perfect truth), apparently believed that he was the worst duke in the world, and Great-grandmother at once replied that Lady Margaret's opinion on anything—whether it was about flowers, interior decoration, places in which to hold picnics, or her brother—was deserving of little to no attention.

Perhaps, Great-grandmother went on, the Duke would care to join them on a little expedition to the Royal Academy of Art, and she would not object if he accompanied them to Carlton House, as she would be glad of his arm to lean on among the crowds which were always so dense and bothersome.

With this Jane was more than satisfied.

The *ton* was quick to notice that the fascinating Miss Jane Kent, known by one and all to be the apple of her great-grandmother Mrs. Henrietta Penhallow's eye, was all at once being accompanied everywhere by the equally fascinating Duke of Radcliffe who had never before been seen in London Society.

As the Duke was the possessor of an old and distinguished title, fabulously wealthy, unattached, and in his own unconventional way quite good-looking, he was widely viewed as a stellar new addition to the Marriage Mart and a significant number of ladies privately vowed to set their caps at him.

However, these ladies were destined to be disappointed, for the Duke, while polite, evinced no discernable interest in them as potential objects of his affection, and besides, as soon as his son Wakefield arrived in Town, he—

accompanied by Miss Kent—was seen at fewer Society events and more often at venues of interest to children, such as the Egyptian Hall, the famous maze at Hampton Court, the Tower of London, a balloon ascension at Hyde Park, and (several times) at Gunter's Tea Shop, famous for its pastries, confections, sweetmeats, and ices, where, it was rumored, the three of them racked up some impressively extravagant bills.

Six weeks after his momentous conversation with Jane on that rainy night, Anthony (who had joyfully eaten enough in London to regain all the weight he had lost during his extended period of misery), along with Wakefield and Bunch, returned home to Hastings and to an incredibly emotional reunion (on Wakefield's part) with all the dogs, but most especially Snuffles, and additionally his aunt Margaret's cat whom he had given the sobriquet of "Boots" and which the cat seemed to actually respond to from time to time. Jane and her great-grandmother were leaving London shortly as well, only they were stopping in Bath for a fortnight so that Mrs. Penhallow could drink the rejuvenating waters and introduce Jane to all her acquaintance there.

Summer was at its peak of glory, and vigorously Anthony plunged back into his usual pursuits as well as some new ones.

He oversaw the repapering of the wallpaper in the family dining-room (a soft sunny yellow), he personally helped dig some much-needed drainage trenches beyond the southwestern fields, he went fishing with Wakefield and he strode cheerfully up and down the blooming fragrant lime-walk, relishing the complete and entire absence of Margaret's usual ghastly parade of houseguests.

Moreover, thanks to McTavish's diligence in applying vinegar treatments the caterpillars in the succession house had been vanquished, the pumpkins in their cozy green patches were growing like anything, and the Duchess, who was continuing to plump up nicely, seemed genuinely glad to see him again, manifesting this by a delightful spate of grunts and the wriggling of her curly pink tail.

Plus, Margaret, who in his extended absence had taken to wearing clothes that were somehow an even blacker shade of black (making Anthony wonder if she wasn't taking the defection of her cat rather too hard), had regularly been making her way over to the vicarage where she was, according to Wakefield who had winkled the information out of the dour housekeeper Mrs. McKenzie, spending a good deal of time closeted in Mr. Pressley's study in private conversation, all of which resulted in a curiously subdued demeanor on Margaret's part and therefore considerably less conflict and hostility at home. Wakefield said to Anthony that Mrs. McKenzie said it all started after Mr. Pressley gave a sermon on the theme of redemption and second chances which had rendered the entire congregation spellbound.

Then Jane came back and things got even better.

Quite often she came over to Hastings with Wakefield after lessons were over, and stayed for luncheon, billiards, strolls about the grounds, and, of course, visits to see the Duchess. Wakefield showed Jane how to play battledores and shuttlecocks (after which the three of them had some very spirited games), and also how to roll a hoop, and she showed them both a couple of deft maneuvers to try when skipping stones at the lake.

Anthony rode over to Surmont Hall quite a bit, where old Mrs. Penhallow had more or less stopped eyeing him satirically, and occasionally he and Jane were able to slip away to some private place where they kissed each other like maniacs.

Summer began to wane.

The days were getting cooler, the pumpkins were getting bigger, and the Duchess was getting fatter.

All signs pointed to a glorious autumn.

Even though he wanted to, and had to repress the impulse many times a day, Anthony never said a word to Jane about his proposal of marriage, hoping that, by word and by deed, she would realize that he *was* a constant lover. He had wondered, once or twice when he woke up in the dead of night, if there would prove to be some fatal flaw in his character that made it impossible for him to remain steadfast and faithful in his love for Jane, something along the lines of Romeo's phenomenal stupidity in not poking Juliet with a stick, but as the weeks passed it well and truly became clear that those horribly long months of wretchedness before he had gone to London had taught him a lesson quite thoroughly—one that would last him the rest of his life. About things that *really* mattered.

And so, when the harvest *fête* came around, and the Hastings pumpkin lost out, yet again, to Miss Humphrey's gorgeous *Cucurbita pepo*, Anthony was able to congratulate her warmly and with only the slightest tinge of envy, and to console the depressed McTavish with an order to tear down Margaret's ruin which had begun to reek in a very alarming way—a task which cheered McTavish no end, and while he was busy ripping away dead vines, he entertained himself with ambitious plans for next year's crop of pumpkins and also a new and even more artistic shrub in the shape of Lady Godiva riding on her horse.

To no one's surprise, the Duchess won the Fattest Pig contest again, receiving the large blue silk ribbon around her enormous neck with such humble radiance that Johns actually burst into tears and then he shook the hands of everyone around him, one of whom happened to be Cremwell the Penhallow pigman, and another of whom happened to be Jane. Johns dabbed at his streaming eyes, loudly blew his nose in a giant handkerchief, and also with humble radiance apologized to her for harboring unjust suspicions, saying that it was redonculous of him and he should have known from the start that she was a good 'un.

Jane graciously accepted his apology, congratulated him on his tremendous win, and went back to eating her large Bath bun which was light and sweet and dotted with caraway seeds.

How beautiful Jane looked, thought Anthony admiringly as he stood next to the Duchess in her clean shining pen. Jane was wearing a forest-green pelisse and a charming high-poke bonnet of the same color; her cheeks were rosy in the cool autumnal breeze and her eyes glowed silver.

Then those beautiful eyes came to meet his and she smiled, and Anthony felt so happy that he had to take a few moments to bask in his own happiness before indicating to Jane, with a subtle gesture to the side of his face, that there was a caraway seed lodged in one corner of her lovely mouth. She licked it away and calmly proceeded to take another bite of her bun.

As for the fiercely contested accolade of Best Flowers, the judges made an unprecedented decision by declaring a tie among Lady Margaret (Siberian irises), Miss Humphrey (delphiniums), and Mrs. Henrietta Penhallow (roses de Provins). To Anthony's astonishment, he saw that not only was Margaret being civil to Miss Humphrey, she was also wearing a hat he had never seen on her before, a rather dashing dove-gray confection garnished with a frivolous loop of violet ribbon, and when Miss Humphrey complimented her on it, Margaret actually smiled and said thank you very much, and even asked if Miss Humphrey might be willing to share some tips on winter propagation techniques, for which she was much famed throughout the county.

Would wonders never cease, Anthony thought, and promptly thought it again when five minutes later Mrs. Roger walked past arm-in-arm with her husband and smiled at him, a far cry from the menacing stare with which she had favored him during (as he called it in his mind) his awful Time of the Truncheon, after which he spotted Wakefield rolling a hoop with such newfound dexterity that he rolled it into nothing and no one, a nice change from last year. His eyes met Jane's again and they shared another smile.

All in all, an absolutely splendid *fête*.

Chapter 21

Jane scooped up the last of her blancmange and then put her empty bowl and spoon down onto the tray Anthony had ferried over from the house and which lay on a conveniently placed stump near the pig-cote. Anthony was still eating his blancmange, and the Duchess, over at her trough, still had a ways to go on hers, but this was not surprising as Anthony had given her a much larger amount, which seemed only fair since she was much larger than either of them.

"That was delicious," Jane said, and Anthony looked up from his bowl and smiled at her.

"I'm glad you liked it."

"Oh, I do. Almost as much as apple puffs." She leaned her elbows on the stone balustrade of the Duchess' pen. It was a cold, clear day in February, and a soft blanket of new snow lay on the ground, sparkling a little in the sun. But Jane was warm and snug in her heavy pelisse and cozy hat and sturdy lined half-boots. She watched as the Duchess finally emerged from her stance at the trough, her snout covered in blancmange and looking as peaceful and satisfied as Jane herself had felt after finishing her bowl.

"What are you thinking about?" asked Anthony, and Jane turned her head to look up at him. He had put his own bowl and spoon onto the tray and now stood straight and tall, looking incredibly handsome in his greatcoat and tall hat with the ends of his tawny hair splayed out across his collar. It was strange to remember that when she had first met him—a year ago now—she hadn't at once found him delightfully attractive. Which just went to say something important about first impressions.

"I was thinking about you."

"Were you really?"

"Yes." Jane straightened up and smiled at him.

"In a good way?"

"In a very good way. Anthony, do you remember that night, all those months ago, when you climbed up to my room back in London?"

"I'll always remember it."

"So will I. Do you also happen to recall wanting to give me a gift—something that was in your greatcoat pocket? Something to commemorate our private understanding?"

Jane watched as Anthony's dark-blue eyes did that marvelous thing again: somehow both darkening and filling with light. She would never, ever tire of seeing them do that.

"Yes," he answered. "I certainly do."

Anthony was already standing fairly close to her, but Jane took a step that brought them even closer, which was much better. "Well," she said, "I'd love to have it, whenever you're ready to give it to me."

"Funny you should ask, Jane, as I've been carrying it with me everywhere. And this is the perfect place to give it to you."

"How so?"

"You'll see." Anthony pulled from his greatcoat pocket

a small square box which was about the size of his palm, and held it out to Jane. She took it, blew off the dog hairs, and looked up at him again. "Chocolates?" she said softly, teasingly.

The corners of his attractive mouth quirked. "No, not chocolates this time."

Jane lifted the lid, and saw, nestled on crimson velvet, a necklace made of perfect, iridescent pearls. She caught her breath. "Oh, Anthony, how beautiful."

"I saw it in a shop window in London and knew right away that it was meant for you."

"I love it. I love *you*. Thank you *very* much. Will you put it on me?"

"With pleasure."

Jane held the box and watched in awe as Anthony delicately worked the clasp, put it behind her neck to fasten it, and then brought the gleaming strand to lay on the breast of her pelisse. "Oh, Anthony, thank you. I'll cherish it forever. And you also." She slid her arms around him, went up on her toes, and kissed him soundly.

When finally they broke apart, Anthony said, his eyes filled with light, "Jane, does this mean you're accepting my proposal?"

"Yes. I'm sure now. If you are?"

"Very sure. Oh, Jane, very, very sure." Now he was the one kissing her, and Jane felt so happy that she had to end the kiss so she could laugh out loud with the joy that was filling her up to the brim and beyond.

"Jane, would you say it again?"

"That I love you?"

"Yes."

"I love you, Anthony Farr."

"And I love you, Jane Kent. With all my heart and soul. Have you figured out why this is the perfect place for you to receive your gift?"

Jane shook her head, smiling, and Anthony tilted *his* head toward the Duchess, who was now lying against the brick wall of the pig-cote, ensconced in clean, fresh straw, snoring gently, and as humble and radiant as ever. He said:

"Pearls before swine."

Jane laughed again, and Anthony did also, and after that they had to kiss again for a while but broke apart when they heard pleasant crunching sounds and saw Wakefield loping toward them, his boots flattening the dry winter leaves, all the dogs trotting and adorably lolloping alongside him. He had gotten taller this winter, and now, at nine years old, his fine-boned face had lost a little of its boyishness, but none of its charm. He came near and said:

"I say, were you two kissing?"

"Yes," answered Anthony.

"Does this mean you're going to get married?"

It was Jane who answered this time. "Yes. We love each other very much. I do hope you don't mind, Wakefield."

"Not a bit of it. You're much better than all those other ladies Aunt Margaret brought over. They were awfully boring, and you're not. Jane, does this mean you love me too?"

"Yes, dear Wakefield," Jane said, and went over to where he stood with Joe the dog who had happened to sit on his boot, and she continued: "Very much. May I give you a hug?"

"Yes."

Jane hugged him, and he hugged her back, and then he said:

"Well, that's jolly. I'll like having you for a mother, Jane. What shall I call you?"

"Whatever you like."

"Now, that's going a bit too far," said Anthony. "What if Wake chooses 'Sniffer-crumble,' or 'Lollygriggin'? Or 'Tootle-face'?"

"Oh, Father, don't be ninsonsical."

"Do you mean nonsensical?"

"Yes, that's what I said. I'll keep on calling you 'Jane' for now, Jane, but I might change my mind later on."

"That's fine."

"I say, were you eating blancmange?" He was peering at the empty bowls on the tray.

"Yes," Anthony replied. "Do you want some?"

"I should say I do. Is there any left?"

"Of course there is. Shall we go back to the house? I could do with another bowl of it myself. What about you, Jane?"

"Oh yes, I'd love that."

So the three of them, with the dogs in tow, strolled back to the house and ate blancmange in the cheerful family dining-parlor, and had a merry time together suggesting even more preposterous names for Wakefield to call Jane, and Jane had to several times look down at the shimmering necklace of pearls which looked so beautiful against the deep burgundy bodice of her gown, all the while thinking that being filled with love and joy and certainty (and blancmange) was quite possibly the most marvelous sensation in the whole entire world.

A month later, Anthony and Jane were married.

Mr. Pressley performed the ceremony, of course, Titania and Lucy were flower-girls, and Wakefield carried the rings with the poise and dignity of a prince, an impression he rather undid when, at the wedding-breakfast, he stood on his head and waved his legs in the air, this delightful feat greatly impressing Titania, Lucy, and little Daniel who insisted on trying it himself, much to the hilarity of the young folk gathered around him.

Mrs. Henrietta Penhallow was smiling and gracious and genuinely pleased throughout, and Lady Margaret, rather surprisingly, wore a soft plum gown which made everyone suddenly realize that she was very pretty with her shining light-brown hair and blue eyes and graceful figure, and also that she had, in recent months, stopped scowling and frowning quite so much which was such a pleasant change that nobody made the gauche mistake of actually mentioning it in front of her.

When the breakfast was over and people were saying thank you and congratulations again and what a wonderful ceremony and goodbye, Jane was thankful that her own goodbyes to Great-grandmother, Livia, Cousin Gabriel, and the children only really meant *à bientôt*, which was "see you soon" in French, a phrase she had memorized early on in her French lessons with Mr. Pressley and which would be continuing even after she became a duchess, because she still had a lot she wanted to learn, and mastering French was one of her new ambitions along with really getting the hang of trigonometry.

That night, in Anthony's capacious bedchamber at Hastings that was now her bedchamber also, Jane gave Anthony her wedding-present to him, which was a telescope and which Anthony instantly adored, and he gave her *his* wedding-present, which was the announcement that he had had a large light-filled room on the same hallway as his library made over to her for her very own library and study, with plenty of shelves for books as well as a magnificent desk and comfortable chair, all of which Jane was sure she would adore the moment she set eyes on them, besides instantly adoring the very idea of it, and they thanked each other copiously. Then, after that, Jane finally learned what Anthony had longed to do that day when he was driving her home to the Hall for the very first time and he had admired her boots and blurted out, *I'd like to—well, never mind.* Which was that he knelt before her as she sat on the edge of the bed, still clad in her exquisite gown of carnation-pink silk and her beautiful pearl necklace which complemented it so well, and he gently pulled off her pink satin slippers, and slid his hands up along her legs in a way that made Jane shiver with delight, and then he undid her garters and drew off her stockings and kissed her bare ankles, and after that he kissed his way up her legs and so on and so forth with a wonderful slowness and skill which was remarkable in someone who had never had the chance to do this before, ever. But, as he modestly told her later on in the evening, when they lay entwined in each other's arms and magnificently naked and splendidly sweaty and also utterly replete, and she complimented him on how delicious it all was, it must have been, he said, his own pleasure in giving Jane pleasure which made him so good at it, and, of course, practice makes perfect and he was looking forward to a great deal of practicing with Jane.

Jane immediately said that perhaps they could practice some more right now.

And they did.

On successive nights Anthony got to try all the interesting things he had wondered about that evening he and Jane paced around the Hastings ballroom, and Jane showed him some other equally interesting things she liked and thought he might like too. Not only was Anthony a quick learner, he had some innovative ideas of his own, which, as it turned out, Jane liked very much indeed, and so as the nights passed in immense pleasure and bliss and laughter, and the days in more laughter and also work, learning, meals (along with plenty of snacking), reading, riding, billiards, pig-admiring, star-gazing, stone-skipping, and all sorts of other enjoyable pastimes and occupations which included absolutely no sewing at all on Jane's part, there was also no denying the fact that Anthony and Jane were totally, completely, thoroughly, and entirely right for each other.

They knew it, and would never forget how lucky they were.

So Jane became the Duchess of Radcliffe, and for a long time there was pleasant confusion when people talked about the Duchess, because they had to make it clear whether they were talking about the magnificent award-winning pig or Jane, the Duke's wife and stepmother to Wakefield and also the mother of three additional and equally marvelous children who came along in due course and filled Hastings with laughter, shouting, occasional shrieking, a judicious amount of toys and no more than that, and also a considerable amount of mud and dirt which nobody minded, not even the Duke's sister Margaret who wasn't even there anymore, as she had, a year after her brother's wedding, married Mr. Pressley, with whom she had slowly fallen in love after his spellbinding sermon about redemption and second chances.

For, secretly stricken by the absence of both Anthony and Wakefield who had gone to London, and who, deep down, she genuinely loved, as well as by guilt at the cruel triumph she had felt at Jane's departure, *and* as the final blow the unexpected decampment of her cat to a happier life in Bunch's pantry, ashamedly she had made her way to Mr. Pressley's vicarage (having absolutely no one else in whom to confide) and with incredible stiffness and behind a mask of haughty pride had asked if she might speak with him.

Mr. Pressley had received her with all the kindness and courtesy with which he welcomed all his congregants, and patiently listened, week after week, to Margaret's grievances, which started out being articulated with a sense of angry ill-usage, gradually shifted to bitter self-pity, and finally evolved into a painful awareness that she had really been wearing black all these years to disguise an even more painful truth, which was that she had loathed her husband the late Viscount Peete but had only married him to please her parents, not herself, and what she had really wanted was an enjoyable Season or two in London during which she could flit from one Society event to another, dance all night, and, hopefully, meet a handsome and intelligent and charming man with whom she could find true love.

Skiffy Featherington had not been that man.

He was not only exceedingly stupid, he had also been vain, arrogant, and among the most extreme of the so-called Dandy set—notorious throughout half of England for the immense shoulder-padding in his coats, the soaring height of his shirt-points, the half-dozen fobs jangling from his waist, and the jeweled quizzing-glass he carried with him everywhere including (it was rumored) bed, bathtub, and privy.

The rumors had been true.

How many times had Margaret longed to stab him with that ghastly quizzing-glass! His death had not really freed her, but had only allowed her to come back to Hastings and suffer through years of enduring her sister-in-law Selina's gleeful and vindictive barbs, all concealed beneath a tone of such unctuous concern that Margaret wished she could stab Selina with a quizzing-glass too.

It was during these conversations with Mr. Pressley that Margaret began to peel away the ugly onion-like layers of guilt, grief, rage, and deceit in which she had been encased for a long, long time, enabling her gradually to see, with fresh eyes, that life could actually be rather a pleasant thing, and that she had never really given her cat the affection it deserved and so it truly was much better off with Bunch and she wished it (and Bunch) well. Also she gradually came to see that Mr. Pressley was clever and learned and kind, with an exceptionally nice face as well as broad shoulders just right for resting one's weary head upon, *plus* he was a marvelous dancer, and the moment he confessed that his dour housekeeper Mrs. McKenzie ran roughshod over him, never had the maids dust, and insisted on serving foods which made him bilious, Margaret realized that the love of her life had been right in front of her for years.

So very bravely she told him that she loved him, and to her enormous relief and even more enormous joy he told her that he loved her too and would like nothing better than to make her his wife and cherish her forever, but could a duke's daughter find happiness with a mere younger son who was only a country parson?

Mr. Pressley would have gone on expressing his very noble and honorable doubts at some length, except that Margaret, with even more bravery, stopped his mouth with a kiss, and that was that.

Shortly thereafter they got married, Margaret moved into the vicarage, found Mrs. McKenzie a better situation elsewhere (with a family which, curiously enough, thrived under her stern and eccentric rule), stopped wearing black and instead wore the pretty colors which suited her so well, had fewer and fewer of those awful headaches, went to London with Mr. Pressley (who, as the son of an earl, knew a great many Society people and could mingle like anything), and did indeed dance all night, several times, which was a lot of fun. She also became, with amazing rapidity, a splendid vicar's wife who could beautifully organize any event, small or large, at a moment's notice, was indefatigable in visiting sick parishioners and listening to them sympathetically and offering good advice (which was sometimes even acted upon), and managed to gracefully extract funds for worthy causes from even the most clutch-fisted misers in Somerset. Eventually, thanks to the happiness she had found through love and plenty of meaningful work, she even became friends with her sister-in-law Jane, the Penhallow ladies, *and* Miss Humphrey and Miss Trevelyan, discovering that as wonderful as it was to have a husband whom she loved with all her heart, it was wonderful to have women-friends, too.

As for Miss Trevelyan, no sooner had she finished writing up the last of her biographies of Henry Tudor's wives, the one about Catherine Parr who managed to somehow not get thrown upon the block and have her head chopped off, than she divagated from her usual course as a historian and did indeed try her hand at a novel as she had mentioned, speculatively, upon first meeting Jane.

She used the Viscount Whitton as the model for her hero, who was a duke and extremely rich and handsome and moody and enigmatic, and who had a tendency to lean elegantly and provocatively against doorway jambs, curl his lip with disdain, fold his arms across his excessively muscled chest, and smolder just like the ashes on a good cigar. Miss Trevelyan also used Jane (with her permission) as the model for her heroine, who was born in the most horrid slum imaginable but turned out to be a princess and who was so delightful and feisty and entrancing that the moody, enigmatic, heavily muscled duke fell head over heels in love with her, stopped being such a dreadful ass, and proposed to her in the middle of a crowded ballroom, falling to his knees with incredible grace and not even wrinkling his superbly tailored breeches as he did it. Everyone in the ballroom applauded, the duke kissed the princess right then and there, and not only was there not a ghastly scandal as there would be in real life, they got married the very next day and soon had a dozen perfect children and lived happily ever after.

The book, with the rather unimaginative but at least helpfully explanatory title of *The Princess and the Duke*, was an immediate success, went through several printings, was translated into seven languages, enabled Miss Humphrey to add on another extension to her flourishing greenhouse, and ultimately earned so much in profits for Miss Trevelyan that she had to go to Jane to help her figure out all the obscure and confusing statements she had been receiving from her publisher, Jane having become well known in the county for her mathematical abilities and how she took over the Hastings accounts and whipped them into shape in no time; which was how Jane discovered that Miss Trevelyan's publisher had not been dealing fairly with her. So Jane, with all the firmness and resolution native to her both by temperament and experience—one could take the girl out of Nantwich, but one couldn't entirely take the Nantwich out of the girl, nor should one even try—wrote a couple of very sternly worded letters to Miss Trevelyan's publisher who was soon reduced to sending long replies of abject apology along with the cheques which were due to Miss Trevelyan accompanied by earnest promises to never do it again. Also the publisher humbly requested additional novels, possibly even something with the enticing title of *The Duchess and the Prince*, but Miss Trevelyan wrote back with a polite refusal, saying she was returning to history where she really belonged, and thought she would have a go at solving the mystery of King Richard the Third and whether or not he had villainously had his own young nephews murdered in the Tower of London where they had been imprisoned, and if Henry the Seventh was responsible for the widespread and convincing propaganda that his predecessor really had done it, all in the service of glorifying himself and making secure his rather precarious hold on the throne.

After that quite a few other people in the county came to Jane asking for her help with their tangled accounts, which she very much enjoyed untangling, and Anthony said that she really ought to offer her services to the Crown whose finances were tangled beyond belief, and if anyone could get the Prince Regent to stop spending money on things like his bloated cadre of French chefs, that silly Pavilion in Brighton, garish spangled jackets, and kangaroos, it would be Jane.

Flattered, Jane thanked him, and said that if anybody in Parliament could persuade (or force) the Crown to take her on, it would be Anthony, who had, not long after taking his seat, gained a reputation as a brilliant and fiery speaker whose opponents cowered nervously when he took the floor. This satisfying response, along with his general and exuberant happiness in life thanks to his family and friends and dogs and pig, enabled Anthony to finally stop worrying about what sort of duke he thought he should be, and instead settle in comfortably into just the sort of duke he was, which wasn't, he thought, half-bad. So he never felt obligated to crop his hair to suit someone else, or to wear shoes that made his feet hurt, although he did occasionally let the faithful Evans polish his boots, if only to keep the poor fellow from lapsing into a terrible melancholy.

When Wakefield was twelve, he decided that he wanted to go away to Eton for school, which he did, and learned a considerable amount, played every sort of sport, made a great many friends, got into countless scrapes, and altogether had a marvelous time. He had stopped scrambling his multisyllabic words by then, which secretly made Anthony and Jane a little sorry although they realized it was more because it reminded them that Wakefield was growing up fast, a wonderful and slightly sad inevitability that all parents must accept.

Wakefield went on to Oxford, by then having grown nearly as tall as his father, and (aided by a vocabulary which really was stupendous) he began writing essays and articles which were soon being published in all the local periodicals and occasionally the national ones as well, a pastime he enjoyed so much he thought with real seriousness about making writing his vocation, as it enabled him to speak his mind about things he viewed as important and also allowed him to fulfill his childhood dream of becoming a menace to society, which was even better than being a highwayman or a clown.

And speaking of clowns, neither he, nor his younger brothers and sister, *or* his father and stepmother whom he all loved very much ever, ever went to the circus, a circumstance they never regretted and which, in fact, made them extremely happy and excessively contented, a delightful state of mind that they each and every one entirely deserved.